The pathologist studied the body from head to toe.

"You said there was a bite mark," Peter Roberts mentioned, breaking the silence. "But I haven't seen one yet."

"It's on his back, at the base of his neck. It's deep. Clear. Must've hung on to the kid with his teeth. . . . And there's something else that's strange about it."

The pathologist reached across the body to pull up the left shoulder. "See that? Kind of a signature mark where there shouldn't be any teeth."

Peter observed the elliptical pattern of bruises and abrasions characteristic of a human bite mark. What seemed out of place, however, was a well-defined injury resembling the letter U in back of where the two upper front teeth registered.

"Ever see anything like it, Peter?"

Peter had. He was too shocked to utter a sound. . . .

Bantam Books by Dennis Asen

DEADLY IMPRESSION

ROOT OF DECEPTION

DENNIS ASEN

BANTAM BOOKS
New York Toronto London Sydney Auckland

ROOT OF DECEPTION

A Bantam Book / August 1998

ISBN 0-553-57516-3

Published simultaneously in the United States and Canada

Bantam Books are published by Bantam Books, a division of Bantam
Doubleday Dell Publishing Group, Inc. Its trademark, consisting of the
words "Bantam Books" and the portrayal of a rooster, is Registered in U.S.
Patent and Trademark Office and in other countries. Marca Registrada.
Bantam Books, 1540 Broadway, New York, New York 10036.

PRINTED IN THE UNITED STATES OF AMERICA

OPM   10 9 8 7 6 5 4 3 2 1

For Nancy, my partner in life

I owe a debt of gratitude to those who have given me their time and shared their expertise.

Dr. Isadore Mihalakis, his associates and staff, as well as the coroner's offices of Lehigh and Northampton counties, have graciously supplied me with whatever forensic information I needed.

Robert Steinberg, District Attorney of Lehigh County, and friend, answered all of my questions on criminal law and the judicial system.

I had to learn about the commercial airline industry. Captain Larry Hall guided me from ground to air with a profound desire to be authentic. Likewise, First Officer Mark Wilson, another fine pilot, was extremely helpful.

Emanuel Asen, my uncle, was my Yiddish tutor.

Also, ballistics researcher Edward Clancy unselfishly allowed me to pick his brain until I got what I wanted.

Special thanks to Jerrold Mundis, an author with extraordinary talent, for the pep talks and showing me the way.

I am truly fortunate to have an agent such as Bob Silverstein. He has always been there for me and has done more favors than I can repay.

And finally, a word about Stephanie Kip, my editor at Bantam. Somehow she managed to hold this all together and turn it into something special. Without her guidance and patient kindness, there would be no book.

ROOT OF DECEPTION

PART · 1

1

███████ Squigger didn't realize just how deep he'd gotten himself into it. The fraternity rushes were over, and envious freshmen would have sacrificed a testicle to be in his shoes. *At last, he was going to be a Kingsman, like his father and grandfather. An honor: the most sought after frat on this exclusive university's campus. Prodigious. Priceless. Too good to refuse.* But the darker side had come— as he knew it would, for him to truly belong—and it was darker than he ever dared to dream.

They almost had him. Almost. But the knife slipped, and the boy saw the blade sooner than he was supposed to. Suddenly, there were car doors slamming, feet hitting pavement, tires screeching. Into the woods and away from the road they chased him, leaves rustling under their feet, their hearts pounding, their breath quickening, as their eyes grew wide with fear that they wouldn't catch him . . . and also that they would.

Then, coming from the road, a glimmer of hope: two shining lights. He turned, racing toward them, his arms waving frantically, his voice calling desperately for help. And finally, the headlights on him just as he stumbled. Straightening, he realized that they weren't what he had hoped, what he had prayed for—and they held him there, blinded, paralyzed, until a hand grabbed his throat from behind and a voice yelled: "Game over!"

Kingsman House: smug, arrogant, elite, with a lawless preppie attitude. They wanted you totally, and you had to be consumed. Impressionable young lads would do whatever it took, without regard for morals or emotions, to be bestowed with the indoctrination: *Today you are born a Kingsman. There is no turning back. And with each day hence, you must prove yourself more worthy than the last. Thus forth bound, in spirit and in heart, with brotherhood, in life, at death, and beyond your final breath.*

As a reminder, the oath was hung in the main room of the frat house. Right below it, a banner—an original from the late 1800s—displayed the fraternity's coat of arms: a knight on his horse at the edge of a cliff, gazing down, broken sword in hand. "Looking for more to conquer," it proudly proclaimed. Ancestral tokens taken far too literally.

But it wasn't always this way, Kingsman House—ruthless and fierce. It just evolved, like children of children past who have overstepped their bounds and forgotten their roots.

In the beginning, 1886 to be precise, Kingsman House was officially registered as the first fellowship club of Van Buren University. As a prerequisite for membership, you merely had to be of good stock and strong moral fiber. Among the early alumni of the fraternity were an abundance of bankers, lawyers, doctors, politicians, educators, and other highly regarded professionals.

Over the years, the trend continued, adding two governors and even a Vice President of the United States to the impressive list of Kingsman achievers. And it wasn't long thereafter that being a Kingsman became synonymous with *money, power,* and *intellect.*

The fraternity became more selective, developed an attitude. Accolades served only to feed the impudence. Each year, the limits of self-assumed privilege were tested . . . and then taken a step further.

Most were unaware of the depth to which they had fallen, too caught up in the camaraderie, and the personas they fashioned in order to belong. And those who knew faded into the background like silent shadows, because they feared ostracism, and because they still wanted to hold on to their prize. That's why everyone else was fooled into thinking that all was well. But the fact remained: Kingsman House was out of control.

And that's how it came to pass: Squigger behind the wheel, and another pledge in the backseat with an abducted fifteen-year-old boy.

Academically, Van Buren University was deeply rooted in the political sciences, and the fraternity chose famous criminal cases as themes for their bedeviling. Unfortunately, Squigger and his accomplice got stuck with the Leopold and Loeb card.

Squigger wasn't his real name, of course, but rather the one his future brothers had granted him. This acceptance was the first sign of the consumption. From now on, he would be referred to only by his new name, chosen because of a painfully skinny stature that allowed the ends of his bones to protrude, giving his body a wavy appearance. His thick curly hair added credence to their choice. His companion was known simply as Fats.

They drove along a narrow winding road somewhat north of Philadelphia. It was nearly empty at that time of night—little chance of escape, little chance of being discovered.

Squigger's hands shook so much he could hardly negotiate the curves. Fats downed gulps of vodka. Their prey sat nervously, sweating, whimpering in protest, his hands and feet so tightly tied that the rope cut into his flesh. Blood trickled from the wounds.

"Hey, Squigger, you almost went off the road back there. Here, have a swig. It'll settle your nerves." Fats passed the bottle forward.

Squigger took a long gulp, swallowed hard. The vodka burned his throat and he coughed up half.

Fats laughed. "Better take another, you'll need it by the time this is over. But this time keep it down."

They were to do their dirty deed at an abandoned farmhouse. It was important to follow instructions: Get it done; be quick about it; bring back proof. Everything they'd need would be there waiting.

"There's a trestle ahead," Fats said, reading from a scrap of paper. "You make a right turn before it, then follow the railroad tracks for five miles."

"I know," Squigger shot back. "I memorized the directions like we were supposed to. Now throw that goddamn copy away."

"Hey, don't get testy. I can do it alone. No fucking problem. You want out, just say so."

"No," said Squigger quickly. "Just nervous, that's all. How the hell are we going to bring back proof?"

"Beats me."

The boy started to kick and scream, but Fats grabbed him by his shirt, pushed him back against the seat. "Calm down and maybe you'll get out of this. Okay? Understand?"

Sweat-soaked, fighting the urge to defecate, the boy nodded, but continued to whine softly after Fats let him go.

Squigger wondered what he was doing. Was it really him driving this car? This wasn't like one of his stories, the kind he lost himself in, where he always turned out to be the hero. He was good at that, writing and telling stories. He thought it was what he would like to do in the future, after Van Buren. After Kingsman House.

But his father had never approved. He wanted his son to be an attorney like himself, or maybe something even grander. Fate had trapped Squigger. True, he had choices, but he could no sooner act on them than he could denounce his purpose for being. He felt just like he had that first time his father took him hunting—revolted by the process, but unable to appear anything less than enthusiastic. *That* was what was expected. And when the deer turned and he caught a glimpse of the fear in its eyes, he didn't allow it to touch his heart. Instead, he pulled the trigger deftly and without remorse, thinking: *It's amazing what we allow ourselves to become for the sake of acceptance.* He *would* fulfill his destiny. He *would* achieve the family prophecy. He *would* become a Kingsman. What else could he do?

Fats had no misgivings, at least not now. He was tough. This was simply a new experience, a cheap thrill, just like the coke he snorted and the alcohol he drank. He would come to learn that he had gravely misjudged things. There would be consequences.

And as for the boy, he only wanted to feel important, to control something, anything. He allowed himself to be lured into the car, though he was smarter than that. His mother had warned him. She was all that he had left, a final ally—or so he used to think. But whatever he did, it was never good enough for her. So he offered lies to humor her, and stopped listening a while ago.

His father used to tell the boy he was different, right

before he felt the sting from the back of his father's
hand. And he came to believe that, because others
seemed to see what his father already knew.

A short lifetime of being bullied. The butt of everyone's jokes. It would be a long time before he was
missed.

They traveled another ten minutes, then pulled off
the road. There was a wretched silence, and all of
their hearts beat a little faster as the car came to rest
in front of the empty farmhouse. Because tonight was
the night of the Kingsmen, and they knew that the
course of each of their lives was about to change.

Kingsman House. Was it really worth it?

2

April 1997

It was just before dark when Detective Daniel
Pinchus and Sergeant Sam Milano arrived at Rivington
Street Station. A crowd of reporters, already waiting for
nearly an hour on the station house steps, rushed
toward them as the detectives hustled their suspect
from the car. Word had gotten out: *The Flesh-Eater* had
finally been caught.

Milano stepped forward quickly. "Jesus, it's a
freakin' circus."

Pinchus followed, his eyes on Milano's back. "You
thought it might be otherwise?" His right hand was
locked firmly under the suspect's arm.

The prisoner, a Bartholemew Putnam, was cuffed from behind. His eyes were squeezed shut. His bald head was bent, buried into the side of his jacket.

Ruppert Jones from the *Hamilton Press* fired the first question from the approaching mob. "This the serial killer, *The Flesh-Eater*?"

Cameras flashed.

"Got a name, yet?" someone else shouted.

"Is it true you caught him red-handed?"

"Please," Milano said, pushing his way up the steps. "We've always been fair to you—the press. A statement will be released at the appropriate time. Now move aside. Let us do our job."

A newswoman who had fought her way to the front asked, "What condition was the body in?"

Pinchus looked at her and paused for a moment. She matched the exact profile of Putnam's victims: young, pretty, reddish-blond hair. He envisioned the reporter lying in the woods. *Naked. Dead. Chunks of flesh cut away. Putnam defiling her rotting corpse.* "Condition?"

"I mean, was she mutilated like the others, Detective?"

Microphones leaned in. A camera with *Channel 47* written boldly across it swung around, waited for a response.

"No comment," Pinchus said, waving the others off.

Detective Daniel Pinchus had seen murders before: dismemberments, slashings, torture deaths, sexual mutilations. A homicide detective deals with it every day. He thought he would get used to the grotesque inhumanity. His father had warned him that there would be cases that haunted him, just as this one already did. But they all seemed to leave a mark. It was a different world that he had come to know—one filled with violence and murder. It existed within every city.

Even a *nice* city like Hamilton, Pennsylvania. And now it was a part of Daniel Pinchus's world. He accepted that. He had to. After all, it was what he had chosen to do.

They finally reached the top step. They had just captured the infamous *Flesh-Eater* who had been terrorizing the city for months, but Milano and Pinchus knew they were still in deep trouble. They prepared to face the consequences of their actions.

"Come on, Sergeant," Ruppert Jones called as they slipped inside. "Toss us a bone. Give us something."

"Anything," another reporter pleaded. "What can you confirm about the fourth victim?"

Milano gazed back over his shoulder. "Fourth one that we know about," was all that he would say.

A uniform was waiting at the door to take Bartholemew Putnam to a basement holding cell. Milano went with them to make sure their prize was safely tucked away, while Pinchus signed in with the desk sergeant.

"Could've used a hand out there, Vandy," Daniel said to him.

"Yeah, tell me about it."

"What about Captain Schwenk?"

Vanderhooven remained silent, looking pointedly at the desk.

"Do a background check on our friend, yet?" Daniel asked instead.

"Ran Putnam's name through BCI," Vanderhooven answered, looking up. "Came up clean. No priors. So far, all we have is a quiet accountant from Haverford with a wife and three kids."

"The perfect neighbor."

"Wouldn't be a bit surprised. What about the vic?"

"Same as the others," Daniel said. "Strangled. Hidden in the woods. Patches of skin missing. Found a

fork and knife on Putnam. Dr. Tom Onasis is checking
it out with forensics to see if the marks match."

"Putnam talk about it?"

"Only said that he was sorry. He was very upset.
Puked all over himself when we grabbed him. Onasis
took a sample."

"What the fuck for?"

"To have it analyzed." Daniel shrugged. "A couple
of cuts looked fresh."

Vanderhooven shook his head. "The average citizen
can't fathom how many sick motherfuckers are out
there."

"Lay you odds Putnam's mother was a strawberry
blonde."

"Always back to the mother, huh? I think you're
reading too many psychology books, Danny boy."

Daniel glanced at his watch. "So . . . Schwenk
leave yet?"

"Don't you wish. He has an emergency task force
meeting. Congressman Whitney's due any minute."

"To discuss Whitney's new strategy for his war on
organized crime?"

"More like damage control. We got word that those
missing mob witnesses might have surfaced. Two bodies found up in Coal County match the general description. Whitney's angry. And Schwenk's afraid of being
blamed for the fuck-up."

The thought of Schwenk having to squirm briefly
gladdened Daniel. He smiled. "So Schwenk needs to do
some PR."

"Already has," Vanderhooven replied, lowering his
voice. "Who do you think leaked Putnam's arrest to the
media? Capturing someone like *The Flesh-Eater* will
make a big splash. Take some of the heat off. Not to
mention impress Whitney."

"How? Schwenk had nothing to do with it."

"The arrest did come from his division," Vanderhooven pointed out. "Right now, he's perched by his window, waiting to run down and talk to the press just as soon as Whitney arrives."

Daniel frowned. He hated Schwenk, hated his adeptness at manipulating every situation to his own advantage. "So then Schwenk's okay with the way we handled the Putnam affair?" he asked hopefully.

"You kiddin'? One thing has nothing to do with the other. He's furious. You've got a lot of explaining to do."

"You read the autopsy reports," Daniel argued. "Semen stains—dry ones, wet ones; skin dissected over a period of time. The scumbag didn't just abuse those bodies, he was obsessed with them. Kept returning as long as his secret was undisturbed."

"So you radioed in, *'Just another false lead,'* then went off-line for a couple of hours. I mean, shit, Daniel—do you know how many regulations you broke?"

"But I had to keep it quiet. Otherwise Putnam would never have come back."

"Understood. But you took Schwenk out of the loop. He won't forgive that easily."

"Schwenk would have fucked it all up."

"It's not your call."

"Take a look, Vandy." Daniel angrily pointed toward the entranceway, at the press gathered on the other side. "Can't keep a secret in this town. Especially in Schwenk's division."

"He's talking charges. Suspensions. He wants you in his office right after Whitney leaves," Vanderhooven said. "Both of you."

"Sam? But it was all my idea. I had to talk him into it."

"Thought so," Vanderhooven snapped. "I knew Sam wouldn't pull a stunt like that unless he was pressured.

And you—the young, upstart detective telling him how to get into trouble just so you can show off."

"Is that what you think, Vandy? Maybe Sam knew there was a good chance that Schwenk wouldn't listen. Schwenk's done that before. Maybe Sam didn't want to find out about a fifth victim."

Vanderhooven took a breath and let it out slowly. "Don't get me wrong, Daniel. It's just that Sam's a friend. A good one. I'd hate to see him get burned. He has a lot to lose. I just wish you had considered that."

Vanderhooven was right. And at the time, Daniel hadn't considered it. He only wanted to catch the killer—desperately. "Don't worry about Sam. I'll take the blame," he said.

"Doesn't matter. He's the senior partner. He's still in trouble."

"Not if I give Schwenk what he wants," Daniel said, gazing out the window. Charles Whitney was getting out of his car in front of the station.

"Like what?"

They heard Schwenk clanking down the steps from the squad room.

"Something he wants more than anything," Daniel whispered quickly.

Schwenk rounded the corner. His eyes fixed on Daniel. They were cold eyes, full of contempt. Then he looked away, preparing to go outside.

Daniel moved through the door while Schwenk was still straightening his tie. "Sorry we kept you waiting," Pinchus announced loudly to the press. "As you may already know, *The Flesh-Eater* has been apprehended—"

Sam Milano returned just as Schwenk was rushing after Daniel. He saw his partner addressing the media, saw the look of rage on Schwenk's face. He turned toward Vanderhooven, who shrugged.

Daniel was speaking loudly, smiling at the crowd. "—the real hero, however, is a man who inspired the plan that led to the capture of this fiend. A man whom you've all known for years. That man is our leader, Captain Alex Schwenk."

Sam watched Schwenk's expression soften as Daniel handed him the credit. Sam didn't mind. They got what they wanted, an end to the killing. Neither one of them cared much for notoriety. But Schwenk basked in it. It was a good trade. It kept them out of trouble. And he was happy to see that his young partner had finally learned how to play politics a little.

Congressman Whitney was the first to start clapping. The applause grew as Captain Schwenk stepped forward.

A smile crept across Vanderhooven's face. *Way to go, Danny boy, almost as good as your father was*, he said to himself.

Almost. The compliment was as good as it got.

███████

Schwenk left the station house shortly after meeting with Whitney. Milano and Pinchus were happy for the reprieve, yet still had a long evening ahead, questioning Putnam, doing the paperwork, then going back to the scene of the crime to finish up.

It was very late when Daniel finally got home. He slipped into bed, careful not to wake his beautiful wife. He tried to put the horrors of *The Flesh-Eater* out of his mind. He hoped he wouldn't dream about it anymore.

But what Daniel Pinchus couldn't have known was that the following day held the beginning of an even greater nightmare.

3

Everything was in place, the entire plan complete. It had taken a while to work out, but he was sure it would go smoothly. It already had.

From the second story, he could see the front of the small luncheonette clearly. Any moment the boy would deliver the message. It had to be a child; no one else would be allowed to get that close. But the boy wouldn't give him up. They rarely did. That's how he was able to get away with so much.

He studied the scene from the open window. A cold April breeze cut across his face, but he never felt it. He was too absorbed in what was to come.

It was six-thirty A.M. On the outskirts of Hamilton, inside Carmine's, at a table set for four in the back, sat Dominic Luccetta with three of his lieutenants. Toward the front, four other gumbas waited, keeping a watchful eye on the street.

The Luccetta crime family was well known to Philadelphia. Some say it used to be the biggest, used to

control Philly. But things had changed. Though still a
major player in the city of brotherly love, Luccetta had
wisely seen the future. He didn't dwell on what once
was. He went with the flow and turned his attention to
new horizons—the city of Hamilton. Conveniently just
a stone's throw from Philadelphia, less then twenty-five
miles to the north. Strategically, a haven along the
western corridor to New York, where Luccetta had
business connections.

And, he had always liked Hamilton—the parks, the
suburban atmosphere, the people. He liked it so much,
he moved his wife and kid there. Quite a bit smaller
than Philadelphia—only a quarter of a million people—but the change was refreshing. It was a shame that
he did business there as well.

In his late forties, Luccetta was looking the part of a
young don: a bit of a gut, sharp dresser, slick hair. A
sprinkling of gray around the temples gave him a dis-
tinguished appearance. He was the youngest of three
brothers, but the most intelligent. Each had equal control of the family, but Dominic believed he ran it—and
so did everyone else.

As usual, Dominic was in trouble. He had a court
date in two weeks. The Feds were amassing a case
against him, desperate to make a strike against the syn-
dicates that controlled Philadelphia and its surrounding
cities. Luccetta had been there before and they could
never make anything stick.

This time was different. There were witnesses. An
elderly couple had had the unfortunate privilege of dining next to a drunken Luccetta. They overheard him
brag about specific racketeering operations. Even a *hit*
he personally took care of a while back. The rest of the
case was weak. A lot of hearsay. But with this cor-
roborating evidence, the government felt they had a
shot.

"Hey, boss," one of the wise guys said as he placed his newspaper flat on the table. "Take a look at this— buried on page five."

"What, 'CONGRESSMAN WHITNEY VOWS NEW WAR ON CRIME'? The fuck's looking to get votes. Wants to be governor."

"No, next to that: 'COUPLE FOUND SLAIN IN POCONOS'."

"Oh, *that* headline." Luccetta grinned.

"Says here, they were found late last night after police received a tip. Badly decomposed. They're waiting for confirmation, but they think they might be those witnesses they've been looking for."

"What a shame. Nice people, minding their own business, and someone had to whack 'em. Now, who do you suppose would do something like that?" Luccetta shook his head.

They all laughed.

"Tony," Luccetta said loudly, "make sure you send the family flowers in my name—once the identities are official, of course."

"Of course," Tony said.

Violent and brazen, Luccetta let little stand in his way. Enemies were dealt with swiftly and completely. His ruthlessness led to his success, which led to a sense of invulnerability, and that made him careless. And since he was a creature of habit—and it *was* Wednesday morning—he found himself at Carmine's, drinking coffee and eating pastries as he discussed business with his associates.

After twenty minutes, with breakfast finished and the daily assignments properly reviewed, the entourage prepared to leave.

■■■■■■

His waiting was over. He noticed the glint of sunlight bounce off the glass door as it opened onto the street, and he readied himself.

There was the boy on the bicycle. He rode straight up to the man at the center of attention and handed over the note. A puzzled Luccetta grasped the piece of paper and read. His look turned grave, and by curious reflex he glanced up toward the window—there wasn't time for much else.

The man on the second floor held the rifle with absolute steadiness, the telescopic lens fixed on its target. His pulse never quickened as he met Luccetta's gaze. Rather, he pulled the trigger matter-of-factly, and blew the back of Dominic Luccetta's head off.

4

It was 7:05 A.M. when the phone on Captain Schwenk's desk rang. He had spent a sleepless night worrying that the witnesses—for whom he couldn't deny having some responsibility—might have shown up dead. He snatched the phone up with a sense of dread. It was probably Congressman Whitney, panicking again.

But the caller was from central dispatch, notifying him that Dominic Luccetta had just left his brains all over a Hamilton sidewalk—Schwenk's jurisdiction. Schwenk hung up the phone in disgust. What else could go wrong? He felt as if he had been punched in the stomach. After years of building a career, manipulating subordinates and kissing up to superiors, it was all turning to shit in what seemed like the blink of an eye.

Four months ago, a multiregional task force to fight organized crime had been established. It was Congressman Whitney's pet project—and a coup for the ambitious politician, who had campaigned for it in the press. Its purpose was to pool the efforts of neighboring county, township, and city police departments to stop the criminal infestation that spread commonly across their borders. It would be a test, a model. A triumph.

Three high-ranking officials—Schwenk from Hamilton, Captain Paco Perez from Philadelphia, and Lieutenant Ned Daulkens from the smaller city of Monroe—were chosen to head the force.

Schwenk knew it was a bullshit position. Such associations rarely got results. The inevitable struggle for authority, the constant credit-grabbing, and the utter chaos were more than enough to cripple these impotent enterprises. And then there were the Feds, who had ultimate jurisdiction anyway when it came to organized crime.

Yet Schwenk welcomed the appointment grandly. It would look good on his résumé. After all, isn't that what it was all about? Rumor had it that the Chief of Detectives position would be opening up by year's end. And, like Congressman Whitney, Schwenk wanted to move up.

But the brass ring was slipping from his grasp. First there were the witnesses. The mob should not have known who they were. They were people coming forward anonymously, unknown faces without names. The task force took much of the credit for discovering them, although all they really did was coordinate their protection. However, while they were still patting each other on the back, the witnesses just as quickly disappeared. They had been missing for nearly two months now . . . until yesterday.

And this morning he was being told that someone

made Luccetta's head explode. It meant Whitney would
be involved again, sticking his bloody nose where it
didn't belong, scrutinizing Schwenk's every move.

The next call came only a minute later. Schwenk
was momentarily relieved, although not delighted, to
find out it was Captain Perez.

Perez enjoyed being vindicated, and loved tormenting Schwenk. "Seems like a classic mob hit to me,"
he gloated. "Told you—it's a war."

All along, Schwenk had maintained that the two
witnesses got scared and ran. They were doubtlessly
hiding somewhere halfway across the country. There
were reports of sightings, in Missouri and in Utah, as
recently as two weeks ago.

But Perez was more imaginative in his theory. The
witnesses were a sham, set up by a rival family, probably the Malloys. It was a way of taking Luccetta out,
clean and legal, without starting a spate of violence. But
the couple was betrayed by an informant—and the
mob war that everyone feared might happen had actually already begun.

Above all, it was important for each captain to be
right. They wagered on the outcome: a half-day's assignment in the other's division. If the witnesses were
found alive, Schwenk won; dead—Schwenk didn't even
want to think about it.

"Not necessarily so, Paco," Schwenk said defensively. "All the cards haven't been turned over yet."

"Sure they have. The bodies up in Coal County *are*
those witnesses. As soon as the Malloys realized that,
they moved. Made a stiff out of Luccetta."

"Awfully fast, don't you think? Too fast, if you ask
me. Those bodies were found only a few hours ago.
Takes more time than that to organize a snuff as big as
this one."

"They don't mess around. And it happened in your

area, Schwenk, so you can find out firsthand. Don't forget, Kaminski will be there as an observer—"

How could Schwenk forget? When this whole witness situation blew up in the face of the task force, Inspector Kaminski from the Philadelphia police department was named to oversee the operation. It was an embarrassment. They were usurped.

"—but be careful. Whitney's looking for a scapegoat."

Schwenk's shoulders slumped briefly. Just a few hours ago Whitney, already anticipating the final outcome from Coal County, warned Schwenk about committing any more fuck-ups.

"Doesn't scare me," he told Perez, sitting forward in his chair again. "Didn't you catch this morning's paper? I'm a goddamn hero."

"Yesterday's news, Alex. Gotta run. Remember our bet. Have a nice detail picked out for you." He laughed, then hung up before Schwenk could say another word.

Schwenk never liked losing a bet or anything else, and he saw his promotion fading away. He had to send his most reliable homicide team to the scene of Luccetta's murder. He made a call.

There were very few people Schwenk liked, nor did he endear himself to many. He tolerated Sam Milano. But Daniel Pinchus was too smart for his own good. Just like his father, Seymour—the Fox—who Schwenk loathed even more. He needed to put that aside for the moment. Milano and Pinchus were the best he had, though he hated to admit that even to himself. He couldn't afford another mistake. Especially now. Not if he wanted to become Chief of the Dees.

5

Daniel Pinchus loved his wife dearly, which is why he put up with her miniature Yorkshire terriers nipping at his bare feet in their cramped two-bedroom apartment. They were named Lucy and Ricky—but were the Great Vermin Duo to Daniel. He often threatened Susan, playfully, that he would get the landlord to summon an exterminator to take permanent care of the yapping beasts.

This morning, Daniel was up early, in the kitchen preparing his lunch. It was quiet, and everyone else was asleep. Except for the dogs. They pulled at his pants with their teeth, shaking their heads, growling. He squelched an impulse to step on the hairy caterpillars, and gave them some food instead.

Daniel was getting tired of tuna fish and American cheese sandwiches. But he and Susan were pinching their pennies, saving for a house. After more than two years of trying, Susan had finally become pregnant again. In five months there'd be another child to join their nearly four-year-old son, Adam. Brown-bagging it was part of the program. A young police detective still didn't make very much money—not in Hamilton, not for a growing family.

Just like his father, Lieutenant Seymour Pinchus, Daniel had opted for the homicide division. However, his legendary father hadn't been with the department since three bullets snuffed out his career and nearly ended his life, just before Daniel joined the force.

Daniel was destined to follow in his father's foot-steps, though they were some awfully big shoes to fill. In the beginning, he was simply proud to be the heir apparent to the awesome Lieutenant Pinchus. But soon enough, Daniel had also proved himself worthy of the name. Yet no matter how many cases he helped crack— with wit and instinct reminiscent of his father's—there was always the inevitable comparison from fellow po-lice officers: *"Great case, Daniel, but I bet your father would have nailed it shut last week." "Good job, kid, but you're not quite the old man yet."*

Four years ago he was flattered. Now he was bur-dened. Fuck the comparison. He just wanted to be known as a good, solid detective. And when he didn't quite put one to bed, he couldn't help feeling that ev-eryone in the department thought his father could have—knew the Fox would have. The problem was, Daniel believed it, too.

He put on his coat, tucking his lunch into the side pocket just as Susan entered the kitchen.

"Daniel, why didn't you wake me? I would have made you something to eat," she said, rubbing her big, brown eyes.

"I already took care of it. And the little mangy nip-pers, too. Besides, I wanted to let you sleep. Heard you get up during the night. What was it—two, three times?"

"Four." She sighed.

"Still throwing up?"

"Dry heaves, mostly. Why do they call it morning sickness? I hope I don't feel this way Friday night."

"Friday?"

"Did I forget to tell you? I invited your father over for dinner. I told him I'm going to try to make a real Shabbat meal."

"Susan, I love you, but I think you're taking your conversion to Judaism too seriously. He's not that religious. I'm not that religious."

"Didn't say I was a good Catholic, either," Susan added. "But I want to be a good Jew. I want to do this for me."

Daniel knew not to push. He respected Susan's decision to convert. She felt it was important for their children to be brought up following one faith. She made the commitment, completed her studies thoroughly, and then took pride in the *mikvah* celebrating her accomplishment. She conformed to tradition— made a kosher home, followed Jewish law, and attended services when she could.

"And Kate?" Daniel asked defeatedly. "Is she coming, too, or is she still away?"

"You'll be pleased to know your stepmother will be joining us."

"Peachy."

Daniel hated Kate being called his stepmother, hated that Adam called her grandma. He still had his own goddamn mother, who raised him pretty much by herself after the divorce. He had been only a little more than three years old at the time. It had taken Daniel many years to get close to his father again. And as for his mother, she was out in Denver, remarried for seven years to a filthy-rich door manufacturer—good for her.

"Be civil," Susan pleaded.

"Always am. Just don't try to convert her, too. My father likes to say he's married to a shiksa."

Susan frowned. She knew that wasn't true. Daniel was trying to be funny and it came out mean. It had to do with how he felt about Kate.

"So what's on the menu? Let me guess: chicken soup, of course. And maybe roast beef?" Roast beef was his favorite.

The thought made Susan sick. She curled her lip and swallowed.

"I'm sorry," he said guiltily. "I did this to you."

She smiled. "You bet you did."

Daniel went over, touched her stomach. "Amazing!"

She stood on her tiptoes and kissed him. "You do good work. I think you really nailed this one."

Daniel laughed. "At least I know he's a fighter. He's already giving his mother a tough time."

"You're *so* sure it's going to be a boy."

"He'll need a strong name like Clayton or . . ."

"Courtney?" Susan replied.

Daniel caught the glimmer in her eyes. "What are you trying to say? Know something I don't?"

"Lots—but that's another story."

"The amnio?"

"Correct, Detective."

"But I thought we decided not to—"

"*You* decided. I cheated. After we got the report confirming that everything was okay, I called. Are you disappointed?"

"Not about having a girl." Daniel beamed, then grabbed a handful of her chestnut hair and yanked on it. "But I *am* about your cheating. I'll have to discipline you."

"I hope so." She giggled. "Adam's still asleep. Maybe go in a little late?" Her eyebrows lifted suggestively.

The phone rang. Daniel let go.

Susan reluctantly reached for it.

". . . Oh, hi, Sam. Hold on, he's right here."

"We've gotta roll," Sam told Daniel when he took the receiver. "Someone just blew Dominic Luccetta's head off."

"Where? When?"

"Tremont Avenue. 'Bout twenty minutes ago."

Daniel felt the adrenaline rush. "I'll pick you up in a . . ."

Watching him, Susan shook her head. "My car—the old clunker's on the fritz again. I was hoping to borrow yours."

"Sam, could you—"

"No problem. I heard her. You're closer to Tremont anyway. Be there in fifteen minutes."

"Make it ten."

But Sam was long past the anxious exuberance that still infected his youthful partner. "Relax, Daniel," he said. "Luccetta's not going anywhere . . . except maybe to hell."

6

Dr. Peter Roberts slowed his pace slightly as he hit the four-mile mark. He was looking to do five, but had doubts that he'd make it. It was a cool morning. Perfect. But he wasn't used to the distance. Practicing general dentistry didn't give Roberts as much free time as he liked. At forty-four, he was growing tired of the profession—too many hours, too many patients. But this was Wednesday, the one a month he allowed himself to be off, so he was indulging himself.

Roberts was also involved in forensic dentistry. For that, he always made time. When the coroner or pathologist called, he'd drop what he was doing, shuffle patients to his associates, and make himself available. He loved the work, especially the investigative aspects. It intrigued him. He would determine positive identification of the unrecognizable dead: victims of fire and traumatic accidents; homicide victims that were left to rot before they were found. And sometimes, there would be a bite mark for him to analyze—the telltale evidence incised on a murdered individual, waiting for him to match it to the killer. He enjoyed those cases the most. They had more notoriety, and they made him a star—at least in his own mind.

Roberts turned a corner, his running shoes pounding the pavement. His thighs ached. He vowed to complete the last mile, forced his mind off the monotony and fatigue of the jog and onto a recent case.

Last month, Herb Striklon called from Harrisburg. Striklon was a friend, and a dentist—one of the few Roberts thought knew as much, if not more, about forensics as he did. They were both part of a statewide forensic mass disaster team, working practice drills together and lecturing on the subject. Roberts had great respect for Striklon, liked picking his brain, and felt honored that Striklon was now asking him for advice.

It was a bite mark case and Striklon was baffled. The bite, on the shoulder of a murdered and sexually abused eleven-year-old boy, looked ordinary enough except for the presence of a U-shaped imprint centered behind the area where the edges of the upper front teeth had penetrated. This *signature* was unlike anything Herb had seen before, except for a case nearly two years ago where the bite mark was too faded to tell for sure. Nothing since. He sent Roberts photos of the bite.

Roberts had never seen anything like it either. Together, they ruled out such causes as a denture or retainer worn by the killer. Beyond that, both were stumped.

Yesterday, Striklon phoned again. There was nothing new on the case, but he told Peter that he was going to run pictures of the unique bite mark in the state dental journal and hope for a lead.

"See you at the next drill. Mock disaster, Harrisburg

Airport," Striklon added before hanging up. "Just down the road from me."

Roberts was out of breath, calculated another half mile or so to go before reaching home.

He was looking forward to spending the day with his oldest daughter, Melanie. She was on spring break and he owed her. Two weekends ago was the annual father-daughter dinner dance. Peter had to be in Nashville for an important forensic conference and couldn't attend. Melanie took the disappointment in stride, gave a calculated smile, and simply said, "Don't worry, Dad. It'll cost you." After sixteen years, Peter was getting used to being manipulated by his daughter. They were going on a shopping trip.

Peter reminded himself unhappily that she would soon be driving. He had grown afraid lately, had seen too much. He didn't want her to grow up, wanted her safe at home out of harm's reach. He never wanted to know what it would be like to lose any of his family. Not his children or his gorgeous wife, Diane, with her penetrating green eyes and soft brown hair. Lately, Diane had become fanatical about going to the gym and working out. Lost five pounds she didn't need to, dressed better, and was generally more careful about her appearance. Peter had attributed it to mid-life crisis, but then suddenly realized in mid-stride: He had done those same things when he had his fling with Terri—the affair four years ago that almost finished their marriage.

No. Just being paranoid, he told himself. *Diane would never!* Then again, their sex life couldn't have been better. And *who* taught her all these new things she brought to bed? Wonderful things. Erotic things.

Peter shook his head to dispel the thought. He grimaced, ran his fingers through his sweat-soaked hair, and pushed on. He used to be able to do twice the distance and not be nearly as fatigued. He didn't like knowing that, didn't like getting older. At least none of his friends had had heart attacks, yet. That was *something*, wasn't it? Although this morning he noticed that one of his patients had died—only fifty-four. Roberts had taken him to be much older. Probably bad diet and no exercise.

Roberts hit the front door, waited several minutes to catch his breath, and went in. With a steaming hot shower on his mind, he dragged himself upstairs. Diane, just back from dropping their son, Paul, off at the junior high, met him at the top. She looked stunning.

Jesus, what happened to the worn jeans and oversized sweatshirt? Definitely having an affair. He bent to kiss her.

"Peter, stop. You stink!" she giggled. "Besides you'll mess me all up."

He backed off. *No doubt about it.* "Tell Mel, a fast shower and change, then we're out of here."

"Maybe not. Tom Onasis called a few minutes ago and he wants you to call him back right away. I already warned Mel."

Sighing, but feeling his excitement build, Peter picked up the phone.

Two bodies, badly decomposed, needed a dental, Onasis told him. Up in Coal County.

"Coal County?" Roberts sputtered. "That's an hour and a half away. Since when do you—"

"Covering for a friend on vacation. Like to use my own people. Can I count you in?" Onasis asked. It was a rhetorical question.

"In," Roberts replied.

"Good. I have another homicide to do here this afternoon. Ellen Goray is doing the prelim at the scene now, but the DA wants us both to do the post."

"Must be big."

"Mob hit. But we know who it is. Don't need you on that one. Dental records of the two you're doing should already be up there."

Peter hung up the phone and caught Melanie in the hall.

"Mel, I just got called out."

Her shoulders slumped.

"But don't worry, I'll be back this afternoon. We can still go."

Melanie rolled her eyes. "Sure, Dad."

"No, listen. It's only eight-thirty. I can be out of here in twenty minutes. Three hours total travel time. Another hour in the morgue. I'll be home by one. Don't worry."

"Why should I worry?" Melanie answered with a pout. "If you're not back in time, I'm sure you'll make it up to me."

Peter hesitated, but knew he'd been had.

7

Sam Milano turned onto the street where his partner lived. He knew he wouldn't have to get out of his car or even honk. Half a block away he adjusted his glasses, anticipating the view of Daniel pacing the sidewalk in front of his apartment. He wasn't disappointed.

Sam couldn't help noticing how much Daniel reminded him of his former partner, the Fox. He first met Seymour twenty years ago, when they became a team. For four years now, Milano had worked with his son.

Although Daniel's thick, wavy hair was just starting to recede at the temples, and only a smidgin of gray streaked his sideburns, there was no mistaking the inheritance of strong chin and deep-set eyes. Maybe younger, slimmer, and more muscular, Milano thought, but it *was* Seymour.

As an investigator, Daniel had rare natural instincts, just like his dad. Milano knew that firsthand. Over the years he worked with Seymour Pinchus in homicide, he'd watched him solve an impressive list of cases. Terranova, the Riverside Serial Killer; the Baby Seigel case; the Alice Schaeffer murder. And Daniel had already started to leave his mark on a few of his own. Yet he lacked his father's finesse—he was flamboyant; a risktaker; more impulsive. That could be dangerous. Daniel still needed to learn the tricks of the trade from someone who'd been on the job. Someone steady, someone who may have lacked Daniel's raw talent, but knew how to guide and shape it to its full potential. Someone like Sam.

Sam understood Daniel, his brashness, his desperate need to succeed. There was so much pressure—some from others and some self-imposed. Daniel had to prove himself. It wasn't enough to be *almost* as good, or *just* as good as his father. He had to be better.

Sam barely brought the car to a stop before Daniel hopped in.

"Easy, Danny boy. I said the body isn't going anywhere. What's up?"

"A girl, Sam! We're going to have a girl! Susan just told me."

"*Mazel tov*. But how. . . ?"

"The amnio."

"Thought you didn't want to know?"

"I didn't."

"Oh?" Sam raised an eyebrow. "A girl, that's great.

Got the feeling you were hoping for another son. Disappointed?"

"Not in the least. Secretly I was desperate for a little girl. Didn't want Susan to know that. Didn't want her to think she let me down, so I acted as if I didn't care."

"*Susan* let *you* down? You had something to do with it, partner. If I remember my high school biology correctly, the sperm determines gender."

They both laughed.

"And how does your father feel about having a granddaughter?"

"Haven't told him yet, so don't spill the beans. We're all having dinner together Friday. I'll tell him then."

"My God, a little girl. Your father's face will light up. It's been so long since . . ." Sam caught himself. "Sorry, Daniel, I didn't mean to—"

"It's okay. You were referring to Melissa, weren't you?" His voice was flat. "She was his pride and joy."

"He loved you, too."

"She was extra special to him. I was only two when she died." Daniel was quiet for a moment. "Actually, twenty-six years ago tomorrow. And he still misses her."

"Long time to grieve." Milano sighed.

"Too long," Daniel replied shortly. "Guess for him, you think it'll be like having Melissa all over again."

Milano saw Daniel's pain. "Maybe . . . in a way," he admitted simply. "She was a terrible loss. It took your father a long time to get over it."

"He never did," Daniel snapped.

"Don't hold that against him. Thank God you don't know what it's like. I hope you never do."

"You're right, Sam. I'm sorry."

There was a long pause. An uncomfortable one.

Sam changed the subject. "Listen, Daniel, about this case: It's high profile."

"You don't have to tell me about Luccetta," Daniel said. "He was one hell of a scumbag."

"And it's also the mob. You have to watch your step on this one. Do your job, but be low-key."

"No problem. Have to tell you, though, it's a refreshing change. For once, we're not investigating some innocent old woman who was beaten to death in the middle of the night by some crazed punk. Or some poor schnook who unwittingly got his dick caught in a lovers' triangle. Or any of the other countless victims who didn't deserve to have their life torn from them." He shook his head. "Dominic Luccetta—there is no remorse. This time, no empty feeling in my gut. No pity. He was a bad motherfucker."

"This one's going to bring a lot of heat," Sam warned. "Inspector Kaminski will be at the scene to observe."

"The mob-squad watchdog?"

"The same."

"Knows a lot about homicide, does he?" Daniel asked flippantly.

"Jesus Christ, Daniel, he's close to the police commissioner of Philadelphia." Sam didn't reveal just how close, afraid of what Daniel might think and say. "This isn't about homicide, it's about politics."

"And about saving everyone's ass."

"What do you mean?" asked Milano.

"Luccetta getting whacked. Those dead witnesses they just found. It's all linked together. Kaminski's only here for damage control."

Their car approached the scene of the murder. There was activity, the kind Sam and Daniel had grown used to: several patrol cars, blue and red lights flashing; a few officers containing and controlling the amassing crowd. Yellow crime scene tape marked off a section of sidewalk in front of Carmine's.

Sam parked and the two detectives jumped out of their car, holding out their badges and pushing their way through the onlookers. As they got closer, they noticed the tarp-covered body. Ducking under the yellow tape, they saw the blood spatter on the concrete, arching six feet or more from the tarp back toward the coffee shop. Even the glass storefront was speckled with fine, red droplets. The pattern was consistent with a head shot from long range.

Dr. Ellen Goray was standing near the body, questioning Luccetta's right-hand man, Tony Caputa.

Tony was obviously agitated. He had seen his boss's head explode, still had a sprinkle of Luccetta's blood across his left ear and neck. He was the one that had to call the family to explain what happened. And it was his job to prevent such a thing. He flung his arms out with each response, unable to contain his anxiety.

"Who cares which way he was facing? He's fucking dead. We're fucking dead. That's it! Even you can figure that out, Dr. Gory!"

"That's *Goray,* Mr. Caputa, like I told you before. I'm sorry that your friend has been killed. I can assure you that I didn't do it, so don't take it out on me. Now please answer my question."

Tony pointed. "He was staring up at that building across the street. A second later, I heard the shot, and he was down. Boom. Just like that."

"Thank you," Ellen said politely. She caught sight of the two detectives, stepped forward to greet them. "Sam, Daniel." She nodded to each. "What brings you two out on this fine morning?"

"Guess," Sam replied.

"Hope you brought breakfast."

Daniel held out his hands, palms up. "Sorry."

"Wish Tom Onasis were here," she grumbled. "But he got dragged up to Coal County, so I unfortunately got stuck with the call. He'd be better dealing with this lot. I get intimidated easily."

"That's not what I just saw," Sam said. "You handled yourself quite well, as always." Actually, Sam enjoyed the sight of this petite librarian-looking woman— thick glasses, not much unlike his own, hair wrapped tightly in a bun—putting some two-bit hood in his place. "What's the rundown?" he asked.

"Luccetta walked maybe five steps out of the restaurant, surrounded by his crew of seven cronies. Gazed up across the street and . . . wham. The shot came from that building, second floor, exactly where he was looking. That's all she wrote."

Officer Lauralee Collins, a black police officer, was in earshot of Dr. Goray's account. She turned away from the man she had just finished questioning and addressed Milano and Pinchus. She seemed young, but she was a seven-year veteran of the force. "That's all we have, Detectives. The owner of the place, Carmine Logan, saw the same thing from inside."

"Any other witnesses aside from Carmine and the Seven Hoods?" Daniel asked.

"Logan says a kid on a bicycle stopped in front of Luccetta right before the blast."

Daniel's ears perked up. "Right before? Are you sure?"

Collins handed him her notes. "Thank God the killer waited until the kid was clear before firing. No sign of the kid now, though. Probably peed in his pants all the way home, peddling as fast as he could."

"And the victim?" Milano asked.

"Ain't pretty," Goray answered. She bent, lifted the black tarp. The body of a well-dressed, heavyset man rested on the pavement. Only half of his head was intact. "Entry wound, right temple, ladies and gentlemen," she said dramatically, pointing to a small circular hole, obliquely above and lateral to the eye. "Exit wound—nothing up my sleeves—well, you can see for yourselves."

Instead of the back of Luccetta's head, they saw only what looked like the remains of a smashed pumpkin: skull fragments, naked brain tissue, a torn envelope of scalp, a lot of blood. Luccetta lay exactly as he was taken down, his empty hands outstretched.

"I was checking angles, trying to figure out where the bullet went," Goray continued, motioning toward the coffee shop with her chin. "Haven't found it, yet. But we will. Odd, though. Didn't notice any fragments in the vic, either."

Daniel crouched closer, examining Luccetta's head. "What's this?" he asked, pointing to some fine, white granules clinging to the inside of the wound.

"Hhmm." Goray's mouth twisted to the side. "May have been blown there by the wind. We'll find out at the morgue."

"Bullet could've stayed intact," Milano offered. "Been deflected."

"I'm no ballistics expert," Goray started to say, but was interrupted. The coroner was on the phone inside Carmine's, tapping on the glass, trying to get her attention. "You'll excuse me, guys. Trane got here before anyone else, and he's anxious for me to give the okay to remove the body. That is, if it's all right with you two."

"Tell him he's the boss," Sam answered. "We don't need to look at this anymore."

Trane was a good coroner. He didn't have to have a forensic pathologist on the scene, but often asked for one. He was thorough. Milano and Pinchus appreciated that about him.

"Hey, Sam," Pinchus said, "don't you think it's odd

that Luccetta stared precisely at the spot where the shot
would come from?"

"Must've seen something first."

"Yeah. Something terrible."

"You mean like a rifle poking out of a window?"
Milano suggested.

"Worse. Something from within his heart. Didn't
you see the frozen expression on his face?"

━━━━━

Carmine Logan was sitting on the ground, his back
against the storefront of his business, when Daniel approached him. Sam had gone across the street to investigate the apartment the gunman had allegedly fired
from. "I'm ruined," Carmine was moaning. "This could
only happen to me!"

"What's the matter, Carmine?" Daniel asked sympathetically.

"My business is shot. Who's gonna eat here anymore after what happened? Got a wife and two kids.
Barely making enough as it was. Now I'm fucked." He
lit a cigarette, angrily tossing the match toward the
street.

"Don't look so hopeless," Daniel said.

"Why not? You going to buy this fuckin' place?"

"No, but do you remember Crazy Joe Gallo?"

"Why, is he going to buy this place?"

Daniel smiled. "Joey Gallo, as you know, was a big
mob guy up in New York. A bunch of years ago he got
gunned down in a place called Umberto's, a restaurant
in Little Italy."

"So?"

"So, I bet Umberto's doubled their business after
the hit."

"Why?"

"It became famous. Everyone wanted to see the

place where Crazy Joe Gallo got snuffed. People would brag: *'I ate at the table right next to where Gallo died.'* It gave them a little celebrity status."

Carmine stood. "You really think this will be good for business?"

"Shhh!" Daniel said, a finger against his lips. "You don't want Luccetta's men to hear you say that."

"You're right," Carmine whispered back. "This *is* good news."

Daniel flipped through the notes Officer Collins had taken. "Now . . . tell me more about this kid on the bike."

8

████████ Diane Roberts dialed the telephone number nervously. She knew he would be at work early. He'd be expecting her call. That's how they planned it.

When he answered, she said, "It's me. Peter left a minute ago."

"Relax, you sound so tense. Sure you can handle all of this?"

"I'm sure. It's just that Peter knocked me for a loop. He was supposed to take Melanie shopping this morning. They wouldn't have been back until later this afternoon. I had arranged a sitter for Paige, but then Dr. Onasis called. I knew it was a forensic case and according to Peter, the world stops when that happens. Luckily the case is up in Coal County. So I cancelled the sitter. Melanie can stay with Paige. Peter will be gone for hours."

"I feel a little funny about this," he admitted.

"Having second thoughts? You know you can still change your mind."

"Absolutely not. How about you?"

"I'm fine. Does your wife suspect anything?"

"She doesn't have a clue. Did you get the reservation?"

"I think everything's perfect."

"Knew you could do it, Diane. I can't wait."

"See you in a little while."

"Don't forget anything. Missed details could sink our ship."

Diane giggled. "Don't worry, I won't."

"Bye."

"Bye."

Diane hung up the phone, sighed, and wondered why Peter couldn't be as thoughtful as this man was. Any other woman in her position couldn't help but feel the same way.

9

After questioning Carmine, Daniel circled the tenement the shot had come from, searching for an escape route. The building sat close to the one behind it. A back door faced the alley, but it appeared to be rusted shut. He imagined the killer rushing away, his sense of urgency. He studied the narrow alleyway one more time before moving to join his partner upstairs.

⬛

Milano had already entered the second-floor apartment. Kaminski, Lily Chang from forensics, and a couple of officers were there, but not much else. There was no furniture. Propped against the frame of an open window was a bolt-action Remington .223 sniper rifle with telescopic attachment—presumably the murder weapon.

Chang was busy dusting for prints. Kaminski paced the flat while offering theories to the two officers on how the crime went down. They pretended to be interested in what he had to say.

Kaminski saw Milano enter. "Sergeant Sam Milano. It's been awhile."

They shook hands.

"Nice seeing you again, Inspector."

"Inspector? Why so formal? Call me Russ. After all, I'm out of my jurisdiction. Only here as an observer for the task force. You knew me when I drove for the police commissioner. Remember when you had to come to Philadelphia for those seminars?"

Sam *did* remember Kaminski: red-faced, loud, not that bright, and he sometimes drank too much. But he also recalled Kaminski being good-natured and honest.

"I understand that you're now the Commish's brother-in-law."

"Yes sir, my sister married that fat son of a bitch. Imagine that. How do you think I got this bullshit position, anyway?" He laughed hard, smacked Milano on the back. "Nothing wrong with that. Is there?"

"Guess not, Russ."

"Can't complain, though. Treats my sister real good.

Me, too. How's your family doing? What was it, three kids you had?"

"Two," Sam corrected. "Matthew's in college now and Beth is in high school."

"Great! Wish I had kids. And your wife, er . . . Harriet?"

"Helen. She's doing just fine, thanks."

"I should have gotten married, but who'd have me?" Kaminski laughed again.

Sam politely smiled back.

"About this case, Sam. I think we got it figured out," Kaminski announced and began to summarize, at length, his masterful deductions—most of which Daniel and Sam had already considered and rejected.

Thankfully, Kaminski's explanation was interrupted by the sound of Daniel entering the room.

"Inspector Kaminski, I'd like you to meet Detective Daniel Pinchus."

"So you're the whiz kid I heard so much about," Kaminski complimented.

They clasped hands.

"I was just telling Sam here what I got so far."

"Yes, I overheard," Daniel replied.

"Yeah, old Paco Perez was on target. Has all the markings of a classic mob hit—well planned, very few clues. The location is ideal, once you realize that Luccetta has breakfast every Wednesday morning right across the fucking street. I know this case is yours and Sam's, but I took the liberty of contacting the landlord of this joint. The guy who rented the apartment paid cash. Probably wore a disguise. But you still might want to check out his description. The rifle's serial number was filed off. Don't worry, your gal dusted the piece before I touched it."

Daniel looked toward Chang.

She nodded back, then continued her work.

"You can ask the manufacturer, though. May get lucky with another way to trace it."

"You never know," Daniel said, rolling his eyes at Sam when Kaminski turned away.

"Not likely," Chang offered in her distinct accent. "That piece very popular. Does a good job. Fire maybe twenty-eight hundred feet per second. Hits head—instant guacamole."

Daniel picked the rifle up, drew the bolt back. "Chamber's empty."

"One that's up, is the one you use," said Chang.

Kaminski turned back to them. "Huh?"

"Guy's a pro," Milano explained. "Didn't think he'd need a second shot."

"And the bullet?" Daniel inquired.

Chang shrugged. "Still looking."

"Other than that, I don't think you'll have many leads," Kaminski continued. "Remember, these are only suggestions. Hope I haven't stepped on anyone's toes."

"Not at all," Daniel replied. "Thanks."

Sam could tell Daniel was ready to blow, ready to let Kaminski have it. But his young partner had promised to behave, and so far, was doing an admirable job. *Keep it cool, Danny boy. Keep it cool.*

"Lily, did you dust the window for a possible palm print?" Daniel asked. "Since he didn't have a chair to rest on, he could've used his hand for a prop—placed it on the sill and forgot to wipe it down," he added for Kaminski's benefit.

"Did it. Nada," answered Lily.

"Hey." Kaminski laughed. "Thought you were supposed to be some sort of whiz kid. Jesus. The guy wore gloves. Even I realized that. Ain't gonna leave a print to trace. You're wasting your time."

Milano shot a glance at Daniel, warned him with his eyes. But it was too late.

"So tell me, In-spec-tor," Daniel was already saying. "When did the landlord say he rented out this apartment?"

"Three weeks ago. Got two months in advance. Cash."

"Cash. So you said. But, if this *was* a revenge killing, then how did they plan it so far in advance? The bodies up in Coal County—which haven't been positively identified yet—were only discovered yesterday."

"Don't know." Kaminski shrugged. "Maybe somebody knew about them before now. You can't tell me this wasn't a professional hit."

"Professional, all right, but this wasn't so much a hit as it was an assassination. You said it yourself, Inspector. Luccetta was a creature of habit. You want revenge, why not drive a car down the street and take out the whole lot of them with semiautomatics. Or better yet, blow up Carmine's when they're all drinking coffee and eating doughnuts. Luccetta wasn't worried about a mob war, otherwise he would have never let himself become vulnerable. No, this was an assassination meant only to kill Luccetta for some other reason. Something he wasn't worried about. Seven walked away unharmed. Perez is wrong."

"And *your* Captain Schwenk is right?" Kaminski challenged.

"Didn't say that either. But Perez blew the motive. He still has a lot of responsibility for those witnesses."

"So does Schwenk."

"And so does the whole fuckin' task force."

"That was before I came aboard," Kaminski defended. "Okay, whiz kid, your *assassin* takes out Luccetta, walks out the front door—then who does he go to?"

"What do you mean?"

"If he's not part of a rival mob, where's his allegiance? Who did he do it for?"

"Maybe himself. Too early to tell. But what makes you think he left the building from the front?"

"No other fucking way out of here, whiz kid."

"Sure?"

Milano knew Daniel must have figured something out. He was baiting Kaminski. And Kaminski, true to form, kept putting his foot in his fat mouth.

"Yup. I checked," Kaminski replied. "Ain't such a great neighborhood. All the windows on the first floor are barred. And the back door hasn't opened in years. It's rusted shut."

"So he coolly walked out into the middle of the street in full view of seven of Luccetta's best men? Don't you think they would be staring at this building? Even running over to it?"

"Well, he isn't fucking here. Is he, Detective?" Kaminski yelled back, his arms flung above his head, his face bright red.

"Aha. Very good, Inspector. Maybe he's hiding out somewhere in this building."

Kaminski lowered his arms, for a moment seriously contemplating the possibility.

"But I rejected the idea," Daniel said. "Too risky. He had to get away."

"So he did go down the steps and out the front?" Kaminski asked.

"Not *down,* but up."

"Up?"

"To the roof."

"Had a helicopter waiting, did he?"

"Let's go up and see," Daniel suggested. He led the way. The door to the roof had a dead bolt on the inside, but it had been left in the open position. The trio stepped out onto the flat roof deck.

Daniel pointed to the far end. "The next building's pretty close to this one. Roofs are pretty even. It's a warehouse. I think the township stores its winter stuff there—salt and plows. This time of year it's deserted. It would be perfect."

"I get it," Kaminski replied. "Your assassin jumped to the next building. Hell, it's not that far. Even I can make it."

"Think so?" Daniel asked. "Or do you want to wait for your helicopter?"

"All right, Daniel, that's enough," Milano chided.

Kaminski stared at Detective Pinchus. The look was dispassionate and intense. Then came a grin, which grew to a laugh. "Sam, I love this whiz kid."

Daniel laughed, too, in spite of himself.

"Enough games," Kaminski conceded. "I can tell I'm out of my league. If I didn't get some lucky breaks, I'd still be walking a beat in Center City. Okay, Detective Daniel Pinchus, tell me the rest."

"After the shooter hits his target, he runs up here and jumps across. With all of the commotion on the other side of the building, it's unlikely that anyone would see him. Then he goes into the warehouse—door previously left unlocked—and leaves conspicuously from around the corner. And I think I can prove it."

"Amazing," Kaminski said.

"Grab Lily Chang on the way down," Daniel said. "There's something I want her to check out."

A few minutes later, they congregated at the entrance to the warehouse. Daniel asked Lily to look for prints on *that* front door.

"But he wore *gloves*," Inspector Kaminski stubbornly pointed out.

They all stared at him.

"Okay . . . I'll be quiet."

"If I'm right," Daniel said, "our boy raced down from the top of this building after he'd just killed somebody important. He had to look natural and calm. So, he rested for a moment, checked himself, and took off his gloves *prior* to opening the door. He would look too suspicious doing it on the street. When he pulled the door shut, he left his mark."

"There could be a hundred different prints on that doorknob. How are you going to tell which ones belong to the killer?" Kaminski asked.

"It rained last night, heavy," Daniel explained. "Building's hardly used. I'm willing to bet the only clear ones will be his."

"He's right," Chang announced. "And here they are."

10

▉▉▉▉▉▉ Dr. Peter Roberts drove straight through to Coal County, and with the aid of a little speeding, arrived at the hospital there just after ten-thirty. He was grateful that he hadn't been pulled over. He had a collection of forensic dental evidence—on permanent loan from Dr. Onasis—stored in the trunk of his car because Diane wouldn't allow it in the house: several jaws in formaldehyde, preserved human tissue engraved with bite marks, countless individual teeth. What would a state trooper think if he happened to look? That Peter was a bizarre, mutilating serial killer, no doubt.

Roberts located the morgue, prepared himself for

decomposing bodies of a month's duration, then opened the door. He was immediately overcome by the putrid smell. The sight was even worse. And the room was infested with bugs: crawling, jumping, flying.

On one side of the room, crumpled on a stainless steel autopsy table, were the rotting remains of what had once been a person: hands and feet still grotesquely hog-tied, arms behind the back, knees bent, wrists secured to the ankles.

Tom Onasis, his assistant Kristina, and another person about Peter's age with thinning black hair, were gowned and huddled over the body. They had apparently just finished recording their preliminary findings and were preparing to undo the ropes and undress the victim.

Seated as far away as he could possibly get was a heavyset black man in a police sergeant's uniform. He wore a surgical mask. Roberts recognized the slight oily stain on the front of it. It was not uncommon, for those unused to the proceedings or of less fortitude, to smear Vick's there to camouflage the sickening odor.

Standing next to him, also in uniform and looking peaked, was a young woman, a plain-featured, short-haired blonde. She was holding a clipboard and taking notes.

The morgue was cramped, not like the spacious facility at Hamilton General Hospital that he was used to. Here there was only one autopsy table, set to one side of a room approximately twenty feet square.

Dr. Onasis glanced up from his work. "Hi, Peter. Thanks for coming."

Kristina swiped at a fly near her face. "Hi, Doc. Welcome to Bugs 101. You name it, we got it."

"Jesus. Are these all from the bodies?" Peter asked.

"Yup," Kristina said.

"Due to the season," Onasis explained. "Been unusually warm of late. That, and about four weeks of decomposition—"

"And voilà!" Kristina interrupted. "Recipe for an infestation."

"Grab a gown while I introduce you," Onasis said, pointing to a cabinet in the corner. "Our two tenderfoots over there are Sergeant LeRoy Pentagast, of the Philadelphia Police Department, and Officer Nancy Kirkland, from here in Coal County."

Peter nodded, pulling on a gown. "Nice to meet you."

They nodded back.

"And helping us this morning," Onasis continued, "is Luther Pith, keeper of this morgue. The finest diener I've ever had the privilege of working with."

Kristina turned toward Onasis, gave him an annoyed look.

Luther shook his head and smiled. "Come on, Doc, you've only worked with me once before."

"Yes, I know," Onasis said, "but I'm just not used to such excellence."

Kristina winced. "Thanks a lot, Doc. I'll remember that the next time you need a favor. Like when you called me last Sunday to come in and set the morgue up. An important postmortem, you said."

"And I lied. Why don't you tell everyone why?"

"All right. It was a surprise thirtieth birthday party for me."

"A party in the morgue?" Pentagast croaked through his mask. "You people are sick."

"Wouldn't have it any other way," Kristina said lightly. "But the point is, you snap your fingers and I jump."

Onasis rolled his eyes. "I'm sorry. Kristina, you're wonderful."

Onasis and Kristina were famous for such friendly

bickering. It made their working together, amidst the sadness of human tragedy, a little more bearable.

"What's the rundown?" Peter asked.

"Both victims were beaten about the head," Onasis said. "The lady, waiting in the fridge, also has an apparent gunshot wound to the chest. Odd, though. Radiographs didn't show any evidence of a bullet. And I didn't notice an exit wound when we x-rayed her body."

"Probably missed it," Kristina said. "We'll find it when we get to her. Forensics is still sifting the ground, looking for fragments."

"The coroner will be right back," Onasis told Peter. "He has the antemortem dental records. Sergeant Pentagast turned the files over to him."

"I drove them up from Philly," Pentagast commented as he pulled his mask down, letting it dangle around his neck. "We've been looking for these two for weeks. Thought it might come down to a dental ID, so I got the records a while ago from a clinic in Center City. Both had work done there. Pretty sure these two are the couple we've been looking for, though."

Peter had read about the witnesses in the newspapers. And he knew a lot of people had a lot at stake in their being identified. "How can you be so sure?" he asked.

"Eeassy," Pentagast crooned. "All you need to—"

"Ugh!" Onasis swatted at a group of beetles crawling up his arm. "Luther, can't we do anything about these bugs?"

Luther shrugged. "What can I do?"

"What's the number for maintenance?" Kristina asked, walking over to the wall phone near the entrance to the morgue. Luther gave it to her and she dialed quickly. "Maintenance? This is the morgue. Listen, we have a situation down here. Need a Shop-Vac.

You have one of those? Good. Get it down here, pronto. Who am I? This is by order of Dr. Onasis," she announced with authority, and hung up.

"Cool," Officer Kirkland remarked.

"A Shop-Vac?" Onasis asked.

"*You* come up with something better," Kristina challenged. "We'll suck these varmints up."

"You were saying?" Peter said to Pentagast.

"Oh, yeah. All you need to do is look at these two corpses and you'll realize what *I* did. What *anyone* would."

Peter stared at the victim. Aside from the dark green discoloration of a decomposing body and the movement of thousands of insects and maggots that seemed to make the skin pulsate, there was nothing remarkable about him: a small man, thin and short; age, mid to late fifties; hair, gray.

"So?" Peter shrugged.

"You haven't seen the other one yet. Never did release a description of these two. Needed to protect them—so the task force said. Hah!"

"I'm listening."

"The woman's a giant. About six feet four, and fat. Maybe four hundred pounds." LeRoy Pentagast raised his eyebrows. "You think they weren't noticed in that restaurant?"

11

Roberts turned his attention to the stainless-steel table. The victim was now totally undressed and lying on his back. Onasis and Kristina were taking measurements and calling them out. Pith wrote them down. When Onasis spotted something interesting or noteworthy, he would grab his microcassette recorder—always placed within a step's reach—and dictate his findings.

Roberts had been to enough autopsies to understand what he saw and what needed to be done. Within a few hours of death, certain insects are attracted to the exposed body. Flies lay their eggs there. The eggs incubate and hatch into maggots. Now, there were maggots all over the body. They were swarming, especially in the moist, warm areas: the pubis, armpits, anus, nose, mouth, and ears—entranceways to the inside of the body. As maggots mature they increase in size, in direct relationship to how long they've been there. Depending on the fly species and the general conditions, after a set period of time they move off the body and form a pupa. With metamorphosis complete, they hatch into flies. Every few minutes a new one would swoop up.

Peter watched as Kristina held out a five-inch plastic specimen tube. Dr. Onasis gathered up a few maggots using a pair of tweezers and dropped them into the tube. They repeated this process twice more. An entomologist would study the maggots' sizes with respect to which fly species were present. This would help determine the number of cycles that had transpired, and hopefully, by calculating backwards, give a better idea of the time of death. The entomologist would look at other insects for clues as well. Onasis was about to collect some carrion beetles, known for feeding off of decaying matter.

Roberts knew the ground beneath the body would also be examined: grasses, mosses, leaves, and the like—trapped beneath the body, dating the moment of death with the specific conditions that existed at that point in the season. He was fascinated by the merger of science and mystery. *How did the body get there? How long had it been there? What happened? How did this person die?* The body held secrets waiting to be found. Talented investigators such as Tom Onasis, working with a team of experts, could answer these questions and unshroud the mysteries. That's why Roberts became interested in forensic dentistry: to be a part of the team, to be close to the intrigue. And he admired Onasis. He had learned from him, and remembered the lessons: *No matter how quiet and still the body lies, it always has something to say. Sometimes it shouts, but more often it whispers. Just put your ear to it, coax it gently, and listen . . . carefully.*

Roberts studied the victim. He appeared to be wearing a loose pair of tattered gloves and booties. The condition, he knew, was called degloving—when the dead skin begins to slough off of the decomposing hands and feet. The upper arms, legs, and torso had a greenish tone. This, Roberts had also seen before. It was due to the colonic bacteria proliferating throughout the body and creeping under the skin.

"Holy cow!" Onasis shouted suddenly as he looked through the beetles for a good sample. "They're having an orgy."

Each bug was engaged with another, piggyback fashion. It was difficult to find any asunder.

Kristina's eyes widened. "Now that's *my* idea of a party. Plenty to eat, good sex, and always a load of stuff fermenting. My thirtieth should have been more like *this*," she said, waving a finger at Onasis.

"I'll keep it in mind for your thirty-fifth," he offered.

The rest of the men chuckled. Nancy Kirkland simply smiled, politely.

Onasis lifted one of the victim's pasty eyelids, studied the oculus, then checked the other. There wasn't much left, due to the decomposition and the bugs. Not enough to establish eye color. Just faded remnants of the white, fibrous sclera.

"I read this morning in the obits about one of my patients dying," Roberts mentioned as he watched Onasis continue his external exam. "Recently did a lot of work on him. When it hits home, it makes you think."

"Sure does," Onasis agreed. "Who was it? I remember three being tagged yesterday morning at the morgue."

"Woodrow Fenstermaker."

Onasis shook his head. "You mean Fenster*marker*."

"No, Fenstermaker. From Rivington."

"Fenstermarker from Northrup," Onasis insisted.

"Stroke victim. Fifty-four years young. Read more care-fully next time. This one wasn't your patient."

"Then I'm relieved. I guess I only glanced at the death notice," Roberts admitted. "But who would have thought that there were two Woodrows with such simi-lar last names?"

Pentagast laughed deep from his belly. "Last year my wife had me dead. Had to look in the bed to see if I was still breathing. Saw that a LeRoy Pentagast had died. She was so taken aback that she didn't realize it was LeRoy R. Pentagast. The last name was spelled the same, but I'm LeRoy M."

"Always *observe*," Onasis cautioned.

The door to the morgue flew open. A fastidiously dressed man stepped in: perfectly knotted tie; black pin-striped suit pressed to an edge; sleek Italian loafers. Everything seemed in place, except for the awkward-looking toupee he wore. He headed straight to where Peter stood in the center of the room.

"You the forensic dentist?" he asked as he swiped at an insect that lit on his forehead.

Peter nodded.

He covertly checked his hairpiece, then offered his hand. "Coroner Elliot Brandle."

"Peter Roberts."

They shook.

Brandle looked around the crowded room. "Sorry for the tight quarters." He turned back to Peter, handed him a manila folder. "These are the dental records of Roman and Ethel Johnson. Everything is there. Make your ID. Send your report and your bill to this ad-dress." He reached inside his jacket and pulled out a card.

Roberts took it, opening the antemortem dental file as Brandle continued talking.

"We do things properly in this county. Make sure your report is a reflection of that."

Glancing at the records, Peter let out a groan.

Brandle lost his slick composure for a moment. "What? What's the matter?"

"Maybe nothing," Peter answered. "It's just that these are on NCIC forms. Do you have the *actual* records? Copies of the charts, X rays, treatment notes?"

Brandle looked at Pentagast. "That all you brought?"

LeRoy shrugged. "The clerk at Missing Persons gave me those forms. Said all I needed to do was have the dentist fill them out."

"Sometimes these aren't accurate enough," Roberts explained. "Unless the dentist is familiar with the form, mistakes are easily made. These forms can be very confusing."

The National Crime Information Center had implemented a computerized system to help identify missing persons throughout the country. Law enforcement agencies, with the aid of a dentist, could send in a dental profile of an individual declared missing. These would be stored along with submissions of found individuals—usually discovered dead, but with an unknown identity. The computer automatically compared the antemortem dental record with the postmortem dental findings in an effort to obtain a match. Anything close would get flagged, usually in order of likelihood. Then, a forensic dentist would make the final determination as to whether there is a positive identification or not. The program was a step in the right direction, and was especially helpful with searches across state lines. But Roberts knew, unfortunately, that it was plagued with human error. *He* even found the computer forms to be perplexing at times.

Peter took out the sheet that was labeled Roman

Johnson, placed it on top of the folder, and carried it over to the head of the body.

"Here, let me help you, Doc," Luther said, bringing over a head block and slipping it under the base of the skull to elevate it.

"Thanks," Peter said. He placed the gloved thumb and index finger of his free hand against the chin of the victim, pushed down, and the jaw opened. Glancing from the teeth to the form and back again several times, Peter made mental notes. Then he shook his head. "Shit!"

Brandle was fidgeting with the eraser end of his pencil. "What?"

"I'm pretty sure that this is Roman Johnson. There's enough similarity here."

"But?"

"But, there are also some grave mistakes. The form says that tooth number eleven is missing. It is not. Tooth number twelve is actually missing. One whole quadrant of teeth is mislabeled on the form. I can't give you a positive based on this."

Brandle nodded. He understood.

"Come on, Doc," LeRoy whined. "You just said you're sure it's him. Sign off on the positive. Then do the lady so we can get out of here. My little girl's in a play tonight and I got to drive back to Philly."

"He can't do that," Onasis said, shaking his head. "They'll tear him apart in court. 'Isn't it true, Dr. Roberts, that you found some major inconsistencies in your dental comparison?' a sharp attorney would ask. 'And you made a determination as to identity without proving these inconsistencies to be mistakes? Just how thorough are you, Dr. Roberts?' "

"Okay, I get the picture." Pentagast sighed.

"What if we get the clinic to fax a copy of the dental charts?" Brandle asked.

"Still might need the X rays," Peter said.

"But you might not, right?" LeRoy quickly asked.

"*If* they're very complete. And *if* they don't have the same mistakes that are on the NCIC forms."

"What about the woman?" Onasis said from across the room. "You want us to pull her so you can check the dental now?"

"Christ," Kristina said. "Getting her out will be a major bitch. Don't want to do that until we have to."

"Relax," Peter replied. "We don't know if there are any mistakes on her dental form, but have them fax both charts. I'll get to *her* when you're ready."

"Good," Brandle said. "Sergeant Pentagast, call the dental clinic. Have them take care of it."

LeRoy went over to the wall phone and called the clinic. After he hung up, he turned to Peter, "Sure hope this gives you what you need. My kid's counting on me being there tonight."

"Me, too," Peter replied, suddenly thinking of his own daughter.

"I'm going upstairs to wait for the fax," Brandle said. "Anything else you guys need before I leave?"

"Yeah, a pest strip," Officer Kirkland said as she stamped on a bug that got too close.

"I called maintenance for a Shop-Vac fifteen minutes ago," Kristina said. "Where the hell are they?"

"A Shop—? Never mind. I'll take care of it," Brandle said as he left the morgue.

"Hey, LeRoy," Kristina called out as she picked up an electric saw. "You better get your mask back on. We're about ready to enter the body cavity."

12

Afterward, he had gone directly to the place nobody knew, except the boy. And *he* showed up soon after.

The kid was given a reward: a fifty-dollar bill for a job well done—also for the humping he took five minutes after walking through the door. The lecher couldn't help himself, he was so excited. *Nice young boy. Good boy.* It would be a long time before he had such a chance again . . . if ever.

So far, the plan had moved along superbly, better than expected. He went over the instructions for the next phase, but didn't really have to. The kid knew what to do. He was a good learner. The lecher had seen that right off, and taught him well.

The boy was obedient without question, not unlike so many others who fell victim to his psychological grasp of obsession, fear, and envy: vulnerable youth,

needful of attention, easy pickings for one with an eye
trained for ripeness.

Most people were appalled by such sickness and
wondered how victims allowed themselves to be
claimed. They didn't understand it. Nor did they feel a
need to. It was easier to sit in judgment of the aberra-
tion. They knew it existed, read newspapers and heard
stories—but this was too disparate from *their* reality. *It*
only happened elsewhere: far away from them. And it
was for that same reason that so much of *it* went on,
more than what anyone dared to think, because they
simply failed to look next door.

After the boy left, the lecher listened to his police
scanner for a time, heard that Sergeant Sam Milano and
Detective Daniel Pinchus were assigned to the case. *Excellent!* He had known that this was highly probable.
Now he wouldn't have to call the police making a request. *Crazed assassin taunts authorities by asking for specific investigator.* One less headline—that was fine. One
less thing to do—that was great.

He flicked on the television to catch the late-
morning news. He made the lead story. It caused him
to smile. An on-the-scene reporter was speculating
about a connection between this murder and the two
suspected witnesses, identities still to be confirmed,
that were discovered last night in Coal County. A news
anchorman joined in the discussion with an almost
childlike excitement over the possibility of a mob war
erupting. The reporter agreed with that prospect, nodding vigorously to the camera.

*Idiots! Fools! Spewing out rehearsed deductions on
things they knew nothing about. And even if they did know
the true depth of what took place, they'd still dig a little
deeper like the worms that they were.*

Then there was a glimpse of Congressman Charles
Whitney's news conference. He was telling a crowd that

there was far too much violence in our streets. ". . . whether an innocent victim, or someone like Luccetta, the situation is deplorable. It's still a human life . . ."

It was funny to hear Whitney say those things. Whitney knew the monster Luccetta was, knew he needed dying, and had to be overjoyed at his death. "Fucking politician. Look what you've become, Charles," he said to the TV.

It was time to write the letter and announce just who did this deed. When he was done, he carefully folded the paper, stuffed it into an envelope, and marked it: *FOR THE CONGRESSMAN'S EYES ONLY.*

He headed for the door daydreaming about a time many years ago. He stopped, caught the image of himself in a mirror in the hallway: head partially shaven, eyes bloodshot, features gaunt. The look was chilling. For a moment he had forgotten and it startled him. *What had happened? How did he get here?* He crushed the weakness. Then he furrowed his brow and gazed into the glass. *"Better,"* he mumbled to himself. He saw the scars that were too deep to be reflected. They were softer now than yesterday. And the pain began to ease across his face. It would take more time for it all to disappear. He would go mail the letter and come back. The pieces would fall into place. There wouldn't be much more to do . . . but sit and wait.

13

Sergeant Sam Milano and Detective Daniel Pinchus arrived at the Rivington Street station at eleven-fifteen A.M. The set of prints lifted from the front door of the warehouse had been blown up and faxed to the closest AFIS center, in Lima, Pennsylvania. AFIS, Automated Fingerprint Identification System, was a federal computer bank. If the system wasn't backlogged, they would know whether or not they had a match within minutes. According to Lily Chang, the fax had been sent almost an hour ago.

In the meantime, they discussed a memo from Detective Junior Gibney, who owned a snitch with some connections to the Luccetta crime family. Word was already out that the family was looking for Barney Terzetto—someone who had worked for Luccetta, had gotten close, and now, conspicuously, had disappeared.

They ran a check on the name. It came up clean.

"Either he's the shooter," Milano started.

"Or he's also dead somewhere," Daniel finished.

Sergeant Vanderhooven, who was working the front desk, passed by with a fresh cup of coffee in his hand.

"Hey, Vandy," Milano called to him. "Anything on those victims up in Coal County?"

Vanderhooven turned his head. "Nope. Captain just spoke to the coroner on the phone. ID's gonna take a while. Hear it's a real mess. Bugs everywhere."

"Schwenk tell you that?"

"Didn't have to. Saw his face. He had that look. You know, the one where his lip curls up and quivers."

Milano laughed as Vanderhooven headed back downstairs. "Wish I was there."

"Am I missing something here?" Daniel asked.

"Your father never mentioned it? Schwenk hates bugs. Can't believe you didn't know, De-tec-tive," Milano teased.

"Guess it never came up."

"Not necessarily a phobia, mind you. He's just revolted by them. One of his many quirks. Still thinks nobody's aware of it. Like washing his hands incessantly."

"Now *that* I've seen."

"There's hope for you yet."

Daniel waved him off.

"Speaking of which . . ." Sam whispered to Daniel as he nodded across the squad room.

Daniel turned just in time to see Schwenk slowly heading toward the men's room with his distinctive limp and a scowl on his face.

"Second time since we've been back," Daniel declared. "Got the cleanest hands in Hamilton. Or a bladder infection."

"He's nervous," Milano said. "Worried about those witnesses. They turn up dead, he's fucked. Needs to find out who killed Luccetta, and quick to take some of the heat off."

The phone on Sam's desk rang. "Milano here." He swung his chair to the side, facing Daniel. "Uh-huh . . . That's great . . . See ya soon. . . ."

Daniel raised an eyebrow.

Sam hung up, shaking his head. "That was the DA's office. Search warrant for blood and hair on the Putnam case is ready. Needs to be signed and picked up." He reached inside his pocket, tossed Daniel his keys. "You go. Looks like you could use a break. I'll wait here for AFIS."

Daniel didn't argue. On the way, he stopped at an antique store near the courthouse. There was a Bentley rocker in the window that Susan had her heart set on. Pricey, though. He was able to talk them down, but not enough. Another time. He took care of the warrant and was back within the hour.

As soon as he reentered the squad room, Sam announced that they'd gotten a hit on the prints.

Daniel's eyes widened. "We did? When?"

"Right after you left."

"Damn! Who? Where?"

"Easy, partner. Name is . . ." Milano pulled a pad from his shirt pocket and flipped a couple of pages. "Arthur Sarchick. Forty-three years old. No known address."

"Priors?"

"A couple. AFIS gave us two SID numbers in Pennsylvania." SID numbers were used as jurisdictional arrest labels in some states and could provide them with more details of the charges.

"Anything outside of Pennsylvania?"

"Not as far as we know. Most recent was for racketeering. Nailed him in Philly. Raided a gambling house—backdoor operation. Did eighteen months at

Graterford until his parole, then did a Houdini on his parole officer. The other was some time ago." Milano paused, pursed his lips.

"For?"

"A sex offense."

"A rapist?" Daniel said with surprise. "We're looking for a goddamn rapist?"

"I didn't say rape. I said sex offense. The charge was aggravated indecent assault."

"Same thing in my book," Daniel argued. "What difference does it make what he sticks, or where he sticks it?"

"According to the law it matters," Milano pointed out.

"And in this case?"

"It was some time ago. Near Harrisburg. Eleven years to be exact. Had a relationship with the victim."

"Girlfriend?"

Milano shook his head. "No girls involved. Victim was also much younger. Sarchick was a football coach in a youth league."

"Son of a bitch. How old?"

"Ten."

"Fuck! And he probably got away with it more than once."

"You're right. Several other complaints never made it to court. Don't have to tell you how difficult it is to prosecute cases like that. Cooperation isn't always there. The fear. The shame. For the parents and the kids." Milano put his notepad away. "And there's another strange detail about the Harrisburg arrest. When they went to pick him up, his apartment was filled with magazines. Stacks of them everywhere."

"How did you find that out?" Daniel asked, brow furrowed.

"It was important enough to mention in the arrest report. Shows obsessive behavior."

"Kiddie porn?"

"Mostly. And tons of others. Technical ones, too. Reminded me of you."

"How so?"

"Never throws anything out."

Daniel stared at Milano coldly. "Nothing wrong with being frugal."

"He's also got a juvenile record. Picked up twice for molesting."

"Figures. Where?"

"Hamilton. Grew up here. Moved to Harrisburg somewhere down the line. But Sarchick was only six-teen-seventeen when the incidents occurred. Both times on Halloween."

"Halloween? Used the same MO?"

Milano nodded.

"Caught twice. That wasn't very bright."

"Was only a kid himself then. Young and careless."

"What'd he do, lure the kids into his house when they came calling?"

"No," Milano said. "He was on the street looking for them . . . dressed in costume."

"Shit!" said Daniel, his stomach turning.

Before he could say any more, Vanderhooven came by with a fax for Milano. "Got your pictures, Sergeant."

Milano quickly spread the pages on the desk. "Cop-ies of the actual arrest photos are being sent overnight from Philly and Harrisburg," he explained. "For now, I had them get us the faxes to work from."

"Jesus, looks like he's two different guys," Daniel remarked, staring over Sam's shoulder.

The arrest photo from Harrisburg showed a clean-shaven, robust man, with close-cropped hair, butch style. The accompanying file noted: height 5'9"; eyes and hair, brown.

The one from Philly revealed a long-haired man, painfully thin-featured, with scraggly whiskers. This time the file noted: height 5'11"; eyes green; hair black.

"Do you think they made a mistake?" Daniel asked.

"Not likely. Same birth date. Same fingerprints," Milano answered. "They *are* only faxes."

Daniel studied the two different faces. "You did say there were several years between the arrest in Harrisburg and the one in Philly."

"Yes."

"Much younger man here," Daniel said, pointing to the photocopy from Harrisburg. "This scumbag gets his ass nailed. His cover's blown. Wants to bury his past, maybe loses the weight in prison. When he gets out, he bags it in Harrisburg, starts fresh in Philadelphia. Out with the old. Grows his hair longer. Dyes it black. Colored contacts for the eyes, lifts in his shoes—which of course were all missed by the police in Philly—and you have a different guy."

"Even a different charge," Milano added. "Nothing on file since Harrisburg. Maybe he made another total change."

Daniel shook his head. "Don't think they change that easily—pedophiles, that is. He got wiser. Learned how to manipulate his victims. And Carmine told me that he thought he saw the kid on the bicycle hand Luccetta a note right before he was killed. *That's* what made him look up at the window. It all fits."

"Shit, that's right," Sam agreed. "But still, he doesn't fit the profile of an assassin. Maybe he just happened to be the one who touched that doorknob."

"Yeah, and I'm Mother Theresa. Sam, the guy has a record, jumps parole, and changes appearance. Now, he *just happens* to leave his prints where we expect to find the murderer's? I don't believe in coincidences. It's him."

"That's not enough for a jury."

"We'll get more."

Sam slapped Daniel on the back. "You know, you sound just like your father."

"Sam . . . please."

"I meant it only in the best of ways."

Daniel nodded ceremoniously.

Sam smiled. "At least we have something to go on. That should make Schwenk happy. Kaminski, too."

"You know, the inspector was right about one thing."

"Which was?"

"The killer must've been wearing a disguise," replied Daniel.

"After seeing those two pictures, we may be dealing with someone who's a master at masquerade."

"Trick or treat, baby."

Milano sighed. He envisioned young children at the mercy of such a monster. The thought was terrifying.

14

█████ The attack had been relentless. He even feared defeat for a time—a possibility he rarely considered—until he noticed the weakness. It was the slightest of nuances that revealed what his opponent tried to hide. He didn't give his awareness away, but rather drew the challenger in more deeply. He relied on those instincts, those tactics that seldom let him down. And after a time, when it had become too late to change the inevitable, he delivered the fatal blow.

"Checkmate, Oscar," Seymour Pinchus announced as he slid his bishop into position.

"Damn it, Seymour. Think you could let me win once in a while? You know, it wouldn't kill you."

"Would you really want me to?"

Oscar shook his head. "No."

"But you're getting much better," Seymour conceded. "Almost had me there."

"Seymour!"

"Really, Oscar. You tipped your hand, though."

"How?" Oscar looked unconvinced.

"I really shouldn't give my secrets away. But I will. May even things up for the next time."

"I'm listening."

"When you left your knight vulnerable, I knew you were baiting me. It was the slight quiver in your finger when you moved the piece. That, and the way your tongue grazed across your mustache."

"I wet my lips, Seymour," he said shortly.

"Dry mouth," Pinchus pointed out. "A cardinal sign."

"But you took the piece anyway," Oscar declared.

"Yes, I know. Wanted to see just how important your move was. And you were very happy about that—lit your pipe and sucked hard. That's when I knew. Saw exactly what you were up to."

"You're not talking chess here, you're talking psychology."

"Life is a chess game, Oscar. I thought you knew that. Anyway, I let you have your way with me until your confidence got so great it was blinding. You never saw the end coming."

"Hogwash! You're just playing with my mind. Trembling finger, my ass. You had me from the get-go. I should have guessed when I was up a couple of pieces early it was all part of a plan. You're too good to let that happen. Sorry, Seymour, I don't accept it."

That's how it usually was, or so Seymour Pinchus believed: people giving him more credit than he deserved.

"Ready for a rematch?" Oscar offered.

"Why not. It's nice playing out here in the park. Beautiful day."

"A bit cold for me."

"Not really. You're just annoyed you lost."

Oscar scratched his bald head. "You're right."

They began to reset the pieces.

"Retirement still got you down, Seymour?" Oscar asked, his tone suddenly serious.

Pinchus shrugged. "Mostly. Especially when Kate's away. She's on one of her missions now."

"For how long?"

"A week. I miss her desperately. She'll be back tomorrow night, though. Have to pick her up at the airport. And you, Oscar?"

"Me?"

"Yeah. Ever miss your work at the paper, have the urge to grab your camera and run out to a breaking story?"

"Did it for too long, worked too hard," Oscar answered without hesitation. "I looked forward to retirement. I love photography. Still do it. Difference is, now I don't have to."

"Wish I had that attitude."

"You should, Seymour. What has it been? Four years? You have to learn to enjoy this life—nobody telling you where to go and what to do. You make your own rules: Sleep late, take a drive in the country, or play chess in the park on a glorious day. It's the time you stop and smell the roses."

"Roses give me hives."

"Jesus, Seymour. Why do you always have to be so difficult? In all the years I've known you, you haven't changed."

"Nor have you!" Pinchus retorted.

"Thought we'd soften with age."

"Soften?" Pinchus smiled. "All I know is that we're getting older. I'm getting older and I don't like it."

"The alternative ain't too good, my friend."

"What do they say?" Pinchus said. "The fifties are the old age of youth. And the sixties are the youth of old age. I wasn't too thrilled with my fifty-something status. But at least it was still in the young category. I'll turn sixty in a few months—certified old age." He scowled.

"So that's what this is all about, Seymour? Mourning the passing of your youth?"

"No, not entirely. Trouble is, Oscar, I . . ." Pinchus sighed. "I don't feel needed anymore."

"We're all needed, Seymour," Oscar said sincerely. "You *know* you are. You're too smart not to acknowledge that. The problem is, you don't give it the importance it deserves."

Pinchus aimed a glare at Oscar. "Now who's playing a psychology game?"

"You don't buy it," Oscar said, knowing his friend well.

"Oscar?"

"What?"

"Thanks, anyway."

Suddenly, a child's shout came from the neighborhood of the swings and monkey bars. A woman wheeled around and directed her attention toward the cry.

Seymour and Oscar couldn't help hearing. It didn't take them long to realize that this was a group of six-year-olds on an outing and that the woman was their teacher. The men watched for a few moments as she lined up her students. Apparently, one of the children had flung a rock, hitting a little girl in the back. There weren't any witnesses, but the teacher was determined to find the culprit.

Seymour stood and approached them with Oscar trailing behind.

The woman was grilling her suspects.

"This is a serious matter," she told the group. She demanded to know who did it. "Jane could have been hurt very badly."

"Excuse me," Pinchus interrupted.

She turned, saw what she perceived to be a kind face. "Did you happen to see who did this?"

"No. But maybe I can help."

She furrowed her brow.

"May I see the rock that was thrown?" Pinchus asked.

"I guess so." She handed the offending object to Pinchus.

"Ah, limestone," Pinchus said. He addressed the children. "Limestone has a certain look to it. See the grayish-white color?" He held it up for them to see. "It always leaves a residue. That means it leaves behind a part of itself when you touch it. Not only that, but it has a very unique smell. That's because of the calcium carbonate in it."

Pinchus turned to the teacher. She had an absolutely blank look on her face. He gave her a wink. Then he engaged the children again. "See this nose of mine?" He pointed. "It's very large."

The children giggled.

"It's a super nose. I can smell the slightest trace of

limestone with it." He held the rock up to his nostrils and sniffed deeply.

He glanced back at the teacher and said to her, loudly, "All I have to do now is to look at and smell each one of their hands, and we'll know who did it."

Out of the corner of his eye, Pinchus spied one child peeking at his hand and then quickly holding it up to his nose.

"Aha!" Pinchus turned and pointed to him—the third boy from the end, with chubby cheeks and curly black hair. "Here's your stone thrower."

"I didn't mean to . . ." the boy stammered.

"Johnny, I'm ashamed of you," the teacher said. "When we get back to class, you and I are going to have a talk."

The boy stared at the ground.

"Now, sit over there until it's time to leave." She motioned to a nearby bench. "The rest of you can continue to play." She clapped her hands and things returned to normal.

"I wouldn't be too tough on him," Pinchus advised. "I don't think he meant to hurt her. He probably likes the little girl. Kids do stuff like that."

"Yes, I know. I'm Julie Walker." She smiled, extending a hand. "And you are?"

"Lieutenant Pinchus," he said as they shook. He was embarrassed that he used the old title, didn't know why he had done that. "Actually, it's Seymour."

"Well, thank you very much, Seymour Pinchus. If I have a problem again, may I call you?"

Pinchus blushed.

As Seymour and his friend made their way back to their chessboard, Oscar asked, "Does limestone really leave a mark and have a unique odor?"

Seymour shrugged. "Hell if I know. The important

thing is that the kid believed it. A guilty conscience can make you very careless."

"You're amazing, Seymour. You see, you really are *needed*."

"Yeah," Pinchus groaned. "Now I'm reduced to solving kindergarten capers."

15

████████ LeRoy Pentagast had survived the autopsy thus far. He'd endured the opening of the chest, where a large triangular section of rib cage was cut out, observed the body's inside cavern, muddy-red in appearance, where broken-down blood products seemed to ooze from every rotting organ and vessel, watched as most of the internal organs were removed and weighed—saw their dark colors, brown, red, and green, dull and dark from decomposition—and witnessed the running of the bowel, as the intestines were uncoiled and drawn through slippery gloved hands for inspection. He sat motionless, mask tightly in place, sweat glistening on his massive forehead, vowing never to eat ribs—his gastronomical favorite—again, or for that matter, anything else.

The couple had last been seen alive at a steakhouse near the King of Prussia Shopping Mall two months ago. Tom Onasis and Kristina were busy examining stomach contents spilled across a cutting board that was usually used for cross-sectioning organs. They were hoping to establish a relationship between the presumed last meal and general time of death. Even in light of the length of time that had passed and degree of decomposition, their examination could still be useful since the stomach acted much like a Ziploc bag.

Onasis's fingers fumbled through the heap of partially digested muck. "I'd call *this* steak, wouldn't you?" he said as he stopped to pick up a brown, rubbery morsel.

"That, and a hell of a lot of lettuce, tomatoes, and onions," Kristina noted, poking at some of the larger clumps.

"How could you tell from that pile of shit?" Pentagast said through his mask. His revulsion was obvious.

"We review restaurants on a regular basis," Kristina answered, grinning.

A large plastic tube was filled with some of the stomach contents, sealed, and labeled for analysis.

There were fewer bugs now, since the Shop-Vac had finally been delivered and used to suck up the escaping throngs that littered the floor. However, hoards of insects still clung to the body.

The man who delivered the vacuum had looked around, surmised what they needed to do, and said: "Keep it."

Onasis discarded the rest of the suspected steak dinner, then positioned himself at the head of the victim, which was elevated by a block at the base of the skull. "We have injuries here," he announced. "Kristina!"

Kristina handed him a plastic bag. She had already labeled it with a laundry marker: date and autopsy number.

Onasis grabbed a handful of the corpse's hair. It fell away from the scalp like cotton candy. He stuffed it in the bag, repeated the process. Slowly, the camouflaged wounds to the head became visible. Onasis picked up a

pen, tracing with the capped end the indentations and
color changes indicating the injury pattern caused by
brutal blows to the head. "One . . . two . . . three
. . . four. Four separate and distinct blows."

He stood back so that Pith and Kirkland could take
pictures.

"Can we assume death was due to these injuries?"
Officer Kirkland asked.

Kristina winced.

"Never assume. Our autopsy's not over yet," came
Onasis's scolding bellow. But he quickly softened.
"However, your supposition is probable."

He leaned forward again, picked up a scalpel, and
carefully made an incision into the scalp of the victim,
cutting from the apex of one ear, across the top of the
head, to the apex of the other ear. He then placed a
dull, flat-ended instrument into the seam and gingerly
reflected the skin back—first the front section of scalp,
draping it over the decomposing facial features, then
the back section, leaving it to dangle against the head
block. Exposed was a thin layer of membrane and ves-
sels fixed tightly to the cranium. Areas of hemorrhage
were clearly visible, with crushed and broken skull un-
derneath.

"My God—where was the mercy?" Onasis said angrily. "This man was tied. The violence. The lack of
control." He snatched his microcassette recorder,
flicked it on, and started to dictate his findings.

When Onasis was finished, he turned toward Kristina. "Open the head."

Kristina dissected the remaining soft tissue covering
the skull. When she had finished, she picked up a
small electric autopsy saw with a semicircular blade,
stood over the head of the victim, and switched it on.
The saw hummed and groaned intermittently as it

labored to cut through the hard skull. A cloud of bone dust formed a haze around Kristina as she guided the saw around the circumference of the head. She then reached for an elevator, a hand-sized instrument with a crossbar handle, and placed the tip into the crevice of her cut.

"Love getting into heads," she announced as she gave an abrupt twist. The skull cap dropped off cleanly.

Kristina blinked. Everyone moved toward the exposed cavity.

"There's nothing left," Luther said with amazement. "No maggots. No brain. The little fuckers must have eaten every last bit."

"And I thought blondes were empty-headed," cracked Kristina.

"Watch it," Kirkland warned.

The morgue's door opened then, drawing their attention away from the grisly proceedings.

"Got the fax," Brandle shouted as he waved a sheaf of papers over his head.

"Thank God!" Pentagast said.

"Let's see." Roberts took the papers from Brandle and began to study them, comparing them to the NCIC forms.

"So?" Brandle asked Onasis as he motioned toward the body. "What do you have?"

"Four blows to the head."

"Enough to kill?"

"Easily."

"Weapon?"

"Best guess?"

Brandle nodded.

"Look for a tire iron or crowbar. Something on that order."

Officer Kirkland frantically jotted down notes. "Do you think the lady was done the same way?"

"Do you mean: Does she have the same type of injuries?" Onasis corrected.

"Yeah."

"Haven't looked at her yet. We'll find out."

But Onasis *had* already seen the savage beating to her head. And there was the gunshot wound to her chest, which puzzled him. There could be other surprises. These weren't your average murders. It was overkill. And that worried him.

Roberts carried the NCIC forms, as well as the faxed copies of the antemortem dental records, over to the body. He examined the mouth of alleged victim Roman Johnson again.

Pentagast watched him intently, studied Roberts's body language. LeRoy was not happy.

There was a knock at the door.

Brandle moved to open it. "Bring it in here, boys," he said, clearly expecting the delivery.

Two burly men carried a huge metal box into the morgue, placing it at the far end of the autopsy table.

"It's a metal coffin," Brandle explained. "The top latches down. Tight. Don't want any bugs or odor escaping."

Brandle, like many small-town coroners, was also a mortician who had his own funeral home. In cases like this, the bodies would be held at their mortuary until claimed and transferred for burial. Sometimes, a decision would be made by the family—or, if the corpse remained unclaimed, by the court—for that home to take care of the final arrangements. In either event, the coroner stood to benefit financially.

"Got an even bigger box for the lady," Brandle

beamed. "I'll bring it down later. But as far as this guy goes, you people are just about done. Aren't you?"

Pentagast pulled his mask down. "Better ask the doc over there." He pointed to Roberts. "Something tells me he ain't too happy. And that don't please me at all."

Roberts glanced up, pursed his lips, and shook his head.

"What's the matter, Doc? I gave you all of the fucking records. It's gotta be an easy comparison."

"You're right, it should be. Guy's got a lot of dental work. Just one problem with the comparison, though."

"Which is?"

"I can't give you a match!"

16

████████ "I want every recent case involving a child molestation on my desk," Milano barked. "Start with this district."

"How far back?" asked the assigned officer.

"Two months." Sam pointed a finger at his partner. "Your theory. Said they never change."

"Worth a shot." Daniel didn't look up from stuffing copies of the faxed photos into a folder. "Let's roll."

As they headed for the door, Officer Rifkin stopped them. "Captain Schwenk wants to see you."

They both turned, but Rifkin put his hand on Milano's shoulder. "Just Detective Pinchus," he said. "Only take a minute."

Milano had disliked Rifkin ever since he was transferred to Rivington two years ago from across town. Other cops seemed to share his opinion; it was rumored that Rifkin had been banished from his former precinct.

Milano removed Rifkin's hand from his shoulder. "I'll get two coffees and bring the car around."

Rifkin led Daniel to Schwenk's office and waited at the door until Daniel entered.

"You wanted to see me, Captain?"

"Yes, Detective. Sit down."

Schwenk was seated behind his desk, finishing the last few jelly beans in his hand. An enormous jar of them had been kept close to his chair as long as Daniel or anyone else could remember. The blinds on the window behind him were turned just so, shading his colorful treasure from the morning sunlight—Captain Schwenk's beloved jellies.

"As you know, Detective, I haven't taken any action against you in regard to that stunt you pulled in the Bartholemew Putnam case."

"Yes, I know, sir. Thank you. But I thought that was resolved."

"You thought? Why? I said I haven't taken any action—*yet*."

Daniel squirmed slightly in his chair. He was being set up for something. "You got a lot of good press on that case, Captain," he pointed out. "How would it look if you changed stories now?"

"I don't give a shit how it looks," Schwenk growled. "Right now, I'm not a happy man. Everyone thinks that couple up in Coal County are the missing witnesses. My ass is on the line. Then this Luccetta affair gets thrown in my lap. Unless it's taken care of quickly, I can kiss my career good-bye."

The thought of that prospect briefly gladdened Daniel. "And?" he asked tentatively.

"And if I go down, Detective, so . . . do . . . you."

Daniel gritted his teeth. He didn't like being threatened.

"I want you to have as much at stake here as I do," Schwenk went on. "Milano, too."

"Sam?"

"You like your partner, don't you? Prove it. Milano's from the old school. He wouldn't understand right off."

"And you don't want trouble." Daniel gathered.

"Make sure there isn't any. Explain it to Sam in the right light. Get my drift, Detective?"

"It's blackmail."

"It's a reward!" Schwenk shouted. "An extra incentive to nail whoever did Luccetta."

"We always do our best," Daniel said angrily.

Silence followed. Schwenk regained his composure, and when he began again, his tone was much calmer. "Maybe. But who knows. This may push you to greater heights. Make you dig a little deeper. Hungrier for the kill. I know you've got a name. Make it work—find him."

Daniel felt defeated. There was no way to win this. "Aye, aye, Captain," he said, giving an animated navy salute.

"That's all, Detective," Schwenk fired back. He watched as Daniel stood. "By the way, how's your father doing?"

Daniel tensed. "He's doing fine."

"Hope so," Schwenk said, feigning concern. "Haven't seen him around here in ages. Give him my best."

"Will do," Daniel answered, swallowing hard on a bitter retort.

"You know I always liked your dad." Schwenk smiled broadly.

Liar. Prick. Daniel opened the door to leave and suddenly stamped his foot on the floor.

"What? What's the matter?" Schwenk asked, startled.

"Sorry, sir. Bug. Missed him." And Daniel turned away, hiding a smile of his own.

17

▬▬▬▬ Diane sat at the bar at Mademoiselle's, fidgeting nervously with her glass. She looked at her watch again. He was already twenty minutes late. The restaurant was filling with the lunch crowd. She knew he would come. He would have a good excuse, she told herself. She was tired of nursing her strawberry daiquiri—wasn't used to drinking this early in the day. But she *did* have something to celebrate.

She left her seat for a moment and called home to check on the kids. Everything was perfect. She'd have more time than she thought. She told Melanie to make sure Paul did his homework as soon as he got home.

When she got back, the bartender came over to her seat. "Are you Diane?"

"Yes."

"I have a message for you."

Diane looked up at him, concerned.

"Your friend will be here shortly."

"Thank you." She smiled eloquently.

18

The two detectives were halfway back to Tremont Avenue when Daniel finished telling Sam about his conversation with Captain Schwenk. He left out a couple of things, because he was afraid of what Sam might do.

"That's outright blackmail!" Sam shouted, staring at Daniel, eyes bulging. The car swerved.

"Easy, Sam. Watch the road."

Sam turned his attention back to the street, his teeth grinding together.

"That's what I told him," Daniel continued. "He doesn't see it that way. Says it's more like a reward."

"Didn't think the little prick would resort to shit like this."

"Really?" Daniel raised his eyebrows.

"No, not really. He's desperate . . . and capable of anything. But this time he went too far. We have to stop him."

"I appreciate your wanting to get involved," Daniel said. "But this is between Schwenk and me."

"So take it to Internal Affairs."

Daniel laughed. "Yeah, right. First of all, they'd never believe me—a second-grade detective ratting out his captain? I have no proof, and quite frankly, the complaint has no substance. He didn't ask any more of me than what I'm supposed to do. Even you said so."

"I know, but the suggestion was improper."

"And even if IAB *did* believe me, you think I'll have a career after that? No police department wants a damn crybaby in their division."

Sam nodded slowly. "I guess you're right. But you can't let him—"

"Don't worry, Sam," Daniel interrupted. "I won't." Both men were quiet for several moments before Daniel said, "As much as I hate to ask, what do you think my father would do in this situation?"

Sam rubbed his chin. "Probably let it go for now. Definitely catch the killer. And get even with Schwenk in his own way."

"Exactly." Daniel grinned.

"Ideas?"

He shrugged. "Not quite the old man yet."

They both laughed.

"But seriously," Sam said, "why don't you run this by him?"

Daniel shook his head. "I sometimes talk to him about work. But he changes the subject. If it's about a collar I made, he says: 'Nice job, Daniel. Good boy.' Not much else. Even Schwenk pointed out that he hardly ever comes down to the station. It's as if he doesn't care anymore. His heart's not in it."

"Daniel! Don't ever say that. Your father loves police work. He's extremely proud of you, too. Told me so the other day. But you have to understand, this was his life's passion. For him, it has to be all or nothing. How do you think he'd feel hanging around the station? I'll tell you: Like some washed-up has-been, ready to offer unwanted advice to the Dees who are busting their asses out on the street. He doesn't want that."

"But it's not like that. I'm not like that," Daniel protested.

"I know. But it's what he believes. What's in *his* mind. He feels useless. If you ask him for help, and if you're sincere about it, you'll eventually break down the barrier. But don't ever say he doesn't care. Trouble is—and always has been—he cares too much."

Daniel heard what Sam was saying. And listened to what he already knew.

The yellow tape had already been taken down. Early for some violent crimes, but not unreasonable for those occurring out in the open. In cases like this, expedience was the rule. Consideration had to be given to the local businesses. In addition, the uncontrolled outdoor elements threatened to disturb pertinent evidence. And there was also the nuisance of the gawkers to contend with, crowded around the cordoned-off display of police activity. Morbid curiosity seekers still hoping to catch a glimpse of blood and horror, long after the body had been removed.

Now, six and a half hours since the rifle's echo, things could start returning to normal at the crime scene. Everything relevant had been collected, measured, photographed, and logged. Only the apartment across the street, and the warehouse behind, remained secured and off-limits.

A sea of customers mobbed Carmine's. It was lunchtime, but never had the place been so full—not even on its grand opening five years ago when they had

an accordion player and gave away free spumoni. Luccetta's violent death had given birth to a new landmark:
Carmine's of Tremont Avenue.

Milano and Pinchus parked their car, then squeezed
inside the restaurant.

Carmine, although inundated with orders, noticed
them right away. He waved excitedly from behind the
counter, a large knife in his hand.

"Anything you guys want, you can have, on the
house," he shouted, slicing a block of cheese.

"Thanks anyway," Daniel said, sadly groping in his
coat pocket for his sandwich from home. "But we're
here on business."

"Come on, it's lunchtime. Gonna make you guys up
something. Something special. Joey Gallo, right? I owe
you."

"Fine," Milano answered, enticed by the delicious
smell and his growling stomach. "But anything we take,
we pay for. Department rules." He turned to Daniel.
"My treat, partner. Okay?"

But Daniel had no intention of arguing. "Sure."

Milano handed Carmine the copies of the two
photos they carried. "Recognize either of these faces?"

"They your killers?"

"Don't know," Daniel answered.

Carmine shook his head. "Know a lot of people, but
these two?" He squinted. "Uh-uh."

The crowd was full of locals. They passed the copies
around. Almost all were thrilled to be asked—would
brag later about their part in the celebrated investigation—but Milano and Pinchus didn't come up with
anything solid. A couple of maybes, a few I'm-not-
sures.

Before they left the restaurant, Carmine approached
them with a full shopping bag.

"You're welcome to stay if you can find a table, but

that might take awhile. So I decided to make you a package." He handed the bag to Daniel. To Milano he said: "That'll be a dollar. You said I have to charge, but you didn't say how much."

Milano put up a hand. "Carmine, we can't—"

"Sam!" Daniel said quickly. "Give the guy a buck. If IAB gets wind of it, I'm sure they'll understand. Not to mention, I'm in tight with the captain."

19

██████████ "What I said was *I* can't give you a match," Roberts explained. "The actual records have the same errors in them as the NCIC forms have. That dental clinic really screwed up."

"Just say it's him, Doc," Pentagast pleaded. "You know it *is*. I gotta get home. My girl's playing Wendy in *Peter Pan* tonight."

Tom Onasis started to speak, but Pentagast stopped him. "I know. Court. Murder case. Shit like that." He took a deep breath, let it out slowly. "What do you need?"

"X rays."

"Jesus, that'll take hours," LeRoy moaned. "Gotta be picked up and driven here."

"Do it!" Brandle ordered. "Call whoever you have to, but get it done. This is my county. We do things right."

"What about the body?" Roberts asked. "You were getting ready to take it."

"Right." Brandle nodded. "We need the room. We have a suicide coming in. Cut the jaws out. Keep them for the comparison."

Kristina picked up the autopsy saw. "How do you want them wrapped, Doc?"

Roberts sighed. He dreaded the thought of inheriting more jaws. "I have to call home."

"After me, Doc," Pentagast said, lifting the receiver of the wall phone. "The sooner I call in, the sooner we get the X rays."

"There's another phone in the storage room," Pith offered, pointing to a door in the corner. "Just dial nine for an outside line."

"Thanks."

Roberts opened the door, flipped on the inside light, located the telephone on an old metal desk. In the background, he could hear Kristina manipulating the electric saw.

"Hello," Paige, his three-and-a-half-year-old daughter, answered.

"Hi, sweetheart. It's Daddy."

"Daddy!" she said excitedly.

"Paige, can you put Mommy on?"

"Uh-uh."

"Why not?"

"Mommy's not here."

"Okay. Is Mel there? Can you put her on?"

"Mellie?"

"Yes, Mel. Put her on the telephone."

"Okay, Daddy."

"Wait, Paige. Don't hang u—"

Peter quickly dialed again. This time Melanie answered the phone.

"What's wrong, Dad?"

"I'm going to be tied up here for quite a while.

Sorry. Guess our shopping trip's off. But you know I'll make this up to you."

"Sure, Dad."

Peter could sense his daughter's smile through the receiver.

"Where's your mother?"

"Don't know."

"What do you mean you don't know? She leaves you with your little sister—and you don't know?"

"She's out, Dad," Melanie said matter-of-factly.

"Did she go to the supermarket? To the cleaners? What?" She hadn't been dressed for household errands.

"Dad, she's . . . out."

Peter had a sickening feeling. Both compulsive and possessive to a fault, he was becoming frustrated. Surely Diane would have told Melanie where she was, unless . . . He curled in his lower lip, bit down, then released it slowly. *Stop obsessing, Peter,* he said to himself. "Tell your mother when she gets in that I won't be home until late."

"Will do, Dad."

When Peter came back into the morgue, the decayed and violated remains of Roman Johnson were being placed in a black bag—except for his maxilla and mandible, which were sitting in a pan on a side counter. The bag was hoisted into the metal coffin, and Brandle's two assistants put the cover on and latched it down. The autopsy table was hosed off for the next body.

"Kirkland, you come with me," Brandle ordered, tightening the knot in his tie. "News conference at City Hall. Press has been salivating for some word on these homicides, but I'm not going to tell them shit. And if anybody calls asking questions, don't say a word," he added, looking back at them as he and Kirkland left. "Don't want any premature leaks."

Brandle's men carried the metal casket out. Everything was ready for the second autopsy.

Pentagast had to move his chair so that they could get to the large steel door of the chamber that held the morgue's refrigerated slabs. It took all five of them to transfer the massive dead woman, first onto a gurney, and then onto the table. She appeared to be in much the same condition as the other victim, except for the gunshot wound to the chest.

As Onasis, Pith, and Kristina concerned themselves with the preliminaries, Roberts began to chart the dental findings of the jaws from the first autopsy. He completed his postmortem chart and then, with nothing to do but wait, offered to get coffee for the others. Pentagast eagerly volunteered to go with him.

It took them ten minutes to find the cafeteria. LeRoy wanted to drink his coffee there. Peter didn't object.

Peter discovered that LeRoy liked to gamble. "Atlantic City?" he asked.

"Sometimes. But I'd rather go to Vegas. Vegas is class. Wife lets me go twice a year."

"She go with you?"

"No. Hates it. Allows me my vice, though, and I love her for it. She used to give me some money to put on a number. But the last couple of times she told me to take out flight insurance with it instead. I said, 'You feelin' really lucky or what?' She's a real comedian, knows how afraid I am of flying. It's just her way of rubbing it in. Saves the papers as souvenirs. I told her that's a terrible way to hit a jackpot. She says, 'Bear'— she likes to call me that. *Bear*."

"I wonder why," Roberts said, eyeing LeRoy's massive frame and huge hands.

"Says, 'I already hit two of them. You, and Jasmine.' Jasmine's my little girl. She's my world, Doc. You got any kids?"

"Three. Two girls and a boy."

"Then you know what I mean. Gee, I hope I get to see her play tonight." Pentagast gave Roberts a melancholy look.

"Sorry, *Bear*. Can't help you there. My hands are tied."

"I know." Pentagast sighed. "So tell me, Doc. When you thought your patient died, what was the first thing that ran through your mind?"

"What do you mean?"

"Well, you mentioned that you did all this work on him and you had this worried look on your face. It was more than just remorse. I got a feeling of Shawondasee."

"Shawondasee?"

"Yeah. It means south wind. Back in Oklahoma— that's where I was raised—there was a manure processing plant set near my house. When the south wind blew, you could really smell the shit. Since then, whenever my nose tells me there's more here than meets the eye . . . Shawondasee. What, were you afraid you'd have to give the widow a refund?"

Roberts smiled. "You're quite the detective, LeRoy."

"Thought so." Pentagast snapped his fingers. "Shawondasee."

"Actually, I was trying to remember whether he had paid yet or not."

20

██████ He knew there'd be questions. But he could control the answers. He didn't have to prepare. He only had to close his eyes and remember.

When he was very young, maybe eight or nine, his father had a hummingbird. The bird disappeared one day. Someone left its cage open. And he and his mother were beaten.

But through his father's screams and accusations, he was able to keep his pulse, his breath, steady. And so, his father never really knew—never knew that the bird refused to leave on its own, that he had to reach in and grab it, that it fluttered in his hand before growing still with fear. And also that he felt its little heart racing as only a hummingbird's could, felt it quiver against his palm as his fingers tightened around it, squeezing until the shaking stopped, until its body went limp. Until it was crushed.

It was the same way with the boys—*paralyzed, voiceless, hearts thumping*—and he knew he could do whatever he wanted to them.

His breath remained even. They were all hummingbirds.

21

██████████ Roberts and Pentagast returned to the morgue, with coffee and apologies, a full half-hour later. The others were well into the autopsy. Another large, metal coffin had already been delivered. The tall and terribly obese woman hung over the autopsy table on all sides. Her chest was only an empty cavern now, the organs removed and weighed. The stomach's inventory was noted; this time, more steak than salad.

The reflected incisions revealed a vivid yellow fat layer as thick as nine inches in some areas. A section of remaining abdominal flesh, left uncut, drooped down over her genitalia like an enormous fanny belt of sagging skin.

The victim's scalp had just been peeled away and Pith was taking photographs.

"Make sure you get a few close-ups," Onasis instructed.

"Came back in the nick of time," Kristina said. "We're about to open the head."

"Gosh, almost missed my favorite part," grumbled Pentagast.

"She was a tough lady," Onasis told them. "Counted

fourteen separate blows to the head. That, and something interesting concerning the gun blast to the chest. We found white powder in and around the wound, also in some of the damaged organs. But no bullet. And no exit wound. Kristina thinks she figured it out. She used to be an army brat. Learned a lot about munitions."

"Frangible bullet," she said. "Made out of compressed plaster that disintegrates on impact. It's a phantom—no ballistics; no lead fragments. Only white dust. Shooter had to be an expert to know about it, though."

"Or knew somebody who was," Pentagast volunteered.

"But the guy wasn't shot?" Peter asked.

"No," Onasis answered. "Like I said, she must have been one stubborn gal. The way I see it, whoever did this kept beating her over the head. She was tied and couldn't fight back, but he kept whacking her."

"Jesus!" Roberts said.

"She just wouldn't die," Onasis went on. "So he shot her in the chest to finish her off."

"And he thought he'd be leaving us a puzzle," Kristina added. "But the white traces gave it away."

Pith put the camera down. Onasis nodded to Kristina and she picked up the electric saw.

"Wait. Maybe a little music can help drown that out," Pentagast said. He clicked on an old radio sitting on the desk in the corner.

Ironically enough, "No Way to Treat a Lady" was playing as Kristina began.

At one-thirty, the music was interrupted by the news. They were all startled to learn that the couple they were autopsying had been identified as Roman and Ethel Johnson. The source of the report was coroner Elliot Brandle.

"Son of a bitch." Kristina turned the radio off.

"That's not official yet," Onasis declared angrily. "And it was Brandle who warned us not to say a word."

Kristina turned to Luther. "This prick holds a news conference, sees the reporters, the cameras, the lights, and develops diarrhea of the mouth?"

"Welcome to Coal County," Pith replied with a smile.

"Now I hope, by some strange fluke, it's not them—just to see Brandle's ass in a sling," Onasis voiced what *almost* everyone was thinking.

"Don't say that, Doc," Pentagast cried. "I gotta get home. A fuck-up like that will keep me here all night."

The door to the morgue swung open. An attendant wheeled in a gurney with a body bag on it. "Got your suicide here," he said to Pith. "Room for one more?"

"Sure. Lady over here decided not to stay. You can have her accommodations. The penthouse, slab five. Sign it in before you leave."

"Shit," Roberts said.

"Guess you're inheriting another set of jaws, Doc." Kristina picked up the saw again.

22

█████ The phone by the door was free, but Roberts decided to use the one in the storage room again. He dialed, let it ring several times. Melanie picked up.

"Hi, Melanie. Mom home?"

"No. But she called. When I told her you'd be late, she said she might not be back much before you."

Roberts ground his teeth together.

"She's shopping, I think. With some friends. She told me to make you dinner. How about steak?"

He groaned. After convincing Melanie that corn-flakes would be just fine, he hung up the phone in disgust. Back in the morgue, he noticed that another set of jaws were set aside for him.

Pith, Kristina, and Onasis were struggling to put the woman in the coffin. Her massive girth pressed the body bag against the sides. They were having difficulty getting the lid on properly. An army of bugs that clung to the body bag were marching up the metal walls, trying to get out.

"Sorry, guys," Kristina said to the beetles. She balanced her full weight on top of the lid, pressing it into place as Onasis and Pith latched it down. "Like packing for vacation. God help anyone who opens this. They'll never be able to close it again—and it'll be a buggy surprise."

"You look uptight," Pentagast whispered to Roberts. "Everything okay at home?"

"Fine, thanks. Just anxious to get back."

"Me, too," LeRoy said.

"Luther." Onasis snapped off his rubber gloves. "Kristina and I have to go. Goray will be here eight A.M. tomorrow to do the suicide. You okay to finish up?"

Pith nodded.

Onasis began degowning and washing. "Peter, when you complete the comparisons, call me. For Brandle's sake, pray it's a match." He looked at Pentagast. "LeRoy, it's been a pleasure. Hope you get home on time."

"Thanks, Doc."

When they were gone, Pith called for the body to be removed and began putting the morgue in order. Pentagast watched Roberts chart the second set of jaws.

"Any luck?" he asked when Peter was done.

Roberts pressed his lips together tightly. "Still some inconsistencies. Got a couple of fillings noted on certain teeth—here in the record and on the NCIC forms—but they disappear in the mouth. Rest is a clear match."

"Same old, same old."

"Damn it, I know it's them. I just can't say so officially until I check the X rays. Sorry, LeRoy."

"I understand. Don't sweat it, Doc."

At 3:45, the X rays had still not been delivered but Brandle had called to say he was coming by. Ten minutes later, two officers from the Philadelphia Police Department walked into the morgue carrying a large envelope.

" 'Bout time," LeRoy declared, snatching the envelope from them and handing it to Peter.

Roberts opened it, slipped the radiographs out, and held them up to the light. He glanced back and forth from the films to his own chartings of the victims' dentition.

Pentagast waited, staring intently. It seemed like an eternity passed before Roberts finally spoke.

"Well, I was wrong, LeRoy. The dentist who filled out the NCIC forms did it correctly."

Pentagast's jaw dropped. "You mean—"

"Correctly, according to *their* chart," Roberts clarified. "But the chart was wrong and the dentist never checked the X rays. Otherwise, he would have seen the mistakes."

"Doc, don't scare me like that. We've been through too much today."

"The victims *are* Roman and Ethel Johnson. Officially."

"Hallelujah and amen," Pentagast said. He mentally calculated a two-and-a-half-hour drive back. The play was at seven—running tight, but still doable.

"Promise me one thing, LeRoy."

"Anything, Doc."

"Don't ever go to that clinic for your dental work!"

"No problem. I get it done in New Jersey. Hear those Jersey dentists have better reputations," he teased. "Still gonna have a hard time identifying me, though." With a thrust of his tongue, his teeth slid forward. A set of dentures. LeRoy sucked them back into place.

Roberts shook his head, smiling.

Suddenly, Brandle burst into the room. "See your boys got here with the X rays," he said.

"Guess we didn't need them," Pentagast answered crustily. "Heard your announcement on the radio."

"Now look, Sergeant," Brandle said, aiming a finger at him. "Nothing wrong in letting people know who we felt these individuals were. You knew it was them. I knew it was them. And so did Dr. Roberts."

"So now it's official," Pentagast snapped.

"Right," Brandle said, lowering his hand. "Listen, you boys had a long day. I'd like to thank you. Anything else you need before you leave?"

"Nothing." Roberts shrugged. He looked at Pentagast.

"Wait a minute, Doc. Didn't Onasis say something about those jaws?"

Roberts furrowed his brow. "The jaws?"

"Yeah, you know. About putting them back with the rest of the remains since you don't need them anymore."

"Oh, the jaws," Roberts said, realizing LeRoy's ploy. "That's right, almost forgot. Well, you know how thorough Onasis is. Wants the correct set of jaws in each casket, just in case." He leaned closer to Brandle.

"Onasis runs a tight ship in Hamilton County. By the book. Makes sure all of the body parts are put back properly. Even checks sometimes. Have to follow procedure. The bodies are at your funeral parlor?"

"Yes, they are." Brandle nodded. "But the bugs—I recently redid the place. I can't afford a mess."

"Those metal coffins were a great idea," Roberts complimented him. "We had no problem. Just pop them into the body bag and snap the lid shut. No big deal."

Brandle's smile was broad. "That's why I think of those details. No fuss. No mess."

███████

Outside the morgue, Roberts said, "It's four-fifteen. Think you'll make it?"

"Siren all the way."

"Thanks, LeRoy. You just helped me disinherit two sets of jaws."

"That was my one and only motive," he replied. "After all, what are friends for?"

"Shawondasee," Roberts said.

23

███████ In the 1930s, when many crime organizations across the country were mired in power struggles, there existed in Philadelphia an alliance between two families. Antonio Luccetta and Edgar Malloy, young immigrant crime bosses, had made a pact to protect their territorial riches. Together, as allies, they were strong, and each family grew, overshadowing any and all competitive interests.

It was an agreement that lasted for many years. They even gave each other gifts of friendship. Luccetta had a meat processing plant and often sent Malloy baskets of sausages and other delicacies. Malloy, in turn, would reciprocate with cases of rare wine from his import business.

Life had been good to Antonio. Peaceful and lucrative. So when the time seemed right, in the early 1950s, he turned the operation over to his only offspring, Frank. Antonio then retired to enjoy his wealth, his survival, and his three young grandsons.

But Frank Luccetta was a greedy don, and after controlling the family for a few years, became hungry. Why should he share Philadelphia with an Irish gang like the Malloys?

Edgar Malloy was still firmly in charge of his family, grooming two of his own sons for eventual succession. Then one day he mysteriously disappeared. The Malloys were in turmoil. Frank Luccetta had counted on that, and he offered his sympathy, his help, and even continued sending gifts as he slowly started invading the Malloys' operation. They never suspected.

Once he was satisfied with the strength of his position, Frank Luccetta delivered the final blow. He announced to the Malloys that he had disposed of their father and would do the same to them unless they allowed him to take over the rest of their operations. And not only that, he informed them, they had also devoured their own father's remains in the gifts of sausages he had sent.

Frank Luccetta didn't want an all-out war. He knew his father wouldn't approve. He deemed the Malloys fearful, blundering fools who would fall to pieces upon hearing such horrific news. He never considered that they would react otherwise. That underestimation was the last that he would make, for he was gunned down the following week on a street corner in South Philly.

Antonio Luccetta was devastated. Putting grief aside, he acted quickly to mend fences with the Malloy brothers. The very day of his son's funeral, he promised to give back all that Frank took. He would come out of retirement and lead once again, peacefully, as long as his grandchildren would be allowed to grow up and inherit their birthright.

And since that time, tranquility had reigned. Antonio sent his grandchildren away to good schools, believing education was extremely important if the business was to succeed in the future. But it wasn't a complete answer, he knew. He still saw too much of his son Frank in Marion, and even more in Dominic, yet not enough in Nino. He was spared the ultimate comparison by passing away seven years before his youngest grandson was gunned down.

■■■■■■

Sergeant Sam Milano and Detective Daniel Pinchus had a glorious lunch in Sam's car. Carmine had prepared two huge Italian hoagies, his specialty. Genoa salami, ham, mortadella, provolone cheese, and red peppers . . . and there were sodas and two bottles of iced cappuccino. The coup de grace was a dozen cannoli in a box at the bottom of the bag. They devoured the feast, except for a few of the pastries, which Sam insisted Daniel take home to his wife, or maybe give to his father.

Daniel resisted. They would make Susan puke, and his father was on a diet, strictly enforced by Kate.

"Lost any weight, yet?" Milano asked.

"Nope. Swears he doesn't cheat. Has my stepmother baffled."

"Or so he thinks."

They spent several hours working the neighbor-hood surrounding the murder scene, tracking down a couple of uniforms still on assignment and passing along photocopies of the two faces of Arthur Sarchick—and the rest of the cannoli.

The afternoon had been fruitless. No new leads. No new suspects. At four-thirty they got a call that the bodies up in Coal County had been positively identified as the missing witnesses.

"Told you so," Daniel remarked.

"Poor Schwenk."

"Yeah, my heart aches. Hope Perez gives him the worst fucking detail possible. We'll find out tomorrow."

"That reminds me," Milano said. "I'll be late tomor-row. Department physical. You okay for a ride in?"

Daniel nodded, slowly. He thought Sam had had a physical three months ago, was almost sure of it, but decided not to pry. "Susan's car will be fixed by then," he told him. "She called the mechanic. Ignition switch again. He gave us a rebuilt last month. Said it would save us some money."

"You get what you pay for, partner."

"Yeah, well . . ."

"Just like Luccetta."

"What are you trying to say, Sam?"

"The Malloy gang. Can't rule out a mob war."

Daniel's face wrinkled skeptically.

"Time we found out," Sam said. "Let's shake some trees."

━━━━━

They headed for Luccetta's house. Daniel was still try-ing to remember where it was, but Sam knew a short-cut. A few minutes later, they pulled up in front of a stone Tudor on an acre of land. Modest looking, though, for a wealthy don. A six-foot-high fence of black iron surrounded the property. Cars filled the drive, mostly dark and fancy. The gate, however, was open and conspicuously unmanned.

"Look like they're concerned about a mob war to you, Sam?" Daniel commented.

Sam parked behind a big Mercedes. They got out and walked toward the house.

Two men were standing near the front door. They recognized one of them as Tony Caputa. He was pointing at them, telling the other man something with short, sharp gestures.

"Remember," Milano said in a low voice. "Easy does it."

"Uh-hmm," agreed Daniel. But it sounded hollow.

They approached and took their badges out.

"No need for that," the man with Tony said gruffly. "I know who the fuck you are."

"Good," Daniel replied lightly. " 'Cause we know who you are, too. You're much better looking in person, though. Mug shots don't do you justice, Marion."

Marion Luccetta, tall and slim, with a good build and dark features, looked nothing like his dead kid brother. Although he had the reputation of being more levelheaded and not as clever, Milano knew he was just as ruthless, and just as dangerous.

Caputa lurched toward Daniel, but Marion put out a hand, holding him back.

"You got some goddamn nerve showing up here. Where's your respect?" Luccetta growled. "My brother ain't dead twelve hours."

Milano decided to take charge before Daniel launched another flippant remark. "Our condolences," he said. "We all want to know who did this. Give us some help. We're on the same side this time."

"What do you need?"

"We heard you guys were interested in finding Barney Terzetto," Milano said.

"Who told you that?"

"We hear a lot of things," Daniel said.

"Like you believe he did this to your brother," Milano added. "Is that true?"

"My brother's cold, lying on a slab in the morgue. Beyond that, I know nothing. You wanna enlighten me? Go ahead."

"Terzetto was close to your brother. Now he's nowhere to be found," Milano pointed out. "A little suspicious, maybe?"

"A coincidence," Luccetta said calmly.

"Seem to be a number of coincidences," Daniel said. "Witnesses who were supposed to testify against your brother were found dead a few hours before your brother was taken down."

"My brother didn't have anything to do with that."

"He wasn't afraid of a couple of pieces of lying filth," Caputa snarled.

"I was told how they died. Must've been hell," Daniel fired back.

"Sometimes people create their own hell," Luccetta said, annoyed.

The front door to the house opened. A gorgeous blond woman stepped out, her face pale and strained. She was followed by a thickset man who looked exactly like Dominic Luccetta would have if he had survived five more years. His cheeks were still damp from crying.

"What's going on here?" she asked, her gaze settling on Daniel.

Daniel had heard that a much younger woman married Dominic. After seeing how beautiful she was, Daniel couldn't help but wonder why.

"This doesn't concern you, Sylvia. Nino, take her back inside," barked Marion.

Nino hooked an arm around her waist, tearfully coaxing her back into the house.

"Look what you've done—upset my sister-in-law," Luccetta said, raising his voice again. "On the day her husband dies, you had to do this? I want you sons of bitches to leave. Now!"

Milano gave Daniel a severe look. "We only want to find out who killed your brother."

"When you do, tell us. We can save the taxpayers a lot of money," Marion said, with a smirk toward Caputa.

"Know anything about a note a kid handed to your brother right before he was shot?" Milano asked.

Luccetta looked at his lieutenant. "What note? What kid?"

"A kid passed by on a bicycle," Caputa related, "but I didn't see no note."

"He handed it to Dominic," Daniel said, throwing his arms up in frustration. "You had to have seen it. Other people saw it, for crying out loud."

"He said he didn't," Luccetta snapped. "Now back off!"

Milano winced. "Could you give us a description of Terzetto?"

"Sure," Caputa answered. "Think he was tall."

"No, he was short," Marion said. "I'm sure of it."

"Maybe your guests here have better memories?" Daniel suggested.

"You leave them alone. Everyone here is in mourning."

"Don't you want to know who killed your brother?" Daniel yelled. "Aren't you afraid you'll be next?"

Marion Luccetta turned away in disgust. Caputa started to follow.

But Daniel continued to talk. Milano raised a hand, gesturing for him to stop. Daniel pushed it down. "Just make sure the next time you go out in public you take Tony with you. Hear he's *real good* in stopping assassins."

Milano paled.

Caputa wheeled around, lunging for Daniel.

Instantly, Luccetta reached out and grabbed Tony around the chest. "I'll take care of this piece of shit," he said quietly.

Caputa backed off, eyes wide, full of contempt for Pinchus.

"You think you're such a smart-ass detective?" Luccetta said through clenched teeth as he grabbed the ends of Daniel's open coat and yanked him in close. "I wipe my behind with punks like you."

Daniel swung his forearms up, trying to break the hold.

Milano, at first stunned by the turn of events, now reacted. He threw an arm between the two of them, coaxing Luccetta back. "Let him go, Marion, or I swear, grief-stricken or not, I'll run you in for assault and obstructing."

Luccetta hesitated a moment, then dropped his hands. "Think I don't know who killed my brother, smart-ass? We don't need your help. We can take care of our own mess."

"Maybe we'll find him first," Daniel said, straightening his coat.

"Then, if you know what's good for you, you'll tell us before you pick him up."

"Don't threaten me, Marion. I'm not afraid of you."

"Not a threat. A promise." He pointed a finger at

Daniel before going inside. "Don't create your own hell, Detective."

Milano and Pinchus walked back to their car in silence. Milano shook his head. "You really need to learn a thing or two about diplomacy."

Daniel knew from Sam's tone of voice that he was not only angry, but disappointed as well. Daniel disagreed with the assessment.

"Sam, they weren't going to tell us shit, no matter how polite we were. That was obvious. But we learned something very important."

"Like what? How it feels to be threatened by a mob boss? Believe me, you don't need him for an enemy. I warned you, Daniel," Sam said, trying to check his temper.

"Got him to admit he knows who killed his brother."

"And the price you paid?"

"Just a lot of smoke."

"Better hope so."

"Never would have told us if I didn't shove my ass in his face. Relax, I knew what I was doing. Calculated every step."

Sam eased up, couldn't avoid a grin. "Funny, didn't seem that way. You looked pretty damn scared."

24

He wondered how long he would be kept waiting. It was all part of the game—adding some wrinkles for the sport of it, wanting to see just how smart the young Pinchus was.

He decided to read to help pass the time. He adored the classics. Works by Twain were his favorite: young boys running away, looking for an adventure. It tantalized him.

He also liked contemporary novelists, when they wrote about such things. Except for Benjamin Caldwell, whom he hated—hated him for his lack of originality, hated him for how successful he had become.

He looked at his stack of magazines, his books, finally settling on *Lord of the Flies*. He had read it before, but this time he would fantasize a different ending.

25

It was 5:45 when Sergeant Sam Milano and Detective Daniel Pinchus arrived back at Rivington Street Station. They went up to the squad room, then looked at each other, sniffing. There was an odd but familiar odor permeating the air.

"Insecticide?" Milano asked.

Officer Rifkin passed them on his way out. "Schwenk called the exterminators in. Had the whole place fumigated. Guess he's really bugged." He smirked.

"Aren't you afraid he might hear you?" Daniel asked, surprised.

"Nope. He left an hour ago. Getting ready for his big day tomorrow." Rifkin winked and continued on.

Milano nodded after Rifkin. "Doesn't he ever get tired of playing both sides of the fence?"

"Schwenk should get a refund for the fumigation," Daniel said. "The exterminator left a rat."

"Rifkin? Or Schwenk?"

Daniel laughed.

Sergeant Vanderhooven approached carrying a stack of papers. "Got a bio here on your suspect. Best we can do in only a few hours." He handed each of them a copy. "Also, the photos you wanted will be here in the morning. Had them put a rush on 'em."

"Thanks, Vandy," Milano said. "Anything on Barney Terzetto yet?"

Vanderhooven looked back as he headed for the door. "Nothing."

"Arthur Sarchick," Daniel read aloud, sitting down.

"Went into the military at age eighteen," Milano observed, flipping open the report. "In '73. Served six years, Special Forces. Very impressive!"

"Definitely our boy," Daniel commented. "Whoever killed Luccetta was quite a marksman."

"Don't be in a rush to preclude anybody or anything."

Daniel didn't argue the point. "Why would the military take him in, considering his juvee record? And Special Forces, no less?"

Milano shrugged. "Guess they thought they could straighten him out. Not unusual for the military. They take guys with problems all the time. The training and discipline sometimes turns these misfits around. And if not, they get bounced. Obviously, Sarchick made it."

"Yeah, because there aren't any children serving in the Armed Forces."

"He could still find a way. But six years, Daniel? His record during that period is totally clean."

"And five years after discharge, arrested for molesting."

"Something triggered it," Milano said.

"Or he just got careless again," Daniel countered. "Says here that after he got out of the military he went to college. Van Buren University. Took some engineering courses."

"Pretty good school," Milano noted. "My Matthew was considering it before he decided on Washington. And it's only a half an hour's drive from here. So?"

"So, Van Buren is a four-year school. Sarchick attended for only a little over two."

"He could have dropped out," Milano offered.

"In mid-semester?"

"It happens. Could have been a lot of things."

"Like being expelled?" Daniel asked. "All it would take is a nasty little incident like the type we know he's capable of. Too sticky to prosecute, but enough to get him kicked out." He arched an eyebrow at Sam.

"Interesting theory. Doesn't mention a reason here. We should check." Milano jotted a reminder down in his notepad.

"Then he relocated to Harrisburg." Daniel leaned forward. "Got a job as an airline mechanic. Now how's that possible? Don't you have to be certified or something? Even get a character check?"

"Yeah, you're right. He would have needed an Airframe and Power Plant Mechanic's Certificate or a Repairman's Certificate in order to get an FAA license. The military and some colleges offer programs to prepare you for it," he paused, nodding slowly. "Sarchick may have had both opportunities. As far as a character check, they may not have been privy to anything that went on before Sarchick turned eighteen. Or may not have looked. His military's clean. He could say whatever he wants on an application. Who's to know?"

"Short career. Three years later he's exchanging Harrisburg Airport for Graterford Prison."

Milano shifted in his chair. "And after paying his debt to society he goes to Philadelphia."

"A new town. A new face."

"And a new routine," Milano added. "Racketeering."

"But some things never change," Daniel said icily. "Read the last couple of lines, Sam."

Milano adjusted the way his glasses sat on the bridge of his nose. "Shit! Sarchick volunteered as coach for the youth league there." He tossed the report down. "And the rest we unfortunately know about."

"So where do we go from here?"

"Home. Enough for one day."

"But we barely scratched the surface," Daniel said.

"There's always tomorrow, Daniel. And besides, I can't afford to put in a late night. Got that physical."

"Yeah, right," Daniel mumbled. Then he said, "You go, I'll stay. Something's here that we're not seeing. Sarchick has me intrigued. Different faces. Different titles: child molester, thief, assassin. It's a puzzle."

"Looking for the missing piece?"

"Yup. Motive."

"Or, to put it more completely: What were the desperate circumstances that caused this guy to kill?"

"Desperate circumstances, Sam? Borrowing some of my father's terms?"

"He wouldn't mind. He has a lot to borrow from," Sam said, slipping on his coat. "Your father once found a person with less to go on than we have here. No name. No prints. No face—not even one. It was the Baby Seigel murder case. I'm sure you know about it. Sometimes there are clues just waiting to be noticed. Now, how are you going to get home? You don't have a car."

"I'll catch a ride with Bernie, from vice."

"And if he gets stuck late?" Sam asked, hesitating.

"Then I'll get a ride with someone else. Really, I'll be fine." Daniel waved him away. "Now get going."

And finally, Sam did.

Leaning back in his chair with the report on his lap,

Daniel thought about the Seigel case. He *did* know about it, but not from his father. He'd read about it in the newspapers. When the case broke, Daniel was a teenager, living with his mother. He didn't see his father very much back then, but he stole whatever glimpses he could of the Fox's amazing career through television and the written press. Even if the situation had been different, Daniel wouldn't have learned a lot firsthand, because Seymour Pinchus was a modest man. He would state with a shrug, "Not much to tell. I simply *noticed* . . . and followed through."

The Seigels' son, Jason, had a short life: six months, at the end of which he was bludgeoned to death in his crib. A ladder leading to the second floor nursery window was left behind, and muddy shoe prints were found on the bedroom carpet. Small ones: men's size eight.

Lars Seigel pointed an accusing finger at the estate's former caretaker, Tito Dundabar, who he claimed was loafing on the job and recently had to be fired. Supporting evidence was discovered: Witnesses heard threats of revenge; Dundabar had access to the type of ladder used; and his shoe size fit. All of this was enough to convince almost everyone Dundabar killed Seigel's son. Except for the homicide detective assigned to the case: Seymour Pinchus.

Pinchus learned that advancing arthritis had caused Tito's work to slacken, and after ten years of loyal service, he had been unceremoniously dismissed. The gardener was understandably angry. But he didn't believe Dundabar was agile enough to scoot up a ladder quietly in the night anymore. And if murder was the means of revenge, then why wasn't Lars Seigel the target?

Seigel was a wealthy man, and Pinchus knew that power and money bred enemies. He recanvassed the property and noticed a couple of ash-colored stains in the soil near some bushes that offered a secluded view of the house. He knelt, worked his hands through the clay, and uncovered several cigarette butts. Having been a smoker himself at the time, he became convinced that the spot was where the murderer had stood and smoked, waiting—and casing the house.

And they were special cigarettes, too. A French brand, Le Grande Fumée. Special and rare. Only one tobacco shop in Hamilton carried it. So Pinchus staked the store out, and had the owner signal him when anyone bought that brand.

There were a couple of false alarms, but on the third day he got a hit. It turned out to be a woman— thus the small shoe size. Everything fit. Even the desperate circumstances: She was a factory worker at one of Seigel's plants who was convinced she was screwed out of her pension. Her intention was only to rob Seigel's home. She was acting out of emotion, wanted to get back some of what she believed was hers.

Afraid that the place had an alarm, she figured the only way to get into the house was through an open window on the second floor—the nursery. When the baby awoke and started to cry, she panicked and bashed the kid's head in.

"It's amazing what you can discover if you notice," Daniel heard his father's voice echo as he lifted the pages in front of him once more.

He didn't hear Junior Gibney saunter up behind him, didn't hear him ask what he thought of Tom Onasis's interesting find.

"Huh?" Daniel looked up, trying to clear his head.

"About the frangible bullets," Gibney repeated. "Onasis found evidence that frangibles were used in the murder of those witnesses *and* the hit on Luccetta. I left

the message on Sam's desk. I just got back from a rob-
bery call myself." He glanced at the cluttered surface.
"Not here now. Must've taken it with him. Didn't Sam
tell you about it?"

"No," Daniel answered slowly. "No, he didn't."

26

Peter Roberts lay in bed, unable to sleep, listening to the soft creaks and groans of his house. He
tried emptying his mind, tried to forget the ordeal in
Coal County. Then he thought of LeRoy and wondered
how the play went, imagined his friend's titanic face
beaming as his daughter pranced onstage. It brought a
smile to Peter's lips.

His thoughts wandered to the office, an inevitable
happenstance when he felt tense. Things were different
now: more consuming; busier; colder. Just last year he
had expanded—hired a second associate and added another hygienist. He went with the flow of the times.
The practice became more business oriented. And with
it, the new upscale look for Roberts, Cohen & Afferbach.

Now, there was a fancy coffee machine in the waiting room—one from the Filterfresh company which automatically brewed fresh, gourmet coffee one cup at a
time—along with magazines and pamphlets touting
whiter teeth, implants, and perfect smiles.

They still called him doctor, but he no longer felt
like one. He felt more like a beautician.

Peter wished he could take a step back, but he could only admit that to himself. All of this had become too demanding. He was controlled by the patients and their needs and desires, not his. He should have listened to Diane: "Peter, you simply have to learn how to say no." But now it was too late. He was committed. He had grown fond of the prestige. And the money. And the lifestyle. So each morning before he arrived at work, he pasted on the smile, rehearsed the right things to say, and prepared himself to be trampled on.

Roberts sighed and glanced at his wife, the real source of his restlessness. She was sleeping soundly beside him, the lines of her face now relaxed in gentle relief, her breath flowing easily over soft lips. Innocent. Childlike. God, she was so beautiful, he thought. Most others thought so, too, and often told him so.

When he had gotten back from Coal County she was at the house. She seemed nervous, flighty. He asked about her day. "Shopping" was her reply. Then she became uncomfortably silent, and there were no packages he could see. He let it go. A long time ago he'd learned that sometimes you discover more by being discreet. But he was filled with so many questions; and what about the suspicious phone calls she'd been getting? There were whispers behind closed doors, and quick hang-ups whenever he approached. He had never been so uncertain of her before. His heart ached—was she having an affair? He blanched at the thought. He didn't want to lose her.

And what if she had been unfaithful? His mind filled with images, seedy details of how it would be.

They stood by the bed. Her secret lover touched her and she began to quiver. He softly brought his lips to hers, but she returned the kiss more passionately, driving her tongue past his gentle invitation. They undressed one another, slowly, savoring the moments. And they caressed and gently licked each other, until they could not help themselves any-more.

She dropped to her knees, took him into her mouth. Sultry green eyes, wide and staring seductively up at his face, watching as the pleasure crept across it. And then, when it seemed like he could no longer hold back, he urged her upward with the touch of his hands beneath her arms. She stood, pushed him down on the bed, and climbed on top of him.

He was in her now as she rocked in place. She threw her head back and closed her eyes, surrendering to the sensations.

He was driving, bucking; and she moaned and screamed in ecstasy as Peter thought only he could make her do.

The scene turned even more erotic—their bodies glistening with sweat, their breathing becoming quick and frantic with animal-like passion. Diane began shouting things, things Peter never heard her say before, but secretly wanted her to. The man convulsed, Diane's face contorted, and she released a high-pitched whine. Then, her features eased into contentment as she slowly regained her breath, and she collapsed over him to purr and count the stolen minutes she had left.

Peter envisioned all of this, this other man making love to his desire-filled wife. It was what he desperately feared. He should have been crushed by the vision. Strangely, though, the thoughts excited him . . . intensely.

27

It was late when Daniel Pinchus got dropped off in front of his apartment building. Bernie Fatzinger, his intended ride, got caught doing pussy patrol in a downtown prostitution sweep. So Daniel bummed a lift from Bart Miller, a rookie cop, finishing his four-to-twelve. Bart was single and lived only a mile from Daniel. He invited Pinchus out for a beer. Daniel took a rain check, told him he appreciated the ride but needed to get some sleep. It was that, and the fact he was concerned about Milano.

"Guess you older guys need your rest," Miller cracked as Daniel got out of the car. "Keeps you veterans sharp."

"That's why they pay us the big bucks, sonny," he replied, and slammed the door.

Exhausted, Daniel climbed the steps to his apartment. He had spent the earlier part of the evening calling publishers all over the East, trying to reach those that might still be in. He managed to talk to a few, then worked his way west having more luck. He had generated the lead from one of those clues waiting to be *noticed*. He only hoped it would pan out. In the morning he would try the East again.

He smiled. Once he had asked his father about such a situation—when you're stuck, looking for a thread, looking for anything.

His father had said, "When you believe you're far from a solution and the murderer has you truly baffled, step inside his mind."

"What's his mind like?" Daniel had asked, puzzled. "He's a killer. How could you possibly relate to someone like that?"

"Look within yourself," his father suggested. "Understand what's inside of *you* first. Why you're *not* him. Then, maybe *you* can become *him*. Focus on that, Daniel. It helps you make the leap."

Sam would be proud, Daniel thought, that he had borrowed a few of those famous footsteps tonight, and it didn't hurt his ego a bit.

Daniel entered his home. All was quiet except for the low murmur of a TV. He went into Adam's room, found him soundly asleep with his blanket crumpled to one side. He kissed his son's forehead, fixed the covers, and went to his own bedroom.

Susan had obviously tried to wait up for him, unsuccessfully. The television was on; she still had a book in her hand—Benjamin Caldwell's new best-selling hardcover—and her reading glasses sat cockeyed on her face. Huddled around her were Lucy and Ricky.

Daniel slid the book away, the glasses. Both dogs snarled at him.

Susan opened her eyes. "What are you two doing up here?" she said, half asleep. "You know you're not allowed." She pushed them off the bed and they landed

with a thump, then crept across the floor casting bellig-
erent looks at Daniel.

He stuck his tongue out at them.

"Oh, honey. When did you get home?" She
yawned.

"Just a few minutes ago."

"What time is it?"

"Twelve-thirty. I told you not to wait up."

"I know," she said, eyes closing. "I wanted to."

"Car fixed?"

She nodded. "Love you."

"Love you, too," he told her. But she didn't hear
him. She had dozed off again.

Daniel bent and gently kissed her. "Good night,
Sleeping Beauty," he whispered.

The six years since Susan entered his life had been
the happiest for him, something he often let Susan
know.

When they met, they were both attending schools
in New York: Daniel at John Jay College of Criminal
Justice; Susan at Columbia. It was at one of those social
gatherings college students frequently have, where a
friend of a friend is welcome. He noticed her right
away, standing in a corner—reddish-blond hair, gorgeous face, amazing legs—thought she might be the
one. And as it turned out, she was.

They became inseparable. In four short weeks, she
had moved in with Daniel. They made love a lot. Even
once in the backseat of a crowded Greyhound bus on a
night run to an upstate ski resort.

When Susan became pregnant with Adam, Daniel
was thrilled. It gave him an excuse to get married before they graduated. Like so many young lovers, their
lives seemed enchanted.

However, Daniel knew that Susan was concerned
about the danger of his career. And when his father was

gunned down, the shock put things into perspective. She didn't want Daniel to be a detective, didn't want him to end up disabled like his father—or worse.

He promised Susan that would never happen. He would always be careful. He *had* to be a cop. It was in his blood; it was what he was trained for. But he also knew that no matter what he said, Susan would worry, and try to stay up waiting for him to come home.

Daniel glanced adoringly at his wife, thinking of his unborn child in her womb. The pregnancy seemed to make her even more beautiful. The other day, out of fear and anger, she had said, "You love your job more than me."

God, didn't she know? He loved her so much that he would have given his life for her.

28

September 1970

■■■■■■ Ogden Farms, a thriving agricultural estate during the fifties, met its decline in the succeeding decade. The owners had aged, miserably, and grown tired of the unrelenting tasks involved with managing such an enormous and grueling enterprise. Their offspring had aspirations in other directions, so it became more reasonable, and quite profitable, to sell off much of the land to the greedy, high-class housing developers who had been pursuing them with handsome offers. Now, the only thing left was the main farm dwelling: Ogden

House, an abandoned stone monument to what once was.

It was dark. The setting, perfect. Buried in thicket that cheated the horizon a little bit more each year, the house lay. Any activity inside would be hidden from the roadway. Any screams would be absorbed by its dense stone walls. And, should one get out, it would die in the crisp, chilly air before it reached the fancy homes still some distance away.

Squigger and Fats untied the boy's legs and marched him through the front door. There was barely enough light to see the objects placed on the table in the center of the front room: rope, a pair of handcuffs, a flashlight—essentials for the task. Also a Polaroid camera, with flash—essentials for the proof. They brought only a few additional necessities: booze and cocaine—essentials for the courage.

They pulled a chair away from the table, seated the boy, and tied his legs to the base of it.

He couldn't stop shaking and wet his pants. "Let me go!" he screamed, over and over.

"Shut the fuck up," Fats replied, grabbing a fistful of the boy's hair, and yanking the boy's head back. "Do what we say and maybe we'll let you go."

"How do I know you're telling me the truth?" he sobbed.

"You don't know, fucker. You have no choice. But resist, and I promise you, you'll never see your mama again."

They untied the crude bonds that had held his hands in the car and handcuffed them in front of him. Everything was ready. They got high again, then waited for the coke to pass the blood-brain barrier.

"You go first," Fats ordered, as he wiped his nose with a finger and scooped up the camera.

Squigger hesitated.

"Punking out, shithead? Too late for that."

Squigger knew he was right.

"Do it!"

Squigger undid his belt, unzipped his pants, and let them drop to the floor. Underwear went next. He shuffled over to the boy.

"Nooo! Please, no!"

"Suck his cock, or you're dead."

Squigger bit his lower lip, inched closer and offered it to him.

The boy sat motionless.

"Time's running out," Fats yelled at him.

The boy finally took it with his cuffed hands, closed his eyes, and put it in his mouth.

Fump. A flash of light as Fats snapped the first picture. He drew the film out, waited, then pulled the backing off and threw it on the floor. "Great picture. You should see yourself, Squig!"

As Fats worked the camera, a strange thing was happening to Squigger. His initial revulsion was starting to turn into arousal. He assumed it was due to the alcohol, the coke.

Fump. "Another great shot." Fats discarded the backing, held the picture up.

Squigger became entranced. Cocaine slamming through his system, his own hands embraced the boy's head to guide the pace.

Fump. Fump. Fump. "Unfucking real."

In a few minutes, Squigger finished. He looked down at the boy, who was sobbing and spitting. He realized what he had just done, became momentarily sickened, confused.

"That-a-boy, Squigger. Knew you could do it. See, it ain't so bad. Now, my turn."

Squigger pulled up his pants. Fats handed him the Polaroid.

"There's only three shots left. Make them count," Fats said. "Just fantasize he's a beautiful babe—right?"

At first, Squigger didn't answer, then he said, "Why'd you take so many pictures?"

"One for proof. The rest are souvenirs. Gonna start a scrapbook."

Fats took less time, but was rougher with the kid. Squigger barely got two shots off, pressing the shutter with trembling fingers.

"Let's see the photos," Fats demanded, pulling up his pants. Squigger held them up. "Not bad, but you still got one shot left."

"You said you'd let me go," the boy pleaded.

"Yes, we did." Fats unlocked the cuffs, cut the rope. The boy started to run towards the door, but Fats grabbed his arm. "But we still got one picture left."

"No. You promised."

"Let him go, Fats. We got what we needed."

"Not yet. Bet you got a sweet ass." He pushed the boy down from behind, yanking at the kid's pants.

The boy screamed. His bare backside was sticking up in the air.

"Don't do this, Fats. Let him go. We promised we would."

"And so we shall—after we take the last shot. I want one more picture."

"We have what we need!" Squigger shouted.

"Maybe we'll get extra credit. Who knows? Sweet ass, just like a girl's."

"Please, no," the boy cried.

But it was too late, Fats was on him already. There was a curdling cry of pain.

Squigger was frozen in position, transfixed as he watched. The high had totally worn off, yet he still couldn't take his eyes off what was happening.

"Take the picture. Take the damn picture already," the boy pleaded hysterically.

"Better do as he says," Fats grunted as he drove into him.

Fump.

Fats let him go, then bent down next to the boy's head. "Thanks, lover," he said, thrusting his tongue into his face.

The boy gagged.

Fats stood up quickly.

Vomit flew. It landed across Fats's groin and belly.

"You prick!" he shouted. He drew his pants up, covering the mess, then pivoted, scattering the contents of his pockets on the floor. He launched a driving kick at the boy's face.

It caught him in the mouth. Blood and teeth spurted out as he crumpled to the ground.

Shocked, Squigger looked down at the boy. He was lying very still, a red stream pouring from his face and creeping along the floor boards.

"Gotta get the fuck out of here," said Fats.

They grabbed everything as fast as they could, the cuffs, the rope, the flashlight. They stuffed the pictures in their pockets, scavenged the floor for the photo backings and Fats's possessions. A moment later they were out the door and back in the car. Dirt flew as they took off.

They rode silently for the next few minutes.

Finally, Squigger spoke. "Think he's dead?"

"Don't know. Didn't want to hang around to find out. You?"

"No."

"What the hell happened back there?" Fats asked.

"I told you to stop. You went too far. Now that kid's hurt real bad. Maybe worse."

"No. Not that. The other shit," Fats said. "How

could we have molested the kid like that? Jesus Christ, I'll never get high again."

It didn't surprise Squigger: Fats not caring whether or not the kid was alive or dead, only being concerned with himself, wondering how he was able to commit those unnatural acts. The victim was forgotten. Squigger had hated Fats right from the start. Now, he hated him even more. To Fats, it was the sport of it all. At least for himself, there was a purpose—he needed to do it in order to climb the ladder.

Something else bothered Squigger: He had snorted only a little coke, drank less vodka. Fats said the drugs made him do it. What was his excuse? He despised the violence, or so he thought. Yet, he was left with an odd sense, almost pleasurable. Molesting that boy, having total control, made him feel powerful. *Yes, there was something to that,* he admitted weakly. How else could he have done it? *No! It was the drugs,* he told himself firmly as they made their way back.

"Think we'll get caught?" Squigger said out loud.

"School's twenty-five miles from here. No way he'll ever find us. Doesn't know who we were. And the fraternity will never turn us in."

"And if he's dead?"

"We have to check the farmhouse in the morning," Fats said. "Get rid of the body if he's still there and tell everyone we never completed our mission."

"No body, we hand the pictures in and we're Kingsmen."

"Right," Fats replied. "We got it covered. You scared?"

"Yup. You?"

"Like shit!"

The answer sounded funny coming from Fats after seeing him in action only a half hour ago.

He finally regained consciousness, took his shirt off, and held it up to his face. The blood startled him, how much there was. His backside ached most of all. It was a while before he was steady enough to stand. He had been helpless—used again, just like always.

He looked around the room. It was stripped clean. They took everything with them. But, in the clear space on the floor where his body had lain, something drew his attention—a torn piece of paper. He picked it up. It was a set of directions. He read the heading in the dim moonlight: From Kingsman House to hell. He would find them. And he would get bloody revenge.

29

Dr. Roberts walked past the front desk with a patient's chart in hand. His office manager gave him a woeful look.

"Okay, Nina, let's have it," he said, anticipating the news of impending doom.

"Not starting off to be a good day," she said, shaking her head. "Two more emergencies called. Both insisted on being seen this morning. Had to squeeze them into your schedule as best I could."

"Jesus, they couldn't wait until this afternoon when Cohen and Afferbach are here? I'm overbooked already."

"I know. That's what I told them. Emma Trudeau

was up all night with a toothache. She said if she couldn't get in pronto, she was going to put a gun to her head. The other patient is Jack Kester."

"Shit, Kester? He missed his last two appointments."

"He broke a tooth."

"He in any pain?"

"At first he said no, so I tried to schedule him later. Then, all of a sudden, he says, 'Yes, I'm in pain. Does that make a difference?' He told me if you couldn't see him this morning he was going to find another dentist. All the other time slots I gave him were *inconvenient*."

"Inconvenient?" Roberts seethed.

"His whole family comes here. And his brother's, too."

"So you told him to come in," Roberts said with resignation.

Nina nodded. "Isn't that what you'd want?"

"I guess." He tossed the chart down in front of her and started to walk away.

"Wait. I'm not finished," she sang out with insincere merriment.

"What?"

"Mrs. Wor*shit* is here."

"Nina," Roberts said in a harsh tone, "her name is Wor*chick*." He drew in a breath, let it out slowly. "So?"

"So, she's a half an hour early, again. Demanding to be seen right away, as per usual. She doesn't like to wait."

"Yes, I know."

"Last time, you took her early. Now you've created a monster."

"I can't see her any sooner. I'm already twenty minutes behind, thanks to Mrs. Pilfry, who showed up at eight A.M.—broken denture and no appointment."

"What do you want me to do?" Nina shrugged.

"Appease her."

"How?"

"Find a way," Peter barked.

"I know how you feel about your practice, Dr. Roberts, but *this* person you should definitely lose. She's a horrible old woman."

"Now, Nina, all my patients are important. Some are not happy with their lives and take it out on everyone else. But their money still helps pay our overhead—your salary, as well as mine. Take pity on her."

"Wouldn't mind putting her out of her misery."

"For now, just offer her a cup of coffee," Peter suggested. "Or something. And tell her I'll be with her as fast as I can."

"Okay, Doctor," Nina groaned.

"And Nina . . ."

"Yes, Doctor."

"Remember your smile."

Nina drew her lips back in an exaggerated fashion, showing him her teeth. "Oh, by the way. While you were with Mrs. Pilfry, a Sergeant Pentagast from the Philadelphia Police Department called. Said they found a couple of more bodies up in Coal County. Needs you there this afternoon."

"What?"

Nina laughed. "Also told me to say . . . Shawondasee?" She wrinkled her nose. "Actually, he called to let you know that he made it. The play was wonderful and Jasmine was great!"

Peter's face broke into a grin. He would make certain that he kept in touch with his new friend.

"And he checked in Philly. No record of any odd-looking bite marks with the U imprint that you were so curious about."

"It was worth a shot." He shrugged. "Thanks, Nina."

Roberts walked down the hall as Sallie, his assistant, approached. "Mr. Barbarousk in room four still isn't numb. And I just seated your nine-thirty in number three."

Vivian, a hygienist, poked her head out of the doorway of room two. "Have a patient check here," she called out.

Nina left her desk and walked over to them, agitated. "The old biddy doesn't want coffee or anything else. If she taps on my window again, I swear I'll pop her one."

There was silence. The women stared at Roberts, waiting for orders.

Peter seemed paralyzed for a moment. Then he regained his senses, and swung into action.

"First, I'll dump another carpule into Mr. Barbarousk," he said to Sallie. "Give my nine-thirty patient a magazine to read. Jerry's a friend of mine. Tell him I'm running late. He'll understand." He turned to the hygienist. "Then I'll check your patient."

She nodded.

"Nina, room five is clear. Put Hilda Worschick in there. I'll jump her ahead just to get her out of here."

Roberts slid from one operatory to the next. Finally got Mr. Barbarousk numb and examined Vivian's patient. Tried to placate Mrs. Worschick.

"This tooth bothers me," she said, pointing. "And where the hell were you? I've been waiting a long time."

"Oh, I'm sure it wasn't that long, Hilda. Let me take a look at your problem. Open big."

She opened halfway. Roberts sighed. He aimed his light, manipulated his instruments. "There isn't any decay in the tooth. Not even an old filling," he said. "And last month you were in for X rays and they were negative."

"Well, it hurts when I eat ice cream," she grumbled.

"You do have some gum recession," Roberts noted. "Let me coat the tooth with a desensitizer. Then I'll give you some special toothpaste to use."

"Will it work?" she asked gruffly.

"Only if you let the medicine do its job." He put a suction tip into her mouth, dried the tooth, and painted a solution on. "Now, you have to sit very still and silent, otherwise it won't work," he warned. "It'll take a little time."

Roberts left Mrs. Worschick sitting quieter than he had ever seen her. He hurried to Jerry Taylor, a friend and neighbor. Roberts prepared to cement in a new crown for him.

"Busy morning, Peter," he mumbled over the cotton placed in his mouth. "Guess business is booming."

"Guess so," Peter replied, barely looking up from his work. "How does that feel?"

Jerry bit down. "Feels great," he said through his teeth.

"Good." Roberts took the crown and cotton out, called Sallie in to mix up some cement.

"I saw Diane yesterday," Jerry said. "She looks great."

"You did?" Peter tried not to sound too curious.

"Yeah. She was having lunch at Mademoiselle's with Lance Van Horne. Didn't you know?"

"Sure," Peter said slowly. "Lance Van Horne?"

"Tried to wave, but I don't think she saw me. Gotta tell you, Peter, if I had a wife who looked like Diane, I wouldn't be happy about her having lunch with another guy." He slapped Peter on the knee good-naturedly. "Especially with Lance Van Horne."

"What do you mean?" Peter asked. He felt like somebody had just punched him in the stomach.

"He's a nice enough guy, I guess. But between you

and me, I think he's a bit obnoxious when it comes to women. What was it, a legal matter?"

"Something like that," Peter answered nonchalantly, steadying himself.

Sallie handed Peter the cement. He replaced the cotton, dried the tooth again, and inserted the crown, then instructed Jerry to bite down hard for a few minutes before he bolted from the room.

In his private office, he pushed the speed dial for his home telephone number. After several rings the answering machine picked up. He slammed the phone down. He remembered that Diane had once mentioned that Lance Van Horne wasn't bad looking, had a nice body—but her with him? He winced at the thought. Van Horne was a schmuck. Everyone knew that, even Jerry. Why the hell didn't Diane?

Last summer, when the whole gang was at Roberts's house for a barbecue and swim, Lance had walked up to him, made one of his lewd remarks, the kind he had become famous for. Motioning to Diane in her swimsuit he said to Peter, "Hey, buddy, you're a lucky guy. Wouldn't mind checking her oil out."

Peter had wanted to hit him, but thought better of it. He waited until later and offered Lance a hamburger, one that had fallen on the ground and been licked by the Hoffmans' dog. The revenge wasn't good enough. Now, he wished the mutt had peed on it, too.

A patient's cry snapped Peter back to the present. He hurried out of his private office to the screams of Hilda Worschick.

"Where is he? Where the hell did he get to? You there, girlie," she yelled at Sallie. "Go get him. Tell him I'm not waiting anymore."

When Peter got to the room, Mrs. Worschick was already out of the chair, tearing her bib off. "Are we done?" she roared.

"I guess," he said.

"Good." She threw the bib on the chair. "I want to get out of here." Then she said with less aggression, "So when's my next checkup? Forgot the date."

Roberts took her chart and walked several steps ahead of her up to the front desk. He said to Nina in a low, serene voice, "Tell her there's no charge for today. Check her next appointment. Apologize for keeping her waiting. Escort her to the door. Then . . . kick Mrs. Worshit down the stairs."

Nina wanted to cheer. At the very least, applaud. But then she remembered, and simply smiled, pleasantly.

30

████████ Congressman Charles Whitney sat in his office behind a heavy, oak desk trimmed with touches of brass. The death of Dominic Luccetta had shaken him—how easily it was accomplished, how it could affect his plans. He was so close. Things were going so well. As soon as he heard the news, he went on the offensive to turn it around. But now, unexpectedly, there was also this:

The envelope, with childlike scribbles marking it special delivery, lay crumpled on his desk; the letter was still clutched in his hand. At first, he thought it was a hoax. But the envelope's contents had proven otherwise.

He had dealt with this individual before. Yet, back

then, when he asked for Whitney's help, he had too little to offer in return.

This time was different. Whitney would follow the letter's directions. He needed to. He grabbed for the phone. Arrangements had to be made, people contacted, warned. And the police kept out of it until everything else was set up.

He dialed, got a secretary . . . then nervously waited until Judge Vernon Malchomoty picked up.

31

▬▬▬ Detective Daniel Pinchus walked up the steps to the second floor of the station house. He had phoned in earlier and said he'd be late since he'd logged several hours the night before. He asked Vanderhooven if his extra work had generated any callbacks. There weren't any. Now, as he entered the squad room, he passed Vandy heading down to the front desk. He spread his hands inquisitively at the sergeant.

"Nothing yet, Detective."

"Things look quiet. Thought we had a big prostitution sweep last night."

"Came up empty. Like they were expecting us," Vanderhooven said meaningfully. "Wonder why?"

An expression of uncertainty wrinkled Daniel's face, but before he could respond Vanderhooven added, "Hey, you have a visitor. In the interrogation room. It's a lady. Been here for twenty minutes. Wanted to speak only to you. Told her you wouldn't be in 'til ten. She said she'd wait, so I put her in there."

"Who is she?"

"Didn't leave a name, only her scent." He sniffed the air. "Blue Velvet, I think. Hard to tell over the bug spray. By the way, those photographs of Sarchick just came in." He handed a folder to Daniel. "Nothing special—same faces, only clearer."

Tucking the folder under his arm, Daniel headed for his visitor.

"Be careful, Detective," Sergeant Vanderhooven called after him.

He glanced back, puzzled.

"She's a *real* looker," he said with a wink.

Daniel shook off the jab and opened the door of the interrogation room. There, sitting at a table, drinking a cup of coffee, was Dominic Luccetta's wife, Sylvia. She was wearing black: dress, nylons, and heels. She looked incredible, even in something meant to be widow's weeds. And Daniel had to remind himself of that.

"Mrs. Luccetta, you wanted to see me?" he asked, when he found his voice.

"Don't be so shocked, Detective. The family does let me out once in a while."

"It's not that, it's just . . ."

"I know. My husband was gunned down only yesterday. That, and after the way you hit it off with Marion, you're wondering what I'm doing here."

"Yes, I am," he admitted, placing the folder on the table. He grabbed the chair next to her, twirled it around, and straddled it, resting his forearms on the back. "So tell me why, Mrs. Luccetta."

"Please, call me Sylvia. Mrs. Luccetta sounds like an old Italian lady. Do I look like one?"

Daniel blushed. "No. Not at all."

"I came here to see if I could help you find my

husband's killer. Heard you're looking for a man named Sarchick."

She surprised him. "Who told you that?"

"Why, Marion, of course. Actually, I overheard him talking."

"Marion knows we're looking for Sarchick?"

"Don't be so naive, Detective. Isn't much that goes on here that he doesn't know about." She took a sip of coffee. "Your walls have ears."

"Oh, really? Then aren't you afraid he'll find out you came to see me?"

She laughed. "That's a given." She eased back in her chair, still holding her cup, and cocked her head. "Maybe he sent me."

"Did he?" The possibility intrigued him.

"No. But I'll tell him I was here before someone else does. That way he won't be so angry. You see, he's a bit confused. Doesn't know why you're looking for this Sarchick guy when he's positive Barney did it."

"Terzetto?"

"Yeah. He started working for Dominic a couple of months ago. Dominic liked him. Trusted him completely."

"Short time to earn such confidence."

"Barney just seemed to have all the answers. Did Dominic a lot of favors. Even some he never asked for." She looked down at her empty Styrofoam cup, tilted it forward, then placed it on the table. "Things like that, made them close."

Daniel nodded. "I see."

"Barney never showed up yesterday—before or after the shooting."

"So from that," Daniel said, turning his palms up, "everyone figures he did it?"

"It was more than that," Sylvia continued. "Something important Marion discovered about him."

"Go on."

"Marion never told me."

"Know anything about a note?"

She shook her head, watching him with her luminous eyes.

Daniel stood, meeting her gaze. "Sylvia, I want you to look at something." He took the photographs out of the folder and placed them on the desk in front of her. "Recognize either one of these faces?"

"What is this, some kind of joke?" She glanced at the pictures, then looked up at Daniel. "Is that what this is, Detective?"

His brow wrinkled. "What do you mean?"

"Well, this one I never saw before," she said, pointing to the heavier-looking man. "But you know as well as I do that the other guy is Terzetto."

Daniel bit his lower lip.

"You really don't have to test me like this, Detective Pinchus," she said, rising angrily from her chair. "I meant to tell you the truth right from the start."

"And you have every right to be upset with me." He apologized with boyish charm. And carefully hid his excitement from Sylvia. "But you have to understand I'm running an investigation. I had to be sure."

She hesitated, the tightness in her face easing. "You're lucky I like you."

"Oh?"

"It's not often that I see someone standing up to a Dominic or a Marion—like you did yesterday," she said silkily.

Daniel let the compliment fall away. "I *am* sorry about you losing your husband."

"Don't be, Detective, because I'm not." She hopped up on the table to sit facing him. The move hiked her skirt up, and she crossed her legs.

Daniel couldn't help noticing.

"Dominic was an animal. My life has been a living hell."

"Then why did you. . . ?"

"Marry him?"

"Yes."

"At first, the money attracted me. And the power. I was young. Stupid. When I finally wised up, I was already pregnant. I knew that when Dominic found that out, he'd propose. And you don't simply say no to a don. Nor do you abort his child if you want to live. Funny, that's the only tragedy about yesterday: Me telling our ten-year-old son that his father won't be coming home anymore."

"I'm sure that was tough."

"He'll get over it. He's better off this way," she replied matter-of-factly. "So I played the role of the good wife all these years. But I was more like one of Dominic's trophies. I was there for him to show off, there to entertain his friends. And I was there for his . . . whatever. God! He made my skin crawl."

"Sylvia, you don't have to tell me this," Daniel said. He was unaware that he was staring, eyes fixed on this beautiful woman.

She acted as if she didn't hear him, leaning over the edge of the table. "I played my part well, Detective. Just like I'm doing now," she said softly. "Husband dead, so I dressed in black." Her eyebrows moved provocatively. "Right down to my black lace panties."

Daniel swallowed, fumbled with his thumb for his wedding band. This woman, who lost her husband scant hours ago, was actually coming on to him. She was gorgeous, and it was flattering. But it had to stop— even though he was enjoying it, he admitted to himself shamefully.

What was she all about, this Sylvia? She had implied that there was a mob informant in the station house; cleared up the mystery of Barney Terzetto for him, probably unwittingly; and spoken candidly about her dead husband's dirt. Was she truly a friend? A decoy? Just someone starved for affection? Or maybe she was a Greek bearing gifts. Daniel simply didn't know how to gauge her.

The door to the interrogation room swung open. Rifkin poked his head in. "Oh, I'm sorry. Didn't know anybody was in here." He had a curious look on his face.

"It's okay. I was just leaving," said Sylvia quickly.

"Are you sure?" Daniel asked.

"Yes."

Daniel walked her down to the front door of the station house. Before going, she told him, "I really want *you* to get the man who killed my husband. But I'm afraid, you know, of what Marion might do to you if that should happen. Please be careful."

"If you hated your husband that much," Daniel asked, "why are you so interested in who finds his killer?"

Her expression turned cold. "Maybe I want the chance to thank him, Detective."

Daniel watched Sylvia walk away, still puzzled, but also with a sense of relief. He was anxious for Milano to get back. They had been wrong. Terzetto wasn't dead, because he never existed. He was Sarchick. There was something about the name, though. He grabbed a dictionary. *Barney Terzetto. Son of a bitch, yes!* he said to himself after seeing it in black and white. He slammed the book shut.

Daniel went back to making his calls, trying to establish a solid lead as to the whereabouts of Arthur Sarchick while waiting for Sam. An hour and a half had passed when Officer Rifkin announced to everyone in the squad room that he had just gotten a tip that Captain Schwenk would be dropped off in front of the station house shortly. Captain Perez, as the winner of the bet, made Schwenk pull "decoy duty"—had him dress in drag—and escorting him back to his own division as he appeared on the job was part of the deal.

Rifkin took up a position by the second-story window. He held a camera with a zoom lens in his right hand.

Milano arrived just then, coming to stand next to Daniel. "What gives?"

Before Daniel could answer, Rifkin shouted, "Here he comes."

They all clamored for a view—even a guy in cuffs giving information to two detectives.

Daniel pointed to the street. "Watch," he said to Sam.

A Philadelphia patrol car was at the curb. An angry Schwenk emerged from it. He clutched a handbag in one hand and pulled a wig off his head with the other. He was a sight: earrings dangling; red lipstick on; dressed in a frumpy duster; nylons rolled down to his ankles. He kicked the car door shut with his Hush Puppies.

There were hoots and hollers in the squad room. Schwenk glanced up at the window. Everyone scattered.

"He doesn't make a very pretty woman," Daniel commented.

"Doesn't make it as a woman at all. Did you see how he carried his purse? Grabbing the straps with a fist—a dead giveaway," Milano observed. "No woman would ever hold her bag that way. Learned it in vice. Remember that, Daniel. Never know when you might need it."

The laughter in the room lasted until they heard

Schwenk's footsteps. Suddenly, it grew quiet. Rifkin hid the camera behind his back.

"Not a word. Not even one!" Schwenk warned loudly, staring at the floor as he swiftly limped to his office. His door slammed shut.

"So, how's your blood pressure?" Daniel asked Sam quietly.

"Huh? Oh, the physical. Pressure's fine. Need to lose a couple, though."

Uneasily, Daniel brought up the message Gibney left about the frangible bullets. "Did you see it, Sam?"

"Never got it," he said quickly. "But it definitely ties the murders of the witnesses and Luccetta together."

"Gibney said he put it on your desk. You sure?"

"Listen, I said I never got it," he snapped. "Now that should be enough!"

Daniel was taken aback by Sam's reaction. "Sorry, Sam. You're right. Case must have me frazzled." Puzzled, he dropped the subject in favor of filling Sam in on Sylvia Luccetta's visit.

"Did she sound genuine?" Milano asked.

"She seemed believable."

"Odd she would come to you. Then again, I saw that look she tossed your way at the house."

"What are you implying, Sam?"

"Hard to figure her motivation. That's all. Wouldn't hurt to be a little careful."

"So you don't trust her?"

"Do you?"

Daniel shrugged. "Not sure."

"It's worrisome, though, to think we might have a leak in this department."

"Hhmm." Daniel considered the possibility that someone might have lifted Gibney's message. "But that's not all we have to worry about. The name: Barney Terzetto. I think Sarchick used it as a sick metaphor."

Milano's eyes narrowed.

"I remembered from my piano lesson days. *Terzétto* means three. And *Barney*—well, *Barney* is slang—but synonymous with *deception*." Daniel pulled out the photographs, pointed to the picture of the younger man: heavy face, short hair. "Sarchick number one," he said, then moved his finger to the more recent photo: thin face, long hair. "Sarchick number two."

"Shit!" Milano said. "If you're right, that means we're looking for a third face altogether. *Deceitful three.* No wonder no one has seen him around."

"Makes things a little tougher," Daniel agreed. "But I've been working on a lead, last night and again this morning. I took your advice. Started thinking about the Baby Seigel case. That, and something you said about one of Sarchick's earlier arrests. Had to do with the clutter in his apartment. So I—"

"Sorry to interrupt, fellas," Sergeant Vanderhooven said briskly, handing them a slip of paper. "But I thought you'd want to know right away. You got a call back from the magazine publishers. They have an address for Arthur Sarchick: 519 Rosemont Avenue, apartment 2B."

"Let's go." Milano turned to Vanderhooven. "We'll need two backup units. Take care of it?"

"Done," Vanderhooven replied.

Daniel looked stunned, unable to move. "It actually worked," he mumbled.

"Come on," Milano said. "Don't you want to see your third face?"

32

■■■■■■ "Did you do what you were supposed to?" he asked.

"Yes," she grumbled.

"And?"

"He has no idea. Totally lost."

"Good." Then he said, "Are you sure?"

She gave him an icy look. "If you don't believe me, why don't you ask your pigeon, Marion?"

"We don't own him totally—yet. But it's early. He's only tossed us some unimportant details so far. Like this morning. We met and he gave us the type of bullet used to kill Dominic, but was reluctant to say more. That's why I needed you."

"Who is he?"

Marion chuckled. "Someone who's underestimated who he's gotten into bed with. But give it time," he said confidently. "He'll be in so deep, he'll never be able to say no to anything we ask. That's how we work a snitch."

"Well, I don't like doing your dirty work."

"Thought you'd enjoy yourself, Sylvia. Pinchus is young. He's good-looking. Even righteous. Sounds like your type."

"He's okay," she said plainly.

"Just don't get any ideas. He ain't your savior. Not to mention, he's married."

"Look who's talking. That never stopped *you*," she snapped.

"We did our homework—happily married, Sylvia. It makes a difference," he said with a half smile. "Something you wouldn't know about."

"Bastard."

"Watch your mouth," he warned. "Don't forget I own you, too."

"You think?"

Marion sighed. "What else did you find out? How much do they know about Terzetto? And who's this Sarchick? Why are they looking for him?"

"Not sure, but I think Barney and Sarchick are the same guy."

Marion blinked. "Sarchick's his real name?"

"So much for *your* homework," she scoffed.

"Pinchus tell you that?"

"No."

"So how do you know?"

"Let's just say that was the impression I got from the questions he asked. Give me a little credit for having a brain, Marion."

"And if he should find this guy?" Marion probed.

"No way is he going to tip you off," she said candidly. "You don't scare him."

"But you *did* warn him?"

"Subtly."

"I'm sure. I just wonder what else you told him."
He grabbed her cheek, pinched it hard. "Give away any
secrets, darlin'?"

She pushed his hand away, silent.

"We'll get to Sarchick first, anyway," he said.

"And if you don't?"

Marion aimed his cold gaze at her. "Then we'll have
to do something about it."

"Leave Pinchus alone," she said, her voice low. "Or
I swear, Marion, you'll never see Bobby again."

"Don't threaten me with that ten-year-old bastard,"
he seethed.

"He's the last of the Luccetta males," she reminded
him, then added coldly, "Uncle Marion."

"For now. But I'm still young. There can be more."

"God forbid!"

"I'm growing tired of you, Sylvia. And I don't know
if I can trust you anymore. I think you're lying about
Pinchus."

"I told you the truth. He's not even close."

"Pray that he isn't, Sylvia—for Pinchus's sake, and
for yours. We have to take care of Dominic's killer ourselves."

"Why?"

Marion reached into his pocket and pulled out a
crumpled note. He gave it to Sylvia. "Tony took this out
of Dominic's dead hands. Read it, Sylvia. And maybe
then you'll want to strangle the son of a bitch yourself."

33

Armed with an arrest warrant, Sergeant Milano and Detective Pinchus sped toward 519 Rosemont Avenue. Sam drove. Two unmarked police vehicles followed quietly.

"Can't believe you actually got an address," Milano remarked.

Daniel nodded. "It was the Seigel case. Like you told me, Sam. No face. No name. But my father found the killer anyway. He just happened to notice a couple of ashes on the ground."

"I've seen him do it a hundred times. What was it you noticed here?"

"You mentioned something about one of Sarchick's arrests, about how cluttered with books and magazines his room was."

"That's how you got his address?" Milano asked.

"That, and something my father said about relating

your psyche to the mind of a killer, were my cigarette ashes."

Milano wrinkled his brow.

"You know how you always tease me about being frugal?"

"Cheap is what I said."

"Well, the guy's reluctant to throw stuff out. Must've had several magazine subscriptions before he jumped bail. If it were me, I'd wonder about the undelivered magazines I already paid for."

"And that would bother you," Milano said, nodding for him.

"It would kill me," Daniel admitted. "I figured he'd notify the magazine companies of his new address. Pick an alias that's close to Arthur Sarchick so the mailman would still deliver them thinking that it was just a misspelling."

"Incredible long shot."

"Yeah. I called publishers, starting with the ones I thought Sarchick might have ordered according to his profile. Asked if they had any record of a change of address for an Arthur Sarchick."

"Too bad you didn't have access to the kiddie porn underground. Might have saved you some time," Milano commented, grimacing. "Anyhow, publishing houses are reluctant to give out that kind of information over the phone, even to a cop. How'd you convince them?"

"Told them how important it was. Threatened them. Anything that would work."

"What hit?"

"Mechanic's World."

"That fits," Milano said. "You're definitely Seymour Pinchus's son."

Daniel winced.

"Don't worry, Detective. Someday *he* may be known simply as Daniel Pinchus's father."

"I'd settle for just being the other Pinchus," Daniel lamented.

They came up on the apartment house, passing it to park a short way down the street. Milano and Pinchus went to the trunk and took out their bulletproof vests. One unit was split to cover the back and front exits. The other two officers went inside with them. In the foyer, Milano drew his finger across the mailboxes, rested it on the one labeled 2B. Daniel watched over his shoulder. The name was *A. Solchuk.*

It was an older building. No elevator. They climbed the stairs to the second floor, positioned themselves around the door of the apartment: the two officers with their backs hugging either side of the archway, Milano and Pinchus facing front and a step to the side, guns drawn, pointing up. One of the officers knocked.

There was no answer.

"Sarchick! Police!" Milano yelled. "Open up."

There was silence.

They waited a few moments, then Milano gave Pinchus the nod.

Daniel took a step back, then launched a kick against the door. It held. He kicked again. This time there was a loud crack. The frame splintered by the lock and the door flew open.

In the middle of the room, Arthur Sarchick sat calmly in a high-back easy chair, positioned to watch the show, head and face shaven clean—the last masquerade.

"Finally! I've been waiting for you." Sarchick laughed. Then he looked directly at Daniel. "Detective Pinchus, I presume. I'm impressed." He glanced at his watch. "But I'll have you know, your father would have been here yesterday."

34

"Dr. Roberts." Nina buzzed on the intercom. "Pick up line one. It's Huffnagle. Wants to know why the filling you did the other day is still sensitive."

"Have a patient for you to check, Doctor," Vivian called from room three. "Her kids have early dismissal. Needs to get out pronto."

Roberts had worked through his lunch hour trying to catch up with the morning chaos. His associates, Cohen and Afferbach, had arrived, but the afternoon still looked dismal. And he had Diane on his mind.

Peter was deciding whether to take the call first or do the exam when Sallie approached.

"Had to squeeze another emergency in with you at two," she said. "Mrs. Mitchell. Terrible toothache. Wants only you. Sorry."

Peter sighed, short and powerfully. "I have a god-damn open slot at three. Why not then?"

"Can't. Has a hairdresser appointment. Said she doesn't want to miss it."

Peter threw up his hands. "Enough!" He stormed down the hallway to the front desk. "I'm leaving," he announced abruptly. "I'm leaving and I won't be back for the rest of the day."

Nina was flustered. She'd never seen him like this. "But, Dr. Roberts . . . your patients! What am I going to say to them?"

"Just tell them it wasn't *convenient* for me to see them today," he growled as he disappeared through the front door.

35

Peter drove around aimlessly for the next forty-five minutes. He was obsessed with thoughts of Diane and Lance Van Horne. It shook him. It was awful. It hurt. She didn't even have the decency to find someone he wouldn't know.

He discovered that he had threaded his way downtown. Ironically, he was passing Mademoiselle's. He cringed at the sight. Notions of violence crept into his mind. Then he realized: *Jesus, the guy's a fucking attorney. Lawsuit. Jail.* He fought to maintain control, felt it slipping, and decided he'd better go talk to someone before he did something stupid. *A friend maybe. Somebody close, trustworthy.* Daniel popped into his head. His wife's cousin—and a cop. Rivington Street was only a few blocks away. He quickly turned the car in that direction.

He parked at the corner. As he walked up to the station house he noticed a flurry of excitement at the curb. Daniel, Sergeant Sam Milano, and a couple of officers were hustling an odd-looking gentleman out of one of their vehicles. He was cuffed and his face was twisted with a strange expression. It gave Peter the chills.

Daniel was gripping the prisoner by the arm, urging him forward, when he spotted Peter. "Peter! What are you doing here? Is everything okay?" he asked.

Suddenly, he didn't know what to say. "I, um . . . came to tell you that a . . . you're overdue for your dental checkup."

Daniel furrowed his brow. "Huh?"

"You a dentist?" Sarchick asked, aiming his wild-looking eyes at Roberts. He drew his top lip up and hissed at him through a space between his upper front teeth.

Peter flinched. The guy was scary . . . and should probably consider replacing those ugly caps.

After waiting for the prisoner to be taken inside, Peter had second thoughts about revealing his marital woes to Daniel. He chose to lie, saying he just happened to be next door at the courthouse settling a parking ticket and wanted to stop by and say hello. He went home directly thereafter.

Coming through the garage, Peter noticed Diane's car. He glanced at his watch: two-thirty. The older kids weren't home from school yet, and he remembered Paige was spending the day across town with Susan and Adam. No one else was home. *Perfect,* he told himself. It was time to confront Diane with what he knew.

Peter was suddenly trembling. *Could someone else be taking advantage of the empty house? Like Diane and Van Horne?* He decided to be quiet just in case. He left the garage, entered the kitchen, and poked around on the first floor before creeping upstairs. Their bedroom door was shut, the cat sleeping by it. She yawned at Peter. He could hear Diane giggling inside and his imagination ran away with him.

He threw the door open and yelled, "Aha!"

Diane was sitting on the bed and had just hung up the telephone. She looked up at Peter with round, astonished eyes. "What the hell's wrong with you? Are you crazy or something?"

Peter surveyed the room. Diane was alone.

"Nina called about a half hour ago. Said you left the office in a tizzy. She was concerned. I was concerned."

"Didn't sound that way to me," Peter shouted. "I heard you laughing."

"That was Susan. She was telling me how cute Adam and Paige were together. I didn't want to let on how worried I was about you, so I played along. Where were you? Why are you here in the middle of the day?"

"Because I know what you've been up to, Diane," he said, standing over her, pointing a finger.

"Like what?" A crease formed on her forehead. Her eyes widened.

"Your affair." He folded his arms across his chest.

"I was right. You are crazy—fucking nuts!"

Peter told Diane about the secret phone calls he'd noticed, her unaccounted time, her phony excuses, her lunch date at Mademoiselle's.

When Peter was done, Diane gave a long sigh. "I can't believe it. I knew I should have told you sooner. I wasn't having an affair, Peter. I've been working. A job," she added in response to his blank look.

"A job? Why would you want a job?"

"The kids are growing up. Too fast," she said sadly. "You have your dental practice, your forensic work. What do I have, Peter?"

Peter didn't know how to answer her. It was something he had never considered.

"Joannie Van Horne found out that Parkway Travel was looking for part-time help and were willing to train. Joannie's a good friend. She knew how I felt and encouraged me to apply. It was perfect. I got to pick my own hours.

"When Lance's law partner, Stuart Darcey, mentioned that his twenty-fifth wedding anniversary was coming up and that he wanted to surprise his wife with an expensive, around-the-world cruise, Lance referred Stuart to me."

"Lance knew about all of this, but I didn't?" Peter said, grasping at some of his rapidly disappearing anger.

"Sorry. I was going to tell you right after I got my first commission check. That way you'd know I was serious about it. Do you know how much a cruise like that costs?"

"No."

"Over fifty thousand dollars, Peter. It was one of my first bookings—an impressive start with the agency. And a nice payoff to boot. Lance warned Stuart that I was a novice. It was an important deal. That's why I was so careful about the details. And Stuart knew that I hadn't told you yet."

"The secret phone calls," Peter said slowly.

"I had to contact him several times from the house. When he wasn't busy at the office or when his wife wasn't around."

"And what about Mademoiselle's?"

"I had the final documents ready. They needed to

be picked up. Stuart's wife works near Parkway Travel, so he didn't want to chance having her spot him there."

"What about dropping them off at his office?"

"Same thing. His wife is chummy with the office manager. He didn't want to risk a leak, not after coming this far. So he recommended we meet at the restaurant. I'd casually hand over the documents, give him some last-minute instructions, and he'd slip me a check."

"But how did Lance get into the picture?" Peter persisted. He was beginning to sound like a jerk, even to himself.

"Stuart got tied up with a client. Lance was free, so he offered to go for him. Lance insisted on buying me lunch. Said it was on Stuart. Figures—you know how cheap Lance is. But I settled for a drink instead."

Peter sat down on the bed next to Diane, put his arm around her. "I'm such an idiot," he said. "I'm sorry for not trusting you. Forgive me?"

"Really, Peter," she laughed. "Lance Van Horne? I thought you'd give me more credit than that."

"I love you."

"Nice body, though," she commented, staring off into space.

"Cut it out." Peter went to kiss her.

Diane put up a hand, held it against his face. "Not so fast. You had your fling. That hurt me. Badly. Now you've had a taste of your own medicine. How does it feel?"

"Like shit. But you know I love you. And I know you love me," he added confidently. "You'd never cheat on me."

Diane didn't answer.

"Would you?"

"Certainly not with Lance Van Horne," she proclaimed. "But you'll never be sure of me again. Maybe that will be your punishment."

"I deserve it," Peter said, but he didn't sound sincere.

"You're such a pushover," Diane said, smirking. "After all, look how easily you bought this story."

Peter coughed nervously. With all the confidence he had rediscovered in the last few minutes, there now was the unmistakable inkling of doubt.

"So now what?" Diane's face brightened.

Peter shrugged. He read her smile, knew what it meant.

Her tongue played across her upper lip. "We still have forty-five minutes before any children get home."

Peter pushed her onto the bed. With a desire stronger than he could remember, he tore her blouse open, then furiously struggled to get her jeans down.

"Lance Van Horne?" she blurted out and began to laugh again. "Everyone knows he's a schmuck, Peter. Why didn't you?"

36

▬▬▬▬ Three hours had passed since Arthur Sarchick was arrested. He had been charged and booked for the murder of Dominic Luccetta, then spent most of his time being cleared by federal agents before finally being turned back over to the police. He was now cuffed and seated at a table in an interrogation room.

Sam Milano sat across from Sarchick, elbows resting

on the table, hands supporting his chin. He was staring curiously at Sarchick, his attention drawn to those aspects of Sarchick's appearance that made him look peculiar: the shaven head where stubble was beginning to form; the deep swirl of scar that cut across his upper lip and ended in a knot just below his nose; the empty-looking eyes.

Officer Collins sat next to Sam, recording the session. Detective Pinchus paced back and forth behind them.

Sarchick had waived his right to have an attorney present, and even volunteered some information: *Sure, he killed Luccetta; No, he was working alone.* But not much more than that. They kept asking him questions.

"Why'd you do it, Arthur?" Milano repeated.

"You think you're so smart," Sarchick sneered. "Figure it out for yourself."

"You used the alias Barney Terzetto to infiltrate the Luccetta mob," Daniel said. "Had a secret address, changed your appearance. That means you planned this awhile ago. Now, who are you working for?"

"Like I told you before, nobody."

"Roman and Ethel Johnson—know anything about them?" Milano asked.

"Haven't a clue."

"You're full of shit," Pinchus charged. "Don't see frangibles very often."

"Don't know what you're talking about."

Daniel switched tactics. "Dominic was one mean scumbag. Wasn't he?"

"He was a motherfucker. He needed to die," Sarchick said, becoming more animated.

"So you decided to take him out."

"Somebody had to."

"The Malloys put you up to it? Maybe the Bertelli gang?" Milano pressed.

"No. I did it myself. Like I said, he was a mother-fucker."

"Why were you hanging around your apartment waiting for us? What did you think, we were coming to give you a medal?" Daniel asked.

"Right now, this is the safest place for me," Sarchick maintained.

"Bull," Sam said. "After hitting Dominic the Don, your life expectancy in prison isn't worth crap."

A half smile crept across Sarchick's lips. "We'll just have to see about that. Won't we?"

"And no little boys in the joint for you to fondle," Daniel threw out.

Milano glanced quickly at Daniel, signaling his disapproval.

Sarchick's eyes lit up. "What do you mean?"

"We've seen your record. We know what you are."

"That was a long time ago," Sarchick said bitterly. "I was young. I made some mistakes and I paid for them. I'm not ashamed to admit it because I'm not like that anymore."

Daniel nodded insincerely. "Yeah, right."

"I've been clean."

"Uh-huh."

"Fuck you," Sarchick shouted. "Fuck you all. You let people like Luccetta roam the streets. Sure, you tried to put him away, but you never could. So *I* had to take care of him."

"Judge, jury—" Daniel yelled back.

"That's enough," Milano interrupted.

"—and executioner," Sarchick finished loudly. "That's right. Did everyone a favor when I pulled that trigger. So why should you give a fuck?"

The door flew open and Sergeant Vanderhooven entered the room. "Captain Schwenk wants to see you," he said to Milano and Pinchus.

"We'll be finished with our interview in a few minutes," Milano replied.

Vanderhooven shook his head. "Captain said *now*. I'm supposed to bring Sarchick back down to his playpen."

———

"Nice job, Detectives," Captain Schwenk told them after they were seated in his office.

Milano and Pinchus looked at each other, then back at Schwenk.

"I mean that," Schwenk said, reaching into his jar for a handful of jelly beans. The happier Schwenk was, the more jellies he seemed to eat. The same applied when he was nervous. He appeared to be a little of both.

"Thank you, Captain," they said at the same time.

"About this case," Schwenk began. "I know the press will be hounding us for details. Have been already."

"Don't worry, Captain," Milano said. "We'll be careful with what we give them. Just enough to keep them off our backs."

"Well, throw that out the window," Schwenk said. "Play it up. It's good publicity for the department. The public has a right to know that we won't stand for this sort of shit in our neighborhoods. Innocent people need, and deserve, to feel safe. I've arranged for a press conference tomorrow. Noon. I want you both to be there."

"Yes, sir," said Milano.

Daniel glanced down at the floor.

Schwenk popped a couple of beans into his mouth and chewed hard, staring at Daniel before swallowing. Then he said, "One more thing. I got a call a short while ago. From high up." He leaned back in his chair.

"Seems as though they want our boy Sarchick in the Witness Protection Program."

Daniel jumped to his feet. "What? Who the hell arranged that? And why so fast?"

"Sit down, Detective." Schwenk waited until Pinchus complied before continuing. "Somehow Sarchick made contact."

"How?" Daniel's control was stretched nearly to the breaking point.

"That's not information they're giving out. But it happened recently. Apparently, Sarchick has a lot to offer—dirt on organized crime that could tear them apart. Sarchick knew who to go to, and was able to sell himself."

"So, the son of a bitch had an insurance policy," Milano said quietly.

"The federal prosecutor's office ran the whole deal by me. It's only a formality, but I agreed to turn Sarchick over to the federal marshals tomorrow."

"I don't think that's a good idea," Daniel argued. "He's too smart, too deceptive. He made himself difficult to find, yet he wanted to be picked up all along. Sat there waiting like it was some kind of sick game. I don't trust him. And I bet he's still a pedophile. Hate to think of this guy in some small town out West—with a new identity and the federal marshals' blessing—running around in costume, entertaining little kids."

"I wouldn't worry," Schwenk said. "Feds gave him a polygraph and asked some pointed questions about that. He passed with flying colors. The whole package was considered. I have to go along with it. Anyway, it's out of my hands."

"Can't you at least argue the point?" asked Milano.

"Wouldn't do any good. And it will make them think I'm not a player."

"But, Captain—"

"Discussion closed," Schwenk said firmly.

Milano and Pinchus rose to leave.

"Pinchus—"

They both turned toward Schwenk.

"Just Detective Pinchus. We need to have a word alone."

<hr>

"Don't fight me on this, Detective," Schwenk warned after the door closed behind Sam. He grabbed another handful of jelly beans. "The brass is finally looking my way again."

"And if I do?"

"I still have charges pending against you."

"What?" Daniel forced out, past the rage knotting in his throat. "I thought we had a deal?"

"Deal? I don't seem to remember," Schwenk replied tranquilly.

Daniel was silent a moment. Then he said, "I'm getting to the point where I don't give a shit what you do anymore."

"But you have a partner to worry about," Schwenk reminded him.

"So, that's how it is."

"That's how it is," Schwenk nodded. He threw a few more jelly beans into his mouth.

Daniel wanted to pick up the whole jar and pour them down Schwenk's throat until he choked. Instead, he clenched a fist at his side and said, "Is that all, sir?"

<hr>

Daniel caught Sam just as he was hanging up the phone by his desk.

"Bastard," Milano fumed. "How can he do that? Unless . . . ." He looked at Daniel. "Hey, I hope like hell you're not trying to protect—"

"He only mentioned me," Daniel said quickly. "I think he's afraid of you."

"Well, I'll stand behind whatever you decide to do."

"Thanks, Sam. But I'm going to let this one go. Like Schwenk said, their minds are made up. What good would it do, except get me into more trouble?"

Sam put his hand on Daniel's arm to keep him from saying anything more. "While we're on the subject of dirty deals—"

"Schwenk giving you a hard time, Pinchus?" Rifkin asked with a hint of mockery in his voice as he approached them.

"What's it to you?"

"Got a great picture of Schwenk in drag this morning. Gonna make a few copies. He wants this whole affair to be lost and buried in Philly. But I thought you might want a print."

"Sure." Daniel grinned. "I'd love one."

"Cost you a twenty."

Daniel shook his head. "Rifkin, you'd turn your mother in for a quarter."

Rifkin chuckled. "Next week the price goes up," he said, walking away.

━━━━━

Later, while Sam and Daniel were finishing their paperwork, Chief Foster, head of all police detectives for the city of Hamilton, entered the squad room. He was nearing the end of his career. By no means an impressive one, but conducted with honesty and fairness. He had survived three different mayoral administrations, garnering their respect, as well as that of his own men. The current regime looked toward him to recommend a replacement. He walked directly over to Sergeant Milano and Detective Pinchus.

"What brings you to Rivington Street?" Milano asked the chief respectfully.

"Wanted to thank you boys personally for a job well done on collaring this Sarchick fellow," he told them.

"Thank you, sir," they both said.

"Captain Schwenk in his office?"

"Yes," Milano answered. "Busy as usual. But I'm sure he'll have time to see you."

Daniel secretly made a face at Milano's flowery response.

"Excellent. Keep up the good work." And as abruptly as he entered, Chief Foster headed toward the captain's office.

"So I guess Schwenk's in the running again," Milano whispered. "See what I mean about politics?"

Nodding, Daniel bent his head again. The paperwork seemed to stretch on and on. Finally, Sam told Daniel to leave. There wasn't much left, he said, and he would knock off the rest since Daniel had worked so late the night before.

Daniel accepted the offer.

In the police station parking lot, someone stepped out of the shadows as Daniel was unlocking his car. He recognized the face instantly. Tony Caputa.

"Hear the fucker who whacked Dominic got a buy into Protection," he said, cigarette dangling from his crooked mouth. "In the joint we could have taken him out. Marion warned you. And look what you've done. *Che cazzo.*" He jabbed a sharp finger into Daniel's shoulder. "Now it's your ass on the line."

It had been a long day. First, it was Sarchick. Then Schwenk. And Rifkin. And now, this scumbag—whose premature knowledge of Sarchick and the Witness Protection Program had suddenly confirmed Daniel's suspicions about a rat in the department—threatening him. Poking him. Daniel had had enough. He swung a fist, catching Caputa in the jaw. Caputa went down. Then Daniel calmly got into his car and drove away. Caputa was still on the ground, yelling: "You're a dead man, Pinchus—fucking dead."

In a holding tank in the basement of Rivington Street Station, Arthur Sarchick lay on a cot thinking about tomorrow—his new life and how he would shape it to his desire. *They were all idiots. And so overeager, like children. His mother would have been proud,* he thought, *how he had manipulated everyone. But she left him. Left him by himself, just like the rest. He had become such a disappointment to her.*

Now, he had a chance to prove himself. The assassination of Dominic Luccetta was only the start. Everything would be right again. Soon, they would all pay—every last one of them.

Sarchick was excited. He was having trouble falling asleep. He needed to clear his mind. So he did what he used to do when he stayed with his mother and needed to behave himself, what he did almost every night when he was in prison: He invited a secret friend to share his bed. Tonight, he envisioned him as ten years old, maybe eleven. Sarchick closed his eyes. With blond hair and blue eyes, he decided.

Yes, they were definitely fooled. All with a little help from a hummingbird. He smiled, then gathered his pillow and blanket together, rocked his body rhythmically against it, and drifted deeper into his dark world.

37

When Daniel got home, he was still thinking of Sarchick. He was troubled by the way things ended up, and knew he was powerless to change them. Hitting Tony Caputa had only made matters worse.

"Had to put your son to sleep again before he could say good night to his daddy," Susan said behind him.

He turned. "I'm sorry, Susan. It's—"

"I know." She quickly placed her hand on his mouth. "Don't say another word."

He kissed her hand, took it down with his own, holding on to her.

"I have something I want you to do." She pointed to the *Yahrzeit* candle on the kitchen counter. "It's the anniversary of your sister's passing. I think it would be nice if you lit the candle."

"Susan, that was twenty-seven years ago. There were pictures. I hardly remember her—"

"*Yahrzeit* is a Jewish tradition—a good deed, a *mitzvah* for a family member."

"—and when I do, it only brings back awful feelings. Jesus, I was only two at the time."

"You shouldn't feel that way. It was a life. Don't let it pass without leaving its mark. Look inside your heart, Daniel. I'm sure your father does. I'm sure he's lit one of these for the past twenty-seven years. And it's probably just as difficult each time. But I don't think he dwells so much on the sadness as he does on the memory."

"I'm too tired to argue."

"Someday you'll see it my way," she said confidently.

He struck a match, lit the wick. She kissed him. "Thank you. Now come to bed. Cast that nasty world of yours aside and lie down next to me for a change. I've missed you. I want you back."

Daniel wrapped his arms around her. He tried to empty his mind as he gazed over her shoulder at the flickering candle. Smiling suddenly, he noticed something next to it that he hadn't seen before. Several brightly colored beans trembling in the glow from the candle. He let Susan go.

"What are those?" he asked, pointing.

"Oh, those are Mexican jumping beans. They move when light hits them. Diane gave them to the kids. They're from a promotion her office was doing on Mexican vacations."

"Diane ever tell Peter about the job?"

"Poor Peter," Susan giggled. "I'll tell you about that later . . . after we go to bed."

But Daniel stood a moment longer, staring at the beans. "I didn't know they came in colors."

"They don't. Paige and Adam painted them that way. They look just like jelly beans, don't they?"

38

■■■■■■ He could see it more clearly now, clearer than he ever had before. Slow motion, freezing those moments in time. He heard the man yell: "Pinchus! Got something for you."

He turned, noticed the gun—Desert Eagle, .357 magnum—a second after he placed the face, recognition sinking in too late to save him. And all of a sudden, he realized that the voice was calling him out of anger and misplaced revenge.

Instinctively, he lunged for his own weapon in the top drawer of his desk, a single step, but too far away. Before he could get to it, he saw the first flash from the muzzle.

At the same time he saw Junior Gibney starting to make a leap for the shooter.

The bullet tore into his chest, knocked him backward. His shirt turned red before he actually felt the jolt. It was crushing.

Junior Gibney was in the air, lunging toward his target. Sam Milano screamed for help, heading for his injured partner.

The second shot grazed a railing post, slowed, but never changed direction as it tumbled toward him. He flinched before it hit, tearing into his right shoulder, burning, shattering bone. An arc of blood spurted from the wound, then agony. He began to raise his other arm to grab at the pain, when the next shot came.

The third slug exploded in his head, entering to the side of his left eye, and his knees buckled, sending him to the floor just as Gibney landed on the gunman. This time there was no pain, only the dimming light and fading awareness. The last thing he saw was Sam kneeling over him. He smiled at the familiar face, coughed up blood, then there was only darkness.

It felt like an eternity, there in the black, in limbo for weeks, months. At times there was a light, tempting him to follow. But there were also kind voices that seemed to hold him back. Finally, it was his son that led him out—his presence, his scent, his touch.

Lieutenant Seymour Pinchus's eyes snapped open as morning sunlight crept across his face. He was home, as he had been for four years now. It took him a moment to remind himself of that. No longer a homicide detective. No longer a lieutenant. No longer in the hospital.

He reached for Kate, came up empty. She was already out. The Laughlin job, he remembered. She had told him last night, when he picked her up at the airport after a week of meditation at a Zen monastery, that she promised the Laughlins the new cabinets would be in by this weekend. They were giving a party—lots of guests—and they wanted to show the house off. And true to her word and reputation, Kate had gotten an early start in case there were any hitches. Conscientious to a fault, he knew, this woman that he loved.

He ran his fingers through his silver hair, now shorter and more conservative than the flamboyant way he wore it as a cop. He got out of bed and went to wash, catching his reflection in the mirror over the medicine cabinet. It was a tired look: eyes sagging on either side of his large nose. His forehead had grown since he went to sleep. He said, *"Good morning,"* to himself, and wondered how he was going to fill another day.

When he got to the kitchen, the first thing he looked for was the *Yahrzeit* candle. Just a wet pool of melted wax left, but the glass still glowed with the flickering flame. He stared at it solemnly for a moment.

He tried to linger on the happy times he had spent with his daughter, and not on the tragedy—her death from cancer at the age of five. And when the candle finally did burn out, he would teach himself to let her go for another year.

The *Hamilton Press* was folded neatly on the table by his place setting, as expected. Also expected was the note from Kate:

Love,

Coffee's up. There's oatmeal on the stove. Just warm it with a bit of skim milk. Half a grapefruit in the fridge. Enjoy— doctor's orders. He wasn't impressed with your last cholesterol and triglyceride levels, and God only knows what you've been eating while I was away. Sorry, honey.

Kate

P.S. Nice article about Daniel in the paper.

Pinchus poured himself a cup of coffee, sat down to read about his son and the arrest of Dominic Luccetta's assassin. He was very proud of Daniel and even remembered to tell him so sometimes. But the pride was tempered by a certain jealousy. Seymour still wanted to be out there in the field with him. So in the interest of self-preservation and self-esteem, he tried not to dwell. It was too painful.

He ate the breakfast that Kate had prepared, then decided to hang around the house and wait. Maybe later she would have something he could help her with in the shop.

It hadn't always been this way, not for the Fox. It should *never* have been this way, not after so many years of taking care of himself. He used to be a leader. People looked to him for direction, asked him what to do next. There were challenges but he never shied away, never faltered. In the homicide division, he had *arrived*. Everyone knew it. He knew it, damn it! He would defy the odds, gleaning solutions from the most puzzling of cases with only a smattering of clues. There was nothing he wouldn't attempt.

But now, sadly, Seymour Pinchus had simply surrendered. He was a different man. So many things had changed.

For one, he was no longer obsessed with his own death. Not that he welcomed it either, but some of his zest for life had diminished. He used to doubt he'd reach fifty years of age. It was so important to him that the fear that he wouldn't had been overwhelming. Fifty-five was inconceivable. Now, he was facing sixty in a few months and he looked upon it with resignation. *So, what else is new?*

The depression, he knew, had to do with his retirement. It hadn't been on his own terms. A barrage of bullets had seen to that.

He might have felt differently if he could have picked his time. Maybe after one last case of great importance, a case that showed everyone that the Fox still had it. Then he could step down, gracefully, like some sports legend who bowed out at the top of his game before his skills diminished to mediocrity. They were the ones held in the highest esteem, both for their ability and their good judgment. He mourned not having that opportunity. One more case could have changed things.

That was the essence of Seymour Pinchus. And having been denied that last case, he chose instead to distance himself from all of it . . . or so he made it seem.

He cut out the article about Daniel and discarded the newspaper so that Kate wouldn't see what he had done. He put the clipping with the others he had saved in a shoe box at the back of his closet. This was his secret collection of mementos: old photos of Melissa; her favorite doll; his gun; his badge; and the letter from John Quigley, his old sergeant from before he went into homicide.

He went back to the kitchen, poured a second cup of coffee, and allowed himself to fantasize about one last marvelous case.

39

Daniel Pinchus arrived at Rivington Street Station much earlier than usual, well before the captain was due to arrive. He snuck into Schwenk's office and dumped a handful of the Mexican jumping beans into the captain's favorite jar. Then he adjusted the blinds, just so.

Back at his desk, he busied himself with reports. And waited. Twenty minutes passed before Schwenk appeared. He watched the captain limp into his office. Rifkin came over to sit on the edge of Daniel's desk.

"Change your mind about the picture, Pinchus?"

"No. But you might want to get your camera again."

"Why?"

"Thought you might want to make some more money."

The door to the captain's office flew open, banging as it hit the stopper, and Schwenk raced out. His limp appeared more pronounced as he lugged his jar of jelly beans across the squad room.

"Call the goddamn exterminator again," Schwenk yelled, heading for the steps. He rocked down them unevenly, faster than Daniel had ever seen him move before.

Everyone in the squad room gathered at the second floor window to watch as Schwenk dumped his beloved jar into a trash can on the street corner.

Daniel was happy all morning. Those that seemed to guess he had something to do with the ruckus gave him the thumbs-up as they passed his desk.

He was concentrating on filling out some paperwork when Vanderhooven grunted to him from across the room. His mouth was stuffed with a doughnut. He mimicked holding a phone to his ear and then flashed his index and middle finger into the air.

Daniel picked up the phone and hit line two.

"Pinchus," he said shortly.

"You know who I am, smart-ass?"

Daniel knew exactly who it was, but decided to remain silent.

"Well, smart-ass, you had to do it. Can't say I didn't warn you. But now," Marion Luccetta paused before saying, slow and clear, "you just made your own hell!"

The line clicked, then went dead. But Daniel held on to the phone for another moment, listening to his pulse thump away in his ear.

40

████████ "Try the pastitsio," Seymour suggested. "It's fantastic. Kritalis makes the best I've ever had."

"How would you know?" Kate glanced at him over the top of her menu. "I thought you don't eat out much anymore. The doctors warned you about your cholesterol, and your weight."

"Doctors!" he said, tilting his head. "They only want to rob you of life's little pleasures. But I've been good. Honest. Tom Onasis brought me here once. Awhile back."

"What, did he lose a bet or something?" Daniel asked.

"Of course," Seymour said. "I only gamble on sure things."

"So do I," Kate chimed in. "How about a wager on sticking to your diet?"

"Grandpa's getting yelled at," Adam giggled.

"Amazing," Seymour noted. "I spent my life up-holding the law, but my own wife mistrusts me."

"I think I'll have the moussaka," Susan decided.

"Excellent choice. They do a nice job with that, too." Seymour felt Kate's suspicious eyes on him. "I mean, I imagine they would." He shrugged nervously. "After all, it is a Greek restaurant."

"I'm so sorry we had to go out to eat," Susan said, shaking her head.

"Don't be, dear," Kate told her. "It's the thought that counts. And it was a wonderful gesture. But cooking a special dinner isn't easy when you're not used to it. Don't worry, you'll learn."

"I overcooked the brisket," Susan said sadly.

"Overcooked?" Daniel mused. "Peter Roberts might have trouble identifying it, and he's a forensic expert. Burnt beyond recognition."

"Oh, leave her alone," Kate scolded.

"And my matzo balls turned out like billiard balls," Susan moaned.

"There's a secret to that," Seymour informed her. "Seltzer. Makes them light and fluffy. Here, have a glass of Mavrodaphne. It may be a dessert wine, but it'll make you feel better now."

He reached for the bottle and fumbled it, splattering himself and Daniel with a few red drops before he could regain control.

A waiter rushed over with a bottle of club soda and some extra napkins.

"Ah," Seymour said, somehow keeping his composure. "Another thing seltzer is good for."

Both men excused themselves.

As they washed up by the sink in the men's room, Seymour looked at his son in the mirror. "Read about you in the paper today. I'm very proud of you." He was able to say it without rushing, without mumbling.

"Are you really?"

"Of course I am. I always have been. Why do you ask?"

"I don't know. You seem . . . disinterested at times."

"Well, I'm not," he said sincerely. "I just thought you needed your own space without always worrying about tripping over me."

"It's tough—you're everywhere." Daniel meant it to be a compliment.

"That'll change. Probably already has," Seymour said with mixed emotions. "I didn't want you to feel compelled to come to me if you had a problem. But if you ever really get stuck, I'm here," he said. "For what it's worth. But I shouldn't have to tell you what you should already know."

Daniel smiled, but was unable to meet his father's gaze.

"Now, let's talk about you," Seymour remarked as he worked at his shirt with a wet towel. "What else has you troubled?"

Daniel was silent a moment, but Seymour caught a glimpse of his son's reflection in the glass. "Is it Schwenk?" he pressed.

"He's giving me a rough time. Nothing I can't handle, though."

"My fault. He hated me, and he's taking it out on you now."

"Don't worry. I'm doing my best to make his life miserable."

"From the looks of it," Seymour observed, "I think he's winning. If you want help," he offered, "I still have a couple of things hanging over his head."

"What about your hands-off policy? How else am I going to learn?"

"Touché," Seymour commented, breaking into a

smile. "When you exhaust all of your ideas, then you may ask me." He finished at the sink and leaned a shoulder against the wall. "So, if it's not Schwenk, then what's bothering you?"

"Is it that obvious?" Daniel asked, hesitating.

"No. I'm just perceptive."

"And persistent."

"When it's important."

"The mob," Daniel said finally. "I don't have much experience dealing with them. Sam warned me to be careful."

"Good cop. Smart man. Like I always told you, listen to what he has to say."

"Well, I may have gone too far already."

"How so?"

"I pushed them."

"A little?"

"A lot," Daniel conceded, stopping short of telling his father that he'd decked Caputa. "They wanted information. Information I couldn't and wouldn't give them."

"And?"

"Basically, I told them to go to hell. Then they made some threats."

"That's upsetting," Seymour sighed. "However, I don't think you have much to worry about. Usually, their bark is worse than their bite. They try to get what they want through intimidation. You stood up to them. They didn't like that, so they threatened you. But actually carrying out a threat against an officer of the law is another story. In the future, you'll be more careful."

Daniel brightened a bit. "We better get back to the table. They'll worry."

"Why? Women go to the bathroom together all the time and take forever. They'll understand. I want to tell you one more thing. Something about your work."

"What?"

"When you go home at night, don't bring it with you. *Ver darf es*—who needs it? Don't let the same thing happen to you and Susan that happened to your mother and me. I became too absorbed. Forget those things that you have no control over. I couldn't. Don't let them paralyze you. You have a wonderful wife. Tell her that you love her."

"I do," Daniel said.

"Then tell her some more. You have it all, Daniel. Don't let it slip from your grasp. Spend more time with Adam. In four months you'll have another one fighting for attention."

"Oh my God, I forgot to tell you," he said suddenly. "Susan is going to have a girl. You're going to have a granddaughter."

"A girl," Seymour exclaimed. "A *shaineh maideleh*." His eyes twinkled. "Now, that's something to celebrate. Let's eat!"

"You know, for four years—almost nothing," Daniel said as they left the men's room. "But tonight, you're full of advice. And I've missed your Yiddish expressions."

"Been saving them up," his father confessed. "And I'll give you one more. A final caution about the mob: *Varfen an oyg*—watch your step."

They had a glorious meal. When it was over, Emil Kritalis himself came out to tempt them. "Tonight we have a special treat," he announced. "A Greek apple torte. It's usually served with whipped cream. But for you, my friend," he turned to look at Seymour, "I have some cheddar cheese to put on it instead—since I know how much you like it that way."

Seymour slumped in his chair.

"Only been here once before, my foot," Kate snapped, glowering at him from across the table.

41

That night, Daniel and Susan went home happy. They hurried to tuck Adam in, and a few moments later, he was fast asleep.

Daniel thought about what his father had said and began following his advice right away: He told Susan how much he loved her, then took her to bed. Lying there in her arms he knew how much he wanted to grow old with this woman, knew how much she meant to him.

They made love for a long time. Daniel could feel his unborn child resting between them, never wanting the moment to end. And when it finally did, he kissed his wife and thanked her for everything she brought to him, then dozed off. He had never felt more contented.

Saturday morning, Daniel slept in, and when his eyes opened, the alarm clock by his bed said it was a little after nine. Susan wasn't there. Up and about already. He went into the kitchen to look for her. Adam was at the table, spooning himself dry cornflakes.

"Where's Mommy?"

"She said not to bother you," Adam said over the crunch of his cereal.

The phone rang and Daniel picked it up, nodding at his son's answer.

"Thank God I got you in time," Milano said, his voice thrumming with tension and adrenaline.

"What's up?" Daniel noticed a message from Susan on the kitchen table, and began to read it as Sam talked.

"An anonymous call came into the station house a minute ago—a woman's voice—warning that the officer who arrested Sarchick was in danger," Milano said quickly, still half out of breath. "She said a car bomb had been planted."

Daniel,

Had to run out for milk. Didn't want to upset you yesterday, but my car's on the blink again . . .

"Probably just a crank call," Milano offered, trying to sound less concerned, "but you never know."

. . . so I have to borrow yours—if I can find where you parked it,

Susan.

P.S. You were wonderful last night. How about a repeat performance this evening?

"Bomb squad's on their way. Did you hear me, Daniel?"

Daniel dropped the receiver, never heard it crash to the floor. Milano's voice was still yelling, "Daniel, are you there? Daniel . . ." But he never heard that either.

"Adam, Daddy has to go get Mommy. Promise me you'll stay right there. Don't get up for anything until Daddy gets back."

"Okay," Adam smiled. "I'm a big boy." He continued to eat his breakfast.

Daniel left the apartment, catapulted down the steps, and darted out into the street. He was wearing nothing more than a pair of boxer shorts. Heart racing, mind spinning, he tried to remember where he had parked his car.

Barefoot, he ran down the block, turning left at the corner. Fifty yards ahead he saw the car, still parked. There was no sign of Susan. He was relieved, until he got closer and saw her behind the wheel.

He waved his arms frantically above his head. "Susan, wait!" he screamed as he ran toward her. "Don't start the car!"

Susan heard the commotion and glanced up at him through the windshield, dumbfounded. But she had already begun to turn the key.

"Susan, noooo!"

Their eyes met for a split second. Then there was a terrific explosion.

Shards of glass and pieces of twisted metal showered to the ground, clanging out a final crescendo as Daniel slowly dropped to his knees, devastated.

PART 2

42

Six Months Later

In the middle of the night, Arthur Sarchick dressed in jeans, a khaki shirt, and sneakers. The Witness Protection Program had given him a new life and a new home. But now, the federal marshals wanted the favor he had been forced to promise in return. They hoped he enjoyed his stay, his freedom under their protection. And he truly did. He chuckled to himself as he prepared to leave on his trip.

Last evening, he had decided to allow himself a special treat, a farewell gift. Sarchick took his prize into the woods, told him what he was going to do to him. He found that intensely pleasurable, telling. Then he undressed the boy, fondled him, teased him. And when the time came, he drove into the boy from behind, his hands tight around the small throat, his mouth sucking the soft skin of the small back.

The boy was so young, he tasted like honey. Teeth dig-

*ging into flesh, stifled cries of pain, the pace quickening,
flashbacks of the farmhouse, fingers squeezing . . .* He
felt the boy go limp. And with one last thrust, his own
body convulsed, and stiffened, and then finally relaxed
as ecstasy faded away.

He left the boy there against a tree, covered him
with leaves. In a few days, his little body would be
discovered. There were others, but no one had put it
together yet. He didn't think they ever would. And
even if they did, it wouldn't matter, because Arthur
Sarchick chose not to exist anymore.

43

██████████ Still dark with dawn approaching at Chicago's
O'Hare International Airport, North America Flight
1089 was at its gate. In an hour and a half the 727
would take off for Philadelphia, spend a fifty-minute
turn-time there, and continue on to Miami.

The captain, copilot, and second officer were at a
briefing—the usuals: weather, fuel, load planning. The
rest of the crew met to go over their concerns: who's
working where, how many special meals, where any
VIPs might be sitting.

The flight was often full, serving as a connection
for the red-eyes from the West; shuttling businessmen
between Chicago and the East Coast; and, of course,
transporting the ever-present vacationers. This particular day, however, brought an added category to the
list: A passenger in the Witness Protection Program

was being flown into Philadelphia covertly for his testimony.

The agent assigned to escort the witness came to the terminal early to clear security. He was aware of what had taken place the last time there were witnesses testifying against the Philadelphia underworld. This time would be different—he wanted no possibility of a repeat disaster. There were higher levels of secrecy and protection. Even he was kept in the dark as to exactly who he was transporting until that morning, when he was told to meet federal witness Arthur Sarchick, traveling simply as businessman John Stephens, at Terminal D, Gate 18. He was supposed to wear a dark overcoat and carry a copy of the *Chicago Tribune* folded under his left arm, and Stephens would identify himself. He would fly with Sarchick/Stephens to Philadelphia, where he would meet Agents Murtaugh and Sang at the baggage claim.

So far, everything had gone smoothly. He met his mark, nonchalantly alerted airport security, then discreetly slipped into a private area and confirmed identification. Back at the waiting area, he scanned the other passengers and airport personnel. Nothing seemed out of the ordinary. Nothing suspicious. *Good.* He had had similar assignments before, and had great instincts for spotting trouble. That's why he had been chosen.

Sarchick was a surprise, not the sort of individual he had come to know from previous assignments. Most were quiet, nervous. Or they were boastful, bragging about how they got away with what they had done, of the stamp of importance they now had from the government—instead of their condemnation. But Sarchick seemed relaxed. He only wondered how good the breakfast would be on the plane and if he would get to see a movie. *Jesus, the guy didn't seem to have a clue.*

Some witness! Then again, the agent knew it took all types . . . and there was a better than even chance it was *he* who was being played for a fool.

He didn't like the Federal Witness Program—and he hated the scumbags in it. Sarchick was no exception. But it wasn't his job to judge, only to protect and baby-sit. Most of these assignments were pretty easy. *Cake-runs,* as he called them. This one would likely be no different. He would safely deliver one John Stephens, a.k.a. Arthur Sarchick, and be home with the wife and kids in a few hours.

With the dawn comes a burst of activity at the airport. It happens abruptly, without easing into it. Ground crews complete last-minute preparations for the RONs, those planes which remained overnight. Other crews hustle to turn the first arriving flights of the day. Dealing with sliding ETAs and sometimes shortened turn-around times, assignments are changed strategically, to focus on the birds with the most desperate time demands. And people are shuffled to do their jobs wherever they are needed most urgently; as a result they are often strangers to those working next to them.

At Chicago's O'Hare, as well as at most other major airports, this was almost always the situation. The preparation of Flight 1089 was no exception.

The 727 had already been fueled, and the belt loader was in place. The baggage handlers, commonly known as ramp rats, feverishly jostled the luggage, trying to stay ahead of the growing onslaught. Caterers were preparing the galley, loading food, and the cleaning crew was at work. Like bees servicing the hive, the flight was being readied, slowing only for crews to catch their breath and gauge if they were on track for the given time swing.

So it wasn't surprising that in the usual chaos of the world's busiest airport, nobody noticed that there was an extra person helping them out that morning.

44

████████ Morning sunlight peered through the kitchen window, warming his haggard face. He was sipping coffee, daydreaming again about the first time they met—

"Bored?" he asked as he approached her tentatively.

"Does it show?" she said innocently.

"A little. I was only wondering why such a pretty face looked so sad."

"Corny line."

He gave a boyish grin. "Not a line. Only an observation."

She softened. "Guess I'm just not into this sort of thing."

"Neither am I. Wanna grab a cup of coffee? I know a place that serves the best cheesecake in New York. You look like a cheesecake lover."

"You're right. Another one of your observations?"

"No. Playing the odds. Who doesn't like cheesecake?"

She smiled at him.

"Let's go." He hesitated. "Unless you don't trust me. These are perilous times."

"No, I trust you." She giggled. "I see you're wearing your college pin. If you can't trust a guy from John Jay, who can you trust?"

He shook his head. "Everyone's a detective. By the way, I'm Daniel."

"And I'm Susan."

"I think I'm going to like you, Susan."

"Why, Daniel, you already do," she replied.

He poured another cup of coffee. He had awoken early, to the sound of barking. And for a moment, just a moment, he had forgotten himself and thought it was Susan, out in the next room playing with her dogs. But a moment later he remembered she wouldn't be. Susan was gone.

He sat alone. He had been that way since the dogs left, and since he had given Susan's parents permission to take Adam. Only for awhile—time for Daniel to heal, they had said. They were retired, living in a good neighborhood in Connecticut after a lifetime in the Bronx. They convinced Daniel that they were in a better position to give Adam the attention and care he needed.

Adam would help them get over this, too, Daniel had thought. It would help everyone. And now, nearly six months since that fateful day, he remained alone. Because he wanted to be. Because it was easier. Because he wasn't through punishing himself. And because only alone would he permit himself to cry.

Not long after Susan's funeral, Daniel moved out of the apartment they shared. It was too painful to stay. He spared himself that much—although he felt he didn't deserve to be spared. He found another place, across town on the north side.

Sergeant Vanderhooven took the dogs. Vandy wasn't much of a dog lover, but his wife was. She would take good care of them.

Two weeks after Susan's death, Daniel was back at work. He went through the motions, and not much more. It showed—to him, and to everyone. And when he wasn't brave enough to face the day, or face those he knew he was letting down, he would call in sick. It happened often, because Daniel Pinchus had lost the eye of the tiger; his enthusiasm; his verve.

The morning news lay crumpled on the kitchen table. Headline: SECRET FEDERAL WITNESS TO TESTIFY IN PHILADELPHIA AGAINST UNDERWORLD, now a blur after being read and reread interminably. It provoked the memories. The bad ones. The ones that never really strayed far from his consciousness or his dreams. And sometimes, when things became so still and awesomely quiet that he could hear his own heartbeat, they would reach out to him without warning. Chilling him. Tormenting him. Making sure he remained a prisoner to his own abyss.

There would be flashes of Susan in the car, how she glanced at him that last time. Or scenes from Susan's funeral—the sorrowful mob of people studying the closed casket and his grief-stricken face, morbidly wondering what was left to bury. And there would be visions of Adam crying for his mother when Daniel ran out of reasons to explain why she was being put into the ground.

On one particular evening, when his hauntings had become too much to bear and he knew Marion was in town, he drove to the Luccetta compound vowing to kill him, slowly, wretchedly, without mercy. He had parked on a street beside the house and sat there all night trying to find the courage to storm inside and rip the life from Luccetta. But when morning came, and he hadn't made his move, Daniel simply went home and wept: for Susan; and then for himself, and the coward that he deemed he was.

The newspaper taunted him. He felt cheated. Now, it would be up to the courts to put Marion away. He knew how effective legal shenanigans could be: attorneys chiseling away at obscurities, weaving them into reasonable doubt; defendants wearing innocent expressions and fancy suits, their loving families poignantly watching the proceedings like victims themselves, all in an effort to subconsciously influence the jury. Luccetta could still get off. This wasn't the kind of justice Daniel had hoped for.

But even if the law did prevail this time, it would do little to abate Daniel's anguish. There would be neither solace nor peace in it, for the murder of his wife would still be left unanswered. Unavenged. And, mournfully, Daniel Pinchus knew he had missed his chance. And nothing less would free him. So he chose to do nothing more, except be swallowed deeper by the cold and dark.

He had visited this chasm before, when he was a boy and his father had left. And then again, just a few years ago, when he feared for his father's life after he was gunned down. But he had never realized the true depth of that cavern—the depth Susan's death had led him to know.

Daniel got up to wash out his cup. He remembered when Susan had come home with the set of mugs, how excited she was to find the exact shade of colors that matched the kitchen wallpaper. Simple things like that made her happy. And he also recalled how upset she was with him when he carelessly dropped one of them on the countertop the next day. But he carefully glued the fragments together and saw her face brighten when he proudly presented it to her.

She laughed at the mosaic with the crooked handle, made him promise to only use that particular one from now on for fear he'd damage the rest. It was a promise he had always kept. Sometimes it made him smile with thoughts of her. Other times it made the loneliness unbearable.

There were so many things like that, mortal possessions and deeds. Things that lingered behind long after Susan was beyond his touch, reminders of how she was, who she used to be. Like the afghan Daniel kept folded on a living room chair.

It took Susan all of four months to knit. He recalled how she struggled with the needles and the colored yarn. It was her first effort, but she was proud of it and wrapped it around herself on cold nights.

Daniel picked up the blanket now and brushed the wool against his face, searching for her scent. Now he was with her again, tasted her kisses once more, remembered what it was like to hold her tight.

He thought about those times in the middle of the night, when it seemed as though they both woke up at the same instant, instinctively or out of need, to cuddle and make love. He missed that, making love to her, desperately missed the woman he chose to share his whole life with, have children with, grow old with.

But when he concentrated on her, for a moment, she was with him again. The rest was just a bad dream, something to be awakened from. Until, as always, he would realize that *this* was actually the dream. And waking up meant facing the reality that Susan was no more. He would never have her again. Never feel her warm breath, or her soft touch. Never see the excitement in her eyes. Never hear her say I love you.

He carefully refolded the afghan and put it back in place, returned to the kitchen, and finished cleaning up. He dried the mug, studying the ugly scars—his broken cup, his shattered life. He had to get ready for work, but then he saw the newspaper again and decided to call in sick as he drifted down through the crypt and into the dark.

45

Captain Alan Leeds made his way to the cockpit of the 727 thirty-five minutes before takeoff. Marjorie Duncan, first flight attendant for the trip, was there waiting. They had flown together many times before, liked each other, and often bid on the same routes.

"Good morning," she said as he crossed in front of her.

He nodded back, preoccupied.

"You okay?"

"Sure," he replied unconvincingly as he looked past her. "Just feel a bit odd is all. Kind of cold." He focused on Marjorie then, saw her bright expression begin to fade into concern.

"It's nothing," he barked quickly. "Probably just caught a chill somewhere. It'll pass."

"Coffee's hot, if you want some?"

The second officer, also known as the flight engineer, had arrived a few minutes ahead of Leeds and was already seated, having a cup as he started to take out the log book.

"No, thanks," Leeds yawned. "You know coffee keeps me awake."

"Ha, ha," said Marjorie.

"But save a cup for Jim. He'll be along in a minute."

"Want him to start it off?" the flight engineer asked.

"Over my dead body," Leeds snarled. "I always take the first leg. My takeoffs still equal my landings. You got a problem with that?"

"Hey, I was only asking."

"I said I was fine," he said more calmly. "You think I would take her up otherwise?"

"No. It's your call."

Marjorie respected Leeds. She knew how dedicated he was, something she didn't see in many of the other pilots. That's why she was so comfortable flying with him. She felt safe in his hands.

"Anyway," Leeds joked, trying to break the tension, "Jim's too busy ogling that new flight attendant."

"He's in the back of the airplane now, flirting with her," Marjorie commented.

"Supposed to be checking the emergency equipment," said Leeds.

"Pretty girl," Marjorie admitted. "Was an Arkansas beauty queen."

"If I know Jim, he's looking to join the mile-high club with her."

"Again?" Marjorie blinked.

Leeds's jaw dropped. "I was only kidding."

"Oh, guess you didn't hear. Rumor has it that several years ago Jim got canned from another company for just that reason. On a red-eye. Most of the passengers in dreamland, Jim and a young flight attendant rattling the plastic wall panels of the first-class lavatory."

Leeds shook his head. "And you wanted me to let him start it off?" he said to the second officer, teasing.

"Thought he had enough experience getting it up," the flight engineer shrugged.

Leeds laughed.

"Is there anything we need to know for the flight?" Marjorie asked.

"We're in for a few bumps. Turbulence all up and down the East coast and wind-shear warnings below ten thousand feet. Nothing we haven't dealt with before," he said, unconcerned. "You might want to have things secure before we're too close in. As of now, Philadelphia's still on for one hour fifty-eight minutes. How's your end?"

"Set to board in fifteen. Have a couple of VIPs traveling in first class. Newt Harting in three-A—"

"The college basketball star?" Leeds interrupted. "Like to get his autograph."

Marjorie's eyes narrowed.

"For my son."

"Sure," she said. "And Bobby Travis in five-C. A rock star. Want his autograph, too?"

Leeds put a hand up. "Pass. Anything else?"

"Got a guy with a firearm: federal marshal escorting a witness to Philadelphia. Looks like an important one. Gate agent will be in shortly."

"If you see Jim out there flirting, tell him to come up here."

"Will do." Marjorie smiled and turned to leave.

"One more thing," Leeds called after her. "How many kosher meals?"

"Five," she announced meekly. It was a running bet between the two of them.

"That's more than three. You owe me a drink after we land in Florida."

"I swear you must be ordering them for the passengers," she moaned.

"Hey, it's the Miami run," he said. "Gotta play the odds."

A few minutes later Marjorie was back, along with a burly man in a rumpled suit.

"Henessy from airport security," he said as he entered the cockpit. "Spoke to the federal agent. They'll be occupying twelve-A and twelve-B. You want him to surrender his weapon? Your prerogative."

Leeds sighed. "You run his ID?"

"Of course."

"Have the necessary paperwork?"

"Right here," he said, handing it to Leeds. "It checks out."

"Let him keep it," Leeds said finally. "You can begin preboarding whenever."

"Yes, sir," Marjorie answered.

He was in the men's room now, at the far end of the terminal, hidden in a stall as he changed out of the ground-crew uniform. Earlier, he had climbed up from the tarmac and into the jetway assigned to Flight 1089, faded into the background, then passed unremarkably out into the gate area. Needing to know for sure, he searched for his objective and quickly spotted him, standing with the federal agent escort. He noticed the smattering of disinterested security personnel, too. But he didn't allow their eyes to touch him. He studied the other individuals waiting to board, and didn't allow their lives to touch him either—not the businessmen, the fathers, or the mothers. Not even the faces of the little children. Rather, he fantasized about the travesty—how he would win.

He left the bathroom, headed back to the gate area, and waited until the 727 pushed back. Soon after, he scurried to a vantage point that he knew would give him a nice view. From there he watched Flight 1089 taxi to the runway and take off, a perfect beginning. Then, he boarded the next available flight to Philadelphia.

46

It was eight-twenty A.M. at Rivington Street Station. Officer Rifkin answered the phone, then buzzed the captain on the intercom. It was Sergeant Deacon Fishburn, head of Chief Foster's personal staff.

Schwenk picked up. "How you doin', Fish?"

"Morning, Captain. I'm calling all of the precinct heads to see if there might be an opening in any of the homicide divisions."

"Foster needs a favor, does he?"

"Favor's for me. You know my son, Cliff, don't you? Over at the Tenth."

"Fine boy."

"Well, he'd like to get into homicide. He's been working patrol three years. Thinks he's ready for the big boys."

"There's a waiting list for that, Fish."

"Already on it. And besides, that list is unofficial. You have the prerogative to cherry-pick whoever you want. Like taking guys with more education over more experience."

"True. But no one's closer to Foster than you. There could be a spot opened just on his say-so."

"I don't want that. Neither does he. He doesn't feel any of you captains should have to live with one of his favors after he's gone. Doesn't want anyone losing their position over this, either. He told me to call around and check. If something came up, then that would be okay for everybody. Strictly *me* asking. Simple as that."

"Hhmm." Schwenk rocked back in his chair. Pinchus's name had been crossed off the daily duty roster. Again. "Might have a slot opening up real soon," he said.

"Oh?"

"Yeah. Got a detective whose career is on thin ice. Don't know why I've waited, but a bunch of charges are about to be brought against him."

"Serious ones?" Deacon asked in surprise.

"Insubordination, failure to perform duties, unexcused absences, and maybe—criminal acts."

"First I'm hearing of it. That stuff needs to be documented. And it needs to be reported to Foster. Nothing's crossed my desk."

"Yeah, well, I was just getting ready to send in my report," Schwenk said, a little too quickly. "Tell me, Fish. Has Foster mentioned anything about who he's recommending to replace him?"

"As far as I know, he hasn't decided. And he won't tip his hand until the dinner, anyway. You're in the running. But you don't need me to tell you that."

"Foster thinks a lot of you, Fish, doesn't he? Trusts your opinion."

"Just what are you trying to say, Captain?"

"A kind word about me thrown his way wouldn't hurt. Might help to unbury this report of mine. Could even color it a tad. Not that I would put in anything that isn't true, mind you."

"Not interested, Captain," Fishburn replied abruptly. "You got some real charges to file, that's one thing. But don't be manipulating shit on my account. I can't afford the price tag."

"Don't be stupid, Fish. I've always treated you well, haven't I? Told Foster I thought it was great having a Negro on his personal staff."

"Thank you, sir. We blacks appreciate that," he answered, not trying to hide his sarcasm.

"And when quotas came to this department, I never voiced an objection. Not like some other people."

Fish was silent.

"Nor did I ever say anything to the chief about your problem," Schwenk threw out quietly.

"Sir?"

"Let's cut the bullshit, Fish. I heard about the times you've staggered into work when you thought nobody was looking."

"How did you—?"

"I have my sources," Schwenk boasted. "A guy assigned to your department a while back now works for me. Even told me about the bottle of bourbon you keep in the bottom drawer of your desk."

Fishburn gave an audible sigh.

"Good. So you'll try to sway Foster, bring him around?"

"I don't have a choice. Do I?"

"Then we both agree. I'll take care of my problem, and a position opens up in homicide. A position your son will get. But only after I'm named to succeed Foster as the new Chief of Detectives, of course."

"I see," Fishburn said. "A little insurance policy to make sure I follow through."

"Don't sound so glum, Fish. We're not doing anything illegal here. Nothing that might not happen anyway."

"Did you forget you're talking to a cop?"

"We're only politicking," Schwenk assured him. "Not only that, think about what having your son in the homicide division would mean for you, for your family, for the department."

"Jesus. A fucking credit to his race," Fishburn said in disgust.

"Better than a father's disgrace," Schwenk countered. "One more thing, Fish."

"Yes, Captain?"

"Don't worry. I don't intend to make many staff changes once I'm Chief of the Dees."

"That's comforting, sir. Have a wonderful day."

"You too, Fish."

Schwenk knew he was taking a chance with Fishburn. But the clock was running out on his career. It was worth the risk. He had manipulated men before, when he believed the cards were in his favor. And when he gambled, he almost always won. It had helped him become a captain.

Schwenk replaced the receiver feeling extremely confident.

A moment later, Officer Rifkin hung up his extension.

47

Gunshots echoed through the air, shattering the countryside's morning calm. Seymour Pinchus was behind the barn, target shooting at a white handkerchief stretched and nailed across the trunk of the tree. Twenty paces away and in a combat crouch, he shook his head in disappointment. After six rounds, the handkerchief remained unblemished. And so did the tree. *My God, I'm getting worse.*

Three years ago he had tried to make a comeback. His shattered right shoulder was a multitude of pins surgically placed and painstakingly rehabilitated; his left eye, reduced to seeing only shadows, had been fitted with a special lens to enhance vision; his weak right arm was supported with a brace consisting of a series of leather straps. Only the bullet fragment in his head had remained unaddressed. He knew that any further trauma might push the segment deeper into his brain, causing paralysis, or even death. It was part of the price he would have to pay. A risk he was willing to take, he told Chief Foster.

Foster, being an abundantly fair man, weighed the liabilities against what was owed to Seymour Pinchus, and finally decided to give the former lieutenant a chance.

But Pinchus would have to pass a rigorous police physical, beyond the obvious medical clearances and personal waivers. There would be no other compromises on Pinchus's behalf, which also meant he would have to qualify on the firing range. And that was actually Pinchus's greatest obstacle. Even before his injuries, he deemed himself a lousy shot; it was his one weakness, his Achilles' heel. The few times he had had to use his gun, though, he didn't miss. He considered himself lucky—except one time. Even though it was many years ago, it still haunted him.

There was a standoff. Vince, his partner then, was hustled out of a botched stick-up attempt by the assailant, who was holding a pistol to Vince's head. Pinchus drew his own weapon and dropped into a crouch, aiming. Vince was yelling at Pinchus to shoot as the guy dragged him to the car. Pinchus didn't move, afraid he'd hit his partner. "Don't let him get away," Vince pleaded. "Shoot him, I tell you, or I'm dead!"

Pinchus recalled cocking his gun and then freezing, unable to pull the trigger, afraid to accept the responsibility for his accuracy. The gunman got into the car with Vince, drove about fifty feet, stopped, and shot him through the head. Then he dumped the body and kept going. With nothing left to lose, Pinchus finally squeezed off his shot. It was a very long one: through the back window and through the back of the gunman's head and out between his eyes and then out through the windshield. It *was* a perfect shot.

Seymour now looked at the white cloth on the tree

as if it were ridiculing him. Three years ago he couldn't hit it either, and it was what finally made him give up the fight. But recently he had taken it up again—when Susan was killed. This time, he threw away the leather brace, discarded the glasses, used his good arm, and taught himself how to shoot lefty while aiming with his right eye.

At first, his hand shook, the grip felt alien. But in time it felt at home with the weight, metal, and recoil. And there were even days, when he was especially focused and there was nothing to disturb him, that he actually tore the piece of cloth apart with gunfire. Unfortunately, there were too many other days when he couldn't sever a thread.

Seymour still remembered the way he felt that day with Vince—the hate and remorse, how he vowed that it would never happen again. He took aim at the center of the handkerchief, wet his lips, willed the bullet to pierce the center of the fold, saw the back of the gunman's head, and fired. The shot missed but struck the tree, splintering the bark a half inch above the cloth.

Seymour heard a car approach, swiftly rose and tucked the gun into his pants, then pulled his shirt out to hide it. Kate wasn't due back for an hour yet. He peered around the corner of the barn and was relieved to see Sam pulling up to the front of the house.

Seymour shouted, "Up here, Sam."

Milano waved and walked over.

"What brings you all the way out here, Sam?"

"Daniel."

"Is he okay?" Seymour asked nervously, holding his breath.

Milano saw Seymour's misplaced concern. He hadn't anticipated what his visit alone might appear to mean.

"Relax, Seymour. Physically he's fine."

Pinchus exhaled deeply.

"Sorry. I tried to call. Then I figured you might be tooling around outside, so I drove out."

"That's okay. What's wrong with Daniel?"

"He called in sick again. Fourth time this month. Schwenk wants his head. Last week he had an appointment with the department shrink. Never showed."

"This is a hard time for him."

"Believe me, Seymour, I know. But it's been six months since—"

"I'm sure you caught today's headlines," Seymour said quickly, sounding agitated. "Don't you think Daniel reads the paper? How do you think he feels? The department should understand. They'll have to be patient."

"It's too late. Schwenk's bringing him up on charges. As of now, Daniel has been suspended pending a hearing next Tuesday."

"Suspended? I thought Schwenk and I had a deal."

Milano stabbed a finger at the bulge in Seymour's midsection. "I thought you did, too."

"Ahh!" he said, knocking Sam's hand away. "Only a little target shooting."

"Uh-huh. Kate know about this?"

Seymour was silent.

"Thought so," Milano said. "Anyway, Daniel knows about your little deal—how Schwenk said he would go easy on him as long as you gave up your crazy notion about coming back to the force."

"How'd he find out?"

"How do you think?"

"Schwenk," Seymour growled.

"Told him the other day. Said unless he straightens out, even you won't be able to save him."

Seymour shook his head. "Son of a bitch. Daniel's hanging by an emotional thread and Schwenk's ready to cut it. He was supposed to let me know if Daniel ever got close to the edge. Instead, he tells him this?"

"You thought he would do otherwise? Look who you got into bed with," Milano said pointedly.

"At the time it was a good deal." Seymour shrugged. "Schwenk was scared shitless. But there was no way I could have come back. You and I both know that."

"I guess," Milano said tentatively. "The important thing right now, though, is how Daniel's going to handle all of this. I spoke to him this morning."

"How's he taking the suspension?"

"Angry. Betrayed. Feels like giving up."

"No wonder, after what Schwenk told him, the calculating bastard."

"It's not like Daniel hasn't done anything wrong, Seymour."

"I know. But there isn't enough there for suspension."

"Well, I've heard some other charges flying around that simply aren't true. Schwenk has implied that the suspected leak in the department was coming from Daniel."

Seymour's nostrils flared. "What?"

"Yup. Claims Daniel was feeding the mob tips. Has evidence of several suspicious contacts Daniel made with them. Even one at the station house with Dominic Luccetta's wife right after his murder. He says Daniel found out from them where Sarchick was, then double-crossed the mob by picking him up—and that's why they placed the car bomb."

"Bullshit!"

"I know. Nobody in the squad room believes it. Schwenk's gone too far."

"He's twisting everything around. Actually using Susan's tragedy to hang my son?"

"Wouldn't put it past him," Milano said.

"What about the leak? Did it stop? I mean after?"

"No."

"His wife is killed and he still plays ball with the people who are responsible for it? How does Schwenk explain that?"

"Not sure. Probably he'll claim Daniel feared for his life—that's why."

"Jesus. Daniel's going to fight this. Isn't he?"

Milano sighed. "His heart's not in it."

"That's partly my fault," Seymour admitted sadly. "But *I'm* not going to let this happen. Schwenk's fucking with my son now and I'll make him pay for it."

"Isn't it Daniel's battle, though?" Milano argued. "I think you need to talk to him first."

"Of course. But there's more at stake here than just Daniel. Schwenk's using this to get back at me," Seymour maintained. "Punishing my son for all of those years I taunted him, all the times I showed him up."

"I wouldn't take all the credit, Seymour," Milano said. "Daniel had something to do with it, too, you know."

"But it's still personal," Seymour cried.

"It's always *you*, isn't it?" Sam yelled back. He took a breath, let it out slowly. "Is that what this is about, too?" He motioned toward the hidden gun with his chin. "Susan dies and *you* get this personal vendetta in your head? One-man army avenging her death?"

"What do you expect me to do, Sam? Just sit here?" he thundered.

Milano threw up his hands. "And now, your *son's* career is on the line and it's 'How can they do this to *me*?' When are you going to stop feeling sorry for yourself?"

Seymour took a half step back, squinting at Sam. "Who the hell gives you the right to judge me? This is between a father and a son."

"Is it? Then make it so," Sam shouted, then paused to calm himself. "Forgive me, Seymour. You and I were partners for a very long time. And during that period, we shared the same heartbeat—our life and death woven together. *This* gives me the right to tell you when you're wrong."

Sam saw Seymour's expression ease and knew he was listening. Finally.

"Give Daniel all the help and support he needs, but don't lead him," Sam told him. "Walk with him instead. It's Daniel's fight, not yours. It's time you stepped down."

Seymour nodded gently.

"Talk to Daniel, Seymour."

"I don't know how to. Or what to say," Seymour said softly.

"Oh, I think you do. As partners, you always made me feel equal—a step above where I thought I was."

"You were never anything less."

"See what I mean? Do the same for Daniel. It's tough being the son of the Fox. He has a lot to live up to. You seem to have time and patience for everyone but him."

"Am I that blind?"

"No. Just sometimes we see things as we want them to be, not how they really are."

"Why haven't you told me this before?"

"I tried." Sam gestured helplessly. "More subtly. Not like this."

Seymour put his hand on Milano's shoulder. "Trouble is, Sam, I'm not used to getting advice."

"Nor am I comfortable giving it. Especially to you."

"Must have been tough."

"I'm still shaking," he confessed.

"So, Sam, when did you get to be so wise?"

"Always have been. But I fooled everyone into thinking it was only you," he said with a smile.

"Thanks." Seymour leaned forward, gave his partner a hug.

An hour after Sam Milano left, Kate came home. Seymour was in the kitchen, immersed in thought and emotion—part denial, part guilt. He was drinking a cup of coffee and offered her some.

"No, thanks. You make it too strong," she reminded him.

"Not this time. Knew you'd be by before long. Sit and have some. Talk with me for awhile." He reached over to pour.

She sat. "Sounds serious."

"It is." He waited for her to look up at him. "Sam came by this morning. He had some things to tell me." When he was finished telling her what happened he asked, "What do you think? Do you see the same things Sam does?"

Kate was silent for a few moments, weighing her response. Finally she said, "How could I? Sam knows you in ways I could never hope to. The same goes for Daniel. But if you were to ask me if there was something wrong here, things that my own eyes and instincts tell me, then I would have to say, yes."

"Tell me," Seymour asked. "Help me to understand this."

"Don't get me wrong, Seymour. I don't think it's so one-sided. You and Daniel are so much alike: both stubborn, both driven. You've certainly had your share of baggage, you two.

"I didn't know you when you lost your daughter. That was an awful tragedy, a long time ago. When your career ended, I saw you change. I saw how you tried to isolate yourself from it. I imagine that you reacted the same way after Melissa died."

"I admit I was unfair to Daniel then, but things have healed between us. How could you possibly compare the loss of a career with that of a life?" Seymour shifted uneasily.

"Because *you* did," she said gently. "Because in each terrible instance you lost a part of yourself. Maybe not to the same degree, but you grieved for both. Still do. Don't you think Daniel senses your disinterest now, as he did back then?"

"I don't accept that," he said stubbornly. "Things are different *now*." He swiped at his coffee cup, but knocked it across the table instead. "I've tried to hang on to my son."

"I know you have, darling. And outwardly—to those who don't know both of you well—things seem fine. But when you walk together you each stumble a bit. When Susan was killed, it just got worse. Seymour," she paused, looking at her husband sympathetically, "there's more here than what Sam and I know about, isn't there? Things that only you and Daniel can talk about."

He stared at the spilled coffee, nodding slowly.

"You hold your son secretly, just like those news articles you keep in a box. The ones you didn't think I knew about."

That surprised him. "Yes," he whispered.

"And there's also the fact that you—and God knows you shouldn't—somehow feel responsible for Susan's death."

He looked up, eyes wide. "Know about that, too?"

"Seymour," she said gently. "It wasn't hard to figure out. You don't sleep as easily as you once did. Not that any of us have since, but with you, it's different."

"I told Daniel not to worry about the mob," he said,

running a hand through his hair. "I said they would never go after him."

"You were speaking from experience. Trying to comfort him."

"He let his guard down. I was wrong," he said through his teeth.

"You didn't know," she threw back. "Stop torturing yourself."

"I can't!" He pounded the table with his fist. "Don't you see I can't?" A tear formed in the corner of his eye. "I told Susan right before she married Daniel that nothing would ever happen to him. I gave her my word. My God—who knew?"

"So that's why you go out behind the barn and shoot at trees, like some kid sneaking cigarettes?"

"Don't I have any secrets left?"

"Seymour, I can still smell the gunpowder," she said. "Why is it that great detectives don't learn to hide things better?"

He knew her subtle teasing was meant to break the tension. He gave in to her with a half smile. "Because everything is obvious to us. Why bother?"

"I don't approve, but *obviously* you're getting to be a better shot."

"Oh?"

"More holes in my favorite elm. And fewer handkerchiefs in your drawer."

His grin broadened for a moment, then he got serious again. "You and Sam are right. I have to talk to Daniel."

"You have a lot to tell each other. And you don't need to share it with anyone else, Seymour. Just you and him. Man to man," she said.

"Maybe I should try father to son for a change."

48

████████ "This is Captain Leeds," came the announcement over the P.A. "We're just north of the Lehigh Valley
. . . oh, about sixty miles from Philadelphia. They tell us
it's going to be a bit bumpy on our descent, so I'm going to
put the seat belt sign on now. We'll try to give you as
smooth a landing as possible. Should be on the ground in
about twenty-five minutes. Weather in Philly: clear skies
and a pleasant sixty-two degrees with strong winds from the
west gusting up to thirty miles per hour, so you might want
to hang on to your hats as you go outside. It's been a
pleasure serving you today. From myself and the crew,
thank you for flying North America Airlines, where you're
always at home in our skies."

A thin-faced businessman in first class hurried to
belt down a third Bloody Mary as he proudly showed
pictures of his family to Marjorie Duncan. Newt Harting, the basketball player, nudged her.

"Here are two autographs for the captain. One for

his son, Justin, one for himself." He smiled. "Said I'd give them to you once he got us safely on the ground. This is close enough."

Bobby Travis, the rock musician, was dead to the world, still attached to the headphones of his portable CD player.

Other flight attendants were busy collecting the last of the trash and securing the galleys for landing.

The federal agent looked at his watch, then closed his eyes and mentally calculated how much time he'd have left after meeting his contacts to get something decent to eat before catching his flight back. He thought about his wife and kids. He'd be home early for a change.

His companion stared out the window, like an excited child flying for the first time.

A heavyset African-American man in the twenty-second row was playing blackjack with himself. He was using crumpled balls of paper to keep score, and he was losing—again. He kept shaking his head.

A seven-year-old girl in the back of the plane clutched a brand-new-looking teddy bear. She was fast asleep, head cradled in her mother's lap, dreaming of becoming a ballerina. The mother stroked her daughter's hair, not wanting to wake her, but knowing soon she would have to.

The 727 was on the mazie one approach to Philly. When it descended through five thousand feet, there were three loud pops separated by only seconds. Each made the plane shake, then it continued flying stable.

"What the fuck was that?" the copilot said.

"Don't know." Leeds scanned the instrument panel, spotted the falling hydraulic pressure gauges. Moments later, the warning light came on and the autopilot kicked off. *Beep beep beep.*

Marjorie hit the intercom. *Ding-dong.* "We just heard some loud bangs back here. Everything okay?"

"We're looking. Right now we're fine. Awfully busy up here, we'll let you know."

"The passengers are nervous. I'll take care of it."

"Good girl."

Leeds flicked off the intercom. "All right, let's see what we got here. Looks like we're in manual reversion. Shut off the hydraulics. I've got the airplane, you handle the radios," he said to Jim. He looked back at the second officer, sitting behind the copilot and facing the side of the aircraft. "Get out the checklist. See if you can figure out what happened."

He nodded.

Leeds grabbed the yoke to fly the plane. It didn't budge. "Yoke's jammed," he said to Jim. "Try yours."

The second officer stopped looking at the checklist, turning toward the other pilots.

"Get anything?" Leeds asked.

"Nothing," Jim told him.

"Cable must be jammed. Get on the yoke with me," Leeds ordered. "See if we can free it."

The flight engineer gnawed at his lower lip as he watched his fellow officers struggle.

The yoke broke loose, but the plane didn't respond.

"There's no tension!" Jim said frantically.

"Cable probably snapped." Leeds raised his eyebrows. "And there's also no movement on the rudder pedals."

Jim inhaled slowly, then shot out a breath. "No movement on the yoke? Nothing from the rudder? What about the rest?"

Each pilot hastily checked levers, gauges, switches, dials, everything—to see what was still working. The flight engineer was paging through the checklist in a frenzy, searching for information on the hydraulics and manual reversion. Havoc overtook the cockpit.

"I can't get . . ."

"What the fuck?"

"Jesus."

Leeds tried to operate the elevators electrically. "No response on the electric for the elevators, either," he said.

"Do we have manual?" Jim asked.

Leeds shook his head. "Can't even get this damn elevator wheel to move."

"What the hell is this? Hydraulics out. Controls stuck. Horizontal stabilizer inoperable. How could all of these systems go down at the same time?"

"Calm down." They were now at five thousand feet and descending. "Philadelphia approach," Leeds announced. "Mayday. Mayday. This is North America 1089. We have a problem."

"Okay, what's your problem?"

"We're not sure. Stand by." Leeds tried to focus, to assess the enormity of the situation. He saw that the seat belt sign had remained on and was somehow gladdened that something still worked. "Philly approach, we've lost all control of the airplane: hydraulics and cables—all systems."

"Are you declaring an emergency?"

"Definitely."

"We're standing by. What do you need?"

"Don't know. Right now we're flying stable, but unable to hold altitude."

"What are your intentions?"

Leeds and his copilot glanced at each other nervously, hearts pounding in their ears, sweat dripping. The second officer was overwrought, searching for solutions.

"We'd like to bring her into Philly. Have crash crews ready."

"*We'll take care of it and clear things out for you. Are you able to turn?*"

"We haven't tried to yet. We'll have to use asymmetrical thrust. Stand by."

"*Cleared direct Philly. If able, a heading of one-seven-zero should do it. Standing by.*"

Leeds buzzed Marjorie on the intercom.

"Yes?"

"We're in a very bad situation. Prepare the cabin for an emergency landing."

"What's the problem?" she asked, her voice small and tense.

"We've lost control of the airplane. We're going to do the best we can to bring her into Philly. Just try to keep calm." It was all he would offer.

"Yes, sir."

Leeds was silent a moment, studying the falling altitude. "You know, if the turbulence is as bad as forecasted, we're fucked. We'll have no control." Clenching his teeth, he advanced the left engine's throttle and backed off on the right, keeping the center engine where it was.

The plane responded, gently banking right to a one-seventy heading.

"Philly, here we come."

Right after he spoke, the turbulence that Leeds had so desperately hoped to avoid snatched the plane, tossing it violently side to side.

Passengers screamed. Marjorie Duncan, who was still standing at the time, was thrown to the floor. An unsecured beverage cart bumped its way out of the rear galley and careened down the aisle. A few overhead compartments that were not completely shut opened, contents cascading onto passengers and deck.

Leeds fought to maintain control using only the power from the three engines. The other pilots held their breath. For a moment, there was a painful silence. Then the plane began to roll.

"Mother of Jesus, no!" Jim yelled. A second later, the metal maintenance log book flew up and slugged him in the head, knocking him out.

The second officer screeched at Leeds to do something. But there was nothing he could do.

Everything loose in the cabin went flying through the air. Marjorie Duncan hit the ceiling, crushing her skull, spattering the passengers in rows one to four with blood. Two other passengers and another flight attendant, not buckled in, were thrown about in a similar fashion. Cans from the beverage cart pummeled the people, some exploding as they crashed against side panels, seat-back trays, and heads. The cart eventually landed on top of the blackjack player, pinning him brutally.

Magazines and loose papers littered the floor of the airplane as it completed its revolution. Debris, panic, and hysteria were everywhere. Some people wailed loudly, others gave muffled cries, and a few prayed silently as the plane headed toward the ground at over three hundred miles per hour.

The little girl in the back of the plane lost her grip on her teddy bear. It disappeared, and she began to cry. Her mother hugged her tightly, howling, "No, this cannot be!"

The businessman in first class, resolved that this was the end, quietly said good-bye to his family. Newt Harting kept yelling, "Shit!" at the top of his lungs. The rock star bawled like a baby. And the federal agent, knowing that he'd never come home again, turned to the hyperventilating man sitting next to him and wondered how *they* could have possibly found out.

Captain Leeds battled to the end. He never wavered, still trying to pull up with dead controls, as treetops and ground raced toward him. He simply said: "Forgive me, forgive us all," right before the nose of North America Flight 1089 slammed into the earth.

49

Daniel stood by the graveside, like a statue: arms crossed, head down.

"Figured you might be here," his father said softly, as he walked up behind him.

Daniel turned his head to the side, then back down again.

"I called. I left a message on your machine. Even stopped by the apartment just in case . . . you know."

"Always were thorough," Daniel replied sharply.

"I used to do this, too—visit your sister's grave, that is. In the beginning. When things got too overwhelming and I needed to feel close. Is it that way for you with Susan?"

"Yes," he muttered.

"I heard about the suspension. Sam came by to tell me."

"So?"

"So, you used to be a fighter."

Daniel looked at his father. "Used to be a lot of things. Or at least I thought I was. Maybe I'll let you take care of the problem for me. It would make your day." He shook his head. "Isn't that what you want?"

Air rushed out between Seymour's lips. "Schwenk's deal," he said. "Sam told me you found out about that."

"I didn't need you to do me any favors," Daniel said angrily, then laughed. "All this time, I thought you just gave up. The man who never could, finally did. My God, the great Fox was human after all. Fallible even. I would never have bet on that. Then I hear this. Figures. The ultimate sacrifice for his son."

"It's not what you think."

"Who asked you to give up your career for me?" Daniel snapped. "You made me feel like a little boy. Why should I go back?"

"Daniel, nobody thinks any less of you because of this."

"Why not?"

"Because it's bullshit," Seymour said strongly, eyes narrowing. "They know that. Just like they know the charges against you are bullshit." His expression softened. "Daniel, there is so much I haven't told you. Things you need to hear. Things that people around me already know. Things I finally had to admit to myself."

"Like what?"

"Not here." He glanced over at Susan's grave. "Let's walk."

They stepped across the grass to the pavement. The cemetery had only a few visitors that morning. A gardener's truck was making its rounds. A couple of grave diggers were preparing a plot.

"First, my deal with Schwenk," Seymour began as they walked. "It was very tough trying to come back from the injuries I suffered. The odds were against it, but I felt everyone expected it of me once I made up my mind to try. Like you said"—he furrowed his brow—"I'm supposed to be *infallible*. The legend is always greater than the man. The pressure was enormous. The battle overwhelming. I was tired, not sure that I could measure up. Maybe not wanting to take the risk. Giving in was becoming more attractive. But I couldn't. My ego; my pride. Schwenk's offer gave me my way out. I convinced myself that I was doing it for you. In my mind, that would be okay. But I was really doing it for myself. I know that now. Can you understand?"

"I guess," Daniel said with a touch of skepticism.

"It was supposed to be a secret. A secret Schwenk betrayed. I used you, Daniel, and I'm ashamed."

"Why should I trust what you say now?"

"Because you *know* it's true. You're doing the same thing that I did," Seymour pointed out. "Looking for excuses."

"It was good enough for you."

"Don't make the same mistakes I did," Seymour warned. "When your sister died I abandoned you and your mother, physically and emotionally. I know I can never make that up to you. Think about Adam."

"Adam will survive. He's tough."

"Like you?" Seymour challenged.

"We Pinchuses are used to growing up without our fathers around," Daniel blurted.

"So that makes it okay? Punishing your son for the sins of your father?"

"No, I didn't mean that."

"We're so much alike, you and me—driven snow."

"Pure and innocent?" Daniel's expression clouded.

"No. Compulsive and cold. We wear our tragedy inside out, close to the heart. No one's allowed to touch."

"It's not that way for me," Daniel threw back. "*They* can't imagine the anguish and pain. So why bother?"

"Who's they?" Seymour stopped, turning toward Daniel. "Me? Your son? Don't forget he lost a mother. And your in-laws lost a daughter. Look around, Daniel." He spread his arms. "Headstones as far as you can see. Each with their own story, their own misery."

Daniel glanced around at the rows of marble and granite, at the freshly dug grave, at an old woman placing a pebble atop a monument.

"Death isn't easy," Seymour said, arms dropping to his sides. "But when you can't stop feeling sorry for yourself, you become paralyzed. I had to learn that. Still need to be reminded sometimes. Thank goodness I have friends."

Daniel remained silent. But he was listening to his father. They resumed walking.

"When Melissa died, I quit. Deprived you of a father, your mother of a husband. My work suffered. I let cases slide. Didn't always follow through. God only knows how many people I harmed because I was supposed to be helping them, protecting them. Crime victims, victimized again. This time by me."

"Sounds familiar," Daniel mumbled.

"Almost got thrown off the force," Seymour revealed, then paused to let it sink in. When Daniel looked at him in surprise, he nodded. "Yes—me, too. Never told you about that. Very few people know. I still keep things private." He sighed. "But I'm reforming. Sometimes you need to share."

"What turned your career around?"

"My old sergeant, Stanton Quigley. He didn't have the nerve to tell me face to face what a miserable partner and person I'd become, so he wrote me a letter. I've saved it all these years. It meant that much to me."

"What'd it say?" Daniel asked.

"In a nutshell? It said I needed a purpose in my life since Melissa's death robbed that from me. Some vehicle to channel energy into instead of dwelling on my sad self. Told me he was putting in for a new partner. It was too late to change his mind. He wasn't going to

allow himself to be dragged under. Hoped a fresh start
might pull me out of it."

"Must have been one mean SOB."

"Quigley? Na. Sweetest man you'd ever meet."

"But he pulled the rug out from under you. Deserted you when you needed him."

"Shook me up is what he did. I thought about how
tough it was for him—a man who never meant anyone
any harm. If you *knew* Quigley, you would know it
must have torn his heart out to do that." Seymour
stopped walking again. "He showed he cared enough
about me . . . to let me go."

"What did you do then?"

Seymour motioned to a bench by the walkway,
then lowered himself slowly. "Let's sit. Give an old man
some rest and I'll tell you." Daniel joined him, and he
continued. "I took his advice and went into homicide.
Decided to do the best job that I could. Helped me to
let go a bit, too."

"Of Melissa?"

"As hard as that was, yes. I needed to," Seymour
admitted somberly. "You're right, Quigley *was* a son of
a bitch—a clever one. It took me awhile to figure it out,
but that was the message he wanted me to get all along.
It was the whole point of his letter."

"Why didn't you tell me about this sooner?" Daniel
sounded angry again.

"At first, I hoped you might heal yourself," Seymour
explained, drawing in a breath. "Knew you wouldn't
listen until you sank as deep into self-pity as you could.
And then it was because I was afraid."

"Afraid? You're my father, but at times you act like a
stranger," Daniel fumed, looking down at his hands.

"You're right," Seymour said, staring at him. "That's
why I was afraid. You and I both know there's more to
all of this—beyond Susan's death. Things between us.

Things I knew I would have to confess. To you. To myself."

Daniel looked up, then let his eyes fall from his father. He was unsure if he wanted to hear this.

"I've been so terribly unfair to you, Daniel," Seymour said gently. "Not only when you were a child, but after my disability as well. I shut you out. I only let you in under my terms."

"Why?" Daniel swallowed, staring at the ground.

"To spare myself. It was selfish."

"Yes. But why? To spare yourself from what?"

"I didn't realize you were still blind to what others have seen. Kate, and Sam. They have their own ideas why, but the real truth is," Seymour said, his voice beginning to quiver, "I'm jealous of you!"

"Jealous?" Daniel turned, looking at his father with disbelief.

"Certainly not about what happened to Susan— God, no. But I was envious of what you had, what I once did. Working in homicide. People looking up to you. Feeling important. I was jealous of your youth, your enthusiasm, your life that lay ahead of you. Forgive me, Daniel." He grabbed his son's arm with a shaky hand. "A father should never feel this way."

Daniel saw tears form in his father's eyes, and started to weep himself. "We *are* so much alike. And I have hated you when it wasn't your fault. Every move I made was measured against your shadow. By others in the department, and even by myself. Why did you have to be so damn good?" he groaned. "Better than I could ever hope to become."

"That's not true," Seymour argued.

"It's the reason Susan died," Daniel said, crying harder.

Seymour leaned over and hugged his son. "No one's

to blame for that," he said. Even though he still hadn't forgiven himself.

"I should have seen it coming. The goddamn Fox would have," Daniel shouted.

"No. He wouldn't have," Seymour said, tears streaming down his own cheeks as he rocked his son. "He didn't," he added in a whisper.

"It hurts so much," Daniel sobbed. "If only I never knew her."

His father broke the embrace. "Don't ever say such a thing. Think of all that she's given you—your memories, your son. Don't wish that all away."

"Remembering is painful. I don't have to light a *Yahrzeit* candle to know that."

"It doesn't have to be. Melissa is always with me. Yes, sometimes it's tough. But you can touch a memory without being consumed by it." He looked deeply into his son's eyes, wanted to mend his heart, wanted to find him peace. "When you learn not to hold them so tight, then you can focus on what you once had, not dwell on what you've lost."

"She was my world," Daniel forced out through the tears. "How can I ever let go?"

"I know." Seymour sighed. He placed his palm on top of his son's hand. "Try loosening one finger at a time. I'll help you."

"How?"

"Maybe by taking care of unfinished business. By finding who killed Susan."

"We know *who* already." Daniel seethed.

Seymour shrugged. "If that's so, then let's prove it. Don't let the courts put him away for anything less than murder. *Siz vos iz richtic.* It's what is right. Time to get even, Daniel."

"I thought revenge wasn't virtuous," Daniel challenged.

"We're talking about justice, here. Not vengeance. Remember that. Some might argue that what I'm suggesting isn't healthy or wise. But I think you need closure, or at least the knowledge that you tried."

Daniel considered the idea, nodding slowly.

"You got anything better to do before your hearing next Tuesday?" Seymour added.

"No," Daniel said quickly. "Let's do it."

"Not so fast. We're both full of emotions right now. Think it over a little. You must be absolutely sure you want to do this—but only for the right reasons."

"How will I know when I'm sure?"

"You'll know," Seymour said simply. "Then you'll come to me. Okay?"

"Okay."

"Driven snow, you and me, huh? I think, today, we're more like a summer shower," his father suggested as he wiped an eye.

" 'Bout time, wouldn't you say?" Daniel said.

Seymour nodded, then gave his son a warm smile.

50

He landed at Philadelphia International Airport anxious to find out if he'd succeeded, but no news had been released yet. Except for the hushed murmur of a few airport personnel gathered together, everything appeared normal.

But he needed to know. He walked to the terminal where North America Flight 1089 should have arrived.

At the gate he saw the distraught faces of the people, noticed that the flight monitor marking that particular arrival read: *See airline agent.* He understood what that meant. His body relaxed. His mind eased and contentment washed over him. *Now* he was sure. He smiled to himself. Time to take care of more unfinished business.

51

██████ So far, the day had not gone well. He was already a half an hour behind and his patients were tired of being told that *"the doctor will be with you shortly."* Lunch break was too far off to help right his schedule. Dr. Peter Roberts was fighting to maintain control.

Over the high-pitched whine of his drill, he heard the first report that a commercial airline had crashed somewhere in Pennsylvania. He took his foot off the rheostat and glanced up at the operatory speaker to listen, but there was no further information. The patient mumbled, *"Shit,"* through the cotton rolls stuffed in his mouth.

Roberts shook his head and continued to work. He wondered if he would be called. Since he was a *Go-Team* member of PADIT, the Pennsylvania Dental Identification Team, he probably would be. It was what they trained for. He waited anxiously for more news.

In his excitement, he had forgotten about the plans he had with Diane that week. They would have to be changed if he were summoned. He had also failed to realize the magnitude of the carnage he might be headed for. How could he? A couple of light plane crashes—no more than two or three casualties—and a cursory exercise at Harrisburg Airport where live individuals played the injured and the dead simply couldn't measure up to a real-life commercial airline disaster.

He finished the filling, then hustled to get to his next patient.

It was late morning, and Seymour Pinchus was heading home from the cemetery. He was listening to music on the car radio, feeling good about his talk with Daniel, when the news about the air crash broke: North America Flight 1089 had gone down near Minersville, Pennsylvania. Minersville was a small town situated at the edge of Coal County, resting at the foot of a remote hilly section. *Early reports reveal that rescue efforts are being hampered by the rough terrain.* The flight had originated in Chicago and was bound for Philadelphia. *Details still sketchy. Stay tuned for further information.* The music resumed as if nothing had happened.

Seymour rubbed his chin. He hoped there were survivors. But he knew better. God, he was so sick of death.

Diane Roberts was at home folding laundry, contemplating what she would pack for her trip to Florida. She had become quite busy with the travel agency, and was finally going to experience one of those perks that only top agents were allowed. She had been chosen to witness the christening of a new cruise ship in Miami— and spend two nights on a promotional voyage.

She was thrilled that Peter was joining her. It had been a long time since the two of them had been alone together, and she was becoming a captive of her career.

She felt guilty about that, about not seeing Peter as much as she would like. And about the kids, especially Paige.

Melanie and Paul were growing up and becoming involved in their own worlds. But Paige wasn't in school yet. For her, there were sitters and day care, as Mom's part-time job grew from just a few hours into four full days a week.

Now, Paige was in the adjacent room watching TV. Diane had planned an afternoon just for the two of them. There was a new white tiger exhibit at the Hamilton Zoo. A special treat, before the weekend apart. Paige would stay with Diane's mother, the other two kids with friends. At least, Diane rationalized, they'd all be home to spend Sunday together when she and Peter came back.

It was twelve-fifteen, almost time to leave. First lunch, and then the animals. Diane finished with the laundry and went to get her daughter. As she entered the room, the program Paige was watching was interrupted by a bulletin. The television screen flipped to an anchorwoman sitting in a newsroom. There had been an air disaster. Flight 1089 from Chicago, with ninety-eight people aboard, had crashed. There did not appear to be any survivors. *Basketball star Newt Harting and musician Bobby Travis were reportedly on the ill-fated jet. Thankfully, the plane wasn't full due to severe weather on the West Coast delaying some connecting flights.* There was an interview with a passenger lucky enough to have missed Flight 1089.

Diane stared at the screen, eyes fixed, mouth open. She was to fly that same airline: North America. A similar route: the second leg to Miami out of Chicago, but through Hamilton rather than Philly. The day after tomorrow.

Once again, North America Flight 1089 from Chicago

has crashed near Minersville, Pennsylvania, shortly before ten A.M. Eastern Standard Time. There appear to be no survivors.

Diane blinked. "Oh, my God!"

███████

Walking down the steps of the courthouse, smiling, were Marion Luccetta and his entourage. TV cameras and reporters approached them.

"Mr. Luccetta," one newsman called out. "Do you have anything to say about the temporary halt in the proceedings? We have an unconfirmed report that the prosecution's key witness was aboard that plane."

Luccetta's attorney gently took his client by the arm, shot him a look of caution.

Luccetta shrugged it off. "What's there to say? The government loses one stinkin' witness and now they can't make a case."

"So the reports are true?"

"No comment."

"Awfully convenient, wouldn't you say?" another reporter asked loudly. "There's some talk of sabotage."

"Already? Well, I wouldn't know about that," Luccetta answered calmly. "Terrible thing, though. All those people dying. It's a shame. And also a shame we don't have the opportunity to show what a dirty liar that witness was. I was looking forward to being vindicated. I'm an honest businessman."

"Oh, yeah! Then what's this all about?" one newswoman challenged. "The government's been after you for years."

"And they haven't been able to prove a thing," he barked back. "Hearsay from jealous competitors. There's never been any proof. Look what happened here—dragged my name through the mud, slandered me. Then . . . an act of God." He threw his hands up.

"Pfft—they have nothing? *We're sorry, Mr. Luccetta, that we inconvenienced you?* Tell that to my wife and kids. They still share a name that's been tainted. I should be bringing *them* up on charges."

"So what are you going to do now, Mr. Luccetta?" the first reporter asked.

Luccetta's expression turned saintly. "Go home. Spend the rest of the afternoon with my girls—my wife and two daughters. I'm a family man. Don't get enough time with them. So if you'll excuse me . . ." he pushed his way through the crowd, toward the waiting car.

Inside the car, Caputa turned to Marion. "An act of God, eh?" He smiled.

"A fucking gift from the Almighty," Luccetta said.

Peter jumped each time the phone rang, holding his breath as he waited for Nina to tell him to pick up. But by three o'clock, there still was no word. He decided to call Herb Striklon, the team leader.

"No go," Herb told him.

"Whhatt?" Peter stammered. "But the coroner had to contact PEMA." PEMA, the Pennsylvania Emergency Management Agency, would call in PADIT in a disaster such as this.

"They were contacted, all right," Striklon said, "but as far as the Pennsylvania Dental Identification Team goes, the coroner didn't want us."

"Huh?"

"Yeah. Says he'll get his own team. Probably thinks he can organize a group of local dentists—guys with no experience. He doesn't know what he's getting himself into. Wants to be a general, run the whole deal himself. He has more ego than common sense."

"Jesus, who is it?"

"Elliot Brandle. Coroner of Coal County. Ever hear of him?"

Alex Schwenk held the phone to his ear and closed his eyes.

"Look, Schwenk," Captain Perez was saying. "Even if he was on that plane, it wouldn't matter. All the press cares about is today's news."

"You're wrong," Schwenk told him. "They'll make comparisons and bring up the past. I can't afford the publicity again. Not right now. I've got more at stake here than you."

"Oh? Still looking to become chief? Give it up, Alex."

"Why? What did you hear?"

"Relax, Schwenk. You think Philadelphia cares what goes on in Hamilton? No way. As far as the crash—shit happens. At most, there'll be a vague reference to our little disaster. This was just an accident. Nothing more."

"But there are rumors of sabotage? The media will have a field day."

"Even more reason not to worry," Perez said. "If the Federal Government couldn't protect a witness from the mob, how the hell could we? Either way, we're in the clear. But this wasn't sabotage."

"How can you be so sure?"

"What, take out an entire planeload of people just to silence one witness? Uh-uh. If you knew where this guy was, you'd make your hit long before he decided to get on a plane. Too difficult to get past airport security. And you don't need agencies like the FAA and the NTSB up your ass."

"If you're desperate enough, and the opportunity

arises, I don't think you give a shit," Schwenk maintained.

"Maybe. If you'd like to bet on it, I have the perfect detail lined up: undercover in a gay bar."

"No, thanks."

Perez snickered. "Yeah. Might be quite embarrassing for someone who wants to be chief."

Congressman Charles Whitney was watching aerial footage of the crash site with an advisor. It was the only glimpse of the scene TV cameras had finagled thus far. He was sickened by what he saw.

"You sure the protected witness was on that plane?" Whitney asked anxiously.

"Franklin Marsh telephoned an hour ago and confirmed it. The media has it now."

Whitney hung his head. "This is awful. Shut it off."

"I know," his advisor said sympathetically. "We lose the press on the mob trial, but we can still turn this to our favor."

"You think I give a shit about that?"

"You'd better start if you want to be governor. I don't mean to be cold, Charles, but you're going to have to use things like this. Planes crash; trains derail. There are major fires and floods. All sorts of disasters where people die."

"There's nothing wrong with feeling sorry."

"To a point. But I swear, you look as if you killed those people yourself. Feel remorse, but appear strong. The people of this state need to see that in their leader. Not weakness. Sorry, Charles. Isn't that what you're paying me for? Image?"

Whitney nodded.

"Good. Now in a few months, you should get the nomination. Everyone knows that the governor is good friends with your father. He's entering his last year and soon he'll be throwing his support your way. You're not a shoe-in . . . yet. We have the angry lieutenant governor to deal with. And, you've got to prove to your party that you're electable. You've done a good job keeping yourself in the spotlight with various crusades. That helps regionally. But you need more exposure statewide. This airline crash is a perfect opportunity."

"How?"

"Several of your constituents were on that plane. Newt Harting was one of them. His parents live in your district. Visit them. Pay your respects. Pray for their son with them. Pray for the rest."

"I can't do that," Whitney said, horrified.

"The media will pick it up. This is national magazine stuff."

"I won't use them like that."

"Since when did you get so righteous? This crash really has you spooked."

"I guess," Whitney said, turning to look vacantly out the window.

"Okay, alternate plan," his advisor continued. "Maybe even better. I spoke to a representative of North America Airlines. We still need final approval, but we can have you on a chopper before nightfall and fly you up to the command area in Minersville. You can help out the Red Cross. Hand out supplies, serve meals—"

"No!" Whitney shouted. "I'm not going anywhere near that crash site."

"You don't have to be right there. The command post is a mile away. Try to envision the headlines: CONGRESSMAN LENDS HELPING HAND IN AIR DISASTER."

"No, I said."

The advisor drew in a breath, paused, then let it out. He began again, calmly, like a parent talking to a child. "What happened to our vision, Charles? Yours,

mine—your father's? We've come so far. But we still
have a long way to go. A few years in the governor's
mansion, then maybe on to the White House. You want
to quit? Tell me now. But I refuse to be on a losing
team. It's your call."

Whitney looked his advisor dead in the eyes.
"Given the choice?"

"Yes."

Whitney turned away. "See where the Hartings are
this evening."

It was almost five o'clock when the phone rang. Nina
called for Dr. Roberts to pick up on line one.

"Better take a message," Sallie said. "He's with Nathaniel Bosley."

Little Nathaniel, after ten minutes of crying and
kicking his feet, had finally allowed Peter to place fluo-
ride trays in his mouth. Nathaniel was afraid he would
vomit. Peter had promised to personally hold the trays
steady and only leave them in for a minute. He would
use marshmallow flavor—yummy. He was halfway
through.

"Tell Dr. Roberts it's Herb Striklon," Nina shouted
back.

Peter heard. His hands began to shake. Nathaniel
looked at him with eyes that grew wider with each
quiver.

"No, Nathaniel! No!"

Roberts moved quickly to get the trays out, but it
was too late. Little Nathaniel threw up his lunch, a
McDonald's Happy Meal of cheeseburger, fries, and
chocolate shake, all over himself, the chair, the walls,
and Peter. But he didn't cry. He had a scowl on his
face. "Told you so!" he said, as Roberts wiped the muck
off himself.

Peter snapped off his gloves and tunic, glared at the boy, and stepped out of the room to grab the phone.

"Peter, we just got activated by PEMA," Striklon said.

"What? I thought Elliot Brandle didn't want us."

"He doesn't," Striklon answered. "Turns out, the plane hit a few hundred yards into the next county—Bristle. He didn't realize it when the news broke. Nobody did, except the coroner there, Priscilla Ipollito. She demanded we come. Brandle is furious. They have to set up the temporary morgue in his county, though, due to logistics. In an old airport hangar. So she's letting him help run that part—tossing him a bone to keep the peace. But she's in charge."

"Great. Poor Brandle."

"Team's meeting at six A.M. tomorrow at a ball field on the outskirts of Minersville. Need directions?"

"I'll find it."

"Good. A few of us are going tonight, but there's not much we can do yet. They have to clear a road into the crash site. Terrain's a bit rough. Be prepared. Ipollito made arrangements for us to stay in town at the Lazy Rest Motel. When can we expect you?"

Peter suddenly remembered the message he left on the machine for Diane. He knew she would be wondering if he had been called to the crash site, probably fretting over having their plans ruined. But he had told her not to worry, PADIT wasn't going to be activated, and that he was really looking forward to spending some time alone with her. *Shit! Why did he do that?* "I think I better stay at home tonight," he told Striklon. "See you in the morning."

Groaning, he dialed his house to break the news.

Diane answered. "Peter! I got your message."

"I know—"

"Peter, it's fabulous. I'm so happy that you weren't called."

"Diane, listen—"

"I know how you hate to fly. The crash was terrible and we *are* booked on the same airline. But honey, this is probably the safest time to fly. And I'm so looking forward to this. You're a doll to leave that message. You're great! You're wonderful!"

"Diane, please listen," Peter said abruptly, then paused to make sure he finally had her attention. "The message . . . it was all a mistake. We were activated. I have to go."

"You jerk. You bastard. Why the hell did you leave that message, then?"

"It wasn't *my* mistake. That's what they originally told me," Peter said defensively. "I'm sorry."

"I'm sorry, too, Peter," Diane said. "It's just that I had everything planned."

"I guess you'll have to cancel."

"Not on your life."

"You're going alone?"

"No. I'll take Paige. She'll have a ball. And it will give us some time together."

"But Diane, a trip like that—"

"Peter, my mind is made up. The other two kids are taken care of, so you can feel free to go on your *mission*."

"Mission? Is that what you think this is?"

"No, I didn't mean that." She drew in a deep breath. "Those unfortunate people; their families. You have to go. Are you leaving tonight?"

"In the morning."

"Then we have our work cut out for us," Diane said firmly. "We have to squeeze our weekend into one night. That is, if you're up to it?"

"You're on."

Peter smiled as he got off the phone. "Nina," he yelled, "cancel my patients for tomorrow."

Daniel spent the day driving around town. He thought about what his father had told him, about feelings, about justice, about Adam. He finally came home, put the TV on without the sound, and sat down to call Susan's parents. It was almost dinnertime.

"Adam misses you terribly," his mother-in-law said, as usual.

"Yes, I miss him, too. I want to see him."

"Adam will be so pleased. Which day? Will you be staying overnight again?"

"No. I want to take Adam with me for a few days, if that's all right?"

"Daniel," she cried. "Of course. That's fabulous. I can't wait to tell him. He's out with Dad right now." Her initial excitement waned. "But how are you going to handle things with work?"

Daniel didn't want to mention his suspension—not right now, anyway. But he knew he would need someone to help him. "There's a lovely lady in my apartment house," he said. "Mrs. Kunklemacher, a retired schoolteacher. She needs extra money, ever since her husband died a few years back, and sometimes she baby-sits. Fact is, she's been cleaning my apartment for the past couple of months. Looks in on me to see how I'm doing."

"That's great. When are you coming?"

"I thought I'd pick Adam up Friday night."

"Oh," she said. "Well, it's just that Adam has this really good friend, one of the first kids he met here. The boy's birthday is Friday and Adam was invited to sleep over after the party. He was excited about that."

"No big deal. I'll get him Saturday then."

"Wait, I have an idea," she said quickly. "Dad read about the tiger exhibit at the Hamilton Zoo. It's supposed to be super. He was anxious to go see it before it moved on—he's like a kid. Tell you what, we'll pick Adam up from his friend's house Saturday morning, drive to Hamilton, and visit the zoo. You can meet us there. It solves everything."

"Sounds good," Daniel told her, letting the conversation—its normalcy—wash over him.

"By the way, you know our friends, the Murphys? From Philadelphia?"

"Sure."

"Well, their next-door neighbors know these people who had a relative on that plane that crashed. Isn't it awful?"

"Crash? What plane?"

"Daniel, it's been all over the news," she said. "Haven't you heard?"

He glanced toward the TV. It was a few minutes into the six o'clock news. He saw the aerial footage of the crash site.

"I swear, you must live in a shell. You have to snap out of it, especially if you're going to have Adam over."

Daniel got off the phone with his mother-in-law, noticed the intact tail section of a North America plane among the disintegration on the screen. He turned on the sound.

There was a live interview with Congressman Whitney in the newsroom as the lead story was winding down. Then a film clip outside a courthouse in Philadelphia. It didn't take Daniel long to realize which flight it was, what it meant. As if from a great distance, he recognized Marion Luccetta, saw Caputa standing next to him, heard the reporters' questions—and knew that the government's case had turned to shit.

52

The clock in the basement of Hamilton General read 10:28 P.M. as Peter Roberts quickly stepped past it on his way to the morgue. He had just finished packing for his trip to Minersville when the call came in. It was a kill, a fresh one. One that had to be done that night. The identity they knew. They needed Roberts to look at a bite mark on the body of the fourteen-year-old boy.

Peter had wondered how Diane would take the news. He didn't always know how to gauge her. But surprisingly, she didn't obsess over sacrificing their date. Maybe because she knew the murder involved a child. And for that same reason, Peter declined when Diane offered to wait up for him. Because he was certain that when he got home, he wouldn't have any desire other than to get sick over the experience of the dead kid he was about to examine.

Roberts reached the door of the morgue and

paused. He'd learned to take a deep breath and hold it there, right before he entered.

Tom Onasis was hunched over the autopsy table, Kristina by his side. Coroner Louis Trane was on the phone in the corner. Sergeant Sam Milano was there, too, standing quietly to one side, watching, taking notes. On the table was the boy: body ashen, face purple. His mouth was twisted open, his eyes half shut.

Onasis had just entered the body cavity and was lifting out a section of rib cage. Walls of skin and muscle were flapped to the side—the texture of youth, stained with blood.

The morgue was different that night, and it wasn't just the lateness of the hour. The air was heavier, a little colder. They worked in silence, shaken heads replacing levity, because this was not supposed to happen—not to a child. Playing ball, listening to CDs, or rollerblading down the street should have filled this kid's day. And at ten-thirty at night, he should have been lying home in bed, dreaming about tomorrow, not here on a steel table with his chest grotesquely draped open.

"Thanks for coming, Peter," Onasis said, looking up from the body. "Thought we might have missed you, that you'd be on your way up to the crash site."

"I'm leaving in a few hours."

"So am I," Onasis paused, meeting Peter's eyes. "I was at the Tenerife disaster. I was in the military back then. Awful scene. They'll need all the help they can get up there. Goray will be doing double duty covering for me."

Trane hung up the phone and turned to Peter. "Kid's name is Billy Cooper. He was found around seven P.M. in a cornfield near Maybrook. A guy was chasing his dog and discovered the body." He nodded toward the table. "Just like that."

"Time of death?" Milano asked, hand poised above his notebook.

"Well, we took a core temperature at the scene with a liver probe," Trane said. "Plotting the victim's liver reading against the outside temperature, we believe the kid was killed around four."

"There wasn't much rigor," Onasis mentioned, as he and Kristina were removing organs to weigh and dissect. "A little in the jaw and the joints. But his arms still flopped when he was picked up. Also, he was found at the scene in a prone position, but when they transported the body, he was placed faceup. I noticed on my external examination that blood still pooled to his back. So, lividity wasn't completely set. I'd say the time frame fits."

"Four o'clock," Milano repeated. "That means whoever did this probably grabbed the boy as he was coming home from school."

"That is, if he went to school today," Onasis put in.

"Already checked," Milano said. "He did."

"Cause of death, strangulation?" Roberts asked, staring at the boy's mottled face.

"Probably," Onasis replied. "Face congested and ruddy. Petechial hemorrhages on the cheeks, eyelids, and forehead. Contusions on the neck."

"Tell him what else the bastard did to him," Kristina fumed.

"He had marks on his wrists indicating he was restrained, consistent with a pair of handcuffs. And it looks like the boy was sodomized."

Roberts let out a long breath, trying to steady himself.

"We didn't see any obvious semen, though. Could've used a rubber," Onasis said. "We'll wait for the lab results. Maybe we'll get lucky," he added, looking at Sam.

Sam nodded. "We can use all the help we can get. What about the cuffs?"

"Not found at the scene," said Trane. "He probably took them with him."

"So what we have is a child molester and killer," Sam noted. "Can you tell if the abuse occurred before or after death?"

"Definitely before. But it's interesting that you should ask. There was bruising," Onasis explained. "Yet not a lot. Might have been done during."

Roberts winced. "During?"

"Strangled the kid as he sexually assaulted him," Onasis said grimly. "I've seen it before. Helps these sickos climax. The more excited he becomes, the tighter his grip gets around the boy's throat. Then, the ultimate feeling of power . . . orgasm at the moment of death."

Peter felt sick, and tried not to visualize the scene. "How'd you ID the kid so quick?" he asked.

"He had a wallet on him," Trane answered. "Well, in a pair of jeans we found next to the body. Name and address was in it. We called and spoke to his mother. *'Yeah, he's missing,'* she said. I told her to come down to the hospital. There'd been an accident and we needed some information. *'Now?'* she said. *'Can't you just take care of it?'* No. *'Do you really need me?'* Yes.

"So she came. In private, I told her what actually took place—I didn't go into gory details." Trane paused, turning away for a moment.

"And?" Peter pressed.

"And . . . she didn't give a shit," he growled. Trane pointed to the boy on the table. "She looked at her son to make the ID and said, *'Yeah, that's him. Figures it would come to this. Anything else?'* "

"Jesus Christ," Peter said, eyes wide.

"That's not so surprising," Milano said. "Child molesters are very observant. They look for weaknesses, cracks to slither into. Disruption in the house, parents that don't care," he turned a palm up, "and you have opportunity. Opportunity for the young and naive to be deceived. Often, but not always, those are his victims. They're vulnerable. They need attention. He knows that—it's how he used to be, how he probably still is."

"And he deserves to feel the pain that he caused this young man," Onasis said angrily, curving his hands around the table's edge and leaning forward. He studied the body before him, surveying it from head to toe. *All right, Billy, tell me the name of the son of a bitch who did this to you,* he seemed to ask with his eyes. *Whisper. Scream. I'm listening.*

"You said there was a bite mark," Roberts said, breaking the silence. "But I haven't seen one yet."

"It's on his back," Kristina said. "At the base of his neck. It's deep. Clear. Must've hung on to the kid with his teeth."

"And there's something else about it," Onasis added as he reached across the body to pull up the left shoulder. "See that? Kind of a signature mark where there shouldn't be any teeth."

Peter observed the elliptical pattern of bruises and abrasions characteristic of a human bite mark. What seemed out of place, however, was a well-defined injury resembling the letter U behind where the two upper front teeth registered.

"Ever see anything like it, Peter?" Onasis asked.

Peter didn't answer right away. He was too shocked to utter a sound. The pattern was identical to the pictures that Dr. Striklon had sent him from the unsolved case in Harrisburg over six months ago. Of a bite mark on the body of a murdered, sodomized boy.

53

The remains of Billy Cooper were still being scrutinized, but the autopsy was winding down. Dr. Peter Roberts was documenting the bite mark with photographs and direct transparent overlay tracings, before excising the mark to preserve the evidence.

Sergeant Sam Milano had already left the morgue. He was at a telephone booth, chosen for privacy, at a side entrance of Hamilton General Hospital.

"You sure it was okay to call this late?"

"Anytime, I told you."

"I'm pretty sure the kid is the same one who passed Dominic Luccetta the note right before he got popped."

"Not positive, though."

"No. Red hair. Freckles. Deep-set scar across the right eyebrow. The general description matches, all right. I'll bring a picture around Carmine's, see if the owner can make him. He said he got a pretty good glimpse."

"Could be a lot of kids who look like that. It's easy to confuse a face in front of you now with one that was on that bicycle six months ago."

"Oh, that reminds me," Milano said. "The bicycle. They found one in a field about twenty yards from the body."

"Same color?"

"And type—a green mountain bike."

"Sounds promising. Good work."

"Thanks."

"Good night."

54

At six A.M., a time when ball fields usually lie empty and silent, Clarence Falke Field, chosen as the command post for the recovery operation of North America Flight 1089, was ablaze with activity: buses, fire trucks, ambulances, police vehicles, and EMS units were scattered over the grassy expanse. Some were moving, others remained still, swarming with people. Priscilla Ipollito—coroner of Bristle, and head of the emergency operation—drove around in an open-top jeep barking out orders and kicking up dust.

Falke Field had been chosen for its size, one hundred and seventy-five yards long, almost as wide—and also its location, on the edge of Minersville, along the way to where the plane went down.

Clarence Falke was a local who garnered a certain measure of fame and notoriety by playing baseball.

When he was a kid, the townsfolk gathered at the field on weekends to watch him crush fastballs into the woods. When he was signed to a minor league contract, amidst rumblings about the next Babe Ruth being found up in Pennsylvania's coal country, the towns-people were buzzing with wild confidence about their boy: "Any day he'll be in the bigs." "He'll set records." "He won't let us down." "He's from right here, you know, Minersville."

Three years later, in '85, the Cleveland Indians brought him up mid-season. He was the town's hero. It really wasn't much, but for a small, obscure place born of coal, where the mines had since been closed, they hung on to it.

He lasted five seasons in the bigs before being sent down. Sure, he could hit a fastball a country mile, but a major league curve—uh-uh. He never got a second chance, however, losing his career, and his life, the fol-lowing year in a barroom brawl in Chattanooga.

Still, the devastated citizens of Minersville always believed that Clarence Falke could have been, and should have been, one of the great ones. They took that dinky field he once played on and, with funds better spent on education and housing, built what stood in its place today: four baseball diamonds, one placed at each point, with a fence encircling the entire field to hold back the forest. It was a tribute to Clarence Falke, one of their own. Single-handedly, he had almost brought Minersville, Pennsylvania out of oblivion.

Now, something had happened here which would accomplish what he could not. And if it wasn't spoken, it was thought of sure enough: *If a planeload of people had to go down, it was truly lucky to have happened just outside of their hometown.* Fame and notoriety: For a place like Minersville, it was bliss.

The Red Cross and the Salvation Army set up relief

stations under canopies attached to their trucks. They served doughnuts and hot coffee as volunteers from different agencies huddled together, waiting for their assignments, drinking to keep warm.

North America Airlines had a presence there, too. From the back of a trailer they were handing out packages of protective outerwear to anyone who was authorized to go to the scene: heavy rubber boots, thick vinyl gloves, white Tyvek anticontamination suits, masks, duct tape. And baseball caps with their logo, as if a souvenir might distance them from responsibility for the ninety-eight souls left on a hill in the middle of nowhere.

In the maze of vehicles and people, a small modular home was dropped to serve as an office—the heartbeat of the command post. A sign outside read: *Hepatitis Shots Given Here.* Those who had not been vaccinated previously were encouraged to do so before going to the crash site.

The Federal Bureau of Investigation and the National Transportation Safety Board were on hand as well. They kept a low profile, staying close to the modular office, avoiding conversation.

At a distance, past a row of Porta Pottis, two refrigerated trucks rested. They would house human remains brought down from the crash site, then transport them to the makeshift morgue five miles away.

Trained to handle catastrophic death, Coroner Ipollito had done her job well here. With an incredibly short lead time, she had managed to pull everything together, from chaplains to help cope with the stress of working with the dead, to dogs trained to sniff out hidden human remains. She took control of state and local agencies, dealt with grieving families, the press, and the pressure from the federal groups. But when she needed

to bend, she did, never losing focus on the task at
hand, to get what she wanted, and what she needed.

The wreckage of the 727 lay a mile to the northeast,
in Bristle County. Poor access was delaying the recovery efforts. Fortunately, the previous day and night had
been unseasonably cold. The frigid air would keep the
bodies from turning, and the insects down.

Ipollito had crews working through the night, cutting away timber and brush, widening an existing dirt
path that snaked through the terrain to where the plane
had settled. That area, the crash site, was referred to as
the hill.

Roberts had been at the field for nearly half an hour
already. He had driven through town just as sunlight
was beginning to gather, seen endless rows of mature
homes with peeling paint and unkempt lawns. At the
top of Main Street, a heavyset, moon-faced woman sitting on a rickety porch stared curiously at him as he
passed. The rest of the street was deserted. He noticed
several vacant stores, casualties of a broken economy. A
grocery, an apothecary, a tailor. Blank windows that no
longer showed signs of life. This wasn't what he was
used to. This wasn't like Hamilton. He wondered if
people from Philadelphia and New York thought of
Hamilton this way.

He had driven on, activity pointing the way down a
country road. As he got closer, the busyness intensified.
Parked cars lined the roadside. People rushed by. He
saw, near a swath of trees, a crowd staring. And then
arising in riotous contrast to the rest of the town, stood
their monument: Falke Field.

At the entrance, a section of cyclone fencing had
been taken down for vehicle access. State police moni-
tored the opening, keeping the public and press at bay,
allowing only those with proper authorization to pass
through.

Roberts had cleared security and soon found Herb Striklon standing with four other PADIT members. Together, they waited, their breath misting in the cold as the rest of their group assembled. Everyone who was called had come—twelve men, four women.

The coroner advised them that due to the severity of the scene on the hill, no individual should spend more than four hours at a time there. They would work in shifts. Six dentists would lead off—those with the most forensic experience. The others would report to the makeshift morgue and start working with the antemortem dental records, entering them on computer, and carefully logging the charts and dental radiographs. Using the airplane's manifest, North America Airlines had started contacting the passengers' dentists the night before and had obtained several sets of dental records already. More would be delivered that morning via Federal Express.

Additionally, as human remains reached the morgue, any dental findings would have to be examined and x-rayed. The postmortem dental charts thus generated would be recorded in similar fashion to the antemortem records so that proper comparison between the two could be made.

Often in mass disasters, this was the only way many of the victims could be identified. And in an air crash such as this one, fragmentation of each individual's dentition was possible. Sadly, with ninety-eight aboard, there would be a lot to look at.

The dentists going to the morgue were dispatched. The others got their packages from the North America tractor-trailer and prepared to leave for the hill.

Roberts and Striklon walked over to a vacant patch of grass to put their suits on, sitting on the ground to struggle with the tight rubber boots.

Priscilla Ipollito drove up within a few feet of them

in her jeep. She was about Peter's age, kind of pretty in a rough sort of way. Too pretty to be a coroner, Peter thought. She wore a Dodgers cap. Chunks of blond hair poked out from the sides. A ponytail peeked through the back.

"Got the word," she called to them. "We're almost ready."

Striklon nodded. Ipollito had given him six special armbands for his team to wear at the crash site. She was smart. There were too many impostors who wanted to gain access: curiosity seekers, the press, and worse. Some had already circumvented security. She was putting a stop to it. There would be hell to pay if you were caught at the crash site without the necessary coded emblem.

Roberts pulled a boot over his heel. "Not bad," he said with a tilt of his head as she drove off.

"Don't let that fool you," Striklon warned. "She knows what the fuck she's doing."

"I didn't mean anything by it."

"Sure you did." He aimed a finger at Peter. "And I bet you didn't think a woman could handle all of this. At least not one that looked like that." He handed Peter an armband. "There's lots of money up there: loose, on the ground, and in wallets. Some ghouls were caught pilfering it. Jewelry and luggage, too."

"Christ! Robbing the dead."

"You should've heard Ipollito come down on the state police for it. She doesn't take shit from anybody. Just remember that. Do everything by the book."

"Don't worry," Peter replied.

They stood. A stocky man in his late sixties with a beet-red nose and gray stubble walked toward them. He wore red suspenders over a long-john top and dark green pants. He had a Minersville Volunteer Fireman's cap on. A heavy wad of tobacco pushed out one of his cheeks.

"You guys going up?" he asked in a mumble, then turned to spit some tobacco juice on the ground.

"Yeah," Striklon answered.

"I saw you gettin' ready. You should've stripped down to your underwear before putting them suits on. Know it's cold now, but when that sun starts to beat on you, you'll be sweating like a hog in July. Them suits don't breathe."

"Thanks. Guess we'll find out."

"Don't say I didn't warn ya." He spit again. "So, what are ya? FBI? EMS?"

"We're dentists," Striklon said.

"Shit," he smiled, flashing dark brown teeth. A few of the front ones were missing. "What the fuck do they need dentists for?"

"To identify the victims," Roberts explained. "The crash, the fire . . ."

"Been up there already. Wadn't much fire. Them people were torn apart real bad, though. Ain't got no heads, let alone teeth. Just torsos and limbs. That's all. How ya goin' to identify them without any heads? Tell me that one. Shhhitt!"

Roberts stared at Striklon with his mouth open as the man moved on.

"Rumors," Striklon offered. "Before long, you'll be hearing that everyone on board had a death wish. Pilot included. Or something like that."

"Yeah. Guy's dumb as a rock," Peter said.

Striklon gave him a baleful look and took out the roll of heavy tape. "I'll do you," he said, bending. "Then you can do me."

The top edge of the boot had to be taped to the pants, sealing off that vulnerable area from contamination.

Striklon worked on the boots while Roberts looked distractedly at the crowd behind the fence. They had lounge chairs and picnic baskets. A couple were chugging beers for breakfast.

Striklon noticed Peter's blank expression. "You okay?" he asked over the whine of unraveling tape.

"Yeah . . . No . . . I mean, I don't know," Roberts said, breaking from his reverie. "This town. These people. Something." He made an indefinite gesture.

"You know, I grew up in a town just like this. What do you expect from these people? Trouble is, Peter, you're a snob."

Peter managed a grin. "You always were blunt, Herb."

"Sorry." He smiled back. "But I call 'em the way I see 'em. Known you for a long time. You forget your roots? Those days struggling through dental school and before?"

"I evolved. Became more civilized."

"Not like them." Striklon motioned over to the crowd with his chin.

"No."

"See what I mean?"

Peter didn't answer, let the comment slide away.

The two boarded a school bus commandeered to shuttle people to and from the hill. On the ride up, Roberts told Striklon about the bite mark he had examined the night before, the one on Billy Cooper's shoulder.

"You say it's identical?" Striklon asked.

"No mistake. Same teeth marks. Same nasty little U behind the upper centrals."

"It's been months. I was hoping this guy was locked up somewhere, maybe on another charge, but at least away from kids. Why do you think he waited so long?"

"Who says he waited?"

"The blurb I placed in the journal about the bite mark came up empty."

"But if your victim was the first—"

"Or if the article was missed," Striklon interrupted, "then there could be others. I know."

"Run it again," Roberts suggested. "Contact other states. Somewhere, someone might recall something. Remember Klotz from Oklahoma, put away on bite mark evidence? Had a rotated lateral that left an unusual mark. Twenty years later, the forensic odontologist who testified at his trial—I think Conti was his name—was at a seminar that showed some recent unsolved cases. He recognized the bite right off. Found out Klotz was released two years before. They picked him up the very next day. Obviously, Klotz never changed."

"A leopard and his spots," Striklon noted.

They both sat up as the school bus groaned, climbing one last steep incline to reach the scene.

"You ready for this?" Striklon asked, kneading his brow.

"Too late to wonder now."

The bus halted on a level grade of freshly carved earth. An idle bulldozer slept off to the right, halfway under some trees near the Red Cross relief station. On the left, a refrigerated tractor-trailer stood ready. A fire truck was also there, hoses spilled along its side where a plastic ground cover was draped and fastened into what looked like an enormous kiddie pool. It would serve as a decontamination station where recovery workers returning from the area littered with human remains would be hosed down before having their protective outerwear cut off and disposed of properly.

Blocking the road ahead, leading into the crash site, was a tent: a final checkpoint for last-minute supplies, and first aid.

Two state troopers accosted them at the door of the
bus as they filed off, looking for armbands, reading
their codes.

Ipollito positioned herself on the back of her jeep to
address them. "You all know what to do. Form six
teams, five or six to a group. Each team *must* have a
dentist."

A tall, muscular guy wearing an EMS cap rolled his
eyes at the order. He turned to Peter. "You a dentist?"

"Yes."

"Then come on," he said gruffly.

Peter learned that the guy's name was Zeke, and
that he was the head of their newly formed team. He
also quickly labeled him an ignorant redneck.

Each team passed through the tent, checking themselves. Peter wondered what would be lying on the
other side. Would it be as bad as the rumors said:
crumpled torsos, no heads, commingled remains of
limbs and flesh?

Those concerns were answered as soon as they
stepped around the first bend and saw somebody's liver
sprawled in the dirt by the side of the road.

55

███████ Daniel drove up to the cottage. On the seat
next to him was the morning newspaper with its grim
account of the air crash. Daniel had it bent open to
page seven, where there was a picture of Marion Luc-

cetta smirking on the courthouse steps. The picture had made his mind up. Now, there was no hope of justice.

He saw Kate on the front porch. She waved. "Good morning, Daniel."

"Kate," he said with a nod through his open window.

"He's inside having breakfast."

Daniel shut the car off, pulled out the key. "You know why I'm here?"

"We talked. I figured you'd be around sooner or later."

"And you don't approve."

Her face tightened for a moment, then eased. "It's not as simple as that. Whether I do or don't approve has no bearing, so I decided to let it be."

"Just like that?"

"Yes. Just like that," she said. "But don't mistake my indifference for lack of caring, because I really do . . . care, that is."

Daniel looked up at her, and felt like he was seeing her for the first time.

She reached in to place a hand on his shoulder. "Right or wrong, I know you need to do something, Daniel. You can't go on as you have."

"And my father?"

"He feels your pain. And I understand that. But there's more to it." She gently drew her arm back. "I thought, in time, he could handle losing his career. That he would eventually give in to what he no longer had control over. It was one of the reasons I finally decided to marry him. And he's been good about things. Outwardly. But I was wrong. It changed him. I see it on his face as he rises each day, when he thinks I'm not looking. And then again at night, right before sleep steals him away. He lost more than just a career when those bullets hit. Some dignity, maybe." She shrugged. "I stare into that void and know that this isn't something time alone will heal. He should have been able to decide for himself when to put it down—evenly, on his own terms. Not be torn from it. And as much as I hate the circumstances that are urging his hand now—Susan's death: your loss, his, mine—I still don't want to see him get involved."

"So I was right, you don't approve."

"Except for the fact that this may be his opportunity to achieve peace with himself, and with what happened to him."

"I see. But if it isn't? If it gives him an even greater desire for what he's missed?" Daniel asked pointedly. "Then what?"

"Then I shall stop being selfish," she said honestly, "stop trying to change him, and accept what I should have known all along: You can't corral a wild horse and expect him not to want to run when the wind calls. Not even a lame one."

"I misjudged you," he admitted after a moment. "I'm sorry."

She smiled. "You're supposed to. I'm your step-mother."

He shifted uncomfortably, then sheepishly grinned back.

"One more thing before I go," she said. "Whatever your father revealed to you yesterday was very difficult for him, but he did it anyway. Love him just as much."

Daniel remained seated and thoughtfully watched her get into her pickup, pull out, and clear the drive. Grabbing his paper, he entered the house and found his father sitting at the kitchen table.

"So, what do you have in mind, Pop?" Daniel asked, throwing the picture of Marion Luccetta down in front of him.

"Saw it," his father said, continuing to eat without looking up.

"Dad, I'm here."

"Yes, I know." His father held up another spoonful, made an ugly face at it. "You want some oatmeal?"

"No."

Seymour rose, carried the bowl over to the sink. "Me, neither." He dumped the contents down the disposal. "You decided now? You're ready?"

"Yes!"

"Want some apple pie and cheese?"

"What?"

"Apple pie—"

"I heard you," Daniel shot back with an incredulous look. "Thought you'd be—I don't know—excited?"

"I am. When I get excited, I like to eat. Not that crap, though," he said, throwing a glance at the sink.

"But apple pie and cheese? What about your diet, and what the doctor told you? It's like holding a loaded gun to your head."

"Maybe, but it'll have blanks: low-calorie apple Pop-Tart, nonfat cheddar cheese melted on top."

"Ugh." Daniel winced.

"Not so bad once you surrender to it . . . and make believe."

"You must have one hell of an imagination."

"Hey, when you get to be my age, you're thankful you still have that."

"So where do we begin? How are we going to nail Luccetta?" Daniel watched his father rummage through the refrigerator.

"I thought you were ready?" He let the door close, sighing.

"I am."

"Are you? This is not a vendetta." He threw the cheese onto the counter. "It's a good bet Marion will be implicated in Susan's murder, but we don't know that for sure. For now, he's just a suspect."

"Ah, *vos iz richtic.*"

"Yes, *vos iz richtic.* What is right. This has to be about justice. Otherwise we risk blindness. Remember that, Daniel."

"I'll try."

"First, we have to get organized," Seymour said firmly. "The assassination of Dominic Luccetta was the case you were working on when Susan died. Obviously, the two are intertwined."

"We already know that. The car bomb was meant for me because of my involvement."

"Probably. But I'd like to look into the case again. Actually, I already started."

"Why?" Daniel asked defensively. "You think Sam and I missed something?"

"Sometimes it's hard to find what you weren't looking for. Maybe a different set of eyes?" Seymour furrowed his brow. "Could be more here than the *obvious.*"

"How so?"

"Arthur Sarchick killed Dominic Luccetta. Now Sarchick dies in that crash."

"Nothing bewildering about that. Marion arranged to have that plane go down."

"A commercial airliner full of people?"

"He had a pretty strong motive," Daniel argued. "Don't you think?"

"Maybe." He pointed to the paper resting on the table. "Notice the article about a boy being murdered?"

Daniel shook his head.

"Killed yesterday afternoon. Sexually abused, too. They found a bicycle at the scene, and the general description matches. What if he's the kid with the note you were so curious about?"

"You're looking too deeply," Daniel said. "It's just a coincidence."

"No, a possibility we have to consider," Seymour maintained. "There've been too many coincidences."

"Like a plane crashing with a federal witness aboard who was about to testify?"

His father nodded, conceding the point. "But if I'm right, he's the second person involved with the killing of Dominic Luccetta to end up dead yesterday."

"Maybe it was Marion's handiwork again. Found out who that kid was and offed him that way as sort of a warning? He must have known Sarchick was a pedophile."

"For what reason?" Seymour shook his head. "It doesn't scan. But there is something, or someone, that ties all these events together. For now I'm going to concentrate on the beginning—Dominic's murder. Review every detail and see where it leads. Meanwhile, you find out everything you can about the car bombing."

"But I'll be spinning my wheels," Daniel said glumly. "Nobody at the scene saw anything. Even the bomb squad couldn't come up with a lead. It's all been covered."

"Yes. But not by you. You were in mourning then, and too emotionally involved to investigate it yourself. I have faith. You're a Pinchus. You'll find something."

"Yeah, after six months," Daniel moaned. "And with no witnesses."

"There's one," his father reminded him. "Someone called the station house warning them about the bomb."

Daniel nodded slowly. All that had mattered then was that Susan was dead. He knew who did it—he didn't need any clues. The call was a gesture of kindness, he had come to believe. And he had decided to return the favor by not stirring the ashes. He didn't want to put another in jeopardy. But now he saw how important it was. It was all he had to go on.

"Have any idea who that could have been?"

"Yes," he said with a faraway look in his eyes. "I think I do."

"Then, that's where you'll start," his father said loudly. "It's a long shot. I like long shots. Now, how about some of that apple pie and cheese?"

56

Nobody could have imagined—not in the darkest corner of their mind—the scene on the hill. It was a sight so macabre and grotesque that it couldn't be accepted as real. It was like a make-believe movie set for a horror flick. Human remains in bits and pieces, commingled, on the ground, in bushes, up in trees. Victims with their clothes blown off. Broken bodies. Crushed lives. A field of slaughter. Corpses reduced to fleshy bags of bones, crumpled, naked, organs spilled.

Those who were chosen for the recovery operation worked without thinking, their subconscious protecting them with denial as they sifted through human remains and plane debris. It helped them do the job that needed to be done—until something familiar came into focus: a piece of jewelry, a name on a luggage tag, a picture carried in a wallet. That's when reality flickered back with images of lost lives floating up at them, beckoning for attention, jarring their brains with the horrifying truth of it all.

There was no plane. It had shattered like the bodies of the passengers it had carried. But there were still reminders: a strong smell of jet fuel, and a few recognizable pieces—half a wing, the tail section, landing gear, part of the fuselage with several windows still in place. The rest was reduced to twisted metal that littered the area along with luggage, magazines, seat cushions, and clothes torn from passengers.

A grid, marked in orange spray paint, was drawn over the sloped forest. The dirt road served as the center line, dividing the crash site into east and west. A letter of the alphabet labeled a line every twelve paces along it, crisscrossing the road.

Red flags marked human remains, placed by advance workers when they discovered them, hidden by the brush and debris. Yellow flags were placed near scattered airplane wreckage for the NTSB.

Roberts was working on an embankment, Section J-West. They started at the perimeter and marched forward with an arm's length between each of them, looking for remains. When anything was discovered, they gathered around the spot to investigate. One member of their group was the designated scribe. He recorded what was found, what was left of the victim, including personal effects, if any. Then the morgue runners would be called, a body bag brought, and the remains collected, logged, and tagged with an assigned number and grid location.

Someone spotted a hand, severed, lying by itself. A lot of limbs were found that way: traumatic amputations. Some people were even torn in half, split by their seat belts as they were being jettisoned.

Roberts looked at the hand. The fingernails were neatly painted in red. He envisioned the woman getting ready, putting the polish on, excited about her trip. He crushed the thought.

As they advanced into the section they became busier. Zeke slipped walking up a slope and realized that he had slid on the skin of a victim, camouflaged by fallen leaves. He yelled for the others. Then there was another, and another. Each team member called out his discovery. The scribe barely finished an entry before being summoned again.

The volunteer fireman had been right about a couple of things. Despite the chilly temperature, it was hot under those biohazard suits. They were all sweating. And there were no heads attached to most of the victims, only fragments of faces and pieces of skull still clinging to scalps. But usually there was enough—a section of jaw, a couple of teeth—to hope for identification.

Roberts found an upper torso, a torn T-shirt wrapped around it. There were no arms, but part of the neck remained. Sections of both jaws were still clinging to it. A laundry mark on the shirt read Callaway. Things like that were important. Dental records would still have to be checked, but it was a good lead. He dictated the find to the scribe: "J-W two-fourteen; upper torso; T-shirt—name Callaway written on it; maxilla with teeth two through twelve intact; right section of mandible with teeth twenty-nine, thirty, and thirty-one."

A few yards away, Roberts heard Zeke calling for a body bag. Zeke had just finished examining another victim. The scribe had already recorded it.

"Wait," Roberts shouted, putting up a hand. "I haven't looked for teeth yet."

"Teeth?" Zeke roared. "Ain't no mouth, hardly no head. Where you goin' to find teeth?" He waved Roberts off.

Peter walked over, scanned the area, then dropped to his knees where the victim's head was. He tore at the ground, sifting the dirt with his hands. After a moment, he held up a section of jaw with four teeth attached.

"Here they are," he said.

Zeke gaped, whispering, "Well, I'll be." He bent and worked the earth next to Peter. "Maybe there's more. That would help, right?"

Peter nodded.

"From now on, don't let me catch any of you guys signing off on any remains unless . . . hey, what's your name again?"

"Roberts. Peter Roberts."

". . . unless Dr. Roberts here gives his okay. Understand?"

"Understood," they said in unison.

Over the next few hours they worked that section, and one more—ignoring fatigue and the four-hour time limit—trying to complete the recovery of human remains. Later, they would go over the lists, checking, hoping that the ones they found were identified, offering to do more for the ones who were not.

When they were done, Roberts stood next to Zeke and gazed over into the next zone. They watched one of the other groups at work. It was Striklon's group. Herb was on a ladder with a chain saw, cutting limbs off of a tree, trying to get a torso down.

"Good man," Zeke commented, "risking his own safety for that poor soul."

"The best," Roberts said.

On the way down the hill, Roberts saw a stuffed animal wearing a little ballerina dress resting against the trunk of a tree. Amidst the death and destruction, it had floated there in nearly pristine condition. Roberts nudged Zeke with an elbow and pointed. Zeke stiffened at the sight.

"Don't show me that shit," he said, shaking his

head, eyes red and watery. "I've seen enough. Don't want to see that."

"I know." Peter sighed. Then he whispered, "You're a good man, too, Zeke."

━━━━━

Back at the command post, Roberts found the row of pay telephones slung together provisionally at one end of the field. Seeing people in a more normal setting made him think about the hill, about what they had just done. Reality began to set in. He thought about Hamilton, his kids, Diane. She was going to fly in a plane tomorrow with Paige. God, he didn't want them to do that—not after what he just saw. But he knew he couldn't stop them. He would put it aside. *"Silly. Overreacting,"* he said quietly to himself as he dialed his number.

"Peter, I'm so happy to hear your voice," Diane said. "I can't imagine what you must be going through. Is it as bad as the television reports are making it out to be? They're broadcasting nonstop. And there are reports that the NTSB is going to confirm that it was sabotage."

"I wouldn't know. I just came down from the crash site myself. But I don't want to talk about it. Do you mind?"

"No." She hesitated. "What should we talk about?"

"Anything. Anything at all, Diane. Something totally unimportant. Something normal."

"Okay . . . Well . . . I ran into Mrs. Eisenhart this morning. The one who used to watch our kids before Paige was born. Haven't seen her in years. She got to meet Paige. She gave me a big hug and a kiss, then bought Pepperidge Farm macadamia nut cookies for Paige. . . . Is that what you want to hear—things like that?"

"Things exactly like that," Peter said. "Perfect! How were the cookies?"

"They were damn good!"

"Tell me more."

"Well . . ."

■■■■■

After Peter got off the phone, he looked around the ball field. He saw fresh recovery workers heading for the hill, and some of those who were coming back. Turning away, he walked to an isolated part of the field and sat down.

Those were people on that hill, he had to remind himself. And children, too—no different from the ones in his own neighborhood, no different from the ones he saw in this town. From afar, he could see the crowd behind the fence. Then, the command post disappeared: the trucks, the tents, the modular. The townsfolk filled the stands. Baseball was being played again. Clarence Falke was up at bat, a fastball bearing down on him.

Peter Roberts saw it all, and sitting on the outfield grass, he started weeping in a way he hadn't done since he was a little boy.

57

The gate was open; the circular drive, empty—except for a new BMW parked to one side near a pair of Japanese maples. An autumn wind was blowing and fallen leaves scratched against the asphalt as he knocked softly on the front door, unsure and wary. When it opened, Sylvia Luccetta stood in the doorway, the startled look on her face soon giving way to a smile.

"Why, Detective Pinchus. I mean, Daniel," she said. "What a nice surprise."

She was as lovely as he recalled. "I, um . . . should have called first. Sorry." He looked past her, tentatively.

"Don't worry, Marion's not here. Nor are any of his men. Haven't been for days. The trial and all. Probably off somewhere celebrating. Why don't you come in?"

"Thank you, I will, Mrs. Lu—"

"Sylvia. Remember?"

"Yes, Sylvia. I do."

She moved aside, arching the door wider. He entered, stepping into a large, open foyer with marble floor, curved staircase, and a crystal chandelier above. She crouched to gather up some scattered clothes on the floor: a couple of sweaters; a pair of jeans.

"Excuse the mess. I was waiting for the dry cleaners. I didn't expect company."

He didn't respond, only noticed her bare feet, how her thin dress hiked up above her knees, and how it clung to her body as she bent. It had been so long. From within, he felt something stir—and was nearly overwhelmed with guilt.

"What did you want?" she asked, rising, holding the bundle to her chest.

"To come by and thank you."

"Thank me? For what?"

"For trying to warn me about the car bomb."

"Oh, Daniel," she said, shaking her head sadly. "I was so sorry to hear about your wife. I was going to send you something—a note, or a card. But then I realized that might not look right."

"I understand."

"If you got some kind of warning, though, it didn't come from me." She placed the clothes on the bottom stair.

"You didn't call the station house just before. . . ?"

"No. I would have—that is, if I had known about it."

"They said a woman called. I thought you were the one," Daniel said. "I figured you got wind of what Marion was going to do."

"Marion?" Her head kicked back. "I can't blame you for suspecting him, but I don't believe he had anything to do with it."

"Why not?"

"I just don't, that's all. Not his style. Did you get

any flowers from him? Legend has it that they send flowers after a hit. It's a sign, a warning to others."

"Sylvia, you don't have to protect him."

She laughed. "Is that what you think?"

"Maybe." He paused. "Maybe you've been working with him all along."

"You're wrong," she said angrily. "I hate him. I hate this family. I would never do that."

"Oh? You're not as innocent as you make it seem. I checked. You have a record—arrested for forgery."

"Yes," she admitted. "They said I had a talent. It was exciting. I was foolish. But that was a long time ago. Before—"

"Before you knew who you were getting into bed with?" Daniel finished.

"How dare you!" she cried.

"Your visit to the station house was just a ruse to get information. Information that Marion could use. I saw the look you threw my way when we came here after Dominic was killed. Is that when you and he hatched your little plan?"

"What are you talking about? What look? I was staring at the guy next to you."

"Milano?" Daniel asked, suddenly off balance. "Sergeant Sam Milano?"

"That name doesn't mean anything to me. He looked familiar, though." Her eyes narrowed as if she were trying to recall. "Guess I was wrong."

Daniel couldn't help wondering if Milano *had* been there before. But he would have mentioned it. He shook his head, pushing the suspicious thoughts away.

"As far as coming to see you," Sylvia continued, "you're partly right. Marion did send me. But mainly I did it for myself."

"You'll have to do better than that."

"I don't know why I feel it's so damn important that

you believe me." She hesitated, biting her lip. Then she said, "I have something to show you."

She walked toward a room off the foyer, motioning for him to follow. It was a mannish-looking room, with heavy furniture and dark green carpeting. She went to an escritoire centered in front of a window and opened one of the drawers, withdrawing a folded yellow piece of paper.

"You asked me about a note when I came to the station. I didn't know about it then. But maybe if you read it, you'll realize why Marion didn't want it to get out. You can take it with you. I don't want it in my house anymore." When she handed it to him, her hand trembled.

Daniel spread the paper, his eye falling first on a couple of reddish-brown blotches of what had to be dried blood. Then he read:

I enjoyed fucking your son, and then being his savior. Did you really think I'd forget the party we had at the farmhouse, Fats? Thanks for the frozen memories. Squigger sends his regards. Now look up across the street and wave good-bye.

Daniel stared at the note, his brow furrowing.

Sylvia's voice sounded small and far away. "Bobby was molested on his way home from school one day. Barney Ter . . . Arthur Sarchick—I know his real name now—brought him home. He said he found Bobby cowering in an alley."

"But it was a setup," Daniel guessed, looking up at her, at the beautiful face twisted with fury.

She nodded fiercely. "We were *so* grateful. Sarchick said he needed a job, so Dominic gave him one. Because of Sarchick's good deed."

"And your son, how did it happen?"

"An older boy approached him and asked Bobby to help him look for his lost dog. He led him behind a fence in the alley."

"Did he also abuse Bobby?"

"No."

"Did your son give a description of the boy? Red hair and freckles maybe?"

"It's tough getting details from an eleven-year-old. Especially when you consider what happened to him. The boy left after handing Bobby over to that monster, that fiend, that bastard," she said, voice rising. "Sarchick wore a mask, that's why Bobby didn't recognize him later, when he came back to *help* him."

"I see."

"The family wanted to take care of Sarchick in their own way."

"And you went along with it."

"I wanted them to find Sarchick and gut him like an animal. Not because he killed Dominic, but because of what he did to Bobby."

Daniel tried to read her eyes. He thought they looked sincere. And beautiful. "I'm sorry. I didn't know," he said. "May I talk to your son? We could find out something important."

"Important to who? To you? To some remote connection with the car bombing? I don't think so. Dominic's dead. And now, so is that prick Sarchick. It's best to leave things alone."

"I think the boy who gave Dominic the note was murdered last night."

"Oh, my God." She shuddered. "That doesn't make sense. Why?"

"I'm not sure. But he might be the same boy who lured your son."

"Well, Bobby's not here, even if I thought it was okay for you to talk to him. I sent him to a military academy in Virginia. I wanted him to get away." She sighed. "From all this—what happened to him, his father's death, the Luccetta family influence."

"I understand."

"Wish I could do the same," she said, retrieving a bottle of brandy from the open drawer. With her other hand, she lifted out two glasses. "Want a drink?"

"No, thanks."

"Oh, I forgot: on duty and shit like that."

"I'm—er—not on duty," he stammered. "This is an unofficial call. Just a bit early in the afternoon for me."

"Do you mind?"

"Not at all."

She poured one, carried it over to a leather couch on the other side of the room. Daniel followed her, still carrying the note.

"This is my escape," she said, bringing the glass up to her lips.

Daniel imagined it wasn't the first of the day.

"Sometimes, I want to get so shit-faced that nothing matters, that I forget who I am, what's happened. You ever get that way?"

"Often," Daniel answered, seriously.

"Of course," she said. "I'm sorry."

"It's okay. Why don't you just run away?"

"Leave? Find a new life? Not so easy." She swirled her brandy, looked down at the ruddy liquid. "I used to warn Dominic that one of these days they would arrest him, put him away for good. How I prayed for that. But he'd tell me, 'No way, darlin'. Ain't gonna happen. Got myself an *ace in the hole*.' And now, even though Dominic's gone, I'm still, as they say, married to the mob. It would be unsafe to leave."

"It's dangerous to stay."

"Don't worry. I have a little insurance policy of my own."

He squinted at her. "You got a plan?"

"Not yet. One will come." She smiled unconvincingly.

Daniel fidgeted as if just remembering the note in his hand. "I assume *Fats* was Dominic," he said.

"Yes. It was a nickname given to him by his college fraternity—Kingsman House."

"And *Squigger*—ever hear that name before?"

"No."

"Could've been a fraternity brother?"

"Maybe. It was a weird fraternity, though."

"How so?"

"I once found an envelope marked Kingsman House in one of Dominic's drawers. It was stuffed with old Polaroids. Disgusting pictures. Of Dominic and another guy having sex with a boy. Ugh!" She took a gulp of brandy. "One look was enough. I wouldn't let him touch me after that. The son of a bitch was no better than Sarchick."

"Why did he save them? Unless . . .". Daniel looked up at her over the edge of the yellowed paper. "Unless he was using them to blackmail someone?"

"I have no idea." She shrugged, but something flickered in her eyes. "Wait a minute. Marion did ask me about the envelope right after Dominic was killed. He didn't mention the pictures, didn't know I had already seen them, but he tore the place apart looking for them. I guess they were already gone, because he never found them."

"Frozen moments in time," Daniel read from the note again, then paused. "Sarchick had to be in those pictures. But—"

"Then wouldn't Dominic have recognized him or something?"

Daniel jerked his gaze back to her. "But that was ages ago. People change. Sarchick used an alias, and he's a master of disguise. And we know he's capable of what you saw in those pictures. He's a convicted child molester. And . . ." Daniel suddenly stood. "Sylvia, what college did Dominic attend?"

She blinked. "Van Buren University."

Daniel nodded slowly. "I think I'll have that drink now."

———

"You sure Marion or one of his men won't be stopping by?" Daniel asked casually. As he accepted the brandy, Sylvia's hand brushed against his thigh—innocently, though, he thought.

"Still *my* house, *my* rules. He has to call. And besides, after Dominic died, he doesn't have much business here anymore."

"But he still has *some* reason to come."

She looked down, eyes drowning in her drink. "Yes. A reason," she said quietly.

Daniel felt her discomfort. "I mean the Luccettas have a presence here in Hamilton. And you *are* his sister-in-law."

"But of course." She turned back to Daniel, her gray expression lifting a little.

"It must be tough losing a brother."

"Believe me, there was no love lost between them." She gave a sarcastic chuckle. "Secretly, I think Marion was happy, or at least not too sad, about his brother's death. The men respected Dominic more, his leadership and his ruthlessness. Marion didn't like that. After all, Dominic was his younger brother. But then again, Marion was always jealous of whatever Dominic had."

"Is that why you think Marion wouldn't have retaliated with the car bombing?"

"Partly. But Marion *was* upset with you. He wanted

Sarchick for other reasons. I once heard him say that Sarchick made a fool out of him."

"How?"

"Don't know." She took a big swallow, then held out her empty glass.

"And the tension between Marion and Dominic?" he asked, pouring.

"Seemed to get worse in the few months before Dominic died."

"Around the time Sarchick came on the scene," Daniel observed.

"Yes. But they both trusted Sarchick."

"He could have sensed their conflict. Fed lies to both sides to drive them apart. Remember when I asked you at the station house how Sarchick became so endeared to Dominic in such a short time? Well, aside from rescuing Bobby, I think he might have had something to do with those witnesses who were about to testify."

"Sarchick was the one to find them, and Dominic was eternally grateful."

"Dominic tell you that?"

"No. Guessing," she admitted between sips. "You're not the only one who can add two and two."

"I like your play-calling," Daniel commented.

She smiled back, coquettishly.

He noticed her getting tired—it was in her voice and in her face. "Sarchick could've set the whole thing up from the start," Daniel went on. "Possibly with Marion's help. But Sarchick never intended for those witnesses to live."

"So he double-crossed both Marion and Dominic in the end. Why?"

"I'm not really sure," Daniel said, lifting his hands helplessly. "But it fits. And Sarchick obviously enjoyed the game."

"So do I," she said woozily, draping a leg over one of his. She pressed it against him, riding it up toward his crotch.

Daniel didn't stop her. He didn't want to. Instead, he continued to probe—and kept her glass full.

"Sarchick must've hated Dominic so much that killing him alone wasn't enough. He wanted to destroy his entire empire."

"I know," she mumbled. "Witness protection. Marion was afraid he'd . . ."

"Go on, Sylvia . . . I need you to tell me . . ." But it was becoming more difficult to keep her focused. Her hand joined her leg where she playfully slid them both against his thigh, and she rambled on.

"Good old Marion," she yawned. "I missed my chance with that sicko Freddie."

"Freddie the Welder?" Daniel knew the stories. Freddie was a loose cannon for hire in the world of organized crime, a mean motherfucker who liked to take his victims apart one limb at a time with an acetylene torch. A while back, Freddie's brother was involved in a coke deal that went sour and disappeared without a trace. Rumor had it that Freddie had blamed Marion.

"Yeah, that's the guy." She spoke slowly, trying to concentrate on the words, trying not to slur. "Marion was scared shitless. Claimed that he had no . . . no idea," she yawned. "Swore on his mother's eyes."

"And Freddie bought it?"

"For the time being." She swallowed the last of her brandy. "Honor among thieves and crap like that. No flowers, no body—no hit. But he warned Marion that if he ever found out otherwise, Marion was a fucking dead man."

"You seem to know quite a bit."

"Hah! I could tell you lots of stories about Marion,"

she said, eyes only half open. "Isn't much Marion does that I don't find out about."

"How?"

"Talks in his sleep," she said, smirking. "What did you think?"

Daniel stiffened.

"Oops," she said, sleepily raising a finger to her lips. "Wasn't supposed to tell you that." Her eyes closed.

Daniel nudged her. "Sylvia," he said urgently. "Did Marion have anything to do with the plane crash?"

"Hhmm. What?" she asked, eyelids still shut.

He shook her, repeated the question.

She shrugged. "Don't know about that. Sorry. Shh!" she said, and fell heavily against his shoulder, asleep.

Daniel gently lifted her leg off him and leaned her back against the couch. He stood, took the glass out of her hand, and placed it on a side table. As he left, he looked back at Sylvia and felt ashamed.

He had fed her hearsay and supposition. Even falsely accused her to get her talking. Then drank with her, nursing his own drink, so she would drink more, so she would talk more. He had found out some things that were very important. And other things he had no right knowing at all. He had manipulated her, though there were moments when his instincts were clouded by her beauty. He did his job. He didn't know how he felt about that; didn't know how he felt about her. He folded the note away, and left—disliking himself.

58

As soon as Daniel returned from Sylvia's, he telephoned his dad. Anxious to trade information, he was glad to hear his father's voice and quickly filled him in.

"Party at the farmhouse—there's something familiar about that," Seymour echoed after Daniel recited the contents of the note. "Eh, probably nothing. Too many cases, too many years. If it's important it'll come," he surrendered. "Go on."

Daniel told him the rest, but stopped short of revealing just how Sylvia came to know *some* things.

After a moment, his father asked, "Do you trust her, Daniel?"

Daniel was quiet. When they first met at the station house six months ago, he hadn't been sure. And time had proven her to be less than completely truthful. But then, he hadn't been either.

"Yes, I do," he finally answered. He wanted to believe in her, almost *needed* to.

"She knows things she shouldn't," Seymour said. "You crossed her path before, and Schwenk used that to implicate you as the department leak."

"Schwenk can't prove a thing. He was just trying to substantiate his trumped-up charges. There's nothing there."

"Of course not—on your end. Still, you gave him ammunition," Seymour pointed out. "Don't give him any more. Be careful with her."

"Always the cynic," Daniel said. "You have Sylvia all wrong. She's a woman in over her head, looking for a way out. That's why she decided to keep her eyes open, learn everything she could."

"And she told you what she discovered. Why?"

Daniel didn't inform his father about the brandy, either. "Likes me, I guess."

"That's great! Nice girl—widow of one of the most powerful mob figures of our time—just happens to like my son. Daniel," he said more seriously, "sometimes things appear innocent because we wish them that way. But enough. I made my point."

Daniel breathed a sigh of relief.

"Any conclusions from what Mrs. Luccetta gave you?"

"Well, I think the pictures involved the farmhouse, and Sarchick was the boy."

"Interesting. The abused turns abuser—nothing new there."

"Or Sarchick was Squigger."

"Squigger?" his father blurted out. "Maybe he was the boy, but not Squigger."

"Why not? The whole deal smells of blackmail. Squigger is a better fit."

"Could be lots of reasons why Sarchick wanted

those pictures," Seymour offered. "But he *definitely* wasn't Squigger. Sarchick and Dominic both went to the same university: Van Buren."

"Yes. But I didn't tell you that. How did you—"

"I got Vanderhooven to sneak me a copy of the file on Dominic Luccetta's murder. Spent the day reviewing it," Seymour explained. "Hell of a coincidence."

Daniel thought he heard his father begin to munch on something.

"And your first thought is that Sarchick must have been Squigger. That was the connection."

"Yes," Daniel said, suddenly cagey. "But the fact that Dominic went to Van Buren isn't in the file."

"Old habits," Seymour replied, mouth full. "After all these years they still come back. Whenever I work a murder case I always look at the deceased's obituary."

"His obituary?"

"Like I said—" Seymour swallowed. "Different set of eyes. I take it Mrs. Luccetta didn't mention the year her husband graduated."

"Didn't think to ask," Daniel admitted, a little embarrassed.

"But the obituary did," he said between crunches. "Dominic graduated in '74. Sarchick was still in his teens then."

"Jesus! They couldn't have been in school together. Sarchick didn't attend Van Buren until after military service."

"Exactly."

Annoyed, Daniel listened to his father chomp away feverishly. "You eating corn chips, Dad?"

"Corn chips?" he mumbled. "No."

"Come on. I know you love 'em. I can smell them through the phone."

"Oh, so now my son the detective can smell things

through telephone lines. Well, you're wrong. I'm eating
crackers."

"Crackers, my ass. They're corn chips. And since
you *are* eating corn chips, then Kate must not be home.
Otherwise, she would never permit it."

"Your deductive reasoning is all *farchadat*," Seymour
insisted. "Don't believe me? I'm hurt. Kate's right here.
Want me to put her on?"

"No." Daniel finally surrendered. Then he said,
"Got to hand it to you, Pop—you found out more
through paperwork than I did during an entire afternoon."

"Not true. You discovered things we never knew.
Possibly even the desperate circumstances concerning
Dominic's death. I'd say you've done more than your
share."

"Still, you're amazing."

"You're amazing, too," his father said, loudly crum-
pling a cellophane bag.

Daniel smiled, shook his head at his father's gesture—the clear admission of guilt.

"By the way, Sam called me today," Seymour said.
"Schwenk took him off the Billy Cooper case."

"Who's handling it?"

"No one. He told Sam there are more important
cases right now, to put it aside until he could assign
him a new partner. Sam thinks it's because of the possibility that Cooper was the kid on the bike in the Luccetta murder. And if that were proven, there might be
questions as to whether Cooper was involved with the
killing of those witnesses, too."

"Schwenk's running scared," Daniel commented.

"Can't blame him. Doesn't want reminders of that
fiasco before Monday morning when the chief an-
nounces his successor."

"Think he has a shot?"

"Don't underestimate Schwenk."

"Or politics," Daniel moaned. He took a breath, chose his words carefully. "You and Sam were partners for a long time, right?"

"Why ask what you already know?"

"He ever get jammed up?"

"What do you mean, *jammed up*?" Seymour replied with concern.

"Just a feeling I had. Probably wrong."

"Sam in trouble?"

"Of course not."

"Uh-huh. Well, for sixteen years I've always known Sam to play it straight. That answer your question?"

"Yes. Forget I ever said anything." Daniel sensed his father's irritation with the implication, almost as if he took it personally. He dropped the issue. "So no one's on the Cooper case."

"No. And we're running out of time—your hearing with IAB is on Tuesday. Who knows how many facts Schwenk has twisted. We have to bring something to the table to neutralize that."

"I thought we were looking for Susan's murderer," Daniel reminded him coldly.

"We are. We take what we know, follow it, and see where it leads."

"And you believe it will lead to Susan's killer?"

"In my gut, Daniel. In my gut."

Daniel exhaled sharply into the phone. "Okay."

"Tomorrow, pay a visit to Billy Cooper's mother. Be discreet. Maybe she'll tell you something useful. Then talk to Vanderhooven about the tip he got the morning Susan died. There's someone out there that we still need to find: *our witness*. See if he can remember anything else about the call. Anything at all, no matter how insignificant it may seem."

"Got it." Daniel paused a moment. "Listen, I know I

was wrong about Sarchick being Squigger, but there has to be something in the fact that he and Dominic attended the same school. What was it you said about too many coincidences?"

"Already looking into it," Seymour said. "I'll be at Van Buren tomorrow. I have a ten o'clock appointment with Colin Kirshner, Dean of Students. We'll see if he can enlighten me on Dominic Luccetta, Arthur Sarchick, and that fraternity."

"Kingsman House?"

"Yeah, Kingsman House," Seymour said. "And one more thing I happened to notice. That boy on the bike, Cooper, lived two blocks from where Sarchick grew up. His mother still owns a house there."

"How in hell did you notice that?"

"Familiar neighborhood. Used to work it before homicide. I saw the addresses: Sarchick's, scanning the report; Cooper's, reading the newspaper."

"Christ, is there anything that you miss?" Daniel asked. "Anything that gets by you?"

"Sometimes," Seymour told his son quietly. "Good neighborhood back then. Not much money, but nice. Lots of kids. I imagine it hasn't changed much."

"Playground for a pedophile," Daniel observed.

The phone line was silent for a moment before Seymour said abruptly, "Rest up, we have a lot to do tomorrow. If either one of us strikes a vein, call."

"*Kirshner*, huh. Could be Jewish. Maybe you can dazzle him with your Yiddish?"

"Maybe. But he wouldn't understand. He's a Presbyterian."

"Discover that in an obituary, too?" Daniel kidded.

"No. I simply asked."

59

It was morning, day two of recovery operations. Peter Roberts was to take his turn doing dental comparisons at the temporary morgue five miles west of the crash site. He arrived late, having spent longer than he planned saying good-bye to his wife and daughter on the phone. He wanted them to be safe. He had now seen the fury of an air crash firsthand.

Dr. Heinemann, his therapist—during the time when he thought he needed one—taught him not to impose his anxieties on others. "Dissect them," he had said. "You'll probably discover that your sense of fear is rooted in unrealistic perceptions of imaginary consequences. Don't obsess, Peter. Otherwise, you risk pushing people away."

Peter followed the lesson, and found Heinemann was right. What were the chances of another crash? This one, he knew—although no official announcement had been made—was sabotage. On the hill he overheard a couple of NTSB guys saying just that as they scrutinized broken cable and hydraulic lines from the plane, noting a dark sooty residue at the ends. They became agitated when they realized Peter was so close, practically accused him of spying.

No, after this everyone would be a lot more cautious. There would be extra security. At least for awhile.

In the end, all Peter could do was wish his wife and daughter well on their trip and make small talk, losing track of time while trying to hold on to them.

When he finally did enter the old airplane hangar, he marveled at how it had been transformed into an efficient processing plant for the examination, identification, and disposition of human remains. From his training, he was familiar with the entire operation. Each body bag would make the rounds through a series of stations.

First, general X rays were taken and personal affects logged, along with anything else that might give a clue to the victim's identity.

Next, the pathologists gave their assessment. Any fingers found were rolled for prints by the FBI. If commingling of remains was suspected, an anthropologist was asked to give a determination.

Then, if any dental fragments had been found, the odontologists would chart and x-ray them, delivering a copy of their findings to the comparison section.

Finally, the remains were photographed, then placed in one of the refrigerated trucks for holding until positive identification could be confirmed.

When, and if, identification was made, the morticians took over. They prepared what they could, usually waiting before sending the remains on to their final destination in case more of the same victim was found. Because of the severe fragmentation, there would eventually be one hundred and sixty-seven body bags for ninety-eight passengers.

As Peter searched through the crowded area for the dental comparison section, he spotted Elliot Brandle heading toward him with a glare twisting his unpleasant features. He was wearing a T-shirt that read: *We start when you're finished—Coal County Coroner's Office.*

Peter turned the other way. Out of the corner of his eye he saw Tom Onasis and another pathologist laying the remains of a victim on a metal table for examination. He quickly slid into the empty space next to Onasis, ignoring Brandle.

"Heard you were on the hill yesterday," Onasis said, glancing up at Peter.

"I was there, yes."

The pathologist looked down at the twisted torso in front of them, motioning with his chin. "This was once a human being. They all like that?"

"Mostly."

Onasis sighed. "Did one yesterday: CW-one-eighteen, I think. Just an upper torso. Had a piece of jaw left, too, luckily. Your people ID'd him. Later, another bag came in with a lower half—trousers still on, wallet in the pocket. Same guy. But that half was found in L-East. Nine sections away and across the road." Onasis shook his head. "God, imagine what these people went through before . . . and after impact."

"I try not to," Peter said quietly.

Onasis met his gaze. "You okay?"

"For now."

Nodding, Onasis turned back to the exam table. "You here to do post-exams?"

"No. Comparisons. I was trying to figure out where to go."

"Over there." Onasis pointed to a curtained-off section of the hangar, bending to his task again as Peter headed for his assigned area. Right before he stepped around the curtain, a hand dug into his shoulder from behind, jarring him. He whirled around and found himself face to face with Elliot Brandle.

"I don't like you, Roberts," he said testily.

Peter tried to look puzzled. "What do you mean?"

"Bugs, you son of a bitch," he snapped. "Thought it was cute, huh? You and that fat nigger friend of yours. Do you know how long it took me to get those insects out of my funeral home?"

"Just following protocol."

"I still get flies once in a while," Brandle snarled.

Peter stifled a smile.

But Brandle caught it. "We'll see how long it takes to wipe that smirk off your face. You're on my turf now."

"I thought Ipollito was in charge?"

"Haven't you noticed?" Brandle said, lifting his eyebrows. "You're in Coal County, boy."

"The place where you do things right," Peter mumbled.

Brandle started to stroll away but swung back to face him. "What was that?"

"Tasteful T-shirt, Brandle," Peter said, finally slipping behind the curtain.

The comparison section had more space than the other areas, occupying a good fourth of the hangar. A column of rusty lockers stood close to the curtain; at the far end, a wall of caskets were stacked and waiting. Three long rows of tables were set up between them with passenger names taped down like gruesome place cards, alongside diagrams of their dentition made from records received from hometown dentists.

Phil Polk, a PADIT team member from Erie, was checking names on a list generated from the airplane's manifest. He was the appointed librarian and record-keeper. He sat at one end of the first table in front of cardboard boxes full of charts: antemortem—alphabetized; postmortem—sorted by grid coordinates.

Roberts went over to get briefed.

"We got seven," Polk told him.

"That's all?"

"Hey, it's a start. Pick up a chart and walk the tables. We need the help. Jen is working from a list of computer-generated leads. You can join Linda and Steve doing random scanning."

Random scanning meant roaming among the tables while holding a postmortem chart—a summary of the recovered teeth for a given body bag—playing the possibilities, hunting for a match. It was a tedious process, like doing a giant jigsaw puzzle. When there was a suspected hit, X rays were pulled for a more accurate comparison. Two dentists would have to agree that a match existed within a reasonable degree of certainty before the identification was declared official.

"Brandle been by?" Roberts asked casually.

"Hell, yeah." Polk shook his head. "Told me that each positive must be signed by him where it states who made the ID."

"I thought he'd do something like that."

"He comes by every few minutes, afraid he'll miss his chance. Wants his name where it doesn't belong. I know he's in charge of the morgue, but this operation is a team effort. There's no room for a credit-grabbing egotist like that," Polk declared angrily. "And I'm going to tell Ipollito first chance I get."

"Do that. And Striklon, too. By the way, where is Striklon?"

"Back on the hill with Ipollito. Briefing the green ones. She wants things to go as smoothly as they did yesterday."

"Herb has the experience," Peter said.

"I know. But we could use him here."

Peter glanced over the tables. "Ninety-eight names taped down."

"Ninety-seven," Polk corrected. "FBI scratched one name off—that federal witness. Said they'll do the ID themselves."

"Sarchick?"

Polk shrugged. "I guess. That was the name in the newspaper. But he didn't travel under that name."

"What name did they pull?"

"Let me see." Polk looked at his list. "Stephens. John Stephens. Probably just another alias, though. You have to be careful in the Witness Protection Program. It would have been too risky to use his new identity for the flight. Could have blown his cover."

"Right," Peter agreed. "But if they're doing the identification themselves, then what are they going to compare the dental records to? Without our help they'll have no idea which body bag to look in."

"Already have it."

"What?"

"From a log entry on the hill," Polk explained. "Something about a laundry mark on an undershirt. Heard one of the Feds mention it when they pulled the body bag."

Roberts froze. "I had a body like that," he said slowly. "Section F, Cal . . . Callaway was the name." He pointed to the list. "Got a Callaway?"

Polk looked. "We have a Callahan," he said. "But no Callaway."

"That's it then: Callaway was Sarchick's name in the Witness Protection Program, and he was traveling as John Stephens."

"You sure it wasn't Callahan on that undershirt?"

"Positive. That guy on the hill I found was really Arthur Sarchick." He smiled fancifully—wondering if he would make the news. "You know, I actually ran into him once."

"You did?"

Suddenly Peter blanched, recalling the section of teeth he recovered. "Wait . . . something's wrong. There's been a mistake. A big mistake."

"What do you mean?"

"Is the FBI here?" he asked urgently.

Before Polk could answer, Jen called from across the floor. "We got a match!"

"Confirmed," Steve rang out.

"One second," Polk told Peter. "Name?"

"Purser."

Polk ran a pen down the list as he searched.

Peter waited, trying to calm himself. *Callahan, Callaway—they were awfully close . . .*

"Let's see," Polk murmured. " . . . Pender . . . Pentagast . . . here it is—Purser." He checked it off.

"Pe-Pentagast?" Peter stammered, eyes jerking wide.

"Yeah, Pentagast. LeRoy Pentagast. Why?"

Peter felt himself getting dizzy. "What was the middle initial?" he asked nervously, remembering LeRoy's story. It was a long shot. He held his breath, listening to his heartbeat, waiting for the answer.

Polk wrinkled his brow. "Why?"

"Just tell me," Peter growled.

"M," Polk said, then read: "LeRoy M. Pentagast. He was a sergeant with the Philadelphia police. Took the red-eye from Vegas, connecting with Flight 1089 in Chicago."

Peter's mind went spinning; thoughts about Sarchick evaporated. "Shit!"

The others stopped what they were doing to stare at Peter.

"We already ID'd him," Polk said. "Set of dentures . . ."

Distraught, Peter ran a hand through his hair.

". . . could've been tough to match," Polk continued. "But thank God he had them done in Jersey, rather than here. Jersey law—they had his name in them."

"Shit . . . shit . . . shit." Peter flailed his arms helplessly as he walked over to the lockers. Leaning his forehead against the cool metal, he started kicking them as hard as he could.

Within seconds Elliot Brandle rushed in with one of his deputies in tow. "What the hell is going on here?" he shouted.

Polk held his palms up. "I don't know. I was telling Roberts about one of the passengers and he became upset."

Drawing a harsh breath, Peter turned to give Brandle a penetrating stare. "It was LeRoy Pentagast."

"So?" Brandle said, shrugging.

"*Sergeant* LeRoy Pentagast," he said more loudly. "You signed off on the ID."

Brandle squinted. "What, you knew him or something?"

"Don't you even remember the fat nigger's name?" Peter screamed.

Brandle's jaw dropped. He stood there gaping.

"You bastard," Peter hollered, launching himself at Brandle. "You want me to *bug* you—I'll bug you!"

Polk jumped in between and threw his arms around Peter, holding him back.

Brandle flinched. "You're crazy," he said. "I have no idea what you're talking about." He looked around the room at the others. "No idea at all."

"Shawondasee," Peter replied. "Shawondasee, you fucking bastard."

60

At 10:25, Seymour Pinchus heard Colin Kirshner come over the intercom. He was telling Daphne, his secretary, that he was ready to see Mr. *Puntkis*.

Seymour didn't mind the mispronunciation. Nor did he mind being kept waiting for almost half an hour, having had a delightful conversation with Daphne.

"The dean will see you now," she told him.

"It was nice talking to you," Seymour said as he crossed into the wood-paneled office behind her.

Kirshner stood by his desk, in front of a window that offered a view of the secluded end of campus: There were clumps of trees instead of buildings; a couple of students throwing a Frisbee across the grass. The dean appeared to be in his late forties, with coarse, brown hair, brown eyes, and a lanky, painfully thin build.

"It's a pleasure meeting you, Mr. Puntkis." He arched a hand out in greeting.

"It's *Pinchus*," Seymour said as they shook.

"Oh, really?" the dean asked, wrinkling his brow.

"I should know," Seymour said lightly. He spelled it out: "P-I-N-C-H-U-S. The H is silent and the C sounds more like a K."

"Of course, Mr. Pin . . . chus."

Seymour nodded. "But I prefer Seymour."

"I'm sorry," Kirshner said. "It's been a hectic morning. I was expecting someone from the State Accreditation Committee sometime this month and I thought you were him. They have a Puntkis, but I've never met him."

"Ah. That's why I got an appointment so quickly."

"Yes."

"I didn't mean to mislead you."

Bowing his head in acknowledgement, Kirshner gestured expansively to the chair in front of his desk. "Please, take a seat. The students you inquired about attended Van Buren quite some time ago," the Dean continued.

"Yes, I know—and you still thought I was from accreditation?"

"I'll admit, your request did confuse me."

"And the fact that they've been in the news?"

Kirshner squinted. "You a reporter? Or some kind of detective?"

"A private one, of sorts," Seymour replied.

"Well, these records are confidential. There isn't much I can tell you."

"Tell me what you can."

"Excuse me a moment. Daphne," he called toward the open door. "I almost forgot: Admissions needs that list you were working on by eleven o'clock. Be a dear and run across campus with it."

"Sure," she answered from the front room. "I'll leave right now."

"Thanks." He looked back at Seymour. "Dominic Luccetta graduated in '74. Average student; majored in business. Nothing remarkable on his record, good or bad. But even if there was—"

"I know," Seymour said. "You couldn't tell me."

"Right."

"And Sarchick?"

"Let's see." He picked up a folder. "Attended Van Buren in '79 and '80. Left the beginning of his third year, '81."

"Under what circumstances?"

"Mr. Pinchus, please!"

"He's dead," Seymour pointed out. "In fact both of these men are dead. What harm will it do?"

Kirshner stared at him, heaved a sigh. "Sarchick was expelled."

"For what reason?"

"Doesn't say."

Seymour eyed him doubtfully. "Anything else?"

"Took some engineering courses. He got into Van Buren because of his military service, through an outreach program we had at the time."

"How did that work?" Seymour asked.

"The school had to meet a certain quota of underprivileged students for funding." Kirshner glanced over at the record. "Sarchick qualified because of his early years on the state's assistance rolls. That's what they look for." He aimed a finger at Seymour. "And I really shouldn't be telling you that much."

"Do you see any connection between these individuals?"

"No." Kirshner shifted uncomfortably. "Only what I read in the newspapers."

"What about Kingsman House?"

"Huh?"

"A fraternity you have here, I believe," Seymour said easily.

Kirshner shook his head. "No, you must be mistaken . . . but the name sounds a bit familiar." He gazed up, examining the ceiling tiles with grave intensity. "Let's see, Kingsman House. Yes, I think there used to be a fraternity here by that name. Quite a long time ago, though."

"When Luccetta and Sarchick attended?"

"Possibly. I can check," he offered.

"Thanks. So will I," Seymour declared, watching the pulse in Kirshner's neck.

"Will that be all, Mr. Pinchus?"

"For the moment."

Seymour left the Dean's office looking for a phone. He was disappointed that he didn't see Daphne on his way out. He would have liked to say good-bye, maybe slip her his number. She seemed curious about some of the things he mentioned during their brief chat—a bit more than she should have been. Possibly she would want to talk again.

Seymour found a pay phone on the end of a row next to a message board full of campus news. He got Daniel's answering machine.

"Hi, it's me," he said. "Just came from the Dean of Students at Van Buren. I think I've stumbled onto something. I'm sure he knows more than he's willing to tell. If you're free for dinner, we can discuss it then. Kate's cooking. Hope you like your fish dry." He hung up, staring at the bulletins about student coffees and techno dances and bikes for sale.

A student was looking for change. Suddenly inspired, Seymour gave him a handful and asked where the school library was. The student pointed. It wasn't far, just a couple of buildings down.

At the entrance, he noticed a sign: Students and staff must show university ID. An older gentleman, seventyish with a gray beard, was manning the front desk. The library wasn't very busy. Seymour swaggered past him, eyes scanning the stacks for what he needed, acting as if he belonged.

He reached an information station that said "Ask Ozzie!" above a computer terminal. Seymour stared hesitantly at Ozzie, slowly taking a breath.

"Can I help you, sir?" a man's voice asked from behind him.

Seymour twisted around. It was the guy from the front desk. "Just looking," he answered casually.

"This library is for students and faculty only," the man told him firmly. "May I ask who you are?"

"Of course." Seymour said. "I'm Mr. *Puntkis*—from accreditations."

61

██████ Daniel Pinchus was in Billy Cooper's bedroom. He had no legal right to be there. He had shown his badge to Billy's mother, telling her that his visit was part of the murder investigation. She didn't seem to care much about that, but wanted to know if she was going to get any funds. She heard somewhere that they did that, she said. That they gave you money. Daniel knew she was referring to the Crime Victims Compensation Fund, which reimbursed families for funeral expenses and other things in certain cases. But forms had to be submitted to Harrisburg, he explained. Usually the police didn't get involved. There was, however, an organization that would check to see if you were eligible and help you apply: the Crime Victims Council. He promised he'd look into it.

That seemed to make her happy and she allowed him to question her for a time, but he quickly learned that she couldn't recall anything relevant. She smelled faintly from liquor and Daniel assumed that was the reason she didn't remember much. After a few minutes, he asked to see Billy's bedroom.

The room was like the rest of the house: small, worn, unkempt, dirty. Pushed up against one wall was an old metal cot with flatly strung springs. A naked, beat-up mattress rested on it. Across from the cot stood a plain chest of drawers. A shallow, doorless closet spilled out clothes and shoe boxes full of junk.

Almost intuitively, he headed for the bed and lifted the mattress. There, strapped to the springs, was a spiral notepad. He couldn't believe that someone like Billy still thought you could hide things under your mattress and no one would find them. He shook his head, touched by the childlike innocence of this supposedly streetwise kid.

Snatching the notebook up, Daniel flipped through the pages. It was a diary of sorts, with long gaps between entries. A few of them referred to "Arthur"— always mentioned with a deep sense of regard and a desire to please. Daniel thumbed through it idly, then froze on an entry dated six months ago—the day Susan died:

I did what Arthur told me to do. It was a very bad thing. A terrible thing. Maybe I can stop it before it's too late. It'll make Arthur mad. I hope he's not too disappointed in me.

62

█████████ "It's nice to meet you, Mr. Puntkis." The man introduced himself as Harold Bench and offered his assistance.

Seymour smiled engagingly. Several fraternities had applied to be officially listed with the university, he said. They had to have maintained a presence on campus over the past several years in order to qualify. He needed proof. Fraternity newsletters or the like would be good.

Bench directed Seymour to the basement and told him that *Frat Times* would be helpful. It was a bimonthly put out by the fraternity association, and copies of each issue were bound into volumes and stored in the last aisle.

He looked at Seymour a bit longer than casual interest allowed. "But the library's pretty strict with rules. And I'm only a part-timer here. Accreditations, huh—dean's office know about this?"

"They're familiar with my name."

"Maybe I should check."

"Do that," Seymour said, and slipped quickly downstairs as Bench disappeared.

The basement was empty. Seymour located the volumes that Bench had told him about and soon discovered that they only went back to '85. He searched the shelves, coming across an older periodical. Apparently, *Frat Times* used to be called *Togas, Gabardines and Jeans*. He pulled out a couple of books covering the late sixties through the seventies and carried them to a table between the stacks.

Each issue showed pictures of new fraternity members. Kingsman House was mentioned.

He heard a noise on the stairs. He started turning pages faster. Footsteps were coming toward him.

He found what he was after under *Kingsman House's Newest Faces* in an issue dated October 1970: A young Dominic Luccetta standing with four other inductees, hands clasped and held high above their smiling faces.

He grinned at his discovery even though he knew he was about to get caught—but in the next instant his lips fell open. He gaped in disbelief at the other names listed there: *Congressman* Charles Whitney, *Novelist* Benjamin Caldwell, *Judge* Vernon Malchomoty, and *Dean* Colin Kirshner.

63

Daniel left Billy Cooper's home at a run. He drove directly to Rivington Street Station.

Ironically, he passed Sarchick's mother's house on the way. It looked the same as it had six months ago when they investigated Dominic Luccetta's murder: A run-down two-story with an overgrown yard and an abandoned appearance. This time, however, he thought he noticed a glimmer of light in the basement as he sped by, but on second glance, he saw it was just the sunlight bouncing off the window.

Fifteen minutes later he was at the station house. Bart Miller was leaving on patrol and caught Daniel out front.

"Daniel," Bart said excitedly. "Great seeing you back."

"I'm not back. I'm just visiting," he said, trying to stay calm, desperate to get past the young cop.

"What's your rush?" Bart lowered his eyebrows at Daniel. "Are you okay?"

"I'm fine," Daniel said quickly. He emptied a breath and managed a smile. "Just a little nervous about running into Schwenk. What about you—still impressing babes with that awesome car of yours?"

Bart shook his head. "Need more horsepower."

"The car, or you?"

"Both." He laughed. "But at least I can trade the car in."

"You serious?"

"Only if the bank says so."

"Be careful with your cash flow, Bart," Daniel said, taking a step toward the door.

"Don't worry, they'll let me know before I'm in over my head. Say, when's that hearing of yours?" he asked.

"Tuesday."

"Well, good luck." He gave Daniel a thumbs-up.

"Thanks." Daniel forced himself to walk up the front steps at a reasonable pace. He had expected to find Sergeant Vanderhooven at the front desk. He was not. "Where's Vandy?" he asked the officer filling in.

"Squad room. Getting coffee."

Daniel found Vanderhooven leaving the lunch room with steaming mug in hand. The room behind him was empty, and Daniel motioned for Vanderhooven to step back inside, following on his heels.

"What's up, Danny?" he asked, putting his cup down.

"I want you to play back the call you got the day . . . the day Susan died."

"We've been through that before," Vanderhooven said sympathetically. "I'm sorry, Daniel, there's nothing more I can give you on it."

"Just play it back," Daniel insisted.

"What do you mean, play it back? A lady called and—"

"In your head, Vandy!" he almost shouted. Then again more calmly, "In your head. Concentrate on the voice."

"Okay, sure," he said, making a placating gesture with his hands as he closed his eyes.

Daniel waited until Vanderhooven's eyelids lifted. "You do it?"

"Yes."

"And?"

"Like I said before, a woman called—"

"Could it have been a boy?" Daniel threw out.

Vandy had been sure before. Absolutely positive. But now, Daniel's prompting raised a shadow of a doubt, and Vanderhooven nodded slowly.

64

██████ "You ain't Puntkis from accreditations," Bench announced, standing over him.

Seymour looked up guiltily. "Sorry. You called?"

"Didn't have to. I knew you were lying the moment you fed me that phony excuse."

"And you let me go?"

"Hell, this is a library. What damage could you have done, steal a book? I wanted to see what you were up to. When you're semiretired, you need a little excitement."

"Yeah, tell me about it," Seymour murmured.

"Kingsman House, huh," he said, staring at the page Seymour had opened to. "Could've asked me. I know all the fraternities—their history, the old members. Been here a long time. Taught ethics before they retired me and even used to be a student myself. Still go to most of their games. I guess Van Buren's in my blood."

Seymour sensed an ally. He told Bench the truth about what he was doing there. "Tell me about Kingsman House."

Bench nodded slowly, taking in the gravity of the situation.

"Snooty. Arrogant. Thought they were above the law. A fraternity for the rich and famous, we used to say. All with the university's blessing because of their stellar record."

"Of academic achievement?"

"More important than that. Alumni contributions. Highest in the school."

"So they got away with things."

"Plenty."

"Ever hear of the nicknames Squigger and Fats?"

"Been a while, but yeah, they were sort of a legend."

"Really?"

"Not a good legend," Bench added. "There was a rumor that they picked up this kid and sodomized him. Supposedly brought back pictures to prove it. Most of us didn't believe it. But I wouldn't put it past Kingsman House."

"Who were they?"

"Squigger and Fats? Don't know. Traditionally, all Kingsmen were given a secret name. It was meant to be a source of pride, a special identity known only to you and your brothers. As time went on, Kingsman House changed. The names were more like protection, since they made you do something terrible to get in. Something that could ruin you if it ever got out. It kept them bound to one another. They even had some esoteric vow about remaining silent beyond their final breath. They all had a lot to lose."

"It reads like a list from *Who's Who,*" Seymour said, looking back at the picture.

"Like I said, rich and famous. Each with a nasty skeleton in the closet ready to bite them in the ass. But those horrible deeds weren't only limited to pledging. They were also done as a way of moving up in the fraternity."

"So *any* member could have been Squigger," Seymour said dismally, then brightened a bit. "Remember anyone else from Kingsman House who *fits?*"

Bench's eyes drifted up.

"I'll settle for same time frame," Seymour coaxed.

"Give me a while. I'm sure some possibilities will float back."

Seymour handed him his card. "For when they arrive," he said. "So what happened to Kingsman House?"

"University shut them down; '83, I think."

"Why?"

"Scandal. Kingsman House used to have some pretty wild parties. Well, orgies were more like it. Someone blew the whistle and the campus police raided their frat house. The sixteen-year-old daughter of the then president of the university was found nude in the basement, tied up, spread-eagled. Caught the guy who did it, though."

"They prosecute?"

"Couldn't. President's daughter was a regular at Kingsman House. Didn't want that to come out in court. But Kingsman House was kaput—ordered to disband."

"What happened to the guy?"

"Got expelled," Bench said. He was very still, staring at Seymour. "Artie Sarchick, the same one as in the news."

Seymour let out his breath slowly. Until that moment he hadn't realized he'd been holding it. "It's interesting that an exclusive bunch like Kingsman House allowed Sarchick to join. He was hardly the privileged type."

"They didn't. They let him hang out there only because he did them favors. Like scoring drugs for them when they needed it. He was a campus source."

Seymour arched an eyebrow. "Know that first-hand?"

"Come on, I was a professor back then."

"So?"

Bench smiled. "Anyway, there was a note tacked to the basement door: *Precious is down here, where all precious things should be kept.*"

"He used that word . . . *precious*?" Seymour shuddered.

"Yes. It was a big joke on campus: president's daughter—you know, his little princess. Found Sarchick down there, too. Sitting next to her. He didn't even try to get away."

Seymour now realized why Sarchick had attended Van Buren: to reap revenge against Kingsman House, and against the school's administration that cavalierly allowed them to exist.

"You've been very helpful," Seymour commented. "Wish I could return the favor."

"You could buy me lunch," Bench said without hesitation. "I know where to get the best meal in town. Give an old man some pleasure?"

Seymour patted his pocket. "Expensive?"

"Nah."

Bench led Seymour to a hot dog vendor two blocks from campus. Afterward, he brought him across the street to a Carvel stand for dessert. Bench ordered a vanilla cone; Seymour, a fudge swirl with sprinkles and a cherry.

While they ate their ice cream, Seymour watched Bench, looking for the answer to his last question. "Why did you tell me so much about Kingsman House?"

Bench lifted his napkin and wiped his mouth slowly. Then he said, "Because I hated Kingsman House. Everyone did. Unless you were one of them—smug little rich boys who thought they were God's gift to the world. After all these years, maybe I still feel a need to get even."

Finally, Seymour smiled. "Things must've been different back when you were a Kingsman?" he said quietly.

A long moment passed before Bench returned the smile, nodding. "How did you know?"

"There must be over twenty fraternities on campus. You couldn't possibly have known that much about Kingsman House unless you used to be part of it. And I noticed your eyes glaze over when you mentioned getting even. That's when I knew for sure."

"Being a Kingsman used to be a point of honor, not a disgrace. I despise what they did to it, what it became. But I was powerless to right what was wrong."

"I understand."

"Pretty perceptive," Bench said.

"Old habits." Seymour shrugged. "And I played a hunch. What was your nickname?"

"I can assure you it wasn't Squigger." Bench looked at his watch. "Whoops. Gotta run."

"Wait, you haven't told me your nickname yet."

"Kingsman House secret. I think I've given you enough of those already. Maybe you can pick one."

"Have it your way." Seymour surrendered as his lunch companion turned to leave. "I appreciate the info, Professor Bench."

Bench swung his head around to call over his shoulder. "Thanks for lunch, Seymour *Pinchus*."

65

██████ Polk told Peter Roberts to take a walk and calm down. Then he convinced Brandle, who was threatening to throw Roberts off the rescue operation, not to do anything rash. Everyone was under enormous pressure, and Roberts was obviously grief-stricken over the death of a friend. "Just a little post-traumatic stress syndrome setting in after being on the hill," Polk argued. And besides, it was Ipollito's call anyway.

Brandle finally relented, begrudgingly. He agreed to talk it over with Ipollito. He was afraid of the consequences if he didn't, and aware that he would look better if he played it cool.

Eventually Peter returned, and Polk asked him if he was ready to go back to work. Peter said he was.

"What about Sarchick?" Polk asked. "You mentioned a mistake?"

"I'm not so sure anymore," Peter said unsteadily. "The name I saw on the hill probably was Callahan, not Callaway. Otherwise it would be too bizarre."

Bizarre? Polk didn't press him, just said: "Good."

The next couple of hours passed without incident. Eight more bodies were identified, three by Roberts. One of them, Dellesandro, had also been ID'd through fingerprints. Polk asked Roberts to run the matching charts over to the FBI for confirmation, adding: "Bring back some fresh coffee when you're done."

Roberts found the office just off the entrance to the hangar without a problem: "FBI" had been written on a sheet of loose-leaf paper and taped to the door.

The door was closed. He knocked. No answer. He tried the knob and when it turned, he pushed the door open a crack, positioning his head to peer inside. The room was empty. He saw a desk piled with papers, and decided to leave the charts there. But as he laid the files on the crowded desk, he couldn't help noticing a folder on the top of the stack stamped CLASSIFIED in large red letters. "Arthur Sarchick" was typed on the title tab, and "John Stephens" had been scrawled in pencil near the upper right-hand corner. He glanced back at the doorway—nobody was around. It would only take a second to be sure. He leaned over the desk and fingered the file's cover, flipping it open.

The top page was a fax from the U.S. Marshal's Office. Arthur Sarchick's new identity, it stated, as given to him by the Witness Protection Program, was John Callaway. *Callaway, he was right all along!* He looked back at the door, adrenaline surging, and turned another page: it was the PADIT postmortem dental charting of remains J-W214. There was a Post-It note attached: Remains positively identified as Arthur Sarchick. He quickly flipped again: the next sheet was a copy of the antemortem dental record of John Callaway sent from a dentist in Evanston, Illinois. A full set of dental radiographs was clipped to it.

Roberts bent closer. The two records were a definite

match. *But how could*— Confused, he slipped the X rays out and held them up to the light. *Just as I thought. They got the wrong man!*

"What the hell do you think you're doing?" a voice erupted from the doorway.

Roberts spun around, his gaze resting on a man wearing an FBI jacket and holding a can of Orange Crush.

"Er . . . there's been, um . . . a mistake," Peter stammered. "A huge mistake."

"Only mistake I see, mister, is you being here with your paws on that file," the agent bellowed. "That's federal property!"

Roberts shakily dropped the X rays, trying to explain.

But the agent continued to shout at him.

Priscilla Ipollito, Herb Striklon, and Elliot Brandle appeared at the door. Ipollito and Striklon had just come back from the hill and Brandle had been detailing his complaints about Roberts when they heard the commotion.

"What's going on here?" Ipollito yelled above the noise.

"This man was reading classified documents," the agent told her, raising his voice over Peter's repeated denials.

Brandle tapped Ipollito's shoulder. "See, like I was telling you," he said, pointing at Peter. "He's out of control."

"You don't understand," Roberts said frantically. "They have the wrong man!"

"I've heard enough," Ipollito announced. "Dr. Roberts, your behavior is—"

"At least give him a chance to explain," Striklon interrupted. "I've known Dr. Roberts for years and he must have had a very good reason to—"

"To spy?" the agent cut in.

"To yell profanities at me?" Brandle added.

"I knew Sarchick," Roberts said finally in the sudden silence.

"You knew him?" Ipollito asked, surprised.

"Well, no. I mean I saw him once."

"Say what you mean, Doctor," she said in frustration. "What's this about the wrong guy?"

"Gibberish," Brandle whispered to Ipollito.

"The dental matches okay, but Callaway isn't Sarchick."

"Impossible," the agent roared.

"How do you know?" Ipollito persisted.

"Sarchick smiled at me."

"He what?"

"I told you he was crazy," Brandle said.

"About six months ago he smiled at me, and—"

Ipollito shook her head incredulously. "And that gave you the right to ignore regulations? To come in here and pull out a classified file? You knew that was wrong."

"Yes. But—"

"I'm sorry, Dr. Roberts. I think you may need some help. I want you out of here. Now. I have a major disaster on my hands and I don't have time to entertain your fantasies, or worry about what you might do next."

"Look, if you just let me finish—"

"I said immediately, Doctor!" she snapped. "You're through!"

Ipollito stormed out. Brandle followed, smiling smugly.

Roberts resisted an urge to reach out and snatch the coroner's toupee off.

Striklon stared at his friend, hands spread. "Nothing I can do, Peter," he said. "I warned you about her. Everything by the book, I said."

Roberts shook his head. "It's not your fault."

"Why don't you tell me what this is all about?"

The FBI agent was still seething, putting the file back together behind them. Roberts glanced at him quickly, then said, "What can I say, Herb? I fucked up. I want to go home, think things over for a while. Better get to comparison. They need you there."

Peter Roberts left the room, unsure what he had stumbled onto. Maybe Diane's uncle, the great Seymour Pinchus, would have some answers. He crossed the airplane hangar and strolled out into the sunlight, feeling alone and broken.

66

Dinner was fabulous, they all agreed. Kate and Daniel had pan-fried trout with cream dill sauce, saffron rice, and asparagus prepared with a touch of apple and cinnamon. Seymour had the same, except his fish was broiled with a little lemon and without the sauce— even though he would have rather have had it the other way—but he still extolled the excellence of Kate's culinary skill almost as loudly as Daniel.

"Isn't it better eating well-balanced, healthy meals," Kate said to Seymour, "like you've been doing lately, instead of what you used to put into your mouth without thinking?"

"Yes," Seymour agreed. "You've shown me the virtues of that."

He glanced toward Daniel—who had been expressionless and preoccupied all through dinner—inviting a rhetorical jab. There wasn't one.

"Take lunch, for instance," Seymour continued in the purest tone of voice he could summon. "I had a little dairy, a portion of vegetables served over a few ounces of protein, and some carbohydrates. Something from all the major food groups."

Still nothing.

"How was it, dear?" Kate asked as she cleared the table.

"Just okay." He shrugged. "But I forced it down anyway."

"You know, I should really give you more credit than I do," she said. "You buy low-fat this and fat-free that. The fridge is full of it. You've chosen to sacrifice. I can't swear to it—I'm not with you all the time—but I can see you're making an effort. So . . ."

Seymour looked at Daniel for a reaction: His face was still blank.

". . . wait 'til you see what I've got for dessert." She turned to the table.

"Apple pie and cheddar cheese," Seymour gasped in disbelief. "Real apple pie. Real cheddar cheese." It was his absolute favorite.

"A reward," Kate declared. "For trying so hard."

Daniel finally seemed to pay attention to what was going on in the room. His weakness for apple pie and cheese was almost as great as his father's.

"But only one piece. And Daniel gets to take the rest home."

"Deal," Seymour said.

"Ditto," Daniel said.

"Since I don't necessarily approve of what you two

are about to talk about, and therefore choose not to listen," she added, "why don't you take this into the den while I clean up?"

In the den, they put their desserts on a coffee table. Daniel sat on the couch. The room was small, with a fireplace, a picture window inviting the forest in, and a namda rug on the floor. A set of pocket doors guarded the entrance. Seymour drew them shut, then took a seat across from Daniel in a channel-back chair.

"Thanks for coming, Daniel," he said, pointing with his fork to the mound of apple filling and crust, supporting a slab of cheddar cheese. "If you weren't here, I never would have gotten this. Now, tell me what's wrong."

"What do you mean?"

"Kate and I had a wonderful dinner together . . . alone. You found out who killed Susan."

"Yes," Daniel said, surprised. "But I didn't think I left that in my message. How did you—"

"Vanderhooven told Sam about your conversation when he got back. Sam called me." Seymour paused, looking at his son. "And now you feel cheated. Because Sarchick's dead. Because you think it's over."

Daniel's head drooped.

"Let me tell you something, Daniel: This is far from over. Even if Sarchick had that bomb placed, and I have my doubts about that—scrawlings in a kid's notebook don't exactly amount to proof—there's more to this case. There's got to be a reason. Where's the why?"

Daniel smacked the coffee table with a fist, making the plates jump. "I don't know. That's what's been bothering me."

"There's a lot to be bothered with. Billy Cooper's dead. There's the puzzle of the note and Dominic's death. And the tale of a bizarre fraternity, its members each bound to secrecy through their deplorable acts. You got my messages, didn't you?"

Daniel nodded.

Seymour took a forkful of pie. "Did you have any trouble with Mrs. Cooper?"

Daniel sighed. "She was more interested in getting money from the Crime Victims Compensation Fund than she was in talking to me."

"She let you see Billy's room?"

"Yeah, I just showed her my badge, and—"

"Daniel!" his father shouted, pie crumbs falling from his lips. "You showed her your badge like you were on a routine call?"

"Still had it. Never turned it in."

"But you're suspended. Of all the stupid—"

"Hey, it got the job done," Daniel threw back.

"—idiotic stunts. I warned you: Don't give Schwenk any more ammunition!"

"He'll never find out."

"Don't bet on it," Seymour fumed.

"Vanderhooven is checking to see if Mrs. Cooper is eligible for any dough, and he'll take care of calling her. Relax, Dad." He smiled. "I know what I'm doing. I can read people."

"Well, you didn't a little while ago in the kitchen."

"Who, Kate?"

"Her complimenting me; this pie. She's trying to make me feel guilty because she suspects I'm cheating on my diet. But it won't work, because I'm not."

Daniel's mouth was full, but his expression nearly shouted his disbelief.

"Okay, maybe once or twice," he admitted sheepishly. "But all that stuff I bought should even out the damage."

"She's borrowing a page out of your book—employing the powers of a guilty mind."

"Pie still tastes good," Seymour said innocently, then took another bite. "It's an excellent tactic, though. Used it on Kirshner this morning. We'll see where it leads. I think hearing the name Luccetta on the phone shook him. He got curious. When we met, he purposely got my name wrong and mentioned some bull-shit about an accreditation committee as the reason for giving me the appointment. He wanted to throw me off track, as if he had no idea why I was there. And as an added touch, he left the door open, trying to appear unconcerned about his secretary overhearing what we might talk about." Seymour finished his pie, put his plate down. "But when he realized where my questions were leading, he nonchalantly sent her on an errand."

"Afraid now of what she might hear?"

"Right. I also noticed that when I asked him about Dominic, he didn't glance at his records once. But with Sarchick, he had to read from them."

"So you knew he was lying about not knowing Dominic."

Seymour nodded. "Mannerisms—they can tell you a lot if you're looking. Can even reveal the very essence of what you're trying to hide."

"You think he's Squigger?" Daniel asked sharply.

"Good possibility. But we can't rule out our other esteemed suspects."

"I can't believe Congressman Whitney would be in-volved. I saw him last night on TV at a candlelight vigil for the air crash victims. He was standing with Newt Harting's parents."

"Did you know Whitney was a young assistant DA in Harrisburg before he took that same position in Hamilton?"

"How did you come by that?"

"I worked with him on a few cases. He was a good prosecutor."

"So?"

"So, you and I know that several years ago Sarchick was arrested for molestation over there. Guess who prosecuted him and sent him to jail?"

Daniel's jaw slowly fell open.

Seymour smiled. "I'll find out more tomorrow morning. I have a meeting set up with him."

"The busy, image-conscious congressman granted you an audience?"

Seymour shrugged. "Like I said, we go back a long way."

"Wait a minute," Daniel said suddenly. "It always concerned me how Sarchick got into the Witness Protection Program so easily. What if Whitney was pushing for it?"

"And the program is run by the Justice Department's Office of Enforcement Operations," Seymour added. "Whitney, if I recall correctly, is on a special judicial subcommittee in Congress—and was using his influence to keep his campaign promise about cracking down on crime. Now, I wonder just how much influence he has."

"Could he single-handedly get someone into the program? For his own hidden reasons?"

"I don't know if that's possible. I think he would need a federal prosecutor to go along."

"What about Caldwell and Malchomoty?" Daniel asked.

"I have Oscar helping me with them. You remember Oscar, don't you?"

"Oscar Finch? Of course: news photographer extraordinaire; retired about the same time you did. I was happy to learn you had a playmate."

Seymour gave his son an affected look. "Well," he said, lingering on the word, "Oscar thinks he can get a lot of info from the *Hamilton Press*. Says they have a computer there with the capability to compile news articles from the last several years. Punch a keyword in, or a name, and you got your list."

"Welcome to the nineties, Dad."

"Oscar and I are going to make dossiers. All of these men have been in the news. But first, Oscar is going to see Benjamin Caldwell. Knows him from a piece he once did for the Leisure section. Caldwell was very concerned about how he looked. Wanted Oscar to scoot over with the proofs before they were printed. Coincidentally, Caldwell is going to be in town Saturday to do a signing for his latest novel, but Oscar visiting him will be more discreet, more likely to get some information."

"I understand. But does Oscar know *what*, and *how* to ask?"

"He's covered enough crime stories to know. He also tells me Caldwell's books are quite over the top. He thought I should take a look and dropped off a few for when I get the chance. Anyway, I'm meeting Oscar Saturday morning in the newsroom, right after we brief each other during our workout at the gym."

"Workout?" Daniel asked giddily.

"Yes! Our fitness program. Oscar and I started last month. We try to go three times a week. You got a problem with that?"

The image of his father in a tank top and Spandex shorts stretching at the seams made Daniel want to snicker unmercifully. He swallowed hard, trying to crush it. "No. No problem at all," he forced out. "Glad to see you're making an effort."

Seymour ignored his son's patronizing remark. "We know Squigger was a member of Kingsman House," he continued. "And that the name Squigger was only a nickname. Nicknames are usually derived from some quality a person has—could be physical, could be personal. Fats obviously fit."

"Squigger. *Squiggle*," Daniel muttered. "Like a doodle. Or a line."

"One that's bent over," Seymour offered.

"Doesn't Judge Malchomoty walk with a stoop?"

"Could be from an accident. Maybe arthritis. Might have occurred after college."

"But we don't know for sure," Daniel said.

"Agreed."

The vision of his father standing in athletic shorts flashed into Daniel's mind, focusing on the knees. "What if Squigger means knobby—you know, sort of bony."

"So thin that your bones protrude?" Seymour clarified.

"Gives a nice *squiggly* appearance."

Seymour pondered it. "Hhmm, Kirshner was like that. Very much so."

"Caldwell's also skinny," Daniel noted. "Whitney isn't, though."

"You couldn't tell from the college picture, but maybe he used to be and he's put on a few pounds since," Seymour suggested, then quickly waved a finger at his son. "And be awfully careful with your next comment."

Daniel was kind, only smiling politely. "Anyway, we're just speculating," he said to his father.

"Right. And Squigger may mean something entirely different. Something we're not privy to. Could have fit any one of them."

The phone rang. Seymour snatched the receiver off a side table before the second ring.

"Hello . . . Oh, Tom . . . I see . . . Uh-huh. Well, if you find out anything else, let me know. Thanks for calling." Seymour hung up the phone slowly.

"Onasis?"

Seymour nodded. "Calling from his hotel room. I didn't want to say anything until I knew more. Peter was thrown off the recovery team."

"What?"

"Peter called me when he got back. He was extremely upset. The Feds did a dental ID on Sarchick's remains, but Peter insists they're wrong. Said something screwy's going on. He sounded desperate. Nobody would listen to him." Seymour shook his head, relating the specifics of Peter's dismissal to his son.

"But if Peter is right—" Daniel began.

"Then someone else was on that plane," Seymour jumped in. "Someone whose records were swapped for Sarchick's."

"Is that possible?" Daniel asked, mind racing. "Sarchick alive!"

"An intriguing . . . yet horrifying thought. It's unlikely." His father cocked his head. "At first, I believed Peter. I became excited, thought he might have stumbled onto some incredible plot."

"I've never known Peter to panic or imagine things," said Daniel defensively. "What made you change your mind?"

"Let's just say I have my doubts. Remember, Peter's allegation is based solely on his *recollection* of Sarchick's mouth. And he met Sarchick only once. On the day you arrested him."

"I recall. Peter acted a little weird."

"Claims Sarchick smiled at him. That's when he noticed the space between Sarchick's upper front teeth, and the caps."

"A space? I never saw anything like that. But maybe dentists *notice* teeth."

"And Peter carried that around with him for six months?" Seymour asked skeptically.

"A picture could prove it. At least that Sarchick had spaces."

"Didn't find any mug shots with him smiling," Seymour replied.

"So we don't have anything solid," Daniel said. "But if a switch *was* made, it had to be done recently. What about checking Sarchick's dental records from an older source? He was in the service."

Seymour frowned. "It's doubtful they would keep his dental records this long. And even if they did, do you know what kind of authorization we would need?"

"What about dental work while he was in prison?" Daniel continued.

"Assuming he had any done there, same problem."

"The FBI could look into it."

"But probably wouldn't," Seymour said. "They're convinced Peter's nuts. And Peter practically accused them of a cover-up. Gave a brief interview to a local radio station as he was leaving. Announced that Arthur Sarchick wasn't on that plane, and wanted to know what the FBI was up to."

"I wouldn't put anything past the FBI," Daniel commented.

"But Peter never told me about the interview. Onasis did," Seymour said, annoyed. "The station gave it lots of play. Their affiliates picked it up. It's all over the place. I heard a broadcast just a short while ago."

"How'd it sound?"

"Not good. Peter was pretty distraught after being kicked off the recovery operations. He sounded nervous, out of sorts. They asked him if he knew where Arthur Sarchick was now."

"A reasonable question."

"When Peter didn't answer," Seymour said, his eyes fixed on his son. "They asked him if he knew where Jimmy Hoffa was."

"Shit," Daniel said. "There goes his credibility."

"And everything the FBI claims seems to check out." Seymour sighed. "I spoke to a friend of mine, a federal marshal. Given the circumstances, and the fact that Sarchick is presumed dead, he said he'd look into the matter. He owes me a few favors. Big ones."

"Is there anyone who doesn't?"

Seymour managed a brief smile. "He got back to me. Swears the dental record is authentic. It came from a dentist in Evanston, Illinois. A city near Chicago."

"So?"

"Evanston is where Sarchick was relocated. He had work done there a couple of months ago. The Witness Protection Program has been getting bad press of late. They're trying to tighten things up. Sarchick was printed three weeks ago—part of a new security sweep. Prints matched." Seymour gave Daniel a hard stare. "Same ones we have on file right here in Hamilton from his arrest."

Daniel sucked in air, blew it out against his cheeks. "No wonder the FBI is convinced Peter's nuts."

"Yeah, and there's more." Seymour leaned forward in his chair and told his son the rest, about Onasis seeing Peter so unsettled in the morning, about the scene that followed in the morgue. There was also a report that Peter was eavesdropping on a conversation some NTSB officials were having on the hill the previous day.

"Jesus. I wouldn't believe the guy, either," Daniel admitted, shaking his head.

"Tom Onasis thinks Peter's suffering from post-traumatic stress disorder. He's seen it before—the delusions, the paranoia. But then, I thought about the prints again. The remains—just one finger would nail it down one way or another."

"And?"

"That was Onasis getting back to me. The upper torso had no arms."

"So we can't prove that the Feds were wrong," Daniel noted.

"But, so far, no print of any recovered hand or finger matches Sarchick, either."

"So, the possibility . . ." Daniel said, turning his palms up.

"Has to be considered," Seymour finished.

"What did you tell Peter?"

"He sounded tired, confused. I pointed out that he'd been through a lot. That post-traumatic stress disorder is nothing to be ashamed of and that he might give the psychiatrist he used a few years ago a call."

"A psychiatrist?"

"Midlife crisis," Seymour confided.

Daniel's eyes narrowed. "What did Peter say?"

"That he didn't need a bleeping psychiatrist. He was certain of what he saw. Wanted to get some rest and pursue things in the morning—and tell anyone who would listen. I told him he needed proof first and suggested he should try locating dental records from the private sector. Kirshner mentioned that Sarchick was on public assistance. It's a start. He'll need help, though," Seymour said, aiming an eyebrow at Daniel.

"I'll give him a call in the morning," Daniel surrendered. "We might even try Sarchick's mother for the dental. That is, if I catch her in."

"Worth a shot."

"I thought you didn't believe Peter?" Daniel reminded him.

"Neither did you, a moment ago. But still . . ." Seymour's gaze clouded.

"What if Peter is right?"

"Then we've got a problem."

"Not only is he a pedophile, and an assassin, but

he's a mass murderer as well," Daniel said, footage from the plane crash replaying in his mind.

"Let's not get ahead of ourselves," Seymour cautioned. "But it's imperative that we find out who Squigger is—fast. If Sarchick is alive, Squigger could be in danger."

"I'm not so sure about that. Sarchick spent a lot of time planning Dominic's murder," Daniel said. "Why did he leave Squigger alone? He must have had plenty of opportunities to get him."

"Point," Seymour said. "Finish the thought."

"He's worth more to Sarchick alive. Maybe Sarchick needs his help to carry this out."

"Blackmail?"

"Possibly. Or maybe he had the same desires as Sarchick. Ever wonder about the kind of person who would rape a young boy? Dominic was simply a brutal, violent, unprincipled individual. Squigger might have been different."

"Another pedophile?" Seymour asked, sounding doubtful. "Interesting theory. A stretch, yet interesting nonetheless. But dead or alive, Sarchick's somehow involved in every tangled knot we've come to in this case: Susan's death, the missing witnesses, the Luccettas, Billy Cooper, and Flight 1089."

"The farmhouse, Van Buren University, and Kingsman House," Daniel added. "Sarchick keeps cropping up."

"Like a nasty weed."

"With a twisted root," Daniel added.

"No," Seymour said, after considering it for a moment. "A root of deception."

PART 3

67

He sat alone listening to the radio as a fly buzzed through the air. He was waiting for more news about the air crash, wondering about his companion, Merle Oakley.

He had searched hard for someone like Oakley, through the streets and rescue missions, finally found him in a soup kitchen on the north side of Chicago— same height as himself, same general appearance. A trusting fellow with a simple mind. Perfect.

He had taken care of Oakley, gave him a place to stay, clothed and fed him. He even sent Oakley to the doctors for medical attention. Oakley had never been a subject of his dark desires, rather he was an essential part of the plan. Poor Oakley, it would be a long time before he was missed—if ever.

Suddenly, he heard something new from the stream of radio voices. It was an interview with local dentist Peter Roberts at the crash site. There was talk of mis-

taken identity, that Arthur Sarchick was still alive. It
upset him. He saw everything being ruined.

But it didn't seem as if they believed Roberts. And
Roberts had already been dismissed from recovery operations. That was good. Still, he couldn't afford the
liability.

He reached for the phone book, found Roberts's
address. A wave of calm eased the frown from his face.
Sarchick was dead. One more push would erase all
doubts . . .

The fly lit in front of him. Sarchick smashed it
against the table with his hand, grinding it slowly under his palm.

After all, they were already *nearly* convinced that
Roberts was crazy.

68

████████ Peter wished Diane would call, but knew that
she wouldn't. He was still supposed to be on the hill.
He could try a ship-to-shore connection, but then he
realized it was better this way, with her not knowing.
Why ruin the cruise with a story of how he had been
dismissed, disgracefully, from recovery operations?

He was in the kitchen. The family cat brushed up
against him, meowing loudly. Peter noticed that her
dish was empty.

"Snow Ball," he said reproachfully. "You finished all
the food they left you already?"

"Meeoow," went Snow Ball.

"Oh, well, boredom can do that to you." He headed to the pantry to get more cat kibble, his thoughts roaming back to the hill, to the undershirt marked Callaway, then jumping to the events of that morning. Peter wondered if the incident would make the *Hamilton Press.* Diane had told him before she left that he was already in the paper: AREA DENTIST TRAVELS TO CRASH SITE TO IDENTIFY THE DEAD. At that time, he had been ecstatic over the publicity—but of course, he hadn't said so. Now, he shuddered at visions of tomorrow morning's headlines: DR. PETER ROBERTS BUCKLES UNDER THE STRESS; HAUNTED DENTIST MAKES WILD ACCUSATIONS; ROBERTS EXPELLED FROM CRASH SITE AFTER SPYING ON SECRET FBI FILES.

And he had spoken with the media up in Coal County. It was something he had felt he had to do, needed to do. But it was foolish. It only made matters worse.

He shook his head. *Maybe the* Hamilton Press *won't pick up the story?* Then he recalled that they had reported a traffic violation he had gotten last year, when he went through a stop sign. *Jesus, you call that news? They think they're big-city, but they have a small-town mentality.*

Peter wished it would all go away. Seymour said that he would need proof. He would risk almost anything to salvage his reputation now. A reputation he was certain would otherwise be headed for ruin.

His thoughts were interrupted when he heard a noise outside, close to the house. He went to the back door, opened it a crack, and poked his head out to look. Nothing, just a cool breeze and the darkness. He returned to the kitchen, but a few minutes later he heard something again. This time he slipped his jacket on and went out to search. Again finding nothing amiss, he went back inside.

Before he could get his jacket off, Snow Ball bolted

past him into the living room. He heard the cat hiss violently and he followed her quickly. She had her head ducked under a window shade, facing the night outside.

"What is it? What's the matter, girl?" he asked, peeling the shade up and away from the window.

His stomach tightened, his breath catching in his throat. He blinked, certain that he must be imagining the sight, then quivered with the knowledge that he wasn't. On the other side of the pane of glass was a face, a beam of light illuminating it from below.

"What the hell. . . ?" It was Arthur Sarchick smiling at him again, showing off his teeth.

69

Daniel Pinchus headed home. He boxed up what was left of the cheese and pie as his father watched helplessly, swearing he would absolutely visit his son in the not too distant future.

Now, alone in his car, Daniel again considered the possibility that Peter was right, that Sarchick was alive. The thought was unnerving. It would mean that Sarchick was even more diabolical and deceptive than anyone had imagined. Daniel decided to follow one of his father's lessons again and leaned against the seat, trying to get inside Sarchick's mind.

He started with pedophilia. What was repulsive and alien to him was the motivating force in Sarchick's life.

His experience was limited, having worked only one prior case involving a pedophile: Timothy Wallace.

Wallace was hanging out in a game room looking for victims. He finally found one—young, willing. Later, they met up with a friend, Raymond Boyle, another pedophile. He invited him to come along, but only to watch. After Wallace sodomized the boy, Boyle wanted his turn, but Wallace wouldn't share his prize. Boyle insisted. A fight ensued, with Wallace angrily pushing his friend. Boyle fell, hit his head on the hard cement, fractured his skull, and died. That made it homicide.

Daniel knew certain things about pedophiles from his training. Many come from broken homes, and are often victims of sexual abuse themselves. They tend to be smart, cunning, and deceptive. Sometimes a traumatic event in their life pushes them over the edge, causing them to act on their darkest desires. *The farmhouse.*

They hunt for children in need of attention—vulnerable, not unlike themselves—in parks, schoolyards, and shopping malls. They walk among us, undiscerned, as grandfathers, coaches, ministers, and friendly neighbors—not as the horrendous monsters that our eyes would expect. And it occurs far more frequently than we know about, or have the courage to suspect. Often, they return to old haunts, feeling safe and comfortable in familiar surroundings. They like to be in control, that's the key, wielding such power over their helpless young victims that it keeps these children coming back, keeps them silent. *Billy Cooper.*

This was the ugliness Daniel tried to touch, tried to get inside of. What he didn't realize was that he could barely scratch the surface of the depravity.

A Mobil station loomed up ahead. Daniel stopped for gas and decided to give Peter a call. He thought Peter might take comfort in knowing that he would help him work all of this out. He wanted to tell him now rather than waiting until morning.

He dialed the number, let it ring. There was no answer. His father had said Peter would be home, that he needed some rest after his ordeal at the crash site. Thinking he might have misdialed, Daniel hung up and tried again. This time he let it ring until the answering machine picked up.

It was Melanie's voice: *"Hi. We're not home right now, but if you leave . . ."*

"Peter, it's Daniel. If you're there, answer the phone. We need to talk. Peter . . . Peter . . . hello . . ." He waited for the final beep, then called back and left a message saying he was on his way over.

Daniel got back into his car. He was no longer thinking of Sarchick. Now he only wondered, nervously, just how depressed, or maybe even deranged, Peter might have been.

70

▮▮▮▮ Peter remained paralyzed by the phantasmagoric image on the other side of the glass for several moments. Then he began to fathom its true meaning: Arthur Sarchick was alive; Peter was right all along; and—a wild, impulsive thought—lurking just beyond that window was vindication. He saw only that, not the why or the how. Like the tide rushing out to sea, so went his fear, and he chose, recklessly, to embrace the opportunity.

Darting from the house, Peter spotted Sarchick racing down the street and took off after him, leaving the front door unlatched. He chased him to the end of the block, running faster than he had ever run before. Straining to take longer strides, focusing on his breath, he quickly made up ground.

At the intersection, a startled man walking his dog frantically tried to get out of the way. The pooch yelped violently as the leash yanked it's neck. Peter stumbled to miss them, losing a few steps as he followed Sarchick around the corner.

His lungs burned, his knees and muscles ached, but the thought of this bastard slipping away made Peter push even harder. Air rushed back into his lungs before he could expel the last breath. Another half a block, and a severe pain jolted him below the sternum. It felt as if his rib cage were about to tear loose.

It would have been easy for him to quit just then, and Peter wished he could, but Sarchick was only a few feet ahead now. His heart pounded. He imagined it exploding, sending him tumbling to the pavement, dead. It would happen any moment, he was sure, yet . . . *Just barely out of reach. Proof.*

Sensing how close Peter was, Sarchick veered to the side, hopped a short stone wall approaching an overpass, and slid down the embankment to some railroad tracks.

The shift caught Peter by surprise. He attempted to follow, but awkwardly tripped over the barrier and tumbled to the base of the hill. He regained his footing, saw Sarchick running toward the tracks, and continued the chase—just ahead of him, a murderer; off in the distance, the shriek of a freight train's whistle.

Sarchick crossed the first rail and glanced back, tongue hanging out, eyes staring in disbelief. The toe of his right shoe caught under the curve of the second rail. He stumbled over it, nearly falling down.

Roberts, close behind, dove to knock him completely over. Their bodies crumpled to the ground together, then spilled apart. He scrambled to his feet to face Sarchick.

And the fear rushed back. *What the hell was he doing? Battling a murderer to save his reputation? Trying to be a hero? He was no hero—he was a fucking dentist, for Christ's sake!*

Sarchick, a few inches shorter than Peter, took advantage of Peter's hesitation but missed badly with his left as Peter ducked under it. Peter sprang back up, hands clasped in an upper cut that caught Sarchick in the abdomen. A breath whooshed from Sarchick's lips. He doubled over and something fell from his jacket. There was a glint of metal in the darkness. The train's whistle got louder.

Peter dove for the metal object, thinking it was a gun, but noticed too late it was only a flashlight. Sarchick kicked him in the ribs and sent him hurtling to the ground sideways, his head painfully glancing off one of the metal rails. He was stunned. Sarchick leapt on top of him before he could recover, grabbing him by the shirt.

The train was much closer now, clearly visible to both of them.

"Why?" Peter screamed. "You fucking bastard, why?"

"Because I was dead. It was perfect. I knew you would never leave it alone, you meddling prick. And like a fool you came after me. Now it's your turn to die!" Sarchick laughed, mouth open wide, head cocked back.

That's when Peter saw it, clearly in the light of the moon: Behind Sarchick's two upper front teeth there was a small metal bar in the shape of a U. *The caps . . . the space . . . the bar. It was a bridge! A telephone bridge. A bridge like the one Hitler had.*

Sarchick lifted him up like a rag doll, only to smash him back down against the rail . . . and then again.

Peter, woozy now, could feel the ground beginning to vibrate. The implication of that penetrated his clouded mind: They were on the same track as the approaching freight train. Hopelessly pinned, he struggled for freedom.

"Next time we meet will be in hell," Sarchick hissed. "But don't worry about the wife and kiddies, I'll take care of them for you." He reached back and pulled out a set of handcuffs, slapping one end to Peter's right wrist.

The train lumbered toward them, whistle bellowing.

"Die, you dirty motherfucker," Sarchick spit, eyeing a steel loop buried in the center of the track between two railway ties, a short distance away.

Peter strained to keep his right arm over his head, pulling the cuff out of range. Sarchick could have ended things more simply—by crushing the cartilage in Peter's neck, by savagely shattering his skull against the rail—but that wasn't Sarchick's style. *This* was. And he would do it with morbid panache.

The tracks shook. Sarchick tried to pull the free end of the cuffs toward the loop.

Peter resisted with whatever strength he had left, his thoughts on Diane and the kids. If Sarchick attached the cuffs, Peter was doomed. Then it occurred to him: Sarchick would have to climb off him at some point. With his wrist chained, he could still stretch his body out off the tracks. He would suffer a severed arm, but Peter was willing to accept that terrible consequence in exchange for his life. He waited for his chance.

The train was barreling down. The cuff touched the loop. Peter's arm shook, bent against the force, veins popping. The engine was so close. The noise; the smell of diesel consumed him.

Sarchick, still trying to make the connection that would destroy Peter, waited until the last possible second to save himself. He finally jumped off only after he was certain there was no time for Roberts to avoid being crushed.

But Peter pushed against one of the rails with his leg and rolled off the tracks in the opposite direction as soon as Sarchick's weight lifted. The front of the train slammed against the dangling cuff that trailed behind his body, making a loud clang and delivering a painful jolt to his arm.

As the freight train went by, the gentle breeze from it was like a pronouncement of life. He couldn't stop shaking. He checked himself: fat lip, bruised knees, possible concussion, lacerated scalp. But for the moment, he was safe. Sarchick was trapped on the other side of the tracks; between them there were fifty or more boxcars. And until that moment, Peter was unaware that he had wet his pants during the ordeal. He was mortified.

He could see the last car in the distance, hurtling closer. *What if Sarchick was still there after the train passed, waiting for him?* The side he was on had a hill too steep to climb. Peter stood, frozen by fear, certain that his reprieve from death was a brief one. But when the train disappeared, there was no sign of Sarchick. He scanned the ground on the opposite side of the tracks. Nobody, not a soul. He wanted to run, but hadn't the strength, and instead, he started to limp his way home.

He tugged at the cuffs, used the sleeve of his jacket

to hold them steady as he pulled against them, but couldn't slide them off. He wet them with his mouth, tried again. Only then, with great despair, did he realize what he might have erased. He was sick with himself, and let the cuffs dangle as he moved on, kicking at the ground.

Before he had gone far, he remembered the flashlight: *Sarchick's prints. There could still be proof.* He followed the edge of the rail back, searching—but found nothing. He heaved a sigh, turning back toward the house once again.

There weren't many people out, though there were enough to make him feel safe. He thought about asking a stranger for help, then considered how he must look: dirty, disheveled, bloody. So he stuffed his cuffed hand into his jacket pocket, carefully dragging the chain and other end along, and kept his head down as he walked.

It seemed like an eternity, but he finally arrived at his front door. He recalled leaving it open, pushed against it, and stepped inside.

He was searching for the light when he realized he wasn't alone.

71

From upstairs, Kate heard Daniel leave. She waited for Seymour to come up, passing the time reading in bed. After a half hour she gave up, knowing he wouldn't be along anytime soon.

She had grown accustomed to these occasions,

when things bothered him and he needed to work them through. Seymour would sit in the den with the lights off, sometimes for hours. He claimed that he saw things more clearly that way, in the dark, better than most see in the light. And she never doubted it, knowing from before—although it had been a while—that he would run events over and over again in his mind until every detail was noted, until the obscure became obvious.

But there was a difference this time, and it went beyond the personal importance of solving Susan's murder. He was running with the wind again—hair blowing in the breeze, face flushed with color. Still, she wasn't so sure this was a good thing.

She had a fleeting picture of wild horses led by a large gray stallion. She smiled, then shut the light off and went to sleep.

72

Peter jumped back, his throat too dry to scream. He got a glimpse of a shadowy figure, threw a leg at it, aiming for the groin.

He saw the figure buckle.

"Shit, Peter! Why the hell did you do that?" a familiar voice screeched.

"Daniel? Is that you?" Peter asked, his pupils adjusting to the dim light.

"Yeah," he moaned.

"You okay?"

"I'll live," he forced out, still bent. "I came over because I was worried about you. Found the door open. Called your name a couple of times, but there was no answer. So I went in. I didn't know what to think."

"Jeez, I'm sorry, Daniel. I was scared shitless. I thought you were someone else."

"Like who—Genghis Khan?"

"No. Sarchick."

"Peter." Daniel shook his head and began to straighten. "We have to talk."

Peter hit the hall switch.

Daniel stood erect now, his eyes finally resting on Peter in the light. "My God," he said. "What the hell happened to you?"

Peter was filthy, disheveled. His lower lip looked like a purple balloon. His right hand was tucked tightly into his jacket pocket. The jacket was covered with splotches of blood, and his hair was matted with it.

"It was Sarchick," he said excitedly. "In the window, lit up like a pumpkin. And alive! I thought he was trying to break into the house. But it turned out he was only trying to scare me. He smiled at me again. You see, I was right all along. But nobody would listen. Now they will. They have to."

"Okay. Tell me about it," Daniel said gently, trying to get Peter to sit down.

"I should've called the police. Chased him instead, down to the railroad tracks. We fought. And then I saw it." Peter paused, gulping for breath.

"Easy, Peter. What did you see?"

"When he laughed, opening his mouth wide. There it was, a metal U behind his teeth—a Hitler bridge."

"Hitler?"

"Well, they don't really call it that. I do, though.

Ever since I saw it in the *Forensic Dental Journal*. An article about Hitler's dentition. But I definitely saw it."

"Uh-huh," Daniel said.

Peter shouted. "Don't you get it? It's a link to Billy Cooper's murder, and another boy found a while ago in Harrisburg—the bite marks on their bodies." He swallowed. "I had to prove I was right, but he got away. They never should've thrown me off the hill."

"Don't worry, Peter, we'll catch him."

"God, I hope there aren't others." His eyes jerked open wider. "Gotta call Diane," he said urgently. "Sarchick threatened her."

"Calm down. Diane and Paige are on a cruise. They're safe."

"Melanie and Paul," Peter cried, pacing the living room.

"They're safe, too."

He stopped moving long enough to meet Daniel's gaze. "Think so?"

"Sure," Daniel said, continuing to play along. "So when was it that Sarchick made his threat?"

"On the railroad track."

"On it?"

Peter nodded. "Tried to handcuff me there. He wanted the train to run me over."

"What?"

"He couldn't hook the other end, so he held me down. He thought it was long enough, but I fooled him. As soon as he jumped off, I rolled the other way."

"Really!"

"Wish I could've seen his face," Peter said, eyes staring wildly. "He was so sure."

"Listen, Peter." Daniel placed a hand on his shoulder. "I think you need to see a doctor."

"It's only a bump on the head and a bruised lip." He shrugged. "I'll be all right."

"No, not that kind of doctor." Daniel hesitated a moment. "The one my father gave you the name of. The one you used to see."

"Heinemann?" Peter angrily pushed Daniel's arm away. "You think this was all a delusion, that I'm crazy, or something?"

"Well . . ."

"And that I smacked myself in the head to make the story more believable?"

"Sometimes," Daniel began slowly, "when you're under a lot of stress—like you were with that plane crash—you can have trouble deciding what's real and what's not."

"You're right, I *should* see Heinemann. Then maybe he can explain this," Peter said sarcastically, pulling his hand out of his jacket and dangling it in front of Daniel's face. "And I hope Heinemann has a key so I can get this *figment* of my imagination off my wrist."

73

"Nice drive, Charles."

Whitney pulled his gaze from the ball bounding down the fairway to the man who had just arrived. "Seymour!" He walked over to shake hands. "It's been a long time."

"Yes," Seymour agreed. "Look at you: a congress-man. I remember a young, wet-behind-the-ears assis-tant DA like it was yesterday."

"And you, a hotshot sergeant in homicide. Hoary-headed even then."

"Look who's talking. I see a touch of gray."

"A bit of wisdom maybe. Although some of my de-tractors might argue that." He smiled. "Hey, they still call you the Fox?"

"Only when they reminisce. Time is a bandit," Sey-mour stated somberly.

"I'm glad you made it."

"Not quite. Sixty is still a couple of weeks away."

Whitney's expression clouded. "Then I guess I should say happy birthday?"

"Oh, you meant made it *here*," Seymour said dryly. "Not too complicated. Even for an old man like me: Hamilton Meadows Country Club, tenth hole, seven A.M." He shrugged, glancing at his watch. "Although it *is* seven-twelve. You got impatient?"

"Just a practice swing . . . but I'll take it. It's a tough par five. You have any trouble getting in?"

"No. Not since they changed the rules and began allowing Jews. But they made me wear these shoes." He lifted one up with an unhappy face. "Not my style. Didn't charge me, though."

"I left your name."

"Thanks."

"Wanna play? I can still get you a set of clubs."

Seymour shook his head. "I wouldn't be any good. Never got into the sport—grown men chasing a little white ball around with iron sticks. All right to watch?"

"Have it your way." Whitney replaced his driver, then hoisted the bag over his shoulder. "But I like to walk."

"Okay by me. I can use the exercise."

They headed down the fairway.

"I hope you don't mind meeting me here. It's just that I have a very busy schedule, and you said it was important. Lately, when I'm in town, Friday morning is the only chance I get to play some golf. I come early, catch the back nine. It's quicker that way, less crowded. Especially this time of year."

"You always play alone?" Seymour asked.

"Foursomes take too long. But I usually *do* play with someone. I invited Vernon Malchomoty this morning. He was going to drive up from Philly."

Malchomoty. "Isn't he a judge or something?" Seymour inquired easily.

"A noted one. Presided over some pretty high-profile cases, like the Renfro brothers who butchered their parents—that's where you've probably heard of him. But he cancelled last minute to go out of town."

"I think I saw him on the news once. He plays golf?"

"Yes. Why so surprised?"

"I thought he walked kind of hunched over. Arthritis?"

"Scoliosis. A condition he's had since birth. But don't let that fool you. He accommodated very well. Plays a mean round of golf."

"Did you tell him that I was meeting you?"

"Yes."

"Before or after he cancelled?"

"Before. Why?"

"Just curious."

Whitney squinted at him. They reached the ball. He took out a club, putting his bag down on the ground.

"You know him through politics?"

"No. We went to college together. Van Buren. Same class."

"Mmm." Seymour nodded slowly.

Whitney got into position impatiently. "Wanna tell me why you came? I'm sure it wasn't for a golf lesson, or just to reminisce."

"Two reasons."

Whitney drew back his club, twisted his body.

"The first is Sarchick."

Whitney uncoiled. The ball jumped into the air, curving badly to the left. It landed in the rough, behind some trees. "Damn," he muttered.

"Cut down on your swing, Charles, you won't hook it so much," Seymour suggested. "You're coming in too fast. And your club's closed. Square it up."

Whitney furrowed his brow at Seymour and at the advice, then shook it off. "Sarchick?" he asked nonchalantly and resumed walking. "He died in that plane crash."

"Yes, I know. It was tragic. So many people lost."

"Terrible accident."

"I saw you on TV."

Whitney looked uncomfortable. "Cheap publicity. I didn't want to do it."

"But you did it anyway."

"Pressure from my advisors." He sighed. "They thought it was important."

"The end justifies the means?" Seymour offered.

"Sort of. But I should have held my ground. Politics have no place in a tragedy. My wife is in Miami visiting her mother. Flies back tomorrow night. I can't help but wonder how I would have felt."

"That's understandable. She flying into Hamilton?"

"Yup. On North America Airlines." He paused. "I'll tell you that makes me nervous."

"Makes two of us. My niece is flying in, as well. Maybe they're on the same flight."

"Arrives at eight-oh-five."

Seymour nodded. "Could be."

"So you want to know if Sarchick was the target?" Whitney asked.

"Then it *was* sabotage?"

"No one's committing to that, yet. But off the record—yes."

"You have a history with Sarchick, don't you?"

Whitney abruptly stopped walking, turned to Seymour. "Obviously, this isn't just about the plane crash. You want to tell me about it?"

Seymour began to lift his arms, then let them fall to his sides. "I was looking into my daughter-in-law's death."

"Heard about that. I'm very sorry."

"Thanks." They continued toward the ball. "At first, we assumed it was Luccetta's family that placed the bomb. Now, we have information that Sarchick may have been behind it."

"Sarchick?" Whitney said, confused. "Wasn't he in custody at the time?"

"May have had help."

"But why?"

"I don't know. We're investigating."

"And that's what led you to me."

"Partly," Seymour said. "You pushed to get him into the Witness Protection Program."

"Yes, I did. This isn't for public knowledge, Seymour. I know I can trust you with it. I got a letter from Sarchick. Arrived the day he was arrested, asking for a deal. But it wasn't up to me. The first person I called was Malchomoty."

That surprised Seymour. "Why Malchomoty?"

"Because I knew he was friendly with Franklin Marsh, the Federal Prosecutor. Actually, that's where Malchomoty is now. Marsh has some property a couple of hours west of here and asked him to go pheasant hunting."

"Ah, a judge who likes to play with guns," Seymour remarked. "And he'd rather do that than golf?"

"I guess. He's a firearms buff. Used to be a munitions expert for the military. Anyway, Malchomoty brought the letter to Marsh's attention. Marsh was burned by those two witnesses who got killed, and desperate for someone else to testify. Sarchick was a perfect fit, an insider. Marsh made the deal."

"But a killer?" Seymour threw back. "With a history of child molestation?"

"It was the right decision," Whitney defended. "Organized crime has to be stopped."

"Your platform?"

Whitney shook his head. "Not just politics. It's what I believe. Sometimes we have to pay a price."

"No matter how high the cost, huh, Charles?"

"Listen, Seymour: I'm sorry about your daughter-in-law," he said calmly. "But please don't blame me."

"That wasn't my intention," Seymour apologized, then stopped, pointing. "Your ball."

Whitney set himself and stroked a tremendous shot, driving it over the trees and a water hazard. The ball hit the fairway, bounced, then rolled to where there was a clean approach to the green.

"Not bad," Seymour commented.

Whitney smiled.

"You prosecuted Sarchick once. A long time ago," he continued.

"God, Seymour, you dug deep. No wonder they call you the Fox."

"Nasty habit," he said. "Sarchick ask for any deals then?"

"Most do when they're caught red-handed."

"And?"

"Turned out he had nothing to trade."

Seymour cocked his head.

"You can check—he got an appropriate sentence."

"I will."

"Just what are you fishing for, Seymour?" he asked, annoyed now.

"Maybe nothing," he said. "Maybe everything."

"I wish you would get to the point," Whitney said as they came to the ball again.

"I visited one of your classmates yesterday."

"Who?" He handed Seymour his golf bag.

"Colin Kirshner."

Whitney drew out one of his irons. "How is he? Haven't seen him in years."

"A bit frazzled," he said. "Is that a five iron?"

"Yes."

Seymour glanced at the distance, shook his head. "Too much club. Use the seven."

Whitney gave him a severe look and prepared to hit with the five.

"That's odd," Seymour said, "that it had been so long. And you were going to play golf with Malchomoty today. Weren't all three of you in Kingsman House together?"

Whitney stopped concentrating, looked up. "Know about that, too, huh—Kingsman House?"

"The other reason for my call."

Whitney took his shot. The ball sailed well over the green, landing in a neighboring fairway. He turned his head back to eye Seymour suspiciously.

Seymour shrugged. "I watch a lot of golf on TV."

Whitney grabbed the bag. "Okay, you win. Enough cat and mouse. What do you really want to know?"

"I'm looking for Squigger," he said, walking alongside the congressman.

"Can't help you."

"Come on. I know about Squigger and Fats. I know about the nicknames. I know about the farmhouse. And I know you know, too."

"I wasn't involved in that," Whitney insisted.

"It's curious how your name and Sarchick's keep ending up together."

"By doing my job?"

"He was the one that got your fraternity shut down."

"I never knew that."

"It was out of revenge."

"For what?"

"He was the boy who Squigger and Fats raped," Seymour said.

"I swear, I—"

"And you made deals with him."

"So, that's what this is all about." Whitney leaned forward. "He killed Dominic, and now you think I'm Squigger. Well, you're wrong. Dead wrong."

"I didn't say that."

"You implied it. But Squigger, Fats, and the rest don't exist anymore."

"I disagree. And *you* used to be a DA. Each one of you committed a crime. Crimes that went unpunished and unatoned for. You were all accessories, yourself included."

"There's no legal basis," Whitney argued. "The statute of lim—"

"I know," Seymour cut him off. "The statute of limitations precludes any legal action. Is what you did that bad?"

"No."

"So what are you afraid of? A stupid vow you made over twenty-seven years ago?"

"Jesus Christ, Seymour. Do you know what you're asking me to do?" he cried. "In a year, I want to be running for governor. This will ruin me. And what about everyone else that was in that fraternity? We all did things we're ashamed of now. Things that will get out. Good people, people who are making a difference will be destroyed. Why? Because when we were young and stupid we made mistakes. Got into mischief, needed to feel important, wanted to belong."

"I don't consider sodomizing a young boy *mischief*," Seymour said, his voice steely.

"We were naive," Whitney shouted, his voice pleading. "Impetuous."

"I thought you were a better person than that." Seymour's face was hard.

Whitney bowed his head under that glare. "Don't lecture me."

"Charles," Seymour said quietly. "Have you the courage now to do the right thing?"

"And people will understand?" he finished sarcastically.

"You never know. Don't underestimate your constituents. You say you're not Squigger. I believe you. Take the responsibility for what *you* did. Each of you stands alone. Kingsman House is long gone now."

Whitney drew a huge breath, let it out slowly. "Why is this so important? Can't you let it be?"

"No."

"Why?"

"Because Sarchick may still be alive."

Whitney twitched. "What?"

"My niece's husband, Peter Roberts, a forensic specialist, seems to think so. He says Sarchick wasn't on that plane. That the dental records we have for him are wrong."

"Wait a minute. Isn't he the dentist they expelled from the crash site? The one in today's newspaper?"

"Yes."

"They said he was making wild accusations and suffering from post-traumatic stress disorder."

"They're wrong. Sarchick tried to get to him last

night. To keep him from telling people that *Sarchick is alive.*"

"Do you have any proof?" Whitney asked skeptically, his brow knitting.

Seymour turned his palms up. He thought about what Daniel told him: *a few scratches, a bump on the head, a pair of handcuffs.* "Not yet," he said uncertainly. "But Roberts and my son, Daniel, are working on it."

Whitney glared at Seymour incredulously. "You want me to risk everything I've worked for because Roberts *thinks* Sarchick is alive? Have you considered the possibility that the man might be having a nervous breakdown?"

Seymour nodded. "And I also considered the possibility that he might be right. It means Sarchick downed that plane . . . and it means the murderer of my son's wife and close to a hundred other innocent people is running around free, free to murder and rape and whatever else his sick mind dictates! Charles, don't you see," he said desperately, "you have to tell me who Squigger is."

"Why?"

"He could be helping Sarchick, or involved in the cover-up. Or in danger."

"You're asking a lot." Whitney hesitated a moment. "Tell you what. Bring me proof that Sarchick is alive, and I'll consider it."

"Fair enough," Seymour said. He nudged the politician, pointing to a foursome heading their way. "Better finish up."

Whitney hit a pretty shot, and his ball landed within four feet of the pin.

On the green, Seymour lifted out the flag for him. "Set in motion over twenty-seven years ago," he noted. "Fats: moments before his death, crucified with the knowledge that he was responsible for the perversion set upon his son. Sarchick: the object of a decadent prank, his own depraved soul now emancipated."

"And Squigger, where does he fit in?" Whitney asked, lining up his putt.

"Squigger?" Seymour shrugged. "Maybe another victim caught in the web, too afraid to scream. Or maybe a player, secretly enjoying the card he was dealt. I'm not really sure. But I do know one thing."

"What's that?"

"He's a coward," Seymour said.

Whitney gently stroked the ball. It headed straight for the hole, rimmed the cup, and then skipped past it.

74

████████ Daniel had taken Peter home with him and found a key for the set of Peerless cuffs, placing them in a plastic bag. He then suggested that Peter spend the night.

Feeling anxious and depressed, Peter accepted. But what he felt most of all was lonely. He slept on the couch with an ice bag on his head.

In the morning, Daniel called Lily Chang to ask for a favor.

"Sure," she said. But he would have to get to her early, before she left for work.

Peter was still sleeping. Daniel slipped out of the apartment, leaving a note on the kitchen table.

Chang dusted the cuffs for prints. Unfortunately, Peter had done a thorough job. They were clean.

Then, responding to an odd impulse—part instinct, part curiosity—Daniel drove through Sarchick's old neighborhood. He noticed the children outside playing. Passing Billy Cooper's home he slowed, imagined Sarchick walking with his arm around Cooper, leading him away.

He came to another house he recognized. It was where Sarchick's mother lived. This time he was sure— the sun had barely risen and it was shining the other way—there was definitely a light on in the basement.

He left his car and went to the door. Wondering if she was awake—or, for that matter, if she would even talk to him—he knocked softly. Waiting, he placed his ear to the door, then knocked again, louder. No one answered. He tried the knob, rapped several more times. The door remained closed, no voice on the other side.

After awhile, he gave up and circled around to the side, to the lit window. He bent, stared in: dull cement walls; an unfinished floor; an old table and chairs. No-body.

On his way back to his apartment, Daniel stopped to pick up muffins, a carton of juice, and two contain-ers of coffee. When he came in, he saw that Peter was just getting up. He was sitting on the couch in his un-derwear, yawning, working his shoulders.

"Where've you been?" Peter asked, rubbing his eyes.

"Breakfast," he announced, holding up the bag. "Hungry?"

"Starved."

"How's your head?"

It throbbed. Peter groped for the exact spot. "Ouch," he moaned upon finding it. "I'll live."

"Glad to hear it. Coffee?"

"Please."

They sat at the table, eating, and Daniel told him about having the cuffs dusted, and about stopping by Sarchick's mother's house. He knew there was no phone listing for that address from his investigation six months ago, but called information to check again. There was nothing new. They would have to pay another visit and hope to catch her in.

Peter suggested they follow Seymour's lead about Sarchick and the state's medical assistance program. He treated a few people in the program himself, and had an assigned provider number to get into the system. If there had been any dental treatment—although it would have been awhile ago—the state would have the name of the dentist. Then, if the dentist was still in practice, if he or she had saved the record, and if that unique bridge was on it, they might have something.

Daniel got Sarchick's social security number from the Luccetta Homicide file his father had lent him and Peter made the call. Then quickly hung up.

"What's the matter?" Daniel asked.

"Not open yet. And they only take calls from ten to three."

"Ten to three? Shit!"

"I'm used to it," Peter groaned. "Try calling a dental insurance company sometime. Got any more muffins?"

"Nope. Some apple pie," Daniel offered. "I was saving it for my father, but I really shouldn't. He needs to diet—alter his entire lifestyle. He says he's trying, but it's tough for a leopard to change his spots."

"Leopard," Peter mumbled distractedly. *When had Striklon used that phrase?* "Hold on. Sarchick was relocated near Chicago."

"Yeah. So?"

"The leopard and his spots," Peter said excitedly. "Maybe there were similar cases out there. Bite mark cases that match what I saw on Billy Cooper. If the time frame fits—"

"It would be corroboratory. But not absolute proof," Daniel interrupted.

"Enough to convince the Feds?"

Daniel smiled. "Maybe."

"I know a guy at Northwestern University Dental School. He runs the Forensic Dentistry Department. He was even one of the authors on that article about Hitler's dentition—about the bridge. If there were any bite mark cases in the area, he would know." Peter grabbed the phone.

"Chicago," Daniel reminded, pointing to the kitchen clock. "Still a bit early there."

"You're right." He put the phone down, pacing with uncontained energy.

"What's a Hitler bridge anyway?" Daniel asked.

"Actually, it's called a telephone bridge. One way of restoring a lost tooth is with a fixed bridge," Peter explained. "Usually, the adjacent teeth are capped and they hold a replacement tooth. It's all one piece."

"But you thought Sarchick's teeth were capped when you saw him."

"Yes. But I didn't realize he had a bridge because of the diastema, the space between his two front teeth."

"But if it's all attached, how do you get that?"

"That's what the telephone bridge accomplishes," Peter said. "Some people want to keep the diastema they had because they feel it's distinctive. Or sometimes, because of the diastema, you would need too large a tooth to fill the entire space. That wouldn't look natural. In that case, the units can be connected by a loop arching behind the palate. It's hidden . . . until you bite someone, maybe."

"Ever make any of those?"

"Never even saw one until the Hitler article. It's in textbooks, though, I imagine."

"Why haven't you?"

Peter shrugged. "Modern dentistry has enough tricks to get around the problem. But the fact that *Sarchick* has one—its uniqueness—is in our favor."

"And from what you just told me, I'm guessing it was done quite a long time ago. Maybe by an older practitioner," Daniel mused. "*That,* however, is not in our favor."

"No, it's not." Peter checked the clock again.

While they waited, Peter dressed in what he had worn last night and Daniel grabbed the morning paper, taking it with them when he drove Peter home. Peter rifled through it scanning headlines, cringing when he found the one about him: LOCAL DENTIST DISMISSED—ALLEGEDLY UNDERMINED RECOVERY OPERATION AT CRASH SITE. The article was short, with only the vaguest details, and didn't mention the word crazy. He was thankful for that, and also glad he had remembered to call the kids the night before to warn them.

Back at his house, Peter rushed to his answering machine, expecting to find it full of messages after the report. There was only one: Striklon checking on how he was.

At ten o'clock, they each grabbed a phone: Daniel in the kitchen calling the Department of Public Welfare; Peter on a second line in the den to Northwestern.

Peter finished first and anxiously rushed into the kitchen with the news. Daniel was still talking. He waited for him to set the receiver down, then blurted out: "Two cases within the last six months. A kid in Elgin; another in Aurora."

"Is that near Evanston?"

"Close," Peter said. "Bite marks on the back of the

neck. Identical. Each with the imprint of a U behind the front teeth."

"And the kids?"

Peter shook his head sadly. "One was nine, the other only seven."

"My God," Daniel cried. "How could that happen? Who was watching them?" The words died in his throat. He felt sick, took a breath to steady himself. "If it's Sarchick, he's finding them younger."

Peter stared at him, eyes wide. "What do you mean *if*?"

"And he did it while he was in the Witness Protection Program. Under the noses of the federal marshals."

"They're faxing copies of the bite marks to my office later."

"So you can match them to the one on Billy Cooper?"

"They'll match," Peter assured him. "How did you make out?"

Daniel rolled his eyes. "The first guy I spoke to said he wasn't sure how far their back records went. He thought they only kept them for one year, and he drew a blank on how I would go about getting the name of a treating dentist. He suggested I speak with his supervisor."

"And?"

"She didn't have a clue. Put me in touch with Files and Records. She was positive they would know," he said, frustrated. "Files and Records didn't. But *they* were sure I had to call the Attorney General's Office for that information."

"That doesn't sound right."

"It wasn't. They said they had no idea why I would be calling them for that. They said they only handle criminal cases."

"So what did you do?"

"I called the Department of Welfare again. Got a different guy this time. Someone more enlightened. He told me that they're on a computer system called MAMIS—Medical Assistance Management Information System. It has everything as far back as 1979. That's when it was set up. And Sarchick was under medical assistance when he went to college in the early eighties."

"Did he run Sarchick's social security number?"

"Can't. Not without going through proper channels. They need an official request."

"Such as?"

"A letter from the police would do."

"We don't have time for that," Peter said, thinking quickly. "Wait. You're a cop. What if you showed up in person?"

Daniel balked at the idea, remembering his father's admonition this time. "Peter, did you forget? I've been suspended."

Peter wrinkled his brow. "Does that matter?"

Daniel considered the question, then shrugged. "I guess we don't have a choice."

"Then let's go. We can be in Harrisburg by twelve-thirty."

They left, first traveling across town to check Mrs. Sarchick's house again. She could save them the trouble. But there was still no answer at the door. With the clock ticking, they decided to head for Harrisburg, hoping that Artie Sarchick had had enough good sense to keep up with his dental checkups while he was in school.

75

▄▄▄▄▄▄ She was yelling again. Unable to calm her, Sergeant Vanderhooven called Sam.

"Where's my money?" she screeched.

"Take it easy," Vanderhooven pleaded. "I told you there are forms that have to be filled out. The Crime Victims Council will be in touch. They'll help you. It takes time."

"Not good enough," she shouted.

Milano arrived then, recognizing the irate woman instantly. "Mrs. Cooper . . . can I help you?"

"I know you. You're the one who found my boy."

"Not exactly, but yes, I was there."

"Well, I want my money."

Milano looked at Vanderhooven for an explanation.

Vandy shrugged. "From the Crime Victims Compensation Fund. I tried to explain to her that she has to fill out the forms. I promised Daniel I'd call, try to speed things up."

"Daniel?" Milano asked, surprised.

"I meant to tell you about that," he said in a low voice. "You see, he—"

"I got expenses," she cried. "What's a poor woman to do?"

"What's going on here?" Captain Schwenk bellowed, entering the station house.

Vanderhooven stiffened in his chair, shooting Milano a troubled look.

"I want to see that detective," she demanded. "The one who said I'd get some money."

"Detective?" Schwenk asked. "Who are you? What's this about?"

"This is Billy Cooper's mother, sir. She's inquiring about the fund for victims," Vanderhooven replied quickly, trying to stifle Schwenk's interest. "I'm giving her all the information she needs."

"That detective at my house yesterday said the same thing. Where is he? I need the money."

"What detective?" Schwenk eyed Milano suspiciously. "No one was sent."

"Come on," she barked. "He showed me his badge. Young. Tall."

Schwenk's brow wrinkled for a moment, then the tightness eased. "Detective Pinchus?"

"Yeah. That's him."

"Hhmm. And you say he showed you his badge?"

Milano and Vanderhooven looked at each other helplessly.

"Uh-huh."

"Why don't we go up to my office," Schwenk suggested smoothly. "Straighten this whole mess out."

"And get me my money?" she snapped.

"I'm sure we can work some arrangement," he said as the hint of a smile crept across his face.

76

Seymour Pinchus walked a few more holes with Congressman Whitney, but couldn't rattle his game again. It took him awhile to get back, cutting through trees and fairways, finding himself on the wrong side of a small lake. He worked his way around it, finally locating the clubhouse. There, he returned the shoes and found a phone.

When Daniel called last night to tell him what happened to Peter, Seymour needed no more convincing: Sarchick was alive. It seemed implausible that Peter—whether depressed or on the verge of delirium—would have staged such a bizarre event. And then there were the cuffs, one of Sarchick's tools from his toy chest. He winced at the thought. The fact that Sarchick visited Peter had him concerned. Very concerned. Sarchick had to be stopped, his cover of death removed.

He got Malchomoty's number from Philadelphia information.

"Court of Common Pleas," a woman's voice answered.

"Judge Vernon Malchomoty, please."

"He's not in. What's this in reference to?"

"Oh, darn. I wanted so much to say hello. I'm a friend. Just got into town. Can you tell me where he could be reached?"

"Well . . . he took the morning off to play golf. But he's due back at one to hear a case. Does that help you?"

"You have no idea! Thanks."

"Wait. Won't you leave me your name?"

"But of course. Tell him Seymour Pinchus—an old college chum."

Next, he dialed Daniel's number.

"Hi, this is Daniel. I'll be checking back. Leave your name and number." Beep.

He left a message, then called home. Kate was gone for the weekend. She had taken an early bus to Syracuse to visit her sister. She was going to check in as soon as she arrived. He pressed the code number to retrieve any messages.

There was only one from Daniel—that he and Peter might be heading to Harrisburg in search of the name of Sarchick's dentist. And they came up empty on the cuffs. He frowned and hung up.

The fact that Sarchick was definitely alive meant he had caused the crash of North America Flight 1089, or at the very least, knew it was coming. Whitney had admitted it was sabotage, and hadn't Sarchick been relocated to a city not too far from Chicago's O'Hare Airport? A *coincidence*? Not likely.

The nagging questions continued to pound in his head: How did Sarchick manage to fool the federal marshals? How did he switch identities so completely that his own dental records had been replaced with someone else's? Who was really on that plane? And . . . how do you compromise airport security and single-handedly blow up a major airliner in flight?

Seymour had started looking for the answers the previous night, remembering an old friend. Six years ago Carl Reichenbach's son, Joey, was driving a pal back to school and got stopped going through a red light in Hamilton. One of the officers got a whiff of Mary Jane, searched the car, and found two joints stuffed under the passenger's seat.

Joey claimed they weren't his. He checked out okay. His buddy didn't. However, Joey still faced charges. They were minor, but he was going to be applying to law school in a year and the incident could have affected his chances.

Carl had called Seymour. They were once neighbors, living down the street from each other. Seymour had known Joey since he was a youngster—recalled him being a good kid. He vouched for him, kept his record clean.

Seymour enjoyed doing favors like that, when he had weighed the circumstances and felt it was warranted. For years, Carl had been working security over at Hamilton International Airport. Now, it was Seymour's turn to ask for a favor. They agreed to meet at two. Seymour glanced at his watch, saw he had plenty of time, and decided to swing by Van Buren University first.

Colin Kirshner was in, but refused to see him. "He said he's too busy," Daphne told him.

Seymour twisted his lips skeptically at her, then said stubbornly, "Tell him I'll wait." He scanned a pile of magazines, chose a recent one whose cover already had a photo of the air crash on it, and settled into a chair facing Kirshner's door.

He waited two hours, but Kirshner never came out. "What time does he go for lunch?" Seymour asked.

"Forty-five minutes ago," she replied with a smile. "You still intent on keeping him under siege?"

Seymour scratched his chin. "No. Just give him this." He stood, handing her the magazine. Across the photo of the gruesome fragmentation of Flight 1089, he scrawled: *Tell Squigger we need to have a chat.* Below that he wrote down his home telephone number.

Daphne looked perplexed.

"Inside joke," Seymour said.

"Oh."

"Let your boss know it's safe to come out now," he said as he turned to leave.

████

It took Seymour forty minutes to get to the airport. Carl greeted him at the entrance to Terminal B. They reminisced for a few minutes—about the old neighborhood, about their sons. Joey had passed his Bar exam, Seymour learned. It made him happy.

As they walked, Seymour told Carl what he wanted to know.

"How to get around security?" Carl echoed. "See how it might have been done?"

"Right."

"You're not a terrorist, are you, Seymour?" he asked, gently elbowing him.

"No." Seymour smiled. "But I have an ex-wife who might argue that."

"And I'm sure there are some folks in lockup that would agree with her," Carl said, meaning it to be a compliment.

Seymour shrugged modestly.

"To tell you the truth," Carl said, glancing around to

make sure no one was near, "breaching security ain't that tough."

"But it appears to be."

"Exactly. That's what we rely on—the *perception* of security." Carl motioned toward a group of people marching through a metal detector. "Ever wonder why the alarm goes off sometimes, but not always, even when you're carrying the same stuff?"

"Yeah."

"It's the sensitivity level of the machine. We can turn it up or down," he explained, keeping his voice low. "We get backed up and people start missing their flights, or we have VIPs in a hurry—it doesn't look good. Bad for business. So we turn it down, keep the lines moving."

"I didn't know you were allowed to—"

"We can do whatever we want," Carl said abruptly. "Years ago metal detectors didn't look like they do now. I heard stories about airports not having enough to go around."

"What did they do?"

"Paint a box black, run a wire from it. All of a sudden you have enough."

"Perception," Seymour noted.

"Yup, perception. Of course, we've made a lot of improvements since then. But there are still weaknesses. Anyone familiar with the system can beat it— like that guy Sarchick. You say he worked as an airline mechanic. Then he would know."

"And dressing in the right clothes and wearing an authentic-looking ID would make that knowledge all the more dangerous."

Carl nodded, heading for the security checkpoint. "Follow me. I want to show you something else." He glanced back at Seymour. "Wait a minute. Are you carrying a piece?"

Seymour moved his hands away from his sides, palms up. "Not since I retired."

"Then come on."

They traveled through and continued down a long corridor to the gate area. Carl looked outside as they passed one of the windows. "You see the workers servicing that plane?"

"Yeah."

"Restricted area. To get onto the tarmac from here you need to go through one of those." Carl pointed to a door in a corner. "And you have to know the code," he added, leading Seymour over to stand in front of it. "This is what I wanted to show you, what I've been complaining about. But it falls on deaf ears."

Seymour studied the door, the keypad next to it, the red warning sign forbidding unauthorized entry. "The keypad?" he guessed.

"Bingo. What's unusual about it?"

Seymour squinted, taking a closer look. "Typical telephone button face. Old." He dragged his fingers across it lightly. "Several buttons have more wear than the rest—the two, five, seven, and eight. Four-digit code to get in?" he asked, arching an eyebrow at Carl.

"Right again. And they never change the code. Twenty-four possible combinations. It doesn't take long to run through them. Why don't you give it a try?"

Seymour raised a hand, looking hesitantly back at Carl.

"Don't worry, you're with me."

Seymour began trying the numbers in different sequences as Carl stared at his watch. He was lucky. He hit the right combination on the sixth try.

"You just gained entry to where you shouldn't be in fifteen seconds," Carl declared.

"My God, are all airport security systems this flawed?"

"Some are better, some worse."

"How about O'Hare?"

"Don't know," Carl shrugged. "But they all have kinks in their armor. Without exception."

"Any ideas how he could have gotten explosives aboard?"

"Is that what happened? He tried to blow her up?"

Seymour shook his head. "To disable her. So she would crash. I heard unofficially that there were three small explosions around the same time."

"Could've been triggered by remote," Carl offered. "Or more likely, by an altimeter. Passing through a certain altitude on the way up arms the switch. Come back down through the same altitude, and it detonates. But I'm no explosives expert."

"And getting something like that through security?" he persisted.

"It's not hard if you're using plastics," Carl admitted. "But you're still taking a chance. Best way?"

"Don't hold out on me now."

"It's simple. A seasoned veteran like you should have figured it out," Carl teased good-naturedly. "Simply toss the stuff over a fence in a remote part of the field under the cover of darkness."

"Then clear security and retrieve it before dawn," Seymour finished.

"Simple, right? And they used to call you the Fox?"

"*Gai vais.* Go figure."

77

The phone rang in Chief Foster's office. Sergeant Fishburn stopped typing, swiveling his chair around to answer it.

"Fishburn here."

"Fish, this is Captain Schwenk."

Deacon rolled his eyes. "Chief's not in, Captain."

"But I called to speak to you."

"Listen, Captain. You asked me to have a talk with Chief Foster, and I did."

"I trust it went well?"

"In fact, it went quite well," Fishburn said emphatically. "You'd be surprised."

"Great! Tell that son of yours to get ready for a transfer. And have him cut that 'fro. I like it worn tight to the scalp."

Deacon sighed. "Yez'um," he mumbled.

"What was that, Fish?"

"Bad connection, sir. I said: When I see him."

Schwenk let it slide. "Actually, what I really called about is Detective Pinchus."

"Got your report right here. But I have to tell you, Foster wasn't too impressed. There certainly is not enough here for a dismissal from the force."

"Don't worry, I have a few new charges to add to the list."

"They better be good ones."

"They are," Schwenk assured him. "And *this* time I have a witness."

78

████████ The sentencing proceeding for Rodney Black, an eighteen-year-old convicted of robbing a minimarket, had ended a short while ago. His attorney had argued that Black had no priors, was coerced into the act by others, and had a psychological profile indicating limited mental capacity. He asked for leniency. Expectations were that Black would get probation. The judge sentenced him to two years.

Now he was walking through the courthouse parking garage—hunched over, head bent toward the ground—when someone stepped out of the car parked next to his and blocked his path.

"Excuse me, Your Honor."

Malchomoty shifted his eyes up. They peeked through gray, bushy eyebrows, placing the face as one that had sat in the back of his courtroom. "You a relative?" he asked.

"No. Seymour Pinchus. May I have a word?"

"Hardly. I'm in an awful rush." The judge took out his keys.

"It'll only take a minute. I understand you're an expert on firearms."

"What I am should be none of your concern," Malchomoty said rudely. "I heard about you, and I don't have time for troublemakers."

"You do in court."

"We're not in one now."

"Why won't you let me plead my case?"

"You do something wrong, you pay the price," he said harshly. "It's that simple. Now step aside."

"Sounds odd coming from someone who used to be a Kingsman," Pinchus let fall.

A vein pulsed in Malchomoty's right temple. He stared at Pinchus, working his jaw. "That your car?" He nodded his head to the side, indicating Seymour's blue Oldsmobile. "You're parked in a handicap zone. Move it or I'll call the police!"

Seymour sighed, turned to leave. "By the way, I think you were pretty rough on the boy."

"He got an appropriate sentence," Malchomoty snapped.

"Interesting," Seymour replied, looking back at him. "But he's not the boy I was referring to."

79

████████ It was nearly five o'clock when Daniel and Peter finished at the Pennsylvania Department of Welfare. After speaking with half a dozen employees and two supervisors, and visiting three different departments, they finally got what they wanted: the dentist. On April 12, 1982, Arthur Sarchick had a cleaning and two fillings at the office of Dr. Morris Silverman, 982 Ridge Avenue, Hamilton, Pennsylvania. What was especially noteworthy was that he also had a full set of X rays taken.

They rushed out of the building as it was closing, to a pay phone at a corner diner. Peter called Hamilton information, while Daniel, exhausted, sat and ordered them coffee. Peter came to the counter a few minutes later with a big smile on his face.

"Silverman's still in practice," he said. "Same location, an old converted home. Caught him on the way out."

"Does he have Sarchick's records?"

"He said, 'Hell, I never throw anything away.' You know, he's been practicing for forty-five years?"

"What about the bridge?" Daniel asked anxiously.

"Didn't pull the chart yet. Says he keeps the inactive files up in the attic."

"Forty-five years, huh? The place is probably loaded to the rafters. We can meet him tonight, help him look."

Peter shook his head. "No, he has plans. Couldn't break them. But he's in tomorrow until one. He said to come by then and he'll have it."

"The guy still puts in Saturday hours? Why, he must be at least . . ."

"Seventy-two," Peter said. "He's proud of that fact— that he's still practicing."

"Good for him."

"And lucky for us."

"Wait," Daniel said suddenly. "One o'clock tomorrow?"

"Yeah. Why?"

"I'm supposed to meet my in-laws then to pick up Adam."

"No problem." Peter shrugged. "I'll go to Silverman's office alone."

"No way. I want to be there. Let me see what I can work out." He stood, searching his pockets for coins. He came up empty, and looked at Peter.

"Sorry." Peter turned his palms up. "Silverman."

Daniel changed a few dollars at the register and went to the phone. He called Mrs. Kunklemacher first and was grateful that she was able to help him out. He phoned Susan's parents to explain and spoke to his father-in-law. Susan's mother was out taking Adam to the party, but he didn't believe it would be a problem. Daniel hung up and started to return to the counter, then remembered to let his father know what they were doing, how they made out so far. Seymour wasn't in, so he left the good news on the machine.

"All set," Daniel said to Peter when he came back.

A fiftyish-looking man behind the counter was clearing their coffee cups away. His arms were covered with tattoos. The T-shirt above his apron read: *Elvis Lives!*

"You know, we never ate lunch," Peter said. "You hungry?"

"Starved."

"Then let's get a table."

Daniel looked at Peter dubiously. "You want to eat here?"

Peter glanced around, his gaze resting on a blackboard hanging at the end of the counter. *Today's Special: meatloaf, sauerkraut and peas, bread pudding.* The booths had green plastic tablecloths. A waitress kept snapping her gum and nodding as she took an order from two heavyset hard-hats. Country music was playing on a jukebox in the corner.

Peter turned back to Daniel. "Yes," he said. "Yes, I do."

80

He answered the phone. When he heard the voice on the other end, his stomach tightened. "Why are you calling me?" he asked, trying to keep his own voice steady.

"I thought you might want to talk," the caller prattled in a childish tone.

"And how would you know that?"

"Intuition, Squigger."

"I told you not to call me that!"

"You're in no position to give orders," the caller growled, then added more calmly, "But you *once* were. Remember?"

The memory of the farmhouse flashed through Squigger's mind. With time, he had been able to make the images lose some of their sharpness, but he had never been able to crush them completely. He sighed. "What do you want?"

"Nervous, Squigger?" The caller snickered.

"Why shouldn't I be? This guy Pinchus is very persistent."

"He's fishing. He's got nothing."

"How can you be so sure?"

"A little birdie told me. Haven't you realized by now? I see everything, every move that's made. And that's why I'm calling, to see where you stand."

"I don't know if I can go on like this, covering up for you."

"You should've thought of that sooner. Now you're in up to your ass," the caller said, chuckling again. "And in case you don't agree, let me remind you about Fats. I could do the same to you. In a heartbeat. But don't worry, I won't. Not unless you push me. You're lucky I still need you."

"Maybe there's an easier way out," Squigger said.

"You don't have the guts—even for a coward's way."

Squigger paused, considering. Finally he said, "What are you going to do about Pinchus? He's getting too close. I heard his son's also causing trouble."

"Then, Squigger, we have to stop them from digging," the caller answered matter-of-factly. "And I have just the plan to solve all our problems."

"You usually do," Squigger said sadly. "You usually do."

81

The meal at the diner was pretty good, Daniel had to admit. It was the first time he had had *halupki*—and he hadn't realized that it would be just like the Jewish stuffed cabbage he used to eat at his grandmother's house years ago, with a different name.

At dinner, they talked about the significance of finding Sarchick's dentist. They spoke with guarded optimism: Proving that Sarchick wasn't on that plane would launch an official manhunt; the FBI with all its resources would be on their side. Peter's reputation would be restored; questions about his sanity put to rest.

Afterward, they drove back to Hamilton. Daniel dropped Peter off at his house, but not before arguing with him about staying there alone. "It might not be safe," he insisted.

Peter wouldn't listen. He was looking forward to tomorrow—getting the proof, having his family back.

Everything returning to normal. And he wasn't about to spend another uncomfortable night on Daniel's couch.

It was almost eight o'clock when Daniel got to his apartment. The light on his answering machine was flashing rapidly. He imagined most of the calls were from his father and poked a finger at the play button.

Beep. "Hi, it's me. I met with Charles Whitney. Seemed to be very forthright . . . Maybe a little too forthright. Not sure. Oscar is driving up to Scranton to speak with Caldwell. I'll find out more when he gets back. Maybe I'll stop at Van Buren again. Stay in touch."

Beep. "Hi, it's me. I just pushed Colin Kirshner a little harder even though he wouldn't see me—a sign he might be ready to break. Have to keep up the pressure. Let me know how Harrisburg went. Talk to you later."

Beep. "Hello, Daniel, this is Mrs. Kunklemacher reminding you that I'm free all weekend in case you need me to watch Adam. Just ship him upstairs. I'm looking forward to it. Bye now."

Beep. "Hi, it's me. Airport security has a few flaws . . . like a cheap diamond. Also, I got to meet Malchomoty. Shot my own frangible bullet. I'll explain later. I feel like going to Kritalis's tonight. But not alone. Kate's gone, and Oscar's not back yet. Guess I'll stay home, nibble on a salad—unless you can make it. Call me."

Beep. "Hello dear, this is Mom. Dad filled me in about the plans for tomorrow. I must tell you, I'm a little uncomfortable about leaving Adam with someone I've never met before, but Dad told me that you insisted it'll be okay. This Mrs. Kunklemacher must be somebody special. Make sure she's by the Monkey House at one-thirty. Dad and I have to get back and can't stay much later than that—we have Rotary Club tomorrow night. Oh, and Daniel, make sure she wears something red so we can recognize her more easily. Please call when you get home, unless it's too late. Bye."

Beep. "Hi, it's me. You missed a great meal. The spanakopita and seafood scorpio were out of this world. Oscar's still not back. I went alone. Got your message, by the way. Congratulations. Let's hope he still has the records, and that they match. Call me no matter what time. Speak to you soon." *Beep. Beep. Beeeep.*

Daniel spent the next hour returning the calls—a few minutes trading information with his father, and the rest of the time reassuring his mother-in-law.

It had been a long day. He was exhausted, and he had almost dozed off on the couch by the phone when the front door buzzer jerked him out of it. He jumped up, blinking, and pressed the intercom button.

"Yes."

"Daniel, it's Sylvia Luccetta. I need to see you."

Sylvia? Daniel felt the rush of several different emotions—surprise, concern, excitement—all at the same time.

"Hold on," he said, and buzzed her up.

He scanned the apartment, checking its appearance. *Not too bad. Good.* He waited for her knock, then opened the door.

He was shocked by what he saw. Her clothes and hair were disheveled; her blouse was torn; there was a nasty-looking bruise under her left eye.

"Sylvia, what happened?"

She started to cry. "I'm sorry, Daniel. I didn't know where else to go."

"Don't worry about it," he said quickly. "Come in."

She sniffed. "Thank you."

He led her into the living room, sat beside her on the couch.

Sylvia composed herself, then began talking slowly. "It was Marion. He came back."

"He did this to you?" Daniel said, gently touching her cheek.

"Yes. He found out the note was missing. I don't know why he was looking for it, but he was. I told him that I gave it to you."

"You told him that?"

"I was afraid he'd find out for himself and catch me in a lie. Like I once told you, he owns one of your cops."

"Who?"

"I don't know. But Dominic's been dead for six months. I didn't think he'd care so much about the note."

"But you were wrong."

She nodded. "He started beating me. I broke loose and ran from the house. I hid in a neighbor's bushes. I guess he thought I would run farther and he didn't look for me there. I snuck back later to get my car when he was gone."

"Did you call the police?"

"Get serious," she said with a forced smile. "I'm sorry, but what good do you think that would do? None—except get me killed."

"I'll bet we can pick him up," Daniel said, rising with an expression of rage on his face.

"Don't, Daniel," she pleaded, grabbing his arm. "Listen, I've been too much trouble for you already."

"I think you have that backward."

"Just let me clean up a little. I can't check into a motel looking like this."

"This is my fault. You're staying here, at least for tonight."

"But—"

"I insist. We'll see what we can do in the morning." He looked down at her guiltily. He thought about his visit the other day—how he hadn't been very honest, how he had taken advantage of her. He wanted to kiss her wound. "I'm so sorry, Sylvia. Can I get you any-thing?" he asked. "A brandy?"

"I could use a shower. And a hot cup of tea, maybe?"

"Of course."

He led her into his bedroom, to the bathroom there. "I wasn't expecting company," he apologized.

"Don't worry, this is fine. Honest."

"Clean towels in the closet," he said pointing, then left to put the tea on.

When he returned, the bedroom door was open. He hesitated, knocked by the doorframe. "Sylvia?" he called out before stepping in.

There was no answer, only the sound of the shower behind the bathroom door, her clothes scattered in front of it. He stared at them, especially the undergar-ments, and envisioned her for a moment, wet, naked. He felt something stir, then quickly stifled it, blocking out the image.

Crossing the room, he shot a glance at the morning newspaper still folded on his bureau. Ah, distraction. He remembered there was an article about Dr. Onasis in it, giving an account of his experiences at the crash site. Daniel had meant to look it over but hadn't gotten the chance. Putting the cup down, he began reading the paper as he settled into the rocker in the corner. A few minutes later, he had dozed off.

It was the scent of lavender and soap that awakened him. He opened an eye, saw Sylvia sitting on the edge of the bed, legs crossed, toweling her hair dry. She had on his white terry-cloth robe. It was enormous and seemed to swallow her. But what Daniel noticed most was how incredibly sexy she looked. The urges re-turned. This time he let them grow, let them wander.

He pushed the newspaper aside. "Feel better?"

"Much. How 'bout you? Nice nap?"

"Too short." He yawned, then jumped up, remembering the cup he had brought. "Oh, your tea. Hope it's still hot."

"Relax. I'm sure it's fine."

He found it difficult not to stare. She looked radiant. And when he did pull his gaze away, he found that it kept floating back to her. He nearly tripped getting the tea.

She cleared a spot for it on the night table, moving a pair of handcuffs. "You always keep those near your bed?" she teased, holding them up.

"Only for special occasions," he threw back, eyes fixed on hers as he handed her the cup. He surprised himself with the remark.

She smiled, put the cup down without looking, watching only him. "Well, some people think they're a real turn-on."

"Actually, they were, um . . . never mind, it's a long story." He bent to kiss her.

Her mouth lifted to meet his, her eyes half closed. Suddenly he straightened.

"I'm sorry," he said, raising his hands apologetically. "I'm just . . . I don't think I'm ready."

"Oh, I think you are," she replied steamily. When he didn't respond she realized what he meant. "Haven't you been with anybody since. . . ?"

"No."

"And you're nervous. Right?"

"A little," he confessed. But there was more to it than that. How could she understand?

"Hhmm. Well, I can fix that." She stood and began to unbutton his shirt, but he still seemed unconvinced. His efforts to help her were fumbling and only half-hearted.

"There's another side to me, you know," she confided. Her tongue swept across his ear.

He swallowed. "We all have one."

She stepped back, pulled the robe apart, then allowed it to slide slowly to the floor.

Daniel gasped. He had undressed her before, in his mind, but seeing her now he realized she was more beautiful than he had imagined. His hands began to struggle with his clothes.

She climbed onto the bed, reached for the cuffs, and wove the chain through a post in the headboard, locking one end around her wrist.

"What's your fantasy, Daniel?" she asked with a mischievous look. "For one night, let yourself go. It doesn't have to mean anything . . . not if you don't want it to. It's okay."

He forgot everything else. There was only his desire for her—a desire he had felt from the first time they met, but was too ashamed to admit.

"What's your fantasy?" she whispered, maneuvering her free hand into the other cuff. "I can be whatever you want me to be. Do whatever you want. All you have to do is ask." It snapped shut.

Daniel quickly finished undressing and approached the bed.

"Why, Daniel," she cooed, staring at him with her eyes wide. "You don't look so worried anymore."

At first, Daniel took his time making love to her—slowly tasting her, getting lost in her essence, torturing her divinely. He waited until she begged for him, straining at the cuffs. Then, he fumbled for the key to release her, to feel her embrace.

Their bodies twisted together, pulsing with need for each other; their mouths locked in a caress around probing tongues.

Sylvia toyed with him for a time, her gentle moans

urging him on, until she sensed he was close. Then she rolled on top of him, whispering sexy things, dirty things; rising and falling down again, faster and faster, driving to that point of no return, that final intense rush to ecstasy.

And just then, at that moment, she did become what he wanted her to be . . . almost.

He bucked and twitched in short, uncontrollable waves.

She shrieked, arching her back, and collapsed onto him, quivering.

Daniel held her like that for awhile, catching his breath, listening to her heartbeat. He couldn't remember being more sexually satisfied. The phone rang. He turned toward it and saw a picture of Susan there in the silver frame . . . and the ground opened up.

82

████████ Morning arrived with thick clouds and a steady drizzle. Sylvia lay in bed feeling the fragments of a delicious dream fade. She tried to wrap herself back up in it, to be recaptured by its rapture, but in that juncture between sleep and wakefulness, she sensed someone's eyes upon her; someone watching her every move. She peeked under her lids and saw Daniel gazing at her from across the room, as still as a statue. He was already dressed in jeans and a tennis shirt, holding a steaming cup.

"Good morning," she said, blinking.

"Hi." He smiled back, breaking from his reverie. "I brought coffee. Unless you want tea . . ."

She sat up, dragging the sheet along with her, covering herself. "Coffee's fine."

"Good. Black, right?"

"How did you—"

"From the station house. I happened to notice."

"And remembered? How sweet."

"A detective's compulsion," he confessed, walking over to the bed. He handed her the cup, sitting down by her side.

The phone rang, but Daniel remained seated. It rang a second time.

"Aren't you going to get that?" she asked.

"No. I have a hunch who it is."

They waited through the message, then listened to the caller's voice.

"Yoo-hoo, Daniel. It's Mom. Just letting you know we'll be picking Adam up in about an hour and heading out. He's all packed. It's a lovely day. Nice and sunny. Perfect for the zoo. Remember to tell Mrs. Kunklemacher—something red. Bye, dear."

"See. My mother-in-law. She called last night, too. She's unrelenting. But with the best of intentions," he added quickly.

"Call her back."

"I will. When I'm ready."

"About last night, Daniel. It was wonderful. I needed that. I think we both did."

Daniel tried to change the subject. "So what are you going to do now?"

"I didn't want morning to come," she said, looking out the window. "Go back, I guess. See if Marion has cooled off."

"And if not?"

"Don't you realize," she said hopelessly, "that I have no choice?"

"I never should have taken the note," Daniel lamented.

"Why? Do you think this is the first time he hit me?"

"Sylvia, I'm sorry."

"Don't be. I got myself into this. But I'll get out."

Daniel nodded skeptically. "Don't do anything foolish."

"Not this Sylvia."

"And your other side?" he let fall.

"I thought you enjoyed it."

"I did." He paused, painfully. Then he said, "Something about Marion and the note bothers me. I keep playing it over and over again in my mind."

"What about it?"

"Why he was so protective about the note, and obviously still is." He gestured toward Sylvia's bruise. "It doesn't scan. There has to be more to it."

"A smudge on the family name," Sylvia offered. "It revealed the disgusting things that Dominic did."

"No, it didn't. I pieced that together from what you told me. The note only mentioned Bobby being molested."

"Well, how would you feel if *your* son was sexually abused?" she replied angrily. "The world doesn't have to know."

"So Marion was protecting you?" Daniel asked, confused.

"It was an embarrassment."

"For who? You? Bobby?"

Sylvia lowered her eyes and shook her head. "No. For Marion."

"What are you trying to say, Sylvia?" Daniel knew he didn't want to hear the answer but he asked anyway.

She took a deep breath, held it a moment, then let it out slowly. "Marion is Bobby's father."

It stung. Daniel tried not to let it show. "I see," he said softly.

"Finding out what happened changed things for him. He could hardly look at Bobby anymore—almost as though it was Bobby's fault. Imagine, his own son."

"And he didn't want anyone to know," Daniel said. "That explains it. Everything."

"God, what you must think of me."

"Does it matter?"

"Yes. Very much."

He recalled how she looked last night: bruised cheek, wet hair, lost in his robe—like a little girl, helpless and vulnerable. He had fought the urge to hold her then, to draw her close, to comfort her . . . and more. He felt that same way again, now.

He stroked her face, delicately sweeping away her hair. "Sylvia, it doesn't matter what you did in the past. We've all done things we regret. What's important is who you are now."

"I am what you've come to know," she said simply. *Was she?* "And what do you want, Sylvia?"

"Not what I have, that's for certain." She smiled hesitantly. "Maybe . . . this?" she said, looking at him with a gentle wrinkle of her brow.

Daniel was caught off guard and didn't answer. He didn't know what to say.

She tried to break the tension. "Listen to me running off at the mouth, talking absolute nonsense. It's just that I'm not used to someone being so kind. Now let me up, I have to go."

"So soon? I was, um, hoping you might stay awhile."

"Thanks. I will. But I really have to go. I mean, I have to pee." She giggled.

"Oh. Then how 'bout some breakfast?"

"Great. And call your mother-in-law back. Tell her to bring an umbrella."

"Right."

Daniel tried not to stare, but couldn't help himself as Sylvia jumped out of bed naked and bent to pick up his shirt—still on the floor—before scooting into the bathroom.

In the kitchen Daniel took inventory of what he had: one egg; a handful of Fruit Loops; a couple of swallows of milk. He panicked, then remembered the large slab of Kate's pie that he stowed in the freezer, saving it for a special treat.

A knock on the front door interrupted him as he was pulling out the box. He answered it just as Sylvia entered the room.

"Morning, Daniel." It was his father, holding a large brown paper bag.

Daniel blanched. "Dad, now's not a good time," he said, holding the door only half open, blocking his view.

"Don't be silly." Seymour pushed his way inside. "I've seen the kind of mess you make." Then he saw Sylvia standing there, and what she was wearing. Surprised, he said, "Oh, I'm sorry. I was just . . . I think I should go."

"Don't leave on account of me," Sylvia squeaked.

Daniel sighed. He looked uncomfortable. "Sylvia, this is my father. Dad, this is my . . . *friend*, Sylvia."

"Pleased to meet you, Mr. Pinchus."

"Call me Seymour."

"Okay, Seymour."

"It's Sylvia Luccetta, right?"

"Yes," she answered nervously.

"Uh-huh. Seen your picture in the paper a couple of times."

Shit, Daniel said to himself.

She held her breath, looked toward Daniel for support.

"But you're much prettier in person."

Sylvia blushed. "I like your father," she told Daniel. "Tell him he can stay."

"Well," Seymour started, then read the pleading in Daniel's eyes. "I should be going. I was in the neighborhood and I just stopped off to say hello. I have a friend waiting for me at the *Hamilton Press.*"

Daniel was relieved when his father left, until he heard another knock. The door opened. He was back again. Daniel groaned.

Seymour motioned for Daniel to step out into the hall. "Sorry," he said to Sylvia. "Forgot to tell Daniel something."

Alone with his son, Seymour spoke candidly. "You know, you don't have to act so guilty."

"Rotten timing, Dad. You should have called first. I feel like I was caught making out or something."

"Well, you were. But relax, I don't disapprove."

"Is that what you came back for? Just to tell me that?"

"No. I wanted to talk to you about Caldwell. By the way, did you eat yet?"

"Dad!"

"Didn't think so. Here. Bagels," he said, handing Daniel the brown bag. "Lox and cream cheese, too, in the bottom of the bag."

"Now you're really making me feel guilty. Sure you don't want to stay?"

"Already ate."

Daniel gave him a suspicious look.

"Really. Count them. I bought a dozen. Two are missing. In the car." Seymour shrugged, "I got hungry."

"What about Caldwell?"

"Oh, yeah. He has a book signing at Nostrand's this morning. By the new mall on Hanover. Ten-thirty. I wondered if you could run over there."

"But we already discussed that. There'll be a big crowd. Not the place to confront him, you said. That's why you sent Oscar to Scranton."

"Well, I think it's time one of us rattled Caldwell's cage."

"What made you change your mind?" Daniel asked.

"Oscar *did* go see him. Got back quite late. Called me this morning to cancel out."

"You're not meeting?"

"At the paper, yes. The gym, no. But he filled me in on the phone. Caldwell refused to talk once he found out what it was about. Bound in blood and like that."

"Right."

"Oscar and I compared notes, dug up some things anyway. Your theory about Squigger also being a pedophile?"

"Yeah?"

"I paged through some of his books last night. Very revealing. Always makes his main character an unlikely hero to little kids."

"He writes fiction, Dad. Not autobiographies."

"Most interesting was *Shades of Guilt.* One of his first efforts, the big success that launched his career. In a nutshell, it was about a female army nurse who was raped by her commanding officer. But the officer was very prominent—decorated for saving an orphanage in South America when it mistakenly fell under attack. They made him a role model. Even placed his picture on recruiting posters, hung 'em in the high schools. Others knew about the rape and covered it up. Thought they were doing the right thing. Readers had to decide for themselves."

"Does sound vaguely familiar. But you can't conclude—"

"And Caldwell claims he's gay. I understand it broke his father's heart."

"One thing has nothing to do with the other. Pedophiles and homosexuals are two separate entities," Daniel pointed out.

"Unless Caldwell is using that as a cover. Oscar seems to think so. It's more acceptable."

Daniel looked unconvinced. "What else?"

"He has a sixteen-year-old Jamaican houseboy."

"You think. . . ?"

"Calls Caldwell *uncle*."

"Still . . ."

"And when Oscar was waiting in the library for Caldwell to come down, he flipped through some art books on the shelf."

"So?"

"They were filled with child pornography."

Daniel's jaw was set. "What time did you say that signing was?"

83

In the *Hamilton Press* newsroom, Seymour spotted Oscar wedged into a corner, scanning a computer screen. He walked over to greet his friend, then noticed a picture hanging on the wall that intrigued him. It was an enlarged black-and-white photograph.

"Find out any more?" Seymour asked as he studied

the picture curiously. It gave him an odd sense of déjà vu.

"Lots," Oscar replied. "But nothing relevant. Malchomoty's up for his retention bid in six months."

"You don't say," he murmured.

Oscar swung around to see what had grabbed Seymour's attention. "That's the Ogden estate—how it used to be."

"Looks familiar. Can't seem to place it though . . ."

"It's changed quite a bit since then. I did a picture article on it a few years back. The old and the new. That shot is a restored photo from '53 when the farm was in full swing. I used it as an example of how unbridled development—new houses, roadways, shopping centers—is invading our farmland, devouring the beauty of the countryside. I called it 'All In the Name of Progress.' Won me an award," Oscar said proudly.

"Is the farm still there? Or is it a parking lot now?"

"Only thing left of the estate is the main farmhouse. It's pretty run-down, though. It was condemned and scheduled to be torn down, but after the article ran, there was talk about preserving the old place. Last I heard, they were still trying to get landmark status and money for restorations."

"Still in limbo, huh." Seymour looked closer at the image.

"Something like that." Oscar turned back to the computer. "You want me to continue with this?"

"Yeah. Why?"

"I thought you'd change your mind after what happened to Kirshner."

"Kirshner?"

"Haven't you heard?" Oscar asked, surprised.

Seymour was still staring distractedly at the picture, searching for his connection. He almost had it.

"Colin Kirshner committed suicide."

"Whaat?" Seymour stammered, spinning around.

"Late last night. Jumped out his office window. I thought you knew. There was a small blurb in the morning edition."

Seymour shook his head. "Didn't read the paper yet."

"Well, it looks like you finally found your Squigger."

"And he kept his promise," Seymour mumbled. "*Silent beyond his final breath.*"

"What was that?"

"Nothing," he said, waving it off, although he was visibly upset. "Just a stupid vow. Were they sure? I mean about it being suicide?"

"Apparently. But I guess it's not official until they complete their investigation. Autopsy was scheduled for ten o'clock today."

"I've gotta go," Seymour said. "Have to get to Philly."

"For the postmortem?"

"And to check out Van Buren."

"For crying out loud, Seymour," Oscar shouted. "That'll take all day. Let them do their job. You don't always have to be the one."

"I should have known," he said, wetting his lips, his breath coming heavy. "I feel responsible."

"Jesus, the guy jumped out of a window," Oscar declared, trying to calm his friend. "Not a thing you could have done. Relax. After all, it's not as though you pushed him!"

84

Sylvia turned the shower on soon after Daniel left. As he cleaned up the breakfast dishes, he had explained what he had to do that day, about he and Peter visiting the dentist. He made her promise to wait there until he got back. Not anxious to leave, she agreed.

She was shampooing her hair when she heard the faint ringing of the telephone. Thinking that it might be Daniel, that he had forgotten something, she quickly stepped out from under the spray.

The tape machine was already announcing that Daniel wasn't home. She grabbed a towel, dragging it along behind her as she hurried. But by the time she yanked the bathroom door open, she only caught the tail end of the message. It was a woman's voice, vaguely familiar. *"Tell Mrs. Kunklemacher—something red. Bye, dear."*

She went to the machine, pushed the button that replayed the messages. There was only one—the same one that Daniel's mother-in-law had left earlier that morning.

Daniel had just left, too soon for him to be checking in, Sylvia thought, then wondered if something was wrong with the machine. After a moment she shrugged and let the incident pass.

━━━━

At ten forty-five, there was already an enormous line stretched along the sidewalk outside Nostrand's. Daniel pushed his way through the door. People shouted at him. He told them he was from the press, held up his Polaroid camera.

Inside, he walked past the display of Caldwell's newest best-seller, *The Last Pied Piper,* searching the shelves for a copy of *Shades of Guilt.* He carried it with him to where Benjamin Caldwell sat in an overstuffed armchair, politely thanking each person as he handed back their personalized hardcover. He looked smaller than the pictures placed in the back of his books. Older and thinner, too. His hair was closely cropped, touched with gray, and he spoke in a high-pitched, almost melodious voice.

Daniel elbowed his way to the front, just as Caldwell finished signing for a woman named Doris.

"I really enjoyed this one," Daniel declared loudly, throwing the book he was holding down on the table in front of the author. "I think it's your best."

Caldwell's head shot back, his gaze lifting to Daniel.

A man working for the bookstore stood next to Caldwell, pointing at Daniel. "Excuse me, sir. You have to wait in line like everyone else. And Mr. Caldwell isn't signing *that* one today."

Caldwell raised his hands and smiled. "Sorry."

"Great plot," Daniel continued. "Where'd you get it from—college, maybe?"

Caldwell's expression suddenly turned ugly.

"Sir, I'm going to have to ask you to leave now," said the store employee.

"Can I at least take a picture?" he asked, lifting his camera. "My son's a big fan."

"No unauthorized photographs," Caldwell barked, starting to rise. "Put that camera—"

"Smile for the flash!" *Fump*.

━━━━

Diane and Paige ate an early lunch, then prepared to disembark. They had both had a marvelous time on the cruise. Paige loved the attention, meeting the captain, and ordering whatever she wanted in the dining room—especially the double desserts.

But they were looking forward to getting home and seeing the rest of the family. Diane wondered if Peter had gotten back from the crash site yet and decided to call the house just as soon as they got ashore.

Having been on the boat, she remained unaware of all that he had been through, his dismissal and the perilous chase to the railroad tracks. And it was probably better that way, her not knowing, just as it was better that she remained unaware of the mortal danger that lay ahead . . . for all of them.

━━━━

Daniel heard about Colin Kirshner on the car radio. He was stunned. *Suicide?* He wondered why his father hadn't told him and drove straight over to the *Hamilton Press*.

He caught Oscar just as he was leaving the newsroom. Oscar filled him in. No, Seymour hadn't known about Kirshner when he spoke to Daniel. He would probably be gone for hours.

Daniel got back in his car before it occurred to him

that he hadn't spoken to Peter since last night. Peter was supposed to call around nine o'clock to find out what time Daniel would be by to pick him up. With everything that happened that morning, Daniel had forgotten, and Peter hadn't called. It was now almost eleven-thirty. Concerned, he chose not to waste time looking for a phone and hurried over to the Roberts'.

Max Greely was not a handsome man. He had a pudgy face, tight features that seemed to be upholstered in place, and a bald spot circling his head that left only a tuft of frizzy hair at the top of his brow. They called him *Patch,* a fitting name, because of the line of dolls that he resembled.

He hated it, though. And if it were anyone else in the department, such a nickname would be grossly unkind—but it was Max. And they all agreed he deserved it. He was gruff, rude, and insulting. But mostly he was ugly, and bitter, and jealous, ever since he was passed over for promotion. The position, Chief Medical Examiner, was given to a younger associate, and a black female at that: Bonny Eastridge.

Greely had just finished with the body of Colin Kirshner, and when he left the autopsy room, he was immediately accosted by Seymour Pinchus. He knew Pinchus, but chose to look past him.

"Hey, Max," Seymour called as Greely walked by. "Got a minute to talk about Kirshner?"

Greely turned his head reluctantly. "You have no authority here. And, from what I understand, not even in Hamilton anymore."

"I know. It's a . . . personal matter."

"Then read about it in the morning paper," he growled.

Eastridge was coming down the hall and heard the

exchange. She also knew Seymour. He had helped her out with a case a few years back. "Tell the man what he wants to know, Patch," she ordered.

"Against policy," he argued, his voice whiny.

"Who's it going to hurt?" she fired back.

"Thanks, Bonny," Seymour said.

Greely relented, unhappily. "What do you want to know?"

"Cause of death."

"Fall from height."

"Suicide?"

"Investigation ain't done yet."

"Come on, Greely," Seymour said, lowering his brow.

"Yeah, suicide. He was terminally ill. Found cancer all over the fucking place: stomach, liver, lungs. And there are reports that he'd been depressed the last couple of days. Very depressed."

Seymour shifted uncomfortably. "Did he leave a note?"

"Sort of. On a torn piece of paper. Wouldn't make a fucking difference anyway, though."

"Why not?"

Greely flashed a ghoulish smile. "His last message was pretty clear—he splattered it all over the sidewalk."

━━━━

Daniel was relieved to find that Peter was well. He had had a quiet night, and had simply overslept. They killed some time drinking coffee and trading theories before leaving for Dr. Silverman's office.

When they turned onto Ridge, the street was jammed with traffic. There was some activity at the far end of the block: a flashing light, people milling about. As they drew closer, they noticed a fire marshal's car while they were still about a hundred yards away.

Gradually the burnt remains of the building came into sight.

"Can't be!" Peter said apprehensively.

"What's the address?"

"982."

Daniel glanced to the side, noted a number on a nearby mailbox and started counting down: *994, 992, 990 . . .* He leaned forward to catch a better view. "How the fuck did he know?" he yelled, pounding the steering wheel with his fist.

"Did you tell anybody?" Peter asked.

"Only my father," he replied, but didn't mention that he had also told Sylvia early that morning. *She could've made a call when I was showering.* He felt himself falling, then shook the thought out of his head.

They got to the house and parked behind the marshal's car.

John Duffy, the fire marshal, was standing in front and recognized Pinchus immediately. "Hey, what's shaking, Daniel?"

"Can you give me a rundown, Duff?"

"Since when are you working arson? You change departments?"

"No. But was it? Arson, I mean."

"This an official call?"

"No."

"Under the table?"

"I'd appreciate it."

Duffy shrugged. "Could be. Possible accelerant used on the side wall of the building. We're doing a scan, but it's a good bet. Witness saw some guy running from the scene about ten-fifteen last night, right after the call came in."

"So the fire was last night," Daniel said, hiding a sigh of relief. Then he remembered: he had written Silverman's name and wrote notes about the lead on a

pad. And put it in his bedroom when he got back from
Harrisburg. She could have noticed it. He dozed after
getting the tea. But for how long? *No! There wasn't
enough time. Still* . . .

"You okay?" Peter asked.

"Yeah, sure."

"The owner, Dr. Silverman, can't believe it," Duffy
said. "Thinks somehow it's his fault. He's over there,
sitting on the curb." He pointed to an elderly gentleman in a tweed coat.

Peter and Daniel introduced themselves to him and
told him how sorry they were. He was shaking his
head. "Damn coffeemaker. Should have reminded Elda
to shut it off. She always forgets. Now look what's happened." His eyes filled with water. "My patients—
who'll take care of them? What will they do? What will
I do?"

"Don't blame yourself. It's not your fault," Peter
said.

"Or Elda's," Daniel added.

"I'm not so sure about that. But you're both very
kind. Who did you say you were again?"

"We called yesterday," Peter repeated. "About the
records? Arthur Sarchick?"

"Oh, yes. Of course. Artie. You needed his chart."

"Yes." Peter looked back at the smoldering building,
disheartened. "Guess we're a bit late."

"But I remembered."

Peter sighed. "I'm afraid we need more than that.
The record—treatment notes and X rays."

"That's what I'm trying to tell you. After you called,
I ran up to the attic to fetch the chart. Lucky—found it
in the second batch I went through. I was rushing to
leave, and I happened to carry it along with me. Got it
in the car."

"You have it?" Peter gasped.

Daniel's reaction was guarded. He waited, hope hedging against another disappointment.

"Absolutely," Silverman said. "Did you know he had a telephone bridge? Did it myself. Holds a space between his upper front teeth. Don't see many of those. Beautiful job. Exquisite margins."

"Are you sure?" Daniel couldn't keep himself from asking.

"Sir, I've been practicing dentistry for forty-five years," he replied indignantly. "But don't take my word for it. See for yourself."

"Excuse me?"

"Perfectly positioned casted U right there on the X rays."

▬▬▬

In front of the Monkey House at the Hamilton Zoo, Susan's parents waited with Adam. Susan's father was complaining about having to drag an umbrella along: He knew it wasn't going to rain no matter what Daniel had said. He was also disappointed in the White Tiger Exhibit—the animals stayed in the back, and he never got a close look. A zookeeper had to yell at him because he threw food, trying to coax the tigers over.

Adam was playing with the propeller of a toy plane that his grandparents had given him.

"Be careful, don't break it," his grandmother warned just as she noticed a woman in a red hat approaching.

"Mr. and Mrs. Richmond?" the woman asked with a smile.

"Yes," Susan's mother answered. "Are you Mrs. Kunklemacher?"

"Last time I looked," she giggled. "Daniel described you to a T. And I certainly recognized Adam." She reached out to pat his head.

"Recognized?" Mrs. Richmond asked, her forehead wrinkling.

"From the pictures in the apartment, of course. I also clean for Daniel. Didn't he tell you?"

"Yes, he did," Mr. Richmond replied.

"So how do you like my *chapeau*?" She threw her head back in a pose. "Isn't it smashing? You did say something red."

Susan's mother laughed. "It's perfect."

Mrs. Kunklemacher bent to talk to Adam. "We're going to have lots of fun, you and me. And later, I'll bring you over to your daddy."

Adam took a step back.

"Adam," his grandmother cried. "Mrs. Kunklemacher is very nice."

"Don't worry," she said, waving it off as she rose. "He'll warm up. They usually do. I have a grandson just about his age. Lives in Minnesota, though." She sighed. "I miss him desperately. Oh, my! How could I say that after what you've been through. Please forgive me."

"Don't worry." Susan's mother squeezed Mrs. Kunklemacher's arm. "You're a dear."

"Will we get to spend some time together? It's a marvelous zoo."

Mr. Richmond glanced at his watch impatiently.

"I'm sorry," Susan's mother said. "It's a long drive back to Connecticut and we have plans later."

"What a shame. I hope you didn't miss the White Tiger Exhibit?"

"More like it missed us," Mr. Richmond complained.

"They stayed too far back," Susan's mother told her.

Mr. Richmond looked anxious. "We really must be going."

"Can't we wait a few minutes?"

"Adam will be fine," Mrs. Kunklemacher reassured

her. She offered her hand to the boy. "Come along, Adam."

Adam hesitated.

"Let's go back to the tigers," she said, keeping her hand out. "We'll go, 'Here, kitty, kitty,' and 'psss, psss, psss,' and I bet they'll come right up to us. Then we'll get in your plane and fly right home to Daddy."

This time Adam took her hand.

Mrs. Richmond beamed. "Daniel said you were someone special, and now I know why."

"Your grandson is beautiful," she said softly, and started to lead Adam away.

Susan's parents watched the woman they just met lead their grandson in the opposite direction, never more trusting, never more at ease . . . and never noticing just how awkwardly Mrs. Kunklemacher clutched her pocketbook.

85

Seymour Pinchus faced the rear of Madison Hall, the building that housed Colin Kirshner's office. It was secluded back there, tucked away from the vivacity of the main campus. He wasn't surprised that there weren't any witnesses to Kirshner's final swan dive.

He had gone to the police after leaving the morgue. They were cordial but cool. The old-timers he once knew there were all gone, retired or deceased. It made Seymour feel old. So did a young detective with a military cut who kept calling him Pop in a patronizing way.

Seymour had wanted to twist his ears off, but remained patient, eventually coaxing the younger man into giving him a peek at the official report.

Only Kirshner's window had been found open; the others remained locked. Kirshner had been dead for maybe twenty minutes before the body was discovered, according to his shattered wristwatch. The M.E. backed it up. There was a football game that night in the stadium not too far away, but no one saw anything until it was over.

At approximately ten o'clock last night, in total solitude, the Dean of Students of Van Buren University jumped from his office, smashing himself against the walkway four stories down, Seymour reported to himself. He could still see the faded bloodstains on the stone. It wouldn't completely wash away. Not for a long time. Maybe not ever. He knelt to touch it, feeling as though it were he, with an invisible set of hands, who pushed Kirshner to his death.

Still kneeling, he turned toward the building. His eyes counted four floors up, then rested there. The window was shut. In a dreamlike state he envisioned it open, Kirshner climbing out.

But there was something wrong with the imagery. He shook his head. He distinctly remembered that Kirshner's office was right in the middle of the hallway, fourth door down. He counted seven sets of windows. This one was slightly to the left of center. Seymour squinted. There was a narrow ledge.

He stood. With his eyes fixed on the fourth floor, he walked until he was even with the middle windows, pacing off roughly twenty feet. It would have been a long way to hug a building, Seymour thought. And the football game would have been noisy. If Kirshner had chosen to scream, nobody would have heard it.

He knew the pitfalls of jumping to conclusions, but Seymour Pinchus was beginning to get the distinct notion that maybe someone made sure Squigger kept his pledge. "Sarchick," he said out loud. "That goddamn son of a bitch."

86

Daniel and Peter finally had the proof— Sarchick's dental record. And they were positive Sarchick set the fire. How he found out where they were looking was still a mystery. But as long as he thought that the record was destroyed, it would remain safe. They would keep it quiet, wait for Daniel's father to get back before deciding who to bring it to. For safekeeping, Peter duplicated the chart and X rays at his office and hid the original in one of the operatory cabinets.

While they were finishing up, Daniel phoned his apartment. It wasn't the first time. There was no answer again. He hung up when the machine came on. *Had Sylvia gone home? She had promised to wait. But she wasn't there.* He became disheartened, and was surprised just how wounded he felt. *Obviously, it didn't mean that much to her.*

Other thoughts slowly resurfaced, vague, disconcerting: *Could she have used him, found out all she needed to know, and taken off?* He couldn't believe it, wouldn't believe it. But the thoughts grew beyond what he could bury. He became infected; knowing for sure was all that mattered. He drove Peter home, then rushed to his apartment.

Sylvia met him at the door. He didn't know what to think.

"You missed your father," Sylvia informed him. "He called from Philadelphia. Figured you heard about Colin Kirshner's suicide. He went to check it out. Said the police weren't very informative, but he noticed something . . . *curious*? And then he ran into Kirshner's secretary. Anyway, he told me to tell you he'll be awhile, and he'll call you when he gets back."

"Anyone else call?" he asked suspiciously, glancing over at the answering machine. Nothing was flashing.

Sylvia read the look, but didn't understand. "Daniel, what's the matter with you?"

"Where have you been, Sylvia?" he demanded.

She cocked her head at him in disbelief. "Why, you checking up on me?"

"I called a couple of times. No one answered."

"I didn't think I was a prisoner," she snapped.

"You're not."

"Then why the third degree?"

She had a point. He was allowing his emotions to take control. He tried to smooth it over. "I'm sorry," he said. "I didn't realize how I sounded. I was just . . . concerned."

"Oh," she replied, her voice softening. She paused, then said, "The first time I was in the shower, I think. I heard the phone ring, but didn't get it in time. Afterward, I went out shopping."

"Shopping?"

"Well, I can't keep going around in torn clothes."

It wasn't until then that he noticed that she was wearing a new-looking sweater. "Looks great," he remarked.

"Thanks. Got something else, too," she said, pointing to a wrapped present on the kitchen table. "For your son, Adam. It's a set of Russian nesting dolls. You know, the kind where one fits inside another. I thought he might have fun with it."

"Sylvia, you shouldn't—"

"Tell him it was from you. He'll be expecting something special. I know you've been too preoccupied to think of things like that."

"You're right. I have to learn to be a father again."

"I didn't mean that."

"I know. But I'll tell him the truth."

"You don't have to."

"He won't care. I'll take him to Grossman's tomorrow, let him pick out something grand. Please stay," he asked suddenly, surprised even as he heard himself say the words. "Long enough to meet Adam and give him the dolls yourself?"

Her expression glowed. "I'd love to. What time is Mrs. Kunklemacher bringing him by?"

"About four o'clock. She's supposed to call first, to make sure I'm here."

"Glad you asked. I can't wait to meet your son."

"Sylvia, you're incredible," Daniel said.

He took her in his arms. He was ashamed of what he had thought before—the suspicion, the doubt. He promised himself he would make it up to her.

And because he had promised himself, when she asked how his day went, he told her without hesitation, about Dr. Silverman and the fire, and about Sarchick's dental records being saved. He broke his word to Peter, but he did it out of trust, and also some guilt . . . and he did it without thinking.

Four o'clock came and went without a call. Daniel just assumed Mrs. Kunklemacher had lost track of time and spent longer at the zoo than planned. But when the phone didn't ring by four-thirty, he became anxious. He dialed Mrs. Kunklemacher's number and let it ring several times.

"The zoo must be crowded with that special exhibit," Sylvia said calmly as he gripped the receiver. "They're probably on their way."

Somebody finally picked up on the fifth ring, but the line was quiet.

"Hello? Hello . . ." Daniel waited. He thought he heard a moan. "Mrs. Kunklemacher, are you there?"

Sylvia was at his side, then, concern creasing her brow.

"Ca . . . can't talk," a groggy voice finally replied. "Have to be . . . have to be somewhere."

Daniel stared at Sylvia, his face drained of color. "Help . . . me" were the last words he heard.

He dropped the phone. "Mrs. Kunklemacher—something's wrong," he said, racing out into the hall.

Sylvia followed him as he vaulted up the stairs to the next floor and pounded on Mrs. Kunklemacher's door.

Nobody came.

"Move away from the door. I'm going to kick it in," he said loudly to whoever might be on the other side. Then he stood back and lunged at the door with his foot up. There was a crack of wood and the ping of metal snapping. The door swung open.

Mrs. Kunklemacher was on the living room floor on her side. The telephone was sprawled next to her, its cord twisted. A picture frame was knocked over and a lamp teetered on the edge of an end table.

"Mrs. Kunklemacher, what happened?" Daniel knelt next to her.

She lifted her head, eyes half open, pupils dilated.

She seemed to be regaining some sense of awareness. "Where's Adam?"

Sylvia grabbed the cushion off the couch and placed it gently under Mrs. Kunklemacher's head, then quietly reset the phone and began to dial.

Daniel swallowed. "You don't know where he is?"

"I—I never got to the zoo."

Then who picked Adam up?

"What?"

"A man came. Said he was Adam's grandfather and that there was a change of plans." She took a breath, wet her lips. "I let him in. But he wasn't. How was I to know? He grabbed me, held me down, then stuck a needle in my arm."

"Grandfather?" he muttered through his teeth. *Sarchick. How the fuck could he possibly have found out?*

"Nine-one-one is on the way," Sylvia said.

Daniel swung his gaze to her. His eyes narrowed.

She got up to get Mrs. Kunklemacher a glass of water and his stare followed her, his heartbeat thumping in his ears.

"He told me I was lucky," Mrs. Kunklemacher continued, her voice quivering. "Said he ought to kill me, but—I looked so much like his mother."

Daniel stiffened. Suddenly he knew exactly where to look.

"I'm so sorry, Daniel. I let you down," she said tearfully.

Sylvia returned with the water.

"It's not your fault," he told Mrs. Kunklemacher.

"You have to find Adam," she cried.

"I will. I promise." He rose. "Take care of her," he said to Sylvia as he headed for the door.

"Where are you going? I want to help."

"Maybe you've *helped* enough," he mumbled.

"What?"

"Never mind," he shouted over his shoulder. "Just take care of her."

"But can't you at least tell me where you're going?"

"I'm going to get my son," he roared. And then he was gone.

87

Sarchick's mother—*of course! The perfect cover. It was all falling into place now. His mother's house: the light in the basement, no one ever coming to the door. He needed a safe place to stay. A place and scheme too obvious to consider. And what was it that Milano had called him, a master of masquerade? No wonder he was able to slip through the neighborhood unnoticed. A face children could trust. How many other victims were there?* But Daniel didn't dwell on that. He only wanted his son back— alive and unharmed.

He stood on the porch. Cloud-filled skies made evening arrive early. He had already circled the house, casing it, keeping back in the darkness. The basement light was off, but everything else looked the same— deserted. He wasn't about to be fooled again.

He peered through the edge of the front window, thought he saw a silhouette standing in a corner of the room. He wasn't sure. His eyes strained in the dimness. The object appeared to be still. He moved to the door, grasped the knob, and tried turning it. To his surprise, the latch clicked this time. Reflexively, he reached for his gun with his free hand. A chill came over him—it wasn't there. He had stowed it away with his badge.

He hesitated at the door—

But he wouldn't permit fear to paralyze him. *Adam would be okay. God wouldn't let anything happen to someone he loved,* he told himself. *Not again.*

Adam's image floated up at him, calling to him: *"Daddy, where are you? Daddy, help me. Daddy, I need you."*

He drew in a breath and slowly pushed against the door. It creaked open. His eyes scanned the room, then rested on something hidden in the shadows. It swung gently in the breeze he had let in.

He took a step toward it, trying to see better. *Something suspended from the ceiling. The silhouette he saw from the window?*

He moved closer, unmindful of anything else around him. It appeared to be a figure, a small one. A sense of dread started in his belly, then quickly consumed him.

Jesus, no! It was a body hanging from the ceiling. The realization tore into him. He noticed the small red sneakers. *Oh, my God. Oh, my God. Adam.*

Grief contorted his face. He felt himself going limp, but jerked his body forward. He had to look, had to know for sure. He shot out a hand to steady what was dangling, grabbing it by the pants leg. It collapsed under his grip. He blinked in disbelief. It wasn't real. Then he felt the crack on the side of his head, and everything went black.

88

Peter had taken the copy of Sarchick's dental chart home with him. He studied every pertinent detail. He wanted to make sure there were no surprises. Before, he had faced skepticism and ridicule. This time would be different. Doubts would be erased, people would be convinced, because this time, he had irrefutable evidence. Confident, he put the chart away and began straightening up the house.

The clock in the living room told him it was six-fifteen. Diane and Paige would have taken off already. They would be back in a couple of hours. Tomorrow morning, he would pick up Melanie and Paul. By then, the messy situation with Sarchick would be over. Everything would be back to normal.

Over the noise of the vacuum, Peter heard the phone ring. He switched the machine off, hurrying to get the call.

"Is Dr. Roberts there?"

"Speaking."

"Dr. Roberts, I have something very important to tell you."

"Yes."

"It's about the plane your family's on."

Peter felt his stomach tighten, his knees weaken. "What about it?"

"Remember Flight 1089?" the caller said gleefully. "Same thing's going to happen when they try to land that plane."

"Who is this?" Peter yelled.

The caller laughed. "Told you I'd take care of the wife and kiddies for you."

Peter froze, holding the phone to his ear for several seconds after the final click. Scenes from the crash site flashed before his eyes: bodies torn apart, fragmented, twisted until they no longer looked like people. *My God—Diane and Paige!* He was shaking so badly he needed two hands to hang up the phone. He wanted to vomit.

There might still be time. The plane wasn't due to land until 8:05. Maybe they had learned enough about the North America crash to stop it.

He had to tell someone. He grabbed the receiver and tried to focus. He started to dial, then stopped, and with a trembling finger wondered—who should he tell? Who would listen?

89

He worked swiftly with the wires in the dark, like an experienced tailor looping stitches. The army had taught him well, made him practice until he could do it in his sleep.

It came in handy. Soon, the trigger was set, tied to the front doorknob. *A special present for Seymour Pinchus,* he said to himself, admiring the job.

He had gotten everything he needed without creating the slightest glimmer of suspicion in anyone's eye. It was so easy—a trip to the local hardware store and garden center, dressed as a sweet old lady. And there was no question that it would work. He only wondered how big the explosion would be. *Demolish half the house? Or maybe the whole damn thing.*

90

Peter Roberts tried in vain to find someone who would believe him. He called the airport and the airline. They took the information very calmly, he thought, then placed him on hold. Both times they came back, asked him to state his name and address again.

"Aren't you listening?" he yelled over and over, desperately. "The North America flight from Miami due in at eight-oh-five is going to crash!"

"Have you been feeling okay, sir?" a man from the airport information line asked.

"We'll take care of it," someone from the airline told him nonchalantly. "Are you home? Good. Just stay there. We'll be in touch."

Peter called Daniel. There was no answer. He tried Seymour a few times, but he couldn't get through. He glanced at his watch: It was nearly seven o'clock. He was running out of time. There was only one other way to make them listen. He had to get to the airport, and fast.

He opened the door just as the bell rang. A man in a dark suit was standing there.

"Peter Roberts? Agent Butterfield, FBI," the man announced, flashing an ID.

"Thank God," Peter said, opening the door wider. "You called about Flight 629?"

"Yes. It's rigged. It's going to crash when it tries to land."

"And how do you know about this?"

"I gave that information already," Peter replied, frustrated. "Someone told me."

"Who?"

He hesitated. "Look, we don't have time for a game of questions and answers. I want to know what the hell's being done about the situation!"

"Just calm down. We're taking the necessary precautions."

"Necessary precautions? We're talking about a planeload of people. My wife and daughter."

"Yes, we're aware of that. We also know about you, Doctor," Butterfield said, heaving a sigh. "Spoke with some of our people handling the 1089 disaster. Seems you've got a history of imagining things. Also got a call warning us that you might pull a stunt like this. It came about a half hour before you phoned in."

Peter's eyes lit up. "Don't you see? That was the saboteur!"

"Yes, of course." He nodded gently at Peter.

"You have to believe me. People are going to die. He planned it all."

"Uh-huh. And who might that be?"

"Sarchick," Peter blurted.

"Thought so," Butterfield said, grabbing Roberts by the arm. "Better come along with me."

Peter shook loose. "I'm not going anywhere, except to the airport."

A black limousine screeched to a halt in front of the house. Two men jumped out, leaving the doors open as they rushed up to the porch.

Roberts and Butterfield turned to look. Peter recognized one of them from a campaign poster—Congressman Whitney.

"What's this all about, Cliff?" Butterfield asked one of the approaching men.

"Got Congressman Charles Whitney here. Someone from the airport called him. They knew his wife was on that plane and filled him in as to what's going on. He says he wants Roberts at the airport with him."

Butterfield shook his head. "I don't think that's a good idea."

"I don't give a fuck what you think," Whitney declared.

"Excuse me, sir?"

"You better start believing him," Whitney said, pointing to Roberts, "before we end up with bodies and pieces of fuselage scattered all over Hamilton."

"The plane's been contacted. The captain's checking her out, and it's being searched by the crew. Nothing's showing up. I respect your position, sir, but you don't have the authority to tell me what to do."

Peter tensed.

"You're right," Whitney replied. "However, it just so happens that I'm on the House Judiciary Committee. And by God, if something happens, I'm going to drag your ass before it to explain why."

The other agent shrugged. "We have a chopper flying someone from the NTSB and one of our own down from the crash site of 1089. Thought what they learned might be useful. We're all meeting in the control tower at Hamilton Airport."

"And we got every available piece of rescue equipment heading there, too," Whitney told Peter. "We can be at Hamilton Airport in twenty minutes."

"What else?" Peter asked. "What else can we do?"

"Pray for our families . . . and everyone else aboard."

91

Seymour Pinchus turned into the drive that led to his cottage at precisely seven-thirty. He had discovered some interesting things at Van Buren with Daphne's help. She had let him into Kirshner's office, answered his questions, and showed him whatever he needed. He had seen scuff marks and splinters along the window ledge.

Seymour hadn't spoken to Daniel since that morning, and now he was anxious to get home and talk about what he'd found.

He saw Milano's car off to the side of the driveway. At first, he was delighted at the prospect of having company. But when he saw Sam standing by his door with Sylvia, his elation faded, replaced by apprehension. He parked and got out.

"What's up?" he asked, slamming the car door shut. "Something wrong?"

Sam looked at Seymour gravely. "It's Adam. He's been kidnapped."

Seymour went pale. "What? When? How?"

"This afternoon," Sam told him. "Sarchick drugged

Mrs. Kunklemacher, then someone posed as her at the zoo. Susan's parents never suspected a thing. Handed your grandson right over."

"And now Daniel's missing, too," Sylvia added, her voice shaking.

Seymour sucked in air, making a sound as if he were mortally wounded. He let it out slowly, trying to compose himself. "Tell me," he said through clenched teeth.

"Daniel took off to find Adam. It sounded like he knew where to look, but he wouldn't tell me," Sylvia said. "I stayed behind with Mrs. Kunklemacher, until the ambulance came. Then, I went down to Daniel's apartment to wait, hoping he'd get in touch. He never did. But someone else called."

"Who?"

"I think it was Sarchick," she said, distressed. "At first, he seemed startled that somebody answered at all, and asked me if it was Daniel's apartment. Then he said, 'Tell the old man it's payback time. I got his grandson, and now I have his son, too.' "

"Payback?" Seymour searched for the significance.

"That's what he said."

"Anything else?"

Her lips pressed together. "Something about 'everyone going out with a bang.' After that, he hung up. Then I tried to call you. But your phone's out of order."

"That's right," Milano confirmed. "I tried, too. Several times, before and after picking up Sylvia."

"I got Sam's number out of Daniel's telephone book," Sylvia explained.

"We thought the best thing to do was to drive over and see if you were home," Sam added.

"If Daniel knew where to look for Adam, he would have left word with someone," Seymour pointed out.

"He was concerned about his son. He wasn't thinking clearly," Milano offered.

"He still would have called."

Milano shrugged. "But your phone doesn't work."

"Maybe he got lucky." Seymour turned quickly and unlocked the door. His hand grasped the knob.

"One more thing, Seymour. I guess I better tell you this now," Milano said.

"What?" Seymour sensed it wouldn't be good. He tried to brace himself for it. He couldn't fathom what else could be wrong.

"It's about the plane Diane and Paige are on. Sarchick may have rigged it. He called Peter. Told him it's going to crash when it tries to land."

Seymour shut his eyes tightly, his chest abruptly collapsed. "*Shoyn genug.* Is there no end?"

"At first, they didn't believe Peter. But Congressman Whitney interceded. I got the word from the station house. Half the city's headed over to Hamilton Airport. The cavalry. Plane's due to land shortly."

Seymour's eyes snapped open. "Whitney?"

"Yeah. The Feds thought Peter was pulling another stunt. But Whitney showed up and vouched for him. His wife's on that plane, too."

Seymour was trying to put it all together.

"I have my doubts, though," Milano said calmly. "It doesn't click. Sarchick's here. The plane took off from Miami. How could he have done anything to it? It's impossible."

"Impossible?" Seymour cried. "I would have said the same damn thing about everything else Sarchick was able to accomplish."

He twisted the knob. The door opened with a pop as the latch turned. Seymour immediately went to the phone. There was a clear dial tone. "Seems to be working now," he announced.

The answering machine flashed, indicating only one message. He poked a finger at the playback button, praying.

There was a lot of static, and the words sounded garbled, but the voice was unmistakably Daniel's:

"Hi, this is Daniel . . . Sarchick . . . "—crackle— *"I'll be checking . . . "*—crackle—*"the place"*— crackle—*"it all began."* And then nothing.

"Daniel's answering machine was also acting funny," said Sylvia. "Playing back an old message when I didn't get to the phone on time."

"Hhmm." Seymour scratched his head, hit the button to play it again.

Sam furrowed his brow. "The place where it all began? What does it mean?"

Seymour gazed up, mouthing the words, thinking.

"He used to work for Dominic before all this started," Sylvia threw out. "Could he be at the house?"

Seymour considered it, then shook his head. "Too risky. He needed a safer spot. Sarchick's a pedophile. A psychological profile would tell you they have to feel powerful, and they have a dire need to be in control. I was hoping we could use that against him. But now . . ."

"What about the warehouse across from Carmine's?" Milano suggested. "Sarchick shot Dominic from there—talk about a position of power. And a perfect place to hide. It fits."

"Possibly. But whatever we come to, we better be right. Every minute we lose could mean . . ." Seymour paused, suddenly unable to get a breath.

"Don't even think it, Seymour. We'll find them," Milano assured him.

"Wait!" Sylvia shouted. "I just remembered something. Something Mrs. Kunklemacher said right before

Daniel rushed out. She told Daniel that Sarchick didn't kill her because she reminded him of his mother."

Seymour cocked his head.

"That could be it," Sam said excitedly. "His mother still lives in town. Has an old house over on—on—"

"Yes, I know. It was listed in the report I had given to Daniel. But I can't remember the exact location," Seymour yelled, frustrated.

Milano looked uncertain. "We were there once. Six months ago. But I'm not sure of the address."

"What's her first name?" Seymour prompted.

"Agnes. No, Agatha . . . I think."

Sylvia grabbed the phone book on the desk, rifled through it. "Not in here," she said.

Seymour snapped his fingers. "Oscar. The computers. They have everything. He mentioned he was going back to the *Hamilton Press* tonight." He smiled. "He found a new chess program. Thought he would try to improve his game."

Sylvia looked up the general information number for the paper, called it out as Seymour dialed and switched the phone to speaker. A woman answered. It took him a little less than a minute to get across what he needed, and a couple more for her to track Oscar down. Finally, she relayed the call.

Seymour swiftly filled him in. Oscar seemed to know exactly what to do. Pinchus held his breath.

They heard Oscar groan.

"What? What's the matter?"

"Well, I ran the name search for Agatha Sarchick. It gives the most recent information first," Oscar explained.

"Yeah, so?"

"First thing that popped up on the screen was . . . her obituary. Seymour, she died two years ago."

"Shit!" Seymour slapped the desk.

"But as of six months ago, she was listed as the owner of the house," Milano recalled. "Someone had to be paying the bills. The taxes."

Seymour's eyes grew. "Then, that's it—the answer. Oscar," he said urgently. "Does the obituary give her address?"

"2017 Skidmore Avenue."

"Got it."

"I'll radio the station house. Have half a dozen men there inside of fifteen minutes," Sam declared.

"No!" Seymour said with an abrupt wave of his hand. "Can't risk that. We go alone. You and me."

"I'm coming, too," Sylvia insisted.

Sam shook his head. "No way. Too dangerous."

"Try and stop me."

Seymour looked at Sam, palms up.

Milano suggested they all go in his car, figuring he was in the best shape to drive.

"We better take two cars. Just in case," Seymour told him. "I'll drive Sylvia. You follow."

"Okay, let's roll."

"Wait a second. I'll be right back." Seymour rushed into his bedroom, went to the closet, and reached up for his box of mementoes. He pushed the news clippings aside, the letter from Quigley, and his shield. He found what he was after, and shoved his gun under his belt.

92

■■■■■■ Dr. Peter Roberts and Congressman Charles Whitney were ushered into the control tower at Hamilton Airport. Two men with headsets on were seated at a desk in front of one of the tower windows. Several others were huddled around them, pacing, drinking coffee, asking each other questions as they stared into the empty night sky.

One broke away from the group, introducing himself as Bud Sebring of the NTSB. Sebring had been investigating the crash of Flight 1089 and had been shuttled down to Hamilton to see if he could help. Not only was he a well-respected investigator, he told them, but he also used to fly the 727—knew the aircraft inside and out. He had determined eyes, and a direct manner. He wasn't happy with the way Whitney and Roberts had importuned their way into that room, didn't believe it was any place for civilians. But he did have questions for them.

"Which one of you received the call?" he asked.

"I did," Roberts replied.

"What'd the caller say? Exactly?"

Roberts took a breath. "He told me what happened to Flight 1089 is going to happen here, to this flight. The same thing. When it tries to land," he added shakily.

"He used those words: 'the same thing'?"

Roberts's forehead wrinkled in concentration. "I'm . . . pretty sure."

"Is that important?" Whitney asked.

"Eleven thousand feet; forty miles out," one of the controllers announced.

Sebring swung around for a second, then turned back to Whitney and Roberts. "Maybe," he said, clearly hesitant to add more.

"What do you mean, *maybe*?" Whitney shouted impatiently. "I want to know what the hell's going on here!"

"Look, you'll have to let the experts handle this." He shook his head. "I'm sorry. I just can't tell you any more right now."

"Then I want to speak to whoever's in command," Whitney demanded.

"Can't," Sebring said. "He's busy flying that plane."

"The pilot?"

Sebring nodded. "Above and beyond everyone else, the captain's in charge."

"You mean it's all up to him?" Whitney said incredulously. "What about the experts?"

"He's one of them," Sebring threw back. "We can advise him, and give him information. But he makes the final decisions."

"You have to tell us what's going on," Roberts said desperately. "You've been on the hill. You've seen what can happen. What if it were your wife and daughter on that plane?"

"Ten thousand feet," a controller called out.

Sebring shut his eyes. "I'd want to know," he admitted. After a moment, he opened his eyes, and began to explain. "Flight 1089 had three small explosions. We found evidence of that outside the main body of the aircraft. Each one was strategically placed to knock out hydraulics and cables. We believe an altimeter was used to detonate them. The blasts all happened at an altitude of five thousand feet. We know that from the flight recorders and what the captain reported. Not enough to bring her down immediately, but enough to disable her. Badly."

"That's why you wanted to know if this was exactly the same situation," Peter realized.

Sebring nodded. "The five-thousand-foot mark is critical. Ten eighty-nine was in a descent without controls—engines running. She was vulnerable. Couldn't pull up. Had to try for a landing. But in order to do that, she had to swing around."

"How could she do that?"

"She could still turn by manipulating her engines. However, the weather didn't cooperate. Turbulence grabbed her and caused her to roll—and that was it. But that won't happen here," Sebring insisted.

"Why not?" Whitney scoffed. "You said the explosives were outside. What can anyone possibly do?"

"The captain's taking a straight-in approach—no turns," he pointed out. "Also dumped excess fuel."

"What if those explosives are set for a different altitude?" Whitney voiced what they were all thinking.

"She's already lined up. Captain positioned her sixty miles out for the straight in. And we cleared the way. All other flights have been diverted."

Peter gazed out the window for the first time, saw

the still runways. He noticed the fog creeping in, blurring the lights. "What about the weather?" he said, pointing a trembling finger at the growing shroud.

"Better than 1089 had. Visibility isn't great, but no big bumps. Both aircraft, Flight 1089 and this one, are 727s. If there's sabotage, the explosives would have to be planted in the same location to target controls. Away from passengers."

"Twenty-five miles out; eight thousand feet," the controller called.

Peter tensed. No one had been able to predict what Sarchick would do yet. "And if they're placed in the main cabin this time, or if he used a timer?" he asked fearfully.

"We thought of that, too," Sebring told him. "But he couldn't use a timing device."

Peter blinked. "Why not?"

"You said the caller told you, 'when it tries to land.' The flight's almost over. A timer would be too risky. An altimeter is almost foolproof, though—set for when the cabin depressurizes. But in this case the flight engineer is holding the inside pressure right where it is. The only areas he can't control are the aft stair area and the landing gear compartment. But I don't think—"

"How long can he keep it up?" snapped Whitney.

"Until it lands."

Peter bent his head. "Thank God."

Whitney was breathing heavily. His eyes darted back and forth wildly. "Then what?"

"At least she's down," Sebring said. "We can isolate the most likely areas where explosive devices might be planted. Clear the passengers away from those spots. Then, depressurize. Slowly. Ready for a problem."

"Not good enough," Whitney said, flailing his arms. "This is all supposition. Bomb inside the cabin. Bomb outside. That plane's coming down and you don't really know for sure. Why wasn't it sent to another airport? A bigger one, like JFK. They're more prepared than Hamilton."

People were turning toward the commotion now.

"Just calm down, Mr. Whitney," Sebring ordered. "You're distracting the people who are trying to save your wife. Every possible alternative has been considered. The captain could be afraid he'd bump into the twin towers if he lost control heading for Kennedy. New York is heavily populated. Hamilton has everything he needs—nice long runways, lots of farmland nearby. And we have the necessary support facilities."

"Altitude six thousand feet; eighteen miles." The controller's voice was level, uninflected.

"That plane's going to crash," Whitney cried. He started to hyperventilate. "I just . . . I just know it. Do something," he gasped, tears beginning to run freely down his face.

Peter watched Whitney break down. Somehow he believed what Whitney was saying, even after all of Sebring's reassurances. He froze, helplessly, almost unable to contain his own panic.

Sebring grabbed Whitney and shook him. "Get a grip," he growled. "Because this goddamn bird is going to land safely. And every passenger is going to walk off—alive and well. Do you hear me?"

Whitney nodded.

Sebring let go.

Whitney tried to steady himself. "I'm just afraid for my wife," he sniffed, tears still sliding down his cheeks. "I love her desperately. I'm sorry."

"Fifty-five hundred feet," the controller said.

"I think I see her!" someone else yelled.

Peter strained toward the window. It was odd, searching the dull, empty sky, looking for his family.

Suddenly he saw it, through the mist, a flash of light against the dark horizon. He wanted to reach out with his hand and cradle it in his palm, gently sweeping his wife and daughter down to him, out of harm's way. But all he could do was watch, heart fluttering, as North America Flight 629 descended.

The controller's voice boomed: "Five thousand feet!"

93

Seymour Pinchus raced through streets that he had patrolled before he was ever known as the Fox. Demons kept whispering in his ears, telling him that he was too late, that he was never going to see Daniel or Adam alive again. He had heard those voices before, twenty-seven years ago, when little Melissa was so tragically ill: *There's nothing you can do to save her. No one can. Not even the doctors.* Then, the voices had been right.

Seymour lost his breath, tried to stifle the whispers of doom. But they grew louder, evoking memories of his daughter—how he pleaded with God, hopelessly . . . and how the emptiness had invaded his heart and never left after she was gone.

His panic swelled. He felt himself hurtling out of control, then clutched at the one thing he thought might save him. Driving through the old neighborhood, he could imagine that he was on the force again, and this was just another case. It wasn't his son and grandson in the hands of a maniac. The tightness eased. It helped him keep his head.

He began to scan through everything they knew about the case. Turning stones he had rolled before, he went back to Susan's death, and farther: Kingsman House, Fats and Squigger, the photos, the missing witnesses, Dominic's assassination.

There had to be a solitary link, he believed, a single guiding force behind the crimes, but he never could find it. *Unless . . . unless . . . that link was him,* he thought suddenly. What had Sylvia told him at his house? *Payback time*—it was part of Sarchick's message. But the words meant nothing more to him now than they had before, their significance buried beyond what he could reach.

He kept trying to put the pieces together as he drove, but they remained scattered like shattered glass. He sensed himself slipping again. *Focus, Seymour. Focus.*

He thought about Sarchick: *The son of a bitch left his scent on every step we took. How was he able to find out everything we did—things only we were aware of; and other things we came to only recently?* He turned onto Skidmore, driving by number 2017. Seymour slowed, then continued past it for the same reason that he told Sam not to radio ahead for help. He recalled that Sarchick had a police scanner when he was arrested six months ago, and he wasn't about to risk warning him that they were on their way.

At the end of the block, Seymour noticed Daniel's car. He arched his hand through his open window and across the roof, pointing.

Sam caught the signal, flashed his lights.

Seymour turned to Sylvia. "Looks like we have the right place," he said.

They got out, and Sylvia agreed to stay by Sam's radio in case they needed her to call for help.

"Just like old times: you and me, Sam," Seymour said solemnly as they headed up the street.

"Circumstances aside," Sam replied.

"Don't let that paralyze you," he warned. "Work it the same way."

Milano nodded. The house appeared dark, deserted. "The place is a wreck," he commented in a low voice. "Should've been condemned."

"And torn down," Seymour mumbled, his mind flickering, overcome with an odd sense of something long forgotten that was trying to fight its way back to his consciousness.

"Guess you want to take the front," Sam said.

Seymour broke from the feeling he was chasing. "Wouldn't have it any other way," he whispered.

Seymour gave Sam time to get into position in the rear, and climbed onto the porch.

He paused, staring at the door, wondering what was on the other side, uncertain if he was ready to see.

His stomach knotted as he moved closer. He wanted his family back, wanted to hear their voices once more. The last message on his machine ran idly through his head: *Hi, this is Daniel . . . Sarchick . . . I'll be checking . . . place where it all began.* The message had been garbled, but suddenly he realized why it had seemed so strange: Daniel's voice sounded too even. There was no emotion. His heart jumped. *What had he missed?*

Seymour shook his head, reaching for the door. Unbelievably, the keypad from the airport flashed before his eyes. "Know how many possible combinations?" he could hear Carl say. *Answering machine; keypad?* Fragments of the puzzle swirled through his mind: *payback time . . . Hi, this is Daniel . . . go out with a bang*

. . . place where it all began . . . condemned and torn down . . . Hi, this is Daniel.

He wanted to scream at the fleeting bits and pieces. He was so close, but couldn't quite put it together. He touched the door handle. Finally he knew, just as he twisted the knob.

94

For several moments, as he came to, Daniel thought that it had all been a dream. He was still lying in his bed, Adam safely tucked up in Connecticut. That's what he wished while he slept, and now he was convinced, even before he opened his eyes—

Muffled noises in the background: news report, cops and robbers program. Fell asleep and left the TV on again. Thank God. It was a nightmare.

—But as he slowly regained his senses, the ropes around his limbs and the throbbing of his head told him it was real.

He forced his eyes open, let his pupils adjust to the dim light: *Darkness outside; broken windows; a splintered wood floor; thick paint peeling from the walls, from the ceiling. It's a house—old, decrepit. Tied to a chair in the center of a room. Night.* He noticed a crumbling fireplace. *Must be the living room.*

Daniel's gaze now rested on Sarchick, seated at a table a few feet away. He was engrossed, listening to a portable police scanner. The rest of the room was bare, except for a tattered rug spread on the floor beside him and a couple of kerosene lamps throwing an eerie glow.

"Welcome back," Sarchick greeted him jovially. "Looking for something?"

"Where's my son?" Daniel growled.

Sarchick tilted his head sadly. "I've put *Precious* to sleep," he said, taking pleasure in the words. "But don't worry, not permanently. That would be such a waste. I shall save him for later . . . like a dessert."

"Psychotic bastard!" Daniel yelled. "Where is he?"

"Here with us. But safely hidden. Waiting for me."

"You fucking scumbag," Daniel hissed.

Sarchick stood, picked up the scanner, and kicked the table across the floor at him. It bumped against Daniel's chest, knocking him backward but not over.

"Temper, temper," he said as he followed in the path of the table. He shrugged. "Scream if you want to. No one can hear you."

Past Sarchick's shoulder, Daniel realized he could see the front door from where he sat. It was broken, dangling open by only the upper hinge. Outside he saw only bushes and dark sky. No stars.

"But, it annoys me," Sarchick went on, replacing the scanner on the table in front of Daniel. "And if you continue this behavior, I'll have to take your life sooner than I planned." He grinned. "Or maybe, I'll just get *Precious* right now and let you watch."

Daniel's scream froze in his throat.

"Good boy," Sarchick said, sensing his control of the situation. "You still have time before you die." He reached inside his jacket and pulled out a gun, setting it on the table, next to the scanner.

Daniel recognized it as a .45 caliber Colt. He struggled against the ropes, but it was hopeless to try to free himself, and he sagged back against the chair. "What are you waiting for?"

"For a little birdie to come home," he said anxiously, his eyes shifting toward the scanner.

Daniel heard the radio calls about the airport and twitched. "Another plane?"

"Not just any plane," Sarchick told him. "That prick Roberts almost fucked everything up. Got a little surprise in store for him."

Diane's plane. Daniel felt his rage threaten to leap beyond what he could control. He gritted his teeth and took a deep breath, determined to stay calm for Adam's sake. "Is it going to crash?" he asked, his voice weak with the effort of containing his emotions.

"That's for me to know, and you to find out." Sarchick giggled. "I could have destroyed the other plane instantly. But I didn't. Gave all those people some time to think about it. Can you imagine their terror?"

An emergency call for assistance interrupted the updates about the airport: *Explosion. 2017 Skidmore Drive. One dead; one badly injured.*

Daniel paled. He knew the address. He stared at Sarchick, unable to hide the shock on his face.

"Right you are." Sarchick smirked. "Left enough crumbs for your father to follow. I rigged the joint when we left. I just wanted you to know what I was waiting for. Now—time to say bye-bye."

Daniel was quivering uncontrollably, the grief and fear shredding the last of his strength.

Sarchick picked up the Colt, shook his head, and put it back down. "Too quick; too easy," he said, circling around behind Daniel.

Daniel heard the click of a blade switching open, felt Sarchick grab his chin and yank it up.

"Do you know what it's like to have your neck slit open, your blood rushing out?"

Daniel's heart pounded. "But why are you doing this?" he cried.

"Because of me!" a desperate voice suddenly boomed from across the room. "Let him go, Artie. Right now!"

Sarchick blinked: There in the corner stood Seymour Pinchus, gun in hand.

Daniel's eyes drifted shut. *The Fox.*

"B-but you—" Sarchick stammered, glancing toward the scanner and then back again.

"Place where it all began," Seymour said. "It finally came to me—just in time. I found the present you left at your mother's house."

"The call was a hoax," Sarchick guessed. "To catch me off guard. But it didn't work. Not quite." He flashed the knife.

"He has Adam!" Daniel yelled, staring at the metal blade. "He drugged him."

"Gave him a little fentanyl," Sarchick said, eyes dancing. "Better hope I used the right amount!"

"You motherfucker—"

Sarchick tightened his grip, jerking Daniel's head back until his voice was inaudible, his breath a low whine.

Seymour flinched. "Take it easy, Sarchick. Let's talk."

The madman smiled. "So, you finally remembered. Twenty-seven years ago, when I was butt-fucked in this room, you were the cop assigned to investigate, the cop with the kind face who gave me his word that he would catch whoever did it?"

"Yes." The picture of Ogden House and the sense of déjà vu surrounding the story had brought back sketchy details, enough to lead him here. To the abandoned farmhouse. But the rest had been a blur until now.

"It was an empty promise! You did nothing!"

"I'm sorry, Arthur," Seymour said, his shoulders

bowing under the weight of the memory. "You have to understand: That happened at a time when my daughter was very ill. My mind wasn't on the job. I lost her shortly thereafter." He wet his lips. "You could have asked for another cop."

"It was my life!" Sarchick shouted. "I was only a kid. I wanted you. I needed your help!"

"And I let you down."

"Just like my father." Sarchick seethed miserably.

The comment caught Seymour by surprise. "I'm not your father," he whispered cautiously. "But my son is here and his life is in your hands. Let him go. Let my grandson go. They've done nothing to you. Take me instead."

Daniel was silent, felt his pulse thumping against the ropes.

Sarchick ignored his offer. "I did it alone. It took years, but I finally found Squigger and Fats. By then, all I wanted was a little blackmail. I had the directions to the farmhouse they carelessly left behind that night. I thought it proved everything, but it wasn't any good. I got laughed at. I vowed that would never happen again. Spent enough time in prison to think of a new plan. A perfect one—to make everyone pay!"

Sarchick's eyes were glazed, the expression on his face horrifyingly vacant. Seymour had seen that look before—on the criminally insane. And he knew he was running out of time.

"Don't you see?" Sarchick continued, his voice high. "Everyone has to pay the right price. Fats, the strong, had to be hit hard. Squigger was weak, so I played on his fear. And you, Pinchus—I decided to take what was most important to you: your family. And no one will ever know it was me, because Arthur Sarchick doesn't exist anymore. It's perfect!"

Seymour saw what might be his only chance to rattle Sarchick's sense of invincibility. "No, you're wrong," he said, shaking his head. "You're forgetting the bomb at the house. It never went off. It's being disarmed. People know it was you."

"Liar," Sarchick screamed, nostrils flaring. "Nothing can be traced to me."

"It's over," Seymour yelled back, thrusting his gun forward, his finger tightening around the trigger. His hand trembled.

"What—you gonna shoot me?" Sarchick laughed. "I don't think so. I know why you had to retire. The debilitating injuries. How you almost died. At the time, I prayed that you would. But this is better. Much better. Think you can put a bullet in me without hitting your son? Left-handed? Shaking as it is?"

Seymour squinted in concentration, felt his sweat trickling into his eyes. Sarchick was right. How could he shoot and risk killing Daniel, his own son? The memory of his partner floated up—how his hesitation had cost Vince his life. He relived the moment. It paralyzed him.

"Let's see how good your aim is," Sarchick challenged. "Go ahead and shoot."

But he couldn't. Seymour's finger eased off the trigger.

"We're running out of time," Sarchick declared. "I can open his throat and grab my gun before you ever get a shot off, old man. Shoot—or watch your son die!"

Seymour glanced helplessly at Daniel. His son was mouthing words without sound. *"Shoot him, shoot him now,"* his lips pleaded.

Seymour felt a surge of adrenaline. It made his hand shake worse than before.

Sarchick pressed the knife against Daniel's throat.

Daniel shut his eyes tightly, waiting.

The tip of the blade pierced his skin. A drop of blood trickled out.

And, suddenly, Seymour saw himself at home, behind the barn, saw his handkerchief nailed to a tree—and saw Vince Fitapaldi's head come apart as the killer drove away. In that fraction of a second the trembling eased, his hand grew steady, and he squeezed the trigger.

95

▬▬▬▬ Daniel heard the gunshot. His eyes flew open, he saw the blood, and he sucked in a last, panicked breath. Then, the blade at his throat dropped. Sarchick wobbled, slumped against him. He made a gurgling sound as he slipped to the floor. Daniel caught a glimpse of Sarchick's face as it sank past him. It was twisted in a look of total surprise.

Smoke began to fill the room. Daniel looked around wildly for another trap. But it was a simple accident. When Sarchick struck the floor, he had knocked over one of the kerosene lamps.

Seymour came across the room, ready to fire again if he had to. But the gaping hole in Sarchick's neck had spilled too much blood, and his eyes had the stillness of death. He bent, picked up the knife, and cut Daniel loose. When he had helped his son stand, they saw fire already spreading up the wall behind them.

Daniel grabbed his father. "Adam," he shouted. "We have to find him!"

Seymour's gaze shot around the room, studying every nook and cranny. There was nowhere to hide.

"Not here," Daniel said, letting go. "Somewhere else in the house." He darted out of the room calling Adam's name.

Seymour followed. They each took a different direction. Enough moonlight filtered in to lead their way against the dark as they frantically searched. But the smoke swirling through the house was slowly choking it back.

"Adam, it's Daddy," Daniel cried. "Tell me where you are."

"Are you sure he's here?" Seymour yelled, coughing.

"Yes!" Daniel shrieked back. "Sarchick said 'Precious' was here, waiting for him."

Precious? The word jolted Seymour. Hadn't Sarchick used it before? *Where all precious things are kept.* His mind flashed back to the living room. The rug on the floor—it didn't belong. It was worn, but in better shape than it should have been. He ran back toward the flames, his arms up to ward off the heat.

Daniel found a staircase and started to charge up it. On the fourth step, one of the rotted risers collapsed around his foot. He was trapped.

Fire leaped around the living room. Seymour took a breath, then dropped to his knees and crept toward the rug. Grabbing it, he beat some of the flames back, trying to see the floor it had covered through the haze of smoke. There was a handle. He yanked it up, saw steps leading down into darkness.

"Daniel," he screamed. "Over here. In the living room."

Daniel heard his father, but couldn't move—he was pinned by the chunks of jagged wood hooked into his shin. He pushed furiously against them with his hands. They wouldn't budge. The smoke grew denser. Balanc-

ing himself against the rail, he used his other foot as
leverage and pushed with all his strength. He felt his
skin rip, enormous pain, and his foot finally came free.

The living room. He was having trouble breathing
and his eyes burned from the smoke. He squinted, but
couldn't see. "Dad," he shouted. "Adam?" There was no
response. Fire was everywhere. He called again. Nothing. He thought he heard fire engines outside—but it
was too late. He became overwhelmed with the sense
that it was all hopeless. He was falling again, back into
the hole. He was about to surrender and allow the fire
to consume him, too. Then his father stepped out of
the haze with Adam gathered in his arms.

Seymour rushed ahead, through the front door, carrying his grandson away from the house, until he felt it
was safe enough to put him down.

Hobbling, Daniel caught up with them, and saw his
son's motionless body lying on the grass, his father's ear
against his tiny chest. The relief he had felt just a few
minutes ago melted, replaced by fear. He knelt beside
his father, unable to hold himself up any longer, unaware of anything except the small, still form.

"The drug," Seymour said breathlessly. "I think it's
the drug." He moved his ear away from Adam's chest
and grabbed the boy, shaking him carefully. "Adam,"
he said. "Time to get up."

Daniel held his breath.

Seymour kept talking, trying to rouse his grandson
with gentle motion. "Come on, Adam. You've slept
enough."

Adam's eyelids moved, then fluttered open.
"Daddy," he mumbled woozily.

Daniel's lips started to quiver, his eyes filled with
tears. "Adam. Want to go home?"

"Uh-huh." He nodded.

Daniel grabbed him, drew him in close, never wanting to let him go again.

Seymour swallowed, choking back tears of his own. He swept his arm around the two of them and held on tightly.

"You guys okay?" Milano asked from somewhere behind them.

"We are now." Seymour blinked, a single teardrop slipping out.

"And Sarchick?"

Seymour motioned toward the house. Milano waved the other officers off. Daniel finally looked up and saw Sylvia, her eyes taking in the wound on his leg.

"Nasty gash," she said. "You'll need stitches."

"What are you doing here?" Daniel asked in surprise. "And Sam?"

"She called me," Milano told him. "Said you and Adam were missing. She saved your life. Hell, she probably saved all your lives."

Daniel bit down hard on his lip.

Sylvia smiled at him and winked.

"As it turns out, I know her—well, sort of," Sam said.

"Years ago, when I was arrested," Sylvia explained. "It finally came to me. He was one of the young officers who showed a little sympathy. That's why I thought he looked familiar that time you both came to my house."

Daniel shook his head.

"That bad man broke my plane," Adam said, pouting.

"Don't worry, sport. *That* we can fix. Daddy will buy you a new one."

Seymour looked up at Sam. "The flight?"

Sam grinned. "It was just a decoy. To keep the police from paying attention to the real danger."

Seymour exhaled loudly.

"But I imagine Peter has a lot of explaining to do right now," Milano mused. "The Feds must be hotter than hell about the false alarm, considering his track record."

"Then, we'll have to help him explain things. After all, we need him," Seymour declared, pointing to the inferno. "Who else is going to identify Sarchick?"

"And for the last time," Milano added. "Right?"

But Seymour didn't answer—only pursed his lips and stared pensively at the burning farmhouse as the firemen worked to put out the flames.

PART 4

96

They all celebrated with Sunday brunch at Diane and Peter's. Seymour and Kate were first to arrive, with flowers for the table and chocolates for the kids.

Kate had returned late the night before. Seymour was glad she had been there when he got back from the hospital's emergency room, where Adam was given a clean bill of health and Daniel took twenty-seven stitches in his leg. He needed to hold her, needed to tell her how much he loved her.

Daniel, on crutches, was anxious to introduce Sylvia around—especially to Kate. Paige raced through the house after Adam as the others ate. Melanie and Paul sat in a corner arguing over whether MTV or VH1 was better. And Diane served fresh apple pie for dessert.

Seymour didn't want to leave. It was wonderful. Life was wonderful. It had been awhile. But he had an appointment to get to. There were still questions. Questions that had gnawed at him and had kept him awake the night before. By dawn, he had almost given up searching for answers. He had slipped downstairs and grabbed the paper off the front mat. BOMB SCARE IN SKIES OVER HAMILTON; OGDEN HOUSE BURNS; and, over a picture of Arthur Sarchick, DEAD . . . AGAIN?

In the kitchen, Seymour had stopped at the coffeemaker Kate preset the previous evening and dumped in two extra scoops of grounds before snapping it on.

Details were sketchy. Reporters had fought against a midnight deadline for facts. Seymour's name wasn't mentioned. He was thankful for that. He was looking forward to a peaceful Sunday.

His eye caught a funeral notice for Colin Kirshner—*services 1:30 Tuesday at the First Presbyterian Church of Ardmore. Request donations to the church in lieu of flowers.*

Maybe it was best to leave well enough alone, he had thought then. Suicide or murder, the trail ended with Sarchick. Daniel and Adam were alive, thank God. And the last shadow of a character named Squigger would be laid to rest the day after tomorrow. But, still . . .

He had folded the paper, reached into the cabinet for a cup, and noticed the calendar tacked to the inside of the door. Kate had marked the date of her return and the time of her bus, so he would know when to expect her back from her visit with her sister.

Pinchus had glanced at the paper, at the headline about the bomb scare on North America Flight 629, then back at the calendar—*Greyhound 9:45 P.M.* A dead chill had come over him. He knew he had missed something . . . and there it was!

97

By 2:30 P.M., Seymour Pinchus had left his family brunch and was standing on the front porch of Congressman Charles Whitney's home. The outside was impressive—huge walls of roughcast masonry the color of sand, dark green shutters flanking an even score of windows. With him were Sam Milano and Inspector Kaminski.

"You sure about this, Pinchus?" asked Kaminski. "Philadelphia doesn't need another scandal."

Seymour nodded. The afternoon had become overcast, windy. He turned his collar up against it as Sam reached out and rang the bell.

Early that morning, before going to Diane and Peter's, Seymour had called Sam and gotten him out of bed. He had told Sam what he had in mind, knowing Sam wouldn't refuse him. He asked him to go to the station house and check an old police report. A very old one.

An hour later Seymour had contacted Charles Whitney to set up the appointment. He had said he needed Whitney's help, that it concerned Kirshner's death, and not to say anything about it to Judge Malchomoty or Benjamin Caldwell.

Whitney sounded puzzled, but agreed.

Then Seymour had phoned Daniel and filled him in. Daniel wanted desperately to be included, but Seymour reminded him about the doctor's order to rest his leg.

He had still found a way. At the brunch he told Seymour about something he had realized after their earlier conversation, something his father could use at the meeting.

A silver-haired lady answered Whitney's door. "Yes?"

"We have an appointment with Charles Whitney," Milano said.

"I don't know anything about it." She looked at them suspiciously.

Whitney's voice resonated from the rear of the foyer. "It's okay, Mom. Let 'em in. They're not reporters." He was standing by a grand staircase, an arm hooked around his wife's waist. A man with a camera crouched in front of them.

"One more, Mr. Whitney," the man said.

Whitney pulled his wife in, smiled for the flash.

Introductions followed.

"Nice shot," Seymour remarked as the photographer began packing up. "For the family album?"

Whitney shook his head, looked at the floor uncomfortably. "For the AP. My advisor thinks yesterday's near tragedy will translate into votes. Wants to grab some free publicity."

"And why not, Charles," his mother challenged sharply. "It's news. The public has a right to know."

She looked at the others, flashing a plastic smile. "Always had too much of a conscience to run for office. He needs to learn how the game is played."

"Must've been awful coming in on that plane," Milano said sympathetically to Whitney's wife.

"It was worse on Charles than on me. We never really knew what was happening until after we landed."

"From what I heard, we both had a heck of a night," Whitney said to Seymour.

"Yes. We were all very lucky," he replied.

The younger Mrs. Whitney gestured to her mother-in-law. "Come, Mother. I'm sure these gentlemen have important things to discuss."

The two women started upstairs. The older Mrs. Whitney turned at the landing. "Remember, Charles, we're meeting your father early at the club for cocktails. He has a few friends who want to shake the hand of the next governor of Pennsylvania. What do you think of my boy, gentlemen?"

Whitney covered an embarrassed smile with a wave and his mother continued up the stairs. "Haven't even won the primary yet and she's ready to redecorate the governor's mansion."

They all laughed, following Whitney to a room paneled with light wood and furnished with walnut leather chairs, matching couch, and lots of shelves filled with books, mostly about law. Pinchus noticed a set of Caldwell novels prominently displayed on the corner of a desk, next to a signed picture of the two friends shaking hands. He tried not to stare.

Milano and Kaminski sat. Pinchus stood, resting a shoulder against one of the bookshelves. Whitney closed the door before settling in behind the desk.

Milano spoke first. "Seymour has come upon a few strange details about Kirshner's death. I need to ask you some questions."

"Since Kirshner died in Philadelphia, Milano asked me to tag along," Kaminski explained. "Sort of makes things official. Hope you don't mind."

"Of course not. How can I help?"

"I understand you were with Kirshner shortly before—"

"Yes, that's correct," Whitney replied, cutting Milano off. "So were Vernon Malchomoty and Benjamin Caldwell. As soon as we heard what happened, we alerted the authorities. They questioned us and filed a report. We were all at the football game together. In the alumni box. At halftime, Kirshner left. He was out of sorts, depressed. But, my God, none of us thought he was going to commit suicide." He took a breath. "And now . . . I can't help but feel somewhat responsible."

"Why?" Seymour asked.

"The other day you asked me about Squigger—who he really was. I couldn't tell you then. I had promised I wouldn't."

"And Kirshner was Squigger?"

"We knew you would eventually figure it out. Malchomoty, Caldwell, and I, we all tried to convince Kirshner to come clean. Told him that, legally, he had nothing to worry about. I pushed the hardest. Said Kingsman House didn't exist anymore, that I no longer felt bound. And if he didn't come forward, I would have to turn him in." Whitney lowered his eyes. "Poor Colin. I guess he couldn't live with the shame."

Seymour moved away from the bookcase and took a step toward Whitney. "But Kirshner was murdered!"

Whitney jerked his head up. "What?"

"That's what Pinchus believes," Kaminski cut in. "But hell, as far as I'm concerned, it's still suicide. There was a note. Reasonable evidence. And the M.E. ruled it that way."

"Christ, Russ," Milano pleaded. "Give Seymour a

chance. That's why we're here. To put our heads together."

"Didn't Kirshner jump from his office window?" Whitney asked, still wearing a look of surprise.

"Not exactly." Pinchus started to pace as he explained. "Kirshner hit the ground a good twenty feet down the line from his office. Yet his window was the only one found open."

"So he took a stroll along the ledge," Kaminski commented.

"Seems to me if you're going to commit suicide, you simply jump," responded Pinchus.

"Maybe he wanted to think things over?" Kaminski suggested.

"The ledge is pretty narrow. If he had doubts, I don't think he would have taken the chance that he might fall. And I found scuff marks on it, directly above where Kirshner's body landed."

Kaminski shrugged. "Could have changed his mind. Tried to turn around."

"Or the marks could have been there before," offered Whitney. "Could be any number of reasons."

"Only one," Seymour insisted. "Kirshner went out on that ledge because someone was after him. Nobody heard his cries for help over the roar of the game. So he hugged the building, desperately trying to get away. Until he stumbled to his death."

"What about the note found in his office?" Kaminski asked.

Pinchus made a face. "A torn piece of paper left on his desk, saying, *'Forgive me, Colin Kirshner'*?"

"It was in his own handwriting," Kaminski pointed out.

"I spoke to Kirshner's secretary at the university. She confirmed that it looked like Kirshner's signature, all right. But she also told me Kirshner was a fastidious man. Compulsive. Claims he never would have left a note that way. Certainly not a suicide note." Seymour stopped pacing and faced the inspector. "So there had to be more. It was the end of a letter, torn off from something that would have changed the whole meaning around. And the killer took that piece with him."

"Frankly, I'm convinced," Milano declared. "Kirshner was murdered."

"Have to admit, it's a strong possibility," Whitney agreed. "It had to be Sarchick. He finally got his revenge. First with Fats. Now with Squigger. It fits."

"That's what I thought, too, Charles," Seymour said. "Except for one thing. Even Sarchick couldn't be in two places at once."

"What do you mean?" Whitney said.

"Something my son, Daniel, mentioned. According to the autopsy report, Kirshner died at approximately ten-fifteen P.M., Friday. At the same time, a half hour's drive away, Sarchick was seen running from a fire he set in Hamilton. We have a witness."

Seymour slowly turned his head to look at Whitney. "Want to tell us when you slipped away from the game, Charles?"

98

"Are you mad?" Whitney shouted, rising. "You can't possibly think . . ." He hesitated, staring at Seymour in disbelief. "You *are* mad."

"Your meeting at the game wasn't to get Kirshner to talk," Seymour charged. "Just the opposite."

"No. You're wrong!"

"It was to convince him to keep his mouth shut," Seymour went on relentlessly. "But Kirshner wouldn't listen, so you followed him to his office."

Whitney slammed a fist against the top of his desk. "No!"

"Jesus, Seymour," Kaminski cried. "You're accusing a goddamn congressman."

"Let him finish," Milano demanded.

Whitney slowly sank down into his chair. "Go ahead," he said, eyes wide and furious. "I'd like to hear it. I'd like to know how you got this crazy notion."

"On the golf course you told me you hadn't seen

Kirshner for awhile," Pinchus reminded him. "But just the day before, he called you. The university keeps a close tab on toll calls. Daphne pulled Kirshner's phone records."

"Yes. Your visit had him upset. He asked me what to do. I said, do the right thing. I told you I didn't *see* him. I didn't say anything about not speaking with him."

"You asked me how he was," Pinchus threw out.

"I meant—how did he look? I heard he was ill."

Pinchus paused, but didn't argue. He started to pace again. "Kirshner *was* very ill, which is my next point. He had terminal cancer. He knew he didn't have much longer to live. It had made him religious. He wanted to put his affairs in order, wanted to confess his sins. I understand that in the Presbyterian religion, you don't go to a priest. Rather, you confess to the one you wronged—or, if need be, publicly. He had to get the night of the boy and the farmhouse off his chest."

"The letter," Milano guessed, "that ended with 'Forgive me.'"

Pinchus nodded. "He wrote it that night in his office. Right before you surprised him, Charles."

"And that's why I pushed him out the window?" Whitney scoffed. "But it didn't happen that way. Ask Caldwell and Malchomoty. I was with them for most of the game. They'll tell you I never left."

"I'm sure they will," Seymour replied calmly. "And they'll be lying."

"Why? What possible reason could they have?"

"Because if Kirshner talked, it would ruin them, too. It would ruin all of you."

"That was Kirshner's affair, his disgusting act," Whitney said loudly. "If he felt compelled to reveal it, why would we care?"

Seymour swung around, pointing a finger at Whitney. "Because you all had a hand in the dirty little deed."

"You're wrong," Whitney roared.

"Am I?" Seymour fired back. "Harold Bench, another Kingsman, told me each group of rushees had to help one another. It knitted them together. It wasn't until early this morning that I thought where to look." He moved closer to Whitney, eyes fixed, calculating each step. "Sam dug out the police report—twenty-seven years old. One that I had filed and forgotten. One that mentioned a lonely road, a couple of cars, and *five* young men." He reached the desk, pressed his palms against the edge, leaning forward. "Three of you were chosen to kidnap the boy. The other two had to rape him!"

Whitney glanced away for a moment, then regained his composure. "That's ridiculous," he said, waving off Pinchus's words with both hands.

Seymour straightened, took a step back. "Did you draw straws to see who would go after Kirshner, or was it entirely your idea, Charles?"

This time Whitney didn't even flinch. "Is that all you have, Seymour? Hearsay and supposition? Where's your evidence? An old police report without names—one that even you had forgotten about? If you ask me to explain that report, I can't. But I swear to you, I wasn't with Kirshner on pledge night. Kirshner was a close friend, a fraternity brother. If he committed suicide, I forgive him. But if it was murder, I also want to see his killer caught."

"Bench was at that football game," Seymour pressed. "Third row back, a little to the left. The alumni section."

Whitney's eyes rolled upward.

"Guess you didn't notice him. He says you got up during the second half. Didn't see you much after that."

"He told you the truth," Whitney admitted slowly. "After Kirshner left, I did a little politicking. Worked the crowd a bit. If you like, I can give you the names of a dozen people I spoke with."

Whitney sounded convincing. But Seymour knew he was a murderer.

"I think we've heard enough," Kaminski said, starting to get up. Then he paused. "Wait a minute," the inspector said suddenly. "Malchomoty and Caldwell were your alibi, but you weren't with them for the full second half."

"No. But I explained that."

"So we don't know where *they* were," Kaminski pointed out. "One of them could have paid Kirshner a visit. Seymour . . . maybe you're wrong about Whitney?"

"No. I *know* it was him," Pinchus snapped. There was one more thing he had to tell them—exactly how he knew, what he had been saving.

Suddenly, there was a commotion outside the door. It flew open and Daniel stumbled in.

"I tried to stop him," Whitney's mother said, following closely behind him. "I told him you were having a meeting. But he insisted."

"It's my son," Pinchus said.

"It's all right, Mother."

Nodding disapprovingly, she left, closing the door behind her.

Daniel stood in the middle of the room, one arm slung over a crutch, the other clutching a large envelope covered in soot.

Seymour blinked. "Daniel, what the hell. . . ?"

"I was thinking after you left," Daniel said, catching his breath. "About the missing Polaroids. The Kingsman House photos. Sarchick would have put them in a safe place—where *precious* things are kept. I got in touch with Duffy, the fire marshal. Asked him to check the basement at Ogden. Guess what he found?" He handed the envelope to his father, staring directly at Whitney. "You were right, Pop—there *was* more to all of this. Squigger wasn't Kirshner. Squigger was Kirshner's killer!"

Seymour yanked open the envelope, fumbling through the contents with his fingers. He shook his head, then closed the flap and threw the packet down on the desk. "It's over, Charles. Tell us about it."

"No," Whitney said again and again, each time getting louder. "No . . . *no* . . . NO!"

"Don't make us show these to your mother—see if she can recognize *her boy,*" Pinchus said.

Whitney lunged across the desk, but Seymour snatched the envelope away before he could reach it. Whitney screeched like a wounded animal.

"*You* were Squigger," Seymour charged loudly. "That's why you murdered Kirshner."

Whitney lifted his head. "I didn't mean to," he said, eyes red, voice breaking. "But he wouldn't listen."

"And Sarchick was blackmailing you—wasn't he?"

"Yes," Whitney cried. "I'll tell you whatever you want to know. Just give me that envelope."

"So you did anything he wanted. Like getting him into the Witness Protection Program."

"Who would it hurt," Whitney answered, almost weeping. "A piece of shit like that."

"But Sarchick came back. Took down that plane."

"I didn't know he was going to do that. I swear. My God, all those people. It made me sick. Sarchick claimed it was all on my head. Don't you see why I had to do what he said? Please." He held out his hand.

Seymour tossed him the envelope. "Think you better cancel tonight's plans, Charles."

"Read him his rights," Milano said to Kaminski.

Whitney tore the envelope open and looked inside. His color drained. He started to shake, furiously scattering the contents out onto the desk. There was nothing there but charred paper. "You fucking bastards," he screamed. "You tricked me!"

"A guilty conscience can be easily fooled," Seymour noted. He squeezed the back of Daniel's neck affectionately. *Job well done,* the gesture said.

Daniel clamped his teeth down on his lip to keep from smiling.

"It was all a sham," Whitney groaned. "Bench didn't see me at the game. You never *really* knew."

"But I did," Seymour told him. "Sarchick tipped his hand when he pitched me that phony recording of Daniel's voice and somehow tied up my phone for awhile so no one else could call. I finally realized how Sarchick knew our every move—*phone messages.* Only have to hit one number for a playback on most answering machines when you call in. Mine's a two; Daniel's is a five. Doesn't take many tries to find it."

"So?"

"There *was* one piece of information Sarchick had that was never in any of those messages. How did he know which plane my niece would be on when he planned his little bomb scare? You were the only one I told. That day on the golf course—remember? Just so happens your wife was taking that same flight. And since you were the one giving Sarchick information, I knew you had to be Squigger. You had to help him, or you would have been exposed. Peter mentioned you gave a great performance at the airport. You should have saved it for the courtroom."

"Why couldn't you leave it alone?" Whitney said quietly. "It was over. Sarchick was dead. I was free."

"Because you made us all victims," Pinchus said angrily. "My son. My grandson. Myself. So many others. I couldn't let you get away with that. *Siz vos iz richtic*," he whispered.

"Justice," Daniel echoed.

Congressman Charles Whitney was taken to a waiting patrol car. His wife and mother, shocked, yet convinced there had to be some mistake, got into a unit behind him.

"Why didn't Sarchick simply murder Whitney?" Daniel wondered as they walked toward the cars. "It would have saved him a lot of trouble."

"You can also kill someone by destroying their dreams," his father told him.

"Tell me one thing?" Milano asked Seymour, watching Daniel and the others pull away. "When did you work that whole thing out with Daniel? It was brilliant."

Seymour's lips were pressed together in a little smile. "Years ago I knew a man. Loved to ski. Used to take his young son along. I recently ran into him, inquired if he was still leading his son down the mountain. 'Yes,' he told me. 'But now, I mostly have to follow him.'"

Milano sighed. "Ask a question, get a story. You haven't changed, Seymour. All I want to know is when did you set things up with Daniel?"

"That's what I'm trying to tell you," Pinchus said. He was glowing. "I never did."

99

Daniel arrived late to the police chief's ball. The room was full of people. A band played loudly in the corner. Across the floor he noticed his father standing by the bar with Sam.

He couldn't believe he had ever been suspicious of Sam. His father had finally told him that Sam and Helen were having some difficulties, were seeing a marriage counselor. Sam had tried to keep it secret, lying about his physical and other things to cover the appointments. But Sam and Helen were apparently working things out, taking it a step at a time.

Daniel was glad to hear that. He made his way slowly through the crowd. He had been feeling better and had decided to leave his crutches home, even though his leg still thumped when he didn't watch his step.

There were hoots and congratulatory high signs from his division.

"Yo, Daniel." "Welcome back, kid." "Just like the Fox."

He acknowledged them with a wave of his hand as he walked.

Junior Gibney caught him from behind with a slap on the back. "Nice going, Daniel. Heard about yesterday."

"Thanks," Daniel said, turning.

"Got a surprise for you. We nailed the snitch."

His face lit up. "Who?"

"Well, he ain't here tonight."

Daniel's eyes scanned the room, stopped when they spotted Rifkin. "I thought—"

"We all did," Gibney said. "Got a tip on a fencing operation the Luccetta mob was running from an old warehouse on Delancey."

"Nickel-and-dime shit?"

"Yeah, but it served our purpose. Each day we told a different guy when we were going to bust the joint. Two days ago, the operation was mysteriously shut down." Gibney paused. "Guess who we had fed the info to the night before?"

"Tell me already," Daniel said impatiently.

"Bart Miller."

Daniel nodded slowly. It all made sense: the fancy cars, the lifestyle, the women.

"Got in over his head," Gibney continued. "Ended up borrowing money from the wrong people."

The band started playing a swing. Gibney cracked a smile watching Paul Vanderhooven attempt the two-step, until his own wife came over and yanked him onto the dance floor.

Daniel reached Sam and his father just as Alex Schwenk crossed in front of them.

"Gentlemen," the captain nodded politely. He seemed to be in a good mood, without even a trace of a scowl. He ordered a bourbon from the bar and moved away again.

"Very pleasant," Milano remarked, surprised.

"Guess he still thinks it's his day," Seymour said. "I wonder when Chief Foster will make the big announcement?"

"Think Schwenk has a shot?" Milano asked.

"God, let's hope not," Daniel said.

"By the way, Seymour," Milano said. "I never did hear the entire story—how Sarchick was able to get away with everything, how you managed to put it together."

"To understand it all," Seymour began, smiling, "you have to go way back, even before that night at the farmhouse. Sarchick's father abandoned him and his mother. Probably abused Sarchick before he left."

"The making of a pedophile," Milano noted.

"That's often the case," Seymour agreed. "There are definite trigger points in the life of a pedophile, incidents that make him cross over, make him behave a certain way. His father's abuse was the first push down that path."

"And his rape at the farmhouse was the second," Milano surmised. "His juvee record started soon after that. Picked up for molesting."

"He wanted to feel the same power that others had over him. The utter domination of another human being. But it caused his mother shame. A mother whom he had grown very close to. I bet *she* convinced him to join the army, thinking it would straighten him out. But soon after he returned home, he was back at it."

"And his mother?" Sam asked.

"Probably had enough," Seymour replied. "Told him to leave. Sarchick was devastated. Hated himself, what he had become, the pain he caused her. He felt like the only way to make things right for himself was to get

revenge for that night at the farmhouse. But at first, he
didn't know who, only that it was *Kingsman House*. He
had found a sheet of directions at the scene that told
him that much. Then he got into Van Buren through a
special program and waited for an opportunity to destroy the great fraternity once and for all. But not until
he found out exactly *who*."

"Then he relocated to Harrisburg," Daniel put in.
"With each perverted sexual encounter he became a
little bolder, a little sicker."

"Got arrested for indecent assault," Milano recalled.
"The kid was only ten."

"And the DA assigned to the case was none other
than Charles Whitney," Seymour said, watching Sam's
eyes grow wide.

"Sarchick follow him there?"

Seymour rubbed his chin with a thumb. "Not sure,
but whatever the case, Sarchick tried to bargain his way
out of trouble. Threatened Whitney with those directions he saved from the farmhouse. Whitney wasn't
buying, though. Called his bluff. Prosecuted him to the
full extent."

"So Sarchick was out of the way for a while," Sam
nodded. "Convenient for a DA with aspirations."

"But after Sarchick got out, he didn't forget," Seymour went on. "He couldn't—his mother died right
before his release. Never did get to make peace with
her. It was a final blow to an already twisted mind.
Now, he had to make everyone pay—Squigger, Fats
. . . and the cop who was too busy with his own
problems to help," he added guiltily, though no one
blamed Seymour for that except himself. "Even the
children had to pay. That's when the molestations
turned into killings."

"And Sarchick always remembered the Polaroids."
Sam picked up where Seymour left off. "He had to

make sure they still existed. He tried to get close to Luccetta by infiltrating the mob. But a racketeering charge threw him a curve. After that, he chose a new plan—set everything up. Those pictures must have been Dominic's ace in the hole. He had something over Whitney and Whitney was on the rise. It would be great for business to have a governor in your pocket. Poor Whitney had no clue that he was fucked no matter what. Then Sarchick blows Luccetta away shortly after stealing the Polaroids and sends Whitney a letter telling him what he wants—maybe with one of those photos stuffed inside so Whitney knows he means business."

Seymour nodded, enjoying the recitation.

"Sarchick calculated every step. Getting caught. Getting even with you, Seymour, by arranging to have the bomb planted in Daniel's car and making it look like the mob did it. Gets into the Witness Protection Program and plans his final step—his own death. But there's one more thing. Who the hell was in Sarchick's seat on that plane?"

"I was curious about that, too," Daniel jumped in. "Then I thought about the kind of individual Sarchick would need for his plan to work. Someone who nobody cared about. Someone who wouldn't be missed."

Milano's brow wrinkled. "A homeless person?"

"This morning, I started calling shelters in and around Evanston, where Sarchick was relocated. Got a hit at a mission run by the Salvation Army. Seems they had a regular there named Merle Oakley. Remembered him showing up one day in new clothes, bragging about this friend he found who was taking care of him. Very odd. And no one has seen Oakley since." He lifted an eyebrow at Sam. "Could've also sent him to get his teeth checked."

"The mix-up with the dental records," Sam realized.

"But Oakley would have had to use Sarchick's name—the one he was going by. Why would he do that?"

Daniel shrugged. "Sarchick must've given Oakley a good reason. Maybe he said Oakley could use Sarchick's dental insurance from the witness program."

Suddenly the lights flashed, once, twice, three times. The band stopped playing. Chief Foster was making his way to the podium.

Seymour got a glass of chardonnay for Kate; Sam, a sloe gin fizz for Helen. They all found their seats.

From two tables away, Sergeant Deacon Fishburn shot a thumbs-up at Schwenk just as Foster reached the microphone.

Schwenk nodded back, looking as if he had a canary stuffed in his mouth ready to swallow.

"Thank you for your attention," Foster said into the mike. "I promise to be brief. You've been anxiously waiting for me to announce my retirement, wondering who I'll recommend as my replacement. Some of you will be quite happy with my decision. Most, I like to think. The others, I hope, will at least remember that I always try to do what's best for this police force, the City of Hamilton, and . . ."

"Here it comes," Daniel whispered glumly. "We're finished. He knows Schwenk isn't well liked. He's trying to soften the blow."

". . . I've already discussed this with the city officials and they unanimously approve. I thank them for their trust and confidence. So with a compelling feeling of unfinished business—and isn't that always the case—I'd like to announce," Foster paused for effect, then let his voice boom. "The hell with my retirement. I'm hanging around for one more year!"

The room broke into applause. And loud cheers.

Foster answered them by throwing an arm into the air and waving it back and forth.

Sam's jaw dropped.

Seymour and Daniel both took a peek at Schwenk, who was beside himself.

First, he slumped in his chair. His lips kept quivering, unable to hold the requisite smile he was trying to show. Finally, he got up and headed for the door.

"If you're looking for the men's room, Captain," Daniel said as Schwenk passed, "it's the other way."

"Don't be so smart," Schwenk shot back. "Let's see how you do at tomorrow's hearing."

"You're still going ahead with that?" Seymour cried in disbelief.

"No, he's not," Foster said, coming up behind them. "As of right now, Detective Pinchus is reinstated. *Capisci,* Lieutenant?"

"Lieu . . . Lieutenant?" Schwenk stammered.

"Until *your* hearing, I'm demoting you."

Schwenk's eyes were bulging. "Hearing? But why?"

Heads at nearby tables turned toward the noise.

Foster lowered his voice. "Fish told me you were trying to blackmail him. He came to me about his drinking problem over six months ago. Said he got himself into a program and he's been clean ever since. He doesn't care who knows. He's not ashamed of it, and he had the courage to do the right thing."

"He must've misunderstood our conversation," Schwenk sputtered.

"We have a witness," Foster declared. "The next time you threaten somebody over the phone, make sure nobody else is listening on another line."

Schwenk impulsively glanced around the room and saw Rifkin watching the scene. When his eyes met Schwenk's, he turned away.

"And some funds were misappropriated from your discretionary fund. That money is for paying snitches. Not for bribing people like Mrs. Cooper."

"But Detective Pinchus was—"

"I don't want to hear it, Schwenk," Foster snapped. "And while we're on the subject, what the hell were you doing dressed up like a woman? Someone sent me a picture of you getting out of a Philadelphia patrol car in drag. Some kinda joke?"

"No, sir," Schwenk squirmed uncomfortably.

"In my office, ten o'clock tomorrow," Foster said.

"Yes, sir," Schwenk replied. No one had ever seen him disappear so fast.

Later, Daniel approached Rifkin. "Had you all wrong. I'm sorry," he said, offering his hand.

Rifkin grabbed it. "You and half the department. But you still owe me a fifty for that photo."

"Huh?"

"Price went up," Rifkin told him, poker-faced.

For a moment, Daniel stared at him. Then they both burst into laughter.

Seymour thought about Schwenk long after he had limped away. Schwenk had been his enemy for more years than he cared to count. A cruel man. A jealous man. Seymour should have been happy. But he was not. He felt sorry for his old nemesis.

"You were pretty tough on him," he said to Foster.

"What, you sticking up for Schwenk? I can do what I want. I'm the chief," Foster bellowed. "I owe you, Pinchus. You're a good man. You never complained. Have an opening for a captain if you want it."

Seymour felt his breath leave. The offer was a total surprise. He tried to remain calm, put his hand on top of Kate's and gently rubbed it, thought about how much she meant to him. "I'm flattered," he said. "But I—"

"Don't tell me now," Foster interrupted. "Think about it. Position could be open for a few months. Maybe up to a year," he said with a wink.

When they were alone together on the dance floor, Kate said to Seymour, "Imagine that Foster—actually thinking you might accept his offer."

Pinchus knew she was smarter than that. It was just her way, like a ship moving cautiously out along the water to face a pending storm. Her words sounded confident and clear, but he could feel her body tense against him.

And he had to admit there was a time he would have jumped at the chance. Before. When things looked their darkest. When he thought he was through. But he had promised himself, and Kate, just one more—to solve Susan's murder. And that *one* had grown beyond her death into one, last, fantastic case. It had even fulfilled his dream of working with his son.

"Sounds ridiculous," he answered finally, sweeping the issue aside.

Kate reached up and kissed him. "I love you, Seymour Pinchus," she said.

Seymour pulled her in closer, held her there until the music stopped. Foster may have given him some time to make up his mind, but for the moment, Pinchus had everything he wanted.

EPILOGUE

██████████ Over the next several weeks, things returned to normal in Hamilton. Adam moved in with his dad, and Daniel even fetched the dogs back from Mildred Vanderhooven. He was starting to grow fond of the little pests, letting them sleep in his bed. He knew they missed Susan, too.

Sylvia continued to see a lot of Daniel. She was finally free from the mob—the dismembered remains of Marion Luccetta and Tony Caputa were discovered in the trunk of a car parked along a Hamilton road. Dr. Onasis found evidence that an acetylene torch was used. Authorities were looking for Fred Stillman, a.k.a. Freddie the Welder. Seems as though someone sent him flowers, along with a package of imported meats, signed with Marion's name—by someone with an artful hand.

For the first time, Seymour Pinchus actually seemed to be enjoying retirement. He tinkered around the house a bit, played some chess with his friend Oscar, and, oddly enough, the two of them took up golf. Kate was still skeptical, though. She bought him a fresh box of handkerchiefs to keep him happy—just in case.

Schwenk remained a lieutenant. He was fighting his demotion and had filed a grievance with the PBA. But any decision would be delayed for months. Politics. It turned out that Sergeant Fishburn's cousin was the local rep.

Hamilton got a good deal of national press from Whitney's arrest. People were getting tired of being asked about the fall of their once-beloved congressman who was now awaiting trial. Rumor had it that Whitney was entering a plea of temporary insanity.

In Philadelphia, Judge Vernon Malchomoty kept a low profile. The state's Judicial Conduct Board was reviewing his tenure on the bench, although no criminal charges were filed. He was also up for a retention election. Expectations were that he'd be soundly defeated.

And Benjamin Caldwell began what he hoped would be another best-seller, a sequel to *Shades of Guilt.* It was about a nurse who blew up a federal building at West Point to get even with the military.

▄▄▄▄▄▄▄

On April 7th, nearly six months after a North America jet slammed into a wooded hillside just outside of Minersville, a memorial service was held at the site.

Peter Roberts made the trip and brought his entire family along. He wanted them to see where ninety-eight people lost their lives, wanted them to touch the tragedy, to feel the deep sense of loss and be humbled by it, as he was. His children were young. They were lucky. They needed to learn.

The hill looked different from what Peter remembered. New grass and freshly planted shrubs covered the ground that had been littered with plane parts and broken bodies. Only the trees still wore the scars of what had happened.

Roberts left his family for awhile to wander around alone. Thankfully, he knew he wouldn't run into Elliot Brandle. He had heard that Brandle was caught pilfering supplies and anything else he could carry away from recovery operations. The state police found a whole stash of it at his funeral home—even a missing laptop computer.

But there were people Peter did recognize. Zeke, others from his team, a few guys from PADIT. And others who he did not know. Some were relatives—wives who lost husbands, children who no longer had parents. Sad faces. Solemn nods. And tears.

A stone monument was erected where the supply tent used to be. The names of the passengers and crew of Flight 1089 were struck into it. Peter noticed a little black girl, about seven years old, standing by it. Her mother was a few feet away, facing the other way. The girl's hair was in a braid, clasped with the initial J. He went over to her.

"Are you Jasmine?" he asked.

"Hey, how did you know my name?"

"I, um—I knew your daddy," he said gently, his throat tightening. "He told me how pretty you were."

"Are you one of his friends?"

"I'd like to think so, sweetheart."

"I miss my daddy. A lot."

"I'm sure you do, honey." He felt his eyes begin to water and blinked back the tears.

"He's in heaven now."

"I know."

Her mother turned around. "Child, what are you doing bothering that man?"

"But, Mommy, he knows Daddy."

She looked at him, cocking her head to the side. "You wouldn't be that dentist, Doctor—"

He nodded. "Peter."

"Awfully glad to meet you, Peter. I'm Vivian, LeRoy's wife," she said, coming closer. She handed Jasmine a piece of paper. "Go see if you can find Daddy's name."

Jasmine took it, skipping over to the monument.

"My husband talked about you. He liked you."

"I . . . I don't know what to say," Peter replied sadly.

"Shawondasee," said Vivian.

Shawondasee—it brought a smile to Peter's lips. "I liked LeRoy, too. Is there anything I can do?"

She shook her head. "There's his pension. The insurance he got—poor LeRoy finally cashed in on those insurance machines at the airport. Hit them for the max. Don't worry. We'll be okay." She put her arms around him, and gave him a hug. "Thank you."

"I found it, Mommy. I found it—Daddy's name," Jasmine called.

"Okay, sweetie. Be there in a minute," she said, her voice trembling. She was still hugging Peter, starting to cry.

Peter watched Jasmine trace her father's name onto the paper with a broken crayon. Suddenly, tears slid down his own cheeks. And Vivian's arms became Bear's—the big paws squeezing him. "So long, buddy," he said quietly.

━━━━━

Two evenings later was the anniversary of Susan's death. Daniel took out the *Yahrzeit* candle, said a prayer, and lit the wick. It wasn't without pain, but there was less. He tried to dwell on her life, not her death—about what he was thankful for, what she had given him. Adam. And when those times came, when he found the loss too difficult to handle, he'd simply look into Adam's face—her eyes, her smile. And Daniel knew that she'd always be there.

ABOUT THE AUTHOR

Dennis Asen was born in Brooklyn, New York. A graduate of Brooklyn College and New York University College of Dentistry, he currently resides in Pennsylvania, and is happily married with three children. He is also the author of DEADLY IMPRESSION, the first novel about Seymour Pinchus and Dr. Peter Roberts.

BANTAM OFFERS THE FINEST IN CLASSIC AND MODERN BRITISH MURDER MYSTERIES

C. C. BENISON

Her Majesty Investigates

____57476-0	DEATH AT BUCKINGHAM PALACE	$5.99/$7.99
____57477-9	DEATH AT SANDRINGHAM HOUSE	$5.50/$7.50
____57478-7	DEATH AT WINDSOR CASTLE	$5.99/$7.99

TERI HOLBROOK

____56859-0	A FAR AND DEADLY CRY	$5.50/$7.50
____56860-4	THE GRASS WIDOW	$5.50/$7.50

DOROTHY CANNELL

____56951-1	HOW TO MURDER YOUR MOTHER-IN-LAW	$5.50/$7.50
____29195-5	THE THIN WOMAN	$5.50/$7.50
____27794-4	THE WIDOWS CLUB	$5.99/$7.99
____29684-1	FEMMES FATAL	$5.50/$7.50
____28686-2	MUM'S THE WORD	$4.99/$5.99
____57360-8	HOW TO MURDER THE MAN OF YOUR DREAMS	$5.50/$7.50

Ask for these books at your local bookstore or use this page to order.

Please send me the books I have checked above. I am enclosing $_____ (add $2.50 to cover postage and handling). Send check or money order, no cash or C.O.D.'s, please.

Name _____

Address _____

City/State/Zip _____

Send order to: Bantam Books, Dept. MC 6, 2451 S. Wolf Rd., Des Plaines, IL 60018
Allow four to six weeks for delivery.
Prices and availability subject to change without notice.   MC 6 8/98